ROME'S LOST SON

Robert Fabbri read Drama and Theatre at London University and worked in film and TV for 25 years. He was an assistant director and worked on productions such as *Hornblower, Hellraiser, Patriot Games* and *Billy Elliot*. His life-long passion for ancient history inspired him to write the *Vespasian* series. He lives in London and Berlin.

Also by Robert Fabbri

THE VESPASIAN SERIES

TRIBUNE OF ROME
ROME'S EXECUTIONER
FALSE GOD OF ROME
ROME'S FALLEN EAGLE
MASTERS OF ROME

Coming soon…

THE FURIES OF ROME

SHORT STORIES

THE CROSSROADS BROTHERHOOD
THE RACING FACTIONS
THE DREAMS OF MORPHEUS

Coming soon…

THE ALEXANDRIAN EMBASSY

ROME'S LOST SON

ROBERT
FABBRI

CORVUS

First published in hardback in Great Britain in 2015 by Corvus,
an imprint of Atlantic Books Ltd.

This paperback edition published in Great Britain in 2015 by Corvus,
an imprint of Atlantic Books Ltd.

10 9 8 7 6 5 4 3 2

A CIP catalogue record for this book is available from the British Library.

Paperback ISBN: 978 0 85789 969 9
E-book ISBN: 978 0 85789 968 2

Printed and bound by CPI Group (UK) Ltd, Croydon, CR0 4YY

Corvus
An imprint of Atlantic Books Ltd
Ormond House
26–27 Boswell Street
London WC1N 3JZ

www.corvus-books.co.uk

For my parents-in-law, Eddie and Christel Müller, my sister-in-law, Liane Olbertz, her husband, Sven, and their son, Fabian, with thanks for welcoming me into their family.

Rome

Danuvius

Tyras

MOESIA
THRACE
Via Egnatia
Philippi

Byzantium
Cyzicus

ASIA

Tyra

Pontus Euxinus

Sinope

Phasis

COLCHIS
IBERIA
ALBANIA

Artaxata

PONTUS

ARMENIA

CAPPADOCIA

Melitene

Kentrites

Amida
Tigranocerta
Nineveh

Tigris

Arbela

Euphrates

PARTHIA

Seleucia Ctesiphon

SYRIA

Damascus

JUDAEA
NABATAEI

Caesarea

Mare Internum

PROLOGUE

❧ ❧

Pontus Euxinus, September AD 51

M OONLIGHT SHEENED THE Stygian-dark surface of the Pontus Euxinus and reflected up, silver and bright, into the pained eyes of Titus Flavius Sabinus. He groaned as he leant over the rail of a trireme, bobbing at anchor, water slapping its hull, opposite the mouth of the Tyras River. The moon's reflection was elongated on the swell and then fractured into many replications before re-emerging and contracting back into a near-perfect likeness, as the ship rose and fell in time to the crash of breakers rolling onto the shore just a hundred paces to larboard and starboard.

The constant gyrations of the one point of light in his vision did nothing to alleviate the upheaval within Sabinus' wracked innards. With another strained convulsion, he sent a thin splatter of bile and red wine down the already tarnished planking to drip onto the rearmost pair of the vessel's sixty double-banked starboard oars. His groans blended in with the creaking of straining rope and wood.

From his position next to the two steering-oars at the stern of the ship, the trierarchus affected not to notice the involuntary, high-pitched flatulence that accompanied Sabinus' latest heave, nor did he comment on the fact that he had chosen to vomit on the windward side of the ship; the Governor of the imperial provinces of Moesia, Macedonia and Thracia could be sick wherever he liked on his command as far as the trierarchus was concerned. Indeed, during the two-day run from Novidunum, the home port of the Danuvius Fleet, a hundred or so miles from the river's delta, to this desolate spot on the Euxine's coast, the Emperor's representative had chosen a variety of places in which to spew – not all of them overboard.

Taking quick, shallow breaths, Sabinus cursed the ill-fortune that had forced him to embark on a ship and remain on-board for far, far longer than the contents of his stomach; he had never made any claim to being a mariner. Nevertheless, with his appointment as governor, three years previously, came a responsibility not just to the Emperor but to the Empire itself. If the intelligence that he had learnt from an agent amongst the Getic and Dacian tribes, to the north of the Danuvius, was reliable, the Empire – or at least, the eastern part of it – could be in serious peril.

There had been no question of mistrusting the report; the agent was loyal to Tryphaena, the former Queen of Thracia. The great-granddaughter of Marcus Antonius, Tryphaena was a Roman citizen and fiercely loyal to the Empire. Although she now lived in Cyzicus on the coast of the province of Asia – since she had abdicated at Caligula's request – she made it her business to be well informed about the affairs of her former subjects and their enemies. If Tryphaena's agent made a report concerning a threat to the Empire then it was to be taken very seriously.

By the time the man had made the hazardous, overland journey to Novidunum to give Sabinus his account of the arrival of an embassy from Vologases, the Great King of Parthia, to the Kings of the trans-Danuvian tribes, the news was already four days old. Sabinus had then taken the three biremes and single trireme in the harbour and sailed down to the Euxine. There he had headed north up the coast to lay off Tyra, a Greek colony under the sway of the Dacian King Coson, who was no friend of Rome.

Some duties were so critical that they could not be delegated; Sabinus knew that if he reported to the Emperor Claudius, or, more importantly, to the Empress Agrippina and her lover Pallas, the true powers in Rome, that he had sent a subordinate to intercept the Parthian mission but they had slipped through his grasp, then that failure would be seen as Sabinus'. At least if he were unsuccessful he would have no one to blame but himself; but Sabinus had no intention of being so. He could guess what had been discussed. There was nothing that the Dacian, Getic, Sarmatian and Bastanae Kings, all gathered, according to the agent, in a camp on the grasslands fifty miles west of Tyra, had that was of any interest to Parthia other than one uniting attribute: a hatred of Rome. As that hatred spilled over Rome's northern borders, Parthia, Rome's bitterest enemy to the east, would either sweep west to try once again to take the coast of Syria and gain access to Rome's sea for the first time since Rome came east; or, head north, through the Roman client kingdoms of Armenia and Pontus to gain access to the Euxine.

Either way, Rome's eastern provinces were under threat.

However, Sabinus now had within his grasp an opportunity to find out the timing and direction of such a bold move; with knowledge of how, where and when the blows would fall they could be deflected. It was of vital importance, therefore, that the ambassadors were captured and interrogated as they sailed from Tyra, whose dim lights could be seen on the southern bank of the Tyras estuary.

With another retch and unintentional breaking of wind – one dry this time, the other less so – Sabinus pushed himself upright, sweating despite the cool breeze blowing in from the sea. He watched, in reflection, the ever-shifting image of the half-moon swallowed by a dark bank of cloud; the silver-lined edge undulated on the water's surface for a few moments before fading and becoming one with the darkening sea. Sabinus looked up; the cloud had blocked all light in the sky for the first time since they had begun their dusk to dawn vigil three nights ago. By day they would heave-to just over the horizon, out of sight of the watchtowers of Tyra, but within interception range of any ship that sailed from the estuary to follow the coastline back round to whatever friendly port the Parthians had embarked from. But Sabinus doubted that the Parthians would sail by day as the agent had informed him that they had arrived at Tyra in the dead of night; that, Sabinus knew, was no mean feat for even the most experienced naval trierarchus. Besides, he was under no illusions that, despite their precautions, their presence had not gone undetected and so the Parthians would be waiting for complete darkness, a time such as now, before venturing out to sea.

Still supporting himself on the rail, Sabinus turned towards the trierarchus. 'Have the rowers stand to, Xanthos, and signal the three biremes to prepare for action.' As the trierarchus relayed the order down to the oar-deck below, Sabinus wiped a trail of vomit from his chin and looked towards the bow; he could just make out the shapes of the half-century of marines, sitting around the carroballista mounted on the deck, respecting the standing night-time order for complete silence. He signalled to the centurion commanding them with a hand gesture that they should rise and prepare themselves. From below came the muted sounds of the ship's one hundred and twenty rowers taking their places, one man each on the lower bank of oars and two on the upper. Trying to clear his head, blurred by nausea, Sabinus glanced down and saw the oars being aligned ready for the initial pull that would propel the vessel forward as the first few drops of rain spattered onto the sea and hit the ship's deck with a slow, irregular drumming.

With the ship readied, Sabinus adjusted his red woollen cloak so that it warmed his arms; he tightened the red sash around the midriff of his bronze back- and breastplates and adjusted the shoulder belt in order that his sword hung straight on his right hip. Having replaced his helmet and tied the chinstrap, he picked up his standard-issue semi-cylindrical shield, walked as steadily as possible forward to the bow and stood next to the marine centurion, beneath the towering *corvus* that they would use to board an enemy ship, and prepared to wait for the remaining three hours of the night, peering into the gloom that deepened as the rain intensified.

It was just an intuition at first. There was nothing visible through the torrent and no sound carried over its incessant beating on wood and water but, with less than an hour until dawn, Sabinus was sure that they were not alone. He wiped the rain from his eyes and squinted into the continuing deluge; it was a black wall of water occasionally penetrated by a glimmer of light from the town over a mile away. But then a new sensation pierced his consciousness: a sound, very faint, but certainly a sound other than the driving rain and the creak of timber and stretching rope as the ship strained against the power of the sea. There it was again, long and low. Sabinus counted to five and the noise was repeated; there could be no doubt now: it was a steady rhythm, the massed grunts of exertion of scores of oarsmen pulling in time.

He turned, raised his arm at the trierarchus and signalled to move forward. Deck-hands at either end of the ship hauled on ropes and pulled in the anchors and, within a few moments, the shrill note of the stroke-master's pipe heralded the first heave on the oars; they were under way.

'Have your men load the ballista, Thracius,' Sabinus ordered the marine centurion, 'and check that the deck-hands are manning the corvus and standing by with grappling hooks.'

Thracius saluted and went about his business as the trireme gained momentum with each successive, quickening stroke. Around Sabinus the ship burst into activity as the carroballista's torsioned arms were wound back; deck-hands manned the pulley system that would release the spiked corvus to slam down and pinion an enemy ship, creating a bridge, while marines checked their kit and sailors were stationed along the rails and in the bow with grappling hooks at the ready. The straining groans of the oarsmen intensified as they pulled on creaking sweeps, accelerating the huge vessel; they were augmented by those from the three biremes, one to either side and one behind, creating a cacophony of human effort that Sabinus knew could warn the Parthians of their presence. But that did not concern him; there was nothing that he could do about it as it was impossible for so many men to row in silence. What did concern him, however, was spotting the enemy ship before it evaded them; he stared forward into the night, his nausea forgotten, as the ram below him churned the black waters to foaming grey.

And then it was there; a darker shadow on a dark sea, dimly silhouetted by the port's few lanterns behind it. Shouts from about the ship indicated that other members of the crew had also spotted the spectral blur. Imprecise and non-linear but certainly tangible, it grew more distinct with every grunted heave on the oars as the trireme sped forward towards its prey. Sabinus had given the trierarchus orders to intercept and ram and he felt the ship shift its course slightly to do just that. He smiled to himself and then, with a jolt, realised that the shade was not singular but, rather, split into three as one dark mass fanned out to starboard, another to larboard, leaving the third, the central one, less than fifty paces away, on collision course with the trireme. To either side a bireme split off to intercept the two fleeing ships.

'Release!' Thracius shouted. With an abrupt crack the two arms of the ballista slammed forward, hurling the bolt into the oncoming shadow; its impact registered with a hollow thump but no screams followed.

'Brace!' Thracius roared as the distance between the two vessels lessened dramatically; his men knelt on one leg, bracing themselves with their shields and javeline-like *pila*.

From the stern came a shouted order amplified by a speaking trumpet; it was followed by the mass rasping of oars being hauled inboard to avoid crippling damage should the enemy attempt to rake down one side. Sabinus gripped the rail and went down on his knees as the approaching shadow resolved itself into the outline of a trireme of equal size. And it was with equal weight and equal groaning of timbers that the two vessels ploughed into each other, colliding with their starboard bows. The corvus was released to screech down on its pulleys and crunch through the enemy's rail, shattering it; but the ships were not aligned and the foot-long spike grazed down the side of the hull, failing to penetrate the deck. Their momentum drove the ships on, their rams ricocheting off curved hulls to slew them around, both to their larboard, in opposite rotations, out of control, their crews sprawled out on the deck.

Raising his head over the rail, Sabinus saw that the Roman vessel was spinning on its axis, right to left, its stern heading directly for that of the Parthian's as it rotated, slowly, majestically, inexorably, in the contrary direction as if joining in some strange nautical dance. 'Thracius, take your men back and try and secure us to them with ropes as we hit.'

The centurion picked himself up from the deck, shouting at the sailors with grappling hooks and his men to follow him. Sabinus watched with detached interest as the two ships swung towards each other. With a shuddering impact and the high-pitched grinding of labouring wood, they slammed together at roughly the point that Sabinus had vomited earlier. Thracius and his men tumbled to the ground only to get up again an instant later at the centurion's bellowed commands as, from out of the darkness behind the trireme, surged the third Roman bireme, under full oars and at ramming speed. On it came, the groans of its labouring rowers clearly audible with every swift stroke, its bow ploughing a temporary furrow through churning water directly towards the Parthian's beam.

And without loss of momentum the smaller ship drove into the trireme, punching its bronze-faced ram through the solid timbers of the hull, a foot below the water-line, with an explosive report that drowned the sound of human exertion and the forces of nature. Pushing deep into the Parthian's belly, the bireme's primary weapon ripped through its innards with an eruption of water until its bow, crunching into the vessel's side, prevented further penetration but set the ship rocking, back and forth, grinding on the impaling ram and opening up the wound even more.

Then the grappling hooks hurtled through the air as Thracius formed up his men in preparation for boarding. The ropes were secured as the first arrows thumped in from the trapped ship, cracking into the marines' shields or hissing unseen across the trireme and on into blackness; here and there a cry as a crewman spun to the deck with a fletched shaft quivering in his convulsing body. With a throat-rasping, inchoate roar, Thracius jumped up onto the rail and hurled himself onto the enemy ship; without any hesitation his men followed him as dark figures struggled to form up into a line of defence across the Parthian deck.

Sabinus got to his feet and walked back towards the stern. He was in no rush; it was not his business to risk life and limb in the menial task of clearing an enemy ship and, besides, Thracius and his men seemed to be doing a very competent job of it, having formed up in two lines and slammed into the defenders. Rain sheeted across the heaving deck on gusts of wind, further diluting the blood that slopped onto the soaked planking as iron clashed with iron, resounded on leather-bound wood and sliced through flesh and bone to the piteous screams of the maimed and dying.

To the rear of the marines, the Parthian steersmen and trier-archus lay dead beneath the steering-oars along with a couple of archers caught in the open as Thracius' men had stormed the ship. Near the corpses, their Roman killers, a half-dozen marines, stood guard over the companionway leading down to the oar-deck; with long spears the marines stabbed at the terrified Parthian crew trying to escape the water flooding in below in order to prevent them from coming up behind their comrades, who were now pushing back the eastern, trouser-wearing defenders with the savage discipline that Sabinus expected of regular close-order Roman troops. Finding the route to safety barred, many of the rowers squeezed through the oar-ports to take their chances in the sea. Beyond them, the bireme was backing oars in an attempt to extricate itself from the crippled and visibly listing Parthian vessel; the blades whipped up the already roiling water so that men now floundering found their screams choked and their struggles useless. Many were sucked under while others suffered grim head wounds as the sweeps cracked into their skulls and faces. With the teeth-freezing squeal of grating and tearing wood on wood, the bireme edged back.

Sabinus vaulted the rail and landed on the stricken ship; he drew his sword and strode towards the line of the melee, which had now almost reached the mainmast, past the many dead and wounded left in its wake. The ship lurched, as the bireme managed to pull itself free, and then settled, tilted markedly towards the side with the gaping rend. Sabinus stumbled but righted himself; his stomach heaved again with the rocking of the ship. A slight movement of a dying man just to his left caused Sabinus to pause and press the tip of his sword into the man's throat, grinding the blade left and right, not wanting to be attacked from behind by an enemy feigning incapacity. He withdrew his weapon, with a gurgle of air bubbling through thick liquid, and went to move on but then stopped abruptly. He peered down at the man's face in the gloom. It was bearded; but with a full, Greek-style beard, not the more shaped version sported in Parthia. He looked down at the man's legs: he was wearing eastern trousers and yet they were not partially covered by a long tunic. He glanced around; all the enemy dead wore trousers but none of them had eastern-style tunics or beards, nor were they armed in the Parthian manner – scale armour, wicker shields, bows and short spears and swords – but, rather, in the Greek style of the northern Euxine – oval *thureos* shield, javelin and short sword. Sabinus cursed under his breath and then ran back to where the enemy trierarchus lay; he had a beard the colour of copper, natural, not dyed. That settled it: he was definitely not Parthian.

This was not the ship carrying the embassy.

As panic rose in his throat he ran to the rail and looked out; to larboard he could make out that one of the escort ships had been grappled by a bireme, but to starboard he could see nothing. Behind him Thracius' troops broke the remaining resistance of the ships' marines.

'I want prisoners!' Sabinus shouted as the centurion hacked and slashed his way into the retreating enemy, his men reaping bloody harvest to either side. He sprinted into the rear of the marines and barged his way through, manhandling men out of the way, screaming at them to take prisoners, until he reached Thracius. 'Prisoners! I must have a couple of prisoners.'

The centurion turned back to him and nodded, his eyes wide with killing-joy and his face and arms smeared in blood; he shouted at the men to either side and they charged forward, following up the defeated foe. Sabinus trailed them, checking the bodies of the fallen to see if there was enough life left in one to be able to furnish him with the information he was now desperate for. He cursed himself for allowing his seasickness to cloud his mind: in his weakened state, he had assumed that the Parthian embassy would just try to sneak past his flotilla and had not considered the possibility of a diversion. Which of the other two ships held the ambassadors?

Then that word suddenly echoed in his head: diversion, diversion. Bile surged in his throat and this time it was not from the ship's motion: he had been duped; none of these ships contained the Parthians. He ran forward to the bow where Thracius and his men were disarming the last two dozen or so of the enemy; he looked out to the north as the first vestiges of dawn warmed the thick cloud blanket above.

'Where do you want to question them, sir?' Thracius asked, thrusting a prisoner down onto his knees, pulling his hair back and placing a bloodied blade on the exposed throat.

Sabinus stared, forlorn, at the sleek little liburnian, just visible in the growing light, under full sail and oars, running past them a quarter of a mile away at a speed that neither the trireme nor the biremes could hope to match for very long. 'I don't need to any more. Finish them.'

A scream of terrified pleading erupted from the prisoners as the first was despatched, and Sabinus felt a stab of disgust at himself for ordering their deaths solely out of pique at being outsmarted. 'Hold, Thracius!'

The centurion arrested his stroke as the tip of his sword pricked the throat of a second shrieking prisoner and looked back at his superior.

'Throw them into the water; they can take their chances with the rest. Then get your men back to our ship.'

As the marines obeyed the order, Sabinus walked back to the trireme, calculating just how he would frame what he knew would be a very difficult letter to Pallas, Claudius' favoured freedman and the real power behind the throne of a drooling, malleable fool. Not even his brother Vespasian, who, thanks to the influence of Pallas, was due to become suffect-consul for the last two months of the year, would be able to protect him from the wrath of those in power.

And their wrath would be justified.

Sabinus was under no illusions; he had failed catastrophically and the embassy was now on its way to report back to the Great King in his capital, Ctesiphon, on the Tigris.

There would be no way to hide his guilt. It was a certainty that Pallas also had agents amongst the Dacians and news of the embassy and Sabinus' failure would reach him within the next month or two. It was also a certainty that Narcissus and Callistus, Pallas' fellow freedmen and rivals whom he had outmanoeuvred, by making Agrippina empress, and relegated to second place in

Claudius' pliable estimation, would also hear of Sabinus' failure. They would be sure to use it as a political weapon in the vicious infighting that pervaded the imperial palace.

Sabinus cursed the weakness of the Emperor that gave rise to such combustible politics and he cursed the men and women who took advantage of that weakness for their own gain; but most of all he cursed his own weakness: the nausea he felt each time he stepped onto a ship. Tonight that weakness had addled his mind and caused him to make a mistake.

Because of that weakness he had failed Rome.

PART I

ROME, DECEMBER AD 51

CHAPTER I

Pᴇʀsɪsᴛᴇɴᴛ ᴀɴᴅ sʜʀɪʟʟ, the cry echoed around the walls and marble columns of the atrium; a torment to all who endured it.

Titus Flavius Vespasianus gritted his teeth, determined not to be moved by the pitiful wail as it rose and fell, occasionally pausing for a ragged breath before bellowing out again with renewed, lung-filled vigour. The suffering that it conveyed had to be borne and Vespasian knew that should he not have the stomach for it he would lose the ongoing battle of wills; and that was something that he could not afford to do.

A new cacophony of anguish emitted from the writhing bundle in his wife's arms, its movements caught in the flickering glow of the log fire spitting and crackling in the atrium hearth. Vespasian winced and then held his head high and crooked his left arm before him as his body slave draped his toga over and around his well-muscled, compact frame, watched by Titus, Vespasian's eleven-year-old son.

With the heavy woollen garment eventually hanging to his satisfaction and the howls showing no sign of abating, Vespasian eased into the pair of red leather, senatorial slippers that his slave held out for him. 'The heels, Hormus.' Hormus ran a finger around the back of each shoe so that his master's feet fitted snugly and then stood and backed away with deference, leaving Titus facing his father.

Doing his best to remain calm as the din reached a new level, Vespasian contemplated Titus for a few moments. 'Does the Emperor still come every day to check on his son's progress?'

'Most days, Father; and he also asks me and the other boys questions, as well as Britannicus.'

Vespasian flinched at a particularly shrill bawl and strove to ignore it. 'What happens if you get them wrong?'

'Sosibius beats us after Claudius has gone.'

Vespasian hid his less than favourable opinion of the *grammaticus* from his son. It had been Sosibius' fallacious allegations at the Empress Messalina's behest, three years earlier, that had set in train a series of events that had ended up in Vespasian bearing false witness against the former Consul, Asiaticus, in order to protect his brother, Sabinus. Using Vespasian as a willing tool, however, Asiaticus had had his revenge from beyond the grave and Messalina had been executed; Vespasian had been present as she shrieked and cursed her last. But Sosibius was still in place, his fabricated charges corroborated by Vespasian's false testimony. 'Does he often beat you?'

Titus' face hardened into a strained expression, startling Vespasian by its similarity to his own, older version. The thick nose not so pronounced, the earlobes not so long, the jaw not so heavy and with a full head of hair rather than his semi-wreath about the crown; but there was no mistaking it: Titus was his son. 'Yes, Father, but Britannicus says that it's because his stepmother, the Empress, has ordered him to.'

'Then deny Agrippina that pleasure and make sure that Sosibius has no cause to beat you today.'

'If he does it'll be the last time. Britannicus has thought of a way to have him dismissed and at the same time insult his stepbrother.'

Vespasian ruffled Titus' hair. 'Don't you get involved in any feud between Britannicus and Nero.'

'I'll always support my friend, Father.'

'Just be sure that you don't make it too public.' Vespasian took the boy's chin in his hand and examined his face. 'It's dangerous; do you understand me?'

Titus nodded slowly. 'Yes, Father, I believe I do.'

'Good, now be off with you. Hormus, see Titus out to his escort. Are Magnus' lads waiting?'

'Yes, master.'

As Hormus led Titus away the bawling continued. Vespasian turned to face Flavia Domitilla, his wife of twelve years; she sat staring into the fire doing nothing to try to soothe the babe in her arms. 'If you really want my clients to mistake you for the wet nurse when I let them in for the morning *salutio*, my dear, then I suggest that you plug little Domitian onto one of your breasts and sing Gallic lullabies to him.'

Flavia snorted and carried on staring at the flames. 'At least then they'll think that we can afford a Gallic wet nurse.'

Vespasian pushed his head forward, frowning, unable to credit what he had just heard. 'What are you talking about, woman? We've got a Gallic wet nurse; it's just that this morning you've chosen not to call for her and instead you seem to be intent on starving the child.' To emphasise the point he picked up a piece of bread from his recently abandoned breakfast, dipped it in the bowl of olive oil and then chewed on it with relish.

'She's not Gallic! She's Hispanic.'

Vespasian suppressed a sigh of exasperation. 'Yes, she is from Hispania but she is a Celt, a Celtiberian. She's from the same race of huge tribesmen that all the *finest* women in Rome choose to have breastfeed their sons; it's just that when her ancestors crossed the Rhenus they didn't stop in Gaul, they carried on over the mountains into Hispania.'

'And therefore she produces milk so thin that a kitten wouldn't survive on it.'

'Her milk is no different from any other Celt's.'

'Your niece swears by her Allobroges woman.'

'How Lucius Junius Paetus chooses to indulge his wife is his own affair. However, to my mind, allowing a baby to go hungry because its wet nurse isn't from one of the more fashionable Celtic tribes is the act of an irresponsible mother.'

'And to my mind dragging a wife to live in the squalor of the Quirinal Hill and then not allowing her to purchase the staff that she needs to look after the family is the act of an uncaring and heartless husband and father.'

Vespasian smiled to himself but kept his face neutral now they had got to the nub of the matter. Two and a half years previously Vespasian had used his good standing with Pallas, as the freedman had manoeuvred himself to the most powerful position in Claudius' court, to remove Flavia and their children from the apartment in the imperial palace where they had lived for most of Vespasian's four years as legate of the II Augusta in Britannia. The accommodation had been offered by Claudius ostensibly so that their two sons could be educated together and also so that Messalina, Claudius' then wife, would have a companion in the palace. However, Vespasian knew that the Emperor had been manipulated into making the offer by Messalina's brother, Corvinus, so that his old enemy could have the power of life and death over Flavia and their children. After Messalina's violent end, Pallas had kept his word to persuade Claudius to allow Vespasian to move his family to a house in Pomegranate Street, on the Quirinal Hill, near to that of his uncle, the senator Gaius Vespasius Pollo.

Flavia had resented this.

'If you call protecting my family from the ravages of imperial politics uncaring; and if you call being prudent with money so as not to be subject to the fripperies of the ladies of fashion heartless, then you've understood my character perfectly, my dear. It is bad enough that Titus goes to the palace each day to share Britannicus' education but that was Claudius' price for allowing me to move you out; having executed the boy's mother he didn't want his son to be deprived of his little playmate as well. Surely our son being educated alongside the Emperor's is enough to satisfy your vanity, despite the danger that puts him in; surely that makes up for all this *squalor*?' He indicated with a lazy hand the good-sized atrium around them. Although he would freely concede its decoration was not up to the standards of the palace – it having been built 150 years before, during the time of Gaius Marius – what it lacked in splendour with the mosaic floor's geometric black and white motif or the faded pastoral frescoes, designed to fool the beholder into thinking that they were looking through windows, it made up for with his wife's extravagance. It was filled with furniture and ornaments that Flavia had acquired during her lavish spending sprees while under Messalina's profligate influence.

Vespasian still shuddered every time he surveyed the room's décor surrounding the *impluvium*, the pond with a fountain of Venus at its centre: low, polished-marble tables on gilded legs covered with glass or silver ornaments, statuettes of fine bronze or worked crystal, couches and chairs, carved, painted and upholstered. It was not because of its vulgarity – he could cope with that even though it offended his country-born taste for the simple things in life – it was because of the amount of wasted money that it represented. 'Surely having all the other women jealously arguing amongst themselves as to whether Agrippina will kill Titus along with Britannicus as she clears the way for her son Nero to succeed his stepfather is enough to make you feel special and the centre of attention; like any self-respecting woman would wish for?'

Flavia clutched the bundle of their two-month-old son so tightly that for a moment Vespasian was worried that she would do him some damage. Then she relaxed and stood, holding the child to her breast with tears in her eyes. 'After all that I've done for you, for us, you should accord me a little respect, Vespasian. You are one of the sitting Consuls; I should be able to deport myself as the wife of a consul and not some lowly equestrian upstart ...'

'Which, when you consider the matter, is what we both are.'

Flavia's mouth dropped open but no sound emerged.

'Now, my dear, I'm going to open the door to all this squalor for my clients; they will greet me not only as the master of this squalor but also as the Consul of Rome who can do great favours for them and they will ignore the fact that I come from a Sabine family that can only boast one member of the Senate before me and my brother, just as they will ignore my rough Sabine accent. And then, having dealt out private patronage, I shall, as Consul of Rome, publicly deliver one of Rome's greatest enemies to the Emperor for punishment. If you like, you and our daughter may come to watch, along with all the other women, and you can enjoy the false compliments that they give you. Or perhaps you're too afraid to show your face because your husband bought you a wet nurse who belongs to a tribe that is so out of fashion that she cannot even produce decent milk.'

Vespasian turned and signalled to his doorkeeper to open up; it was with some relief that he heard the brisk clatter of Flavia's retreating footsteps over the mewling of his youngest son.

Vespasian sat on his curule chair in front of the impluvium at the centre of the atrium; the gentle spatter of the fountain, issuing from a vase on Venus' shoulder, remained constant as the dawn light grew, adding a steely tinge to the lifelike, painted skin tones of her naked torso basking in the oil lamps' glow. Hormus stood behind him making notes on a wax tablet. To either side of him were posted the twelve lictors who would accompany him, as consul, everywhere in Rome, carrying the fasces, the axes bound with rods, as a symbol of his power to command and execute. However, it was not civic power that Vespasian was exercising now but, rather, personal power as the last and least important of his two hundred or so clients greeted him.

Vespasian nodded his acknowledgement to the man. 'I have no use for you today, Balbus, you may return to your business once you have escorted me to the Forum.'

'An honour, Consul.' Balbus adjusted his plain white citizen's toga and withdrew to one side.

'How many waiting for a private interview, Hormus?' Vespasian asked, looking around the room filled with respectful men talking in murmurs as they waited for their patron to leave the house.

Hormus had no need to consult his tablet. 'Three that you asked to stay and then a further seven who requested an audience.'

Vespasian sighed; it would be a long morning. However, as the Senate was not due to sit that day it was one of the few occasions that he had the time to deal with personal business before his public duties would call him away; and it was with great interest that he was looking forward to his public duties.

'And then there's a man who is not your client asking for an interview as well.'

'Really? What's his name?'

'Agarpetus.'

Vespasian was none the wiser.

'He's a client of the imperial freedman Narcissus.'

Vespasian raised his eyebrows. 'A client of Narcissus' here to see me? Is it a message or is he trying to ingratiate himself with me?'

'He didn't say, master.'

Vespasian digested this for a few moments before rising to his feet; formality dictated that he would have to see this man last, after his own clients, so it would be a while before his curiosity would be satisfied.

But first, business.

Followed by his slave, he walked with the slow dignity of the leading magistrate in Rome, past the men awaiting his favour, to the *tablinum*, the room curtained off at the far end of the atrium, and seated himself behind the desk. 'I'll deal with the three that I need favours from, first, Hormus; in order of precedence.'

'What the Emperor did while he held the office of censor, four years ago, cannot be undone, Laelius,' Vespasian said, having heard the final plea for favour from a balding citizen wearing a very finely woven crimson tunic under his plain white toga. A heavy gold chain glinted around his neck.

'I understand that, *patronus*; however, the situation has changed.' Laelius produced a scroll from the fold of his toga and stepped up to the desk to hand it to Vespasian. 'This is a receipt from the Cloelius Brothers' banking business in the Forum Romanum. It is for exactly one hundred thousand denarii, the financial threshold for admittance to the equestrian order. When Claudius stripped me of equestrian rank four years ago he was perfectly right to do so as, owing to a series of unwise investments, my combined wealth in property and cash had fallen well below the limit. But now, thanks to your brother, at your behest, securing me the contract to supply chickpeas to the Danuvius Fleet, I've reversed my fortunes and am now financially eligible for readmittance.'

Vespasian glanced at the receipt; it was genuine. 'The Emperor may not revise the rolls for a few years yet.'

Laelius wrung his hands; there was a hint of desperation in his voice. 'My son is now seventeen; only as an eques can I hope to secure him a post as a military tribune and start him on the Cursus Honorum. In two or three years it'll be too late.'

For all his client's outward appearance of confidence Vespasian could perceive that Laelius was just another middle-aged man dogged by the spectre of impending old age with nothing to show for his life. But, if he could get his son started upon the succession of honours, the military and political career that could lead to a seat in the Senate, then he could justifiably claim to have done honour for his family by bettering it. Vespasian could understand his position well; it had been his parents' ambition for their family that had driven Vespasian and his brother Sabinus to the highest office that a citizen could achieve – barring, of course, becoming emperor; that was the prerogative of one family alone. 'Do I take it that there are two favours that you are asking me: firstly to use my influence with the imperial household to have Claudius enrol you in the equestrian order, and then to ask my brother to get your son a post as a military tribune in one of his two Moesian legions? Having already got him to award you the chickpea contract.'

Laelius winced and produced another scroll from his toga. 'I know I ask a lot, patronus, but I give a lot in return. I know that senators are forbidden to conduct trade; however, I know of no reason why a senator should not benefit from trade that is conducted by someone else. This is a legal document that would make you a sleeping-partner in my business with an interest of ten per cent of the profits.'

Vespasian took the scroll, perused it and then handed it over his shoulder to Hormus standing behind him. 'Very well, Laelius, if you make it twelve per cent I'll see what I can do.'

'Have Hormus make the alteration in the contract, patronus.'

'It will be his pleasure.'

Laelius bowed his head repeatedly in thanks and gratitude while rubbing his hands and calling down the blessings of all the gods onto his patron as Hormus escorted him out through the curtains.

Vespasian took a few sips of watered wine while he waited for his final supplicant of the morning, contemplating, as he did, just what a client of Narcissus' could want from him.

'Tiberius Claudius Agarpetus,' Hormus announced, showing in a clean-shaven, wiry man of evident wealth, judging by the heavily jewelled rings on each of his fingers and thumbs. He had the olive skin of the northern Greeks, which was stretched tight over his high-cheekboned, sharp-nosed face. Regardless of having two Roman names he disdained the toga, despite the formality of the occasion.

Vespasian did not offer him a seat. 'What can I do for you, Agarpetus?'

'It's more about what I can do for you, Consul.' The Greek spoke with a measured tone, his dark eyes never leaving Vespasian's nor showing a hint of feeling.

'What can a freedman do for me? I assume that you are Narcissus' freedman since you bear his names that he took from Claudius when he freed him in turn.'

'That is correct, Consul. Narcissus freed me two years ago and since then I have worked for him on a variety of delicate tasks involving the gathering of information.'

'I see. So you spy for him?'

'Not as such; I gather information from his agents in the eastern provinces and make assessments as to its veracity and importance so my patron only sees what he needs to see.'

'Ah, so you're a saver of time?'

'Indeed.'

'And a possessor of knowledge.'

'Yes, Consul; I am a saver of time and a possessor of knowledge.'

Vespasian could see where this was leading. 'Knowledge that could be of value to me?'

'Very much so.'

'At what price?'

'A meeting: you and your uncle with my patron.'

Vespasian frowned and ran a hand over his almost-bald crown. 'Why didn't Narcissus just ask us himself? He may be out of favour with Claudius but he's still the imperial secretary and retains the power to summon a consul and a senator.'

'That is so, but he wants the meeting to be secret; so therefore it has to be away from the palace, away from the eyes and ears of the Empress and her lover.'

'Pallas?'

'As you know, my patron and Pallas are not on the best of terms ...'

'And as *you* know, my loyalty is to Pallas and I won't be a part of Narcissus' schemes against him.'

'Not even if Pallas would knowingly allow the Empress to block your career?'

Vespasian scoffed. 'Block my career? Does it look like it's blocked? I'm Consul.'

'But you will go no further; there'll be no province to govern, no military command, nothing, just political oblivion. My patron asks you to consider this: why were you made consul for only the last two months of this year?'

'Because my forty-second birthday was in November and so it wasn't until then that I was eligible. It was a great honour to be the Emperor's colleague in the office.'

'No doubt that non-entity Calventius Vetus Carminius thought exactly the same thing when he was Claudius' colleague for September and October; in fact I would suspect that he thought it even more of an honour than you did, seeing as he'd done nothing to merit the position.'

Vespasian opened his mouth to refute the claim and then closed it immediately, his mind racing.

Agarpetus pressed his argument. 'But surely it would have been a greater honour for the victorious legate of the Second Augusta to have been made consul in January next year? In only a few days' time you could have been the Junior Consul for a full six months, perhaps even with the Emperor as your colleague, and the year would have been named after you both. But no, you were given a crumb after all your loyal service in Britannia, just a crumb, a two-month consulship, just like the man you succeeded whom nobody had ever heard of; and do you know why?'

Vespasian did not answer; his mind was too busy.

'The Empress hates you because of your son's friendship with Britannicus; and Pallas is powerless to help you against such an enemy. It was she who persuaded her gullible husband that it would be a singular honour for you to be made consul in the very month that you were first eligible and it will be her who'll block any appointment that may be mooted for you when you step down on the first day of January, three days hence. Your only hope for advancement is her demise, and loyalty to Pallas won't bring that about. Narcissus, on the other hand ...' Agarpetus trailed off leaving the last thought dangling.

Vespasian still said nothing as his mind worked and the truth of what he was being told became apparent. He did not argue with it because he realised that deep down he had always known; deep down he had been insulted by being given the consulship for the final two months of a year; deep down, he had known it to be a snub; deep down, the honour that he felt at being consul had been gnawed at by resentment. But he had kept all that buried – deep down. 'How will she block me?'

'Your brother has just failed Rome in quite a spectacular way ...'

'What do you mean?'

'This is the knowledge that we thought would be of interest to you; Narcissus will explain if you meet him. Suffice it to say that Sabinus' mistake is excuse enough to halt all ambitions that any member of your family may have. Pallas cannot help you, so that leaves you with one option.'

Trust Narcissus to reach straight for the truth of the matter; trust him to know how to manipulate. Vespasian looked at Agarpetus, his decision made; it had not been hard to choose between obscurity and disloyalty. 'Very well; I'll meet Narcissus.'

Agarpetus gave the wry smile of a man who has had a prediction confirmed – his first change of expression. 'He suggests that the safest place to meet would be at the tavern of the South Quirinal Crossroads Brotherhood; he believes that your friend, your uncle's client, Marcus Salvius Magnus, is still the patronus there.'

'He is.'

'Very good, his discretion is assured; Narcissus and I will be there tonight at the seventh hour as the city celebrates today's executions.'

'Good morning, dear boy!' Gaius Vespasius Pollo boomed as he waddled fast to fall into step next to his nephew, his expansive belly and buttocks and his sagging breasts and chins all swaying furiously to seemingly different beats. 'Thank you for inviting me to share the honour of conducting the prisoners to the Emperor.' Behind him his clients fell in with those of Vespasian to make an entourage of well over five hundred escorting them down the Quirinal Hill.

Vespasian inclined his head. 'Thank you, Uncle, for lending me your clients to add impact to my arrival in the Forum.'

'My pleasure; it makes a nice change to be preceded by lictors again.'

'"Change pleases",' a voice quoted from just behind Gaius, 'and it makes a nice change for me and the lads not to have to beat you a path through the crowds, seeing as you have them do it professionally today; and don't they do it so well?'

'Indeed, and with more satisfaction too, I'll hazard, Magnus,' Gaius suggested, starting to sweat despite the dignified pace and the chill winter wind. 'After all, a lictor gets paid and therefore mixes business with pleasure.'

Magnus' battered ex-boxer's face screwed into an indignant frown and he looked slantendicular at his patron with his one good eye – the painted glass ball in his left eye socket stared futilely ahead. 'Are you saying that my lads don't enjoy beating a path for you, senator? Because you certainly pay us to do so, although, granted, not in the same way as the College of Lictors remunerates its members. However, you reward us in subtle and much more lucrative ways, which means that our business is far more satisfying, if you take my meaning?'

Vespasian laughed and squeezed his friend's shoulder; despite Magnus being nineteen years his senior and considerably below him socially, they had been friends since Vespasian had first come to Rome as a youth of sixteen. He and his uncle knew far better than most just how satisfying Magnus found his business in the criminal underbelly of Rome as the leader of the South Quirinal Crossroads Brotherhood. 'I do, my friend; and it pleases me that even at your age you still derive satisfaction from your work.'

Magnus ran a hand through his hair, grey with age but still thick. 'Now you're mocking me, sir; I may be sixty but there's still some fight and fuck in me left – although I don't see as well as I used to since losing the eye and that is becoming a bit of a problem, I'll admit. I ain't as sharp as I was and some of the surrounding brotherhoods are getting a whiff of that.'

'Perhaps it's time to think about retiring and taking life easy; take your patron's example: he hasn't made a speech in the Senate for three years now.'

Gaius brushed away a carefully tonged and dyed curl from his face and looked at Vespasian in alarm. 'Dear boy, you wonder why, when the last speech I was forced to make was reading out a list of all the senators and equites accused of crimes with Messalina and condemned to death. That sort of exposure makes one very conspicuous and that's how I still feel three years later, having not even countenanced the possibility of holding an opinion, let alone considered expressing one, during all that time.'

'Well, I'm afraid that you may be dragged out of your self-imposed retirement, Uncle.'

The alarm on Gaius' face intensified. 'Whatever for?'

'Not what but whom, Uncle.'

'Pallas?'

'I wish it were but I'm afraid it's not.'

'Is that wise?' Gaius asked after Vespasian had finished recounting his meeting with Agarpetus. 'If you refuse to meet him, there is still a chance that Pallas may be able to exert some pressure over Agrippina; he might get her to change her mind or at least not oppose you so vehemently just because your boy happens to be her stepson's best friend. But once you go behind Pallas' back to Narcissus then all trust and expectation of loyalty is broken and we lose the best ally that this family has in the palace.'

'But that ally is the lover of my enemy.'

'And so therefore Pallas has become your enemy whilst Narcissus is Agrippina's enemy thus making him your friend? Dear boy, think: Pallas has done nothing more than protect his own position by allying himself with Agrippina; he has made the sensible choice seeing as Nero is a far more suitable candidate to succeed Claudius than Britannicus, purely because he's three years older. Claudius won't last more than two, perhaps three, more years; do you really think that a boy could rule?'

Vespasian considered the question as the party passed under a colonnade and entered the Forum of Augustus dominated by the vividly painted Temple of Mars Victorious resplendent in deep red and strong, golden yellow. Statues, togate or in military uniform, equally as brightly painted, stood on plinths around the edge of the Forum, their eyes – which exposed Magnus' false one for the cheap imitation it was – following the public about their business as if the great men commemorated still guided the city. 'No, Uncle, not without a regent,' he admitted eventually.

'And who would that be in Britannicus' case? His mother, thank the gods, is dead so that leaves his uncle, Corvinus, or Burrus, the prefect of the Praetorian Guard. No one can countenance either option so the weight of opinion is favouring Nero because, since his fourteenth birthday fifteen days ago, he has taken his toga virilis. If Claudius dies tomorrow we have a man to put in his place.'

'If Nero becomes emperor, Agrippina will see to it that I'll never hold office again.'

'Then pull Titus away from Britannicus and the problem is solved.'

'Is it? Claudius would be offended; what happens if he surprises us all and lives for another ten years?'

It was Gaius' turn to contemplate the question as they passed through into Caesar's Forum where the Urban prefect and lesser civic magistrates could be petitioned in the shadow of a great equestrian statue of the one-time dictator himself. 'That would be unfortunate,' Gaius conceded, 'but highly unlikely.'

'But not impossible. If I've earned Agrippina's enmity, would you deem it wise to try to buy her friendship by earning Claudius' as well?'

'If you put it like that, then no.'

'So what choice do we have other than going to meet with Narcissus tonight?'

Massed cheering broke out as Vespasian's twelve lictors came out into the Forum Romanum, their appearance announcing the arrival of one of the Consuls at the Senate House to the thousands of citizenry come to witness the greatest day in Rome since the Ovation of Aulus Plautius four years previously. This would be the day when Rome's great enemy, the chieftain who had led the resistance to her latest conquest, would pay for his temerity and die before the Emperor.

But first, in the absence of his imperial senior colleague who waited at the Praetorian camp, outside the Viminal Gate, it was Vespasian's task to make the sacrifice and read the auspices; it was important that the gods declare the day auspicious for the business of the city to be carried out. Vespasian had no doubt that it would be so.

Blood spurted in heartbeat bursts into the copper basin beneath the white bullock's gaping neck. The beast's eyes barely focused, stunned as it was by the Father of the House's mallet blow to its forehead made an instant before Vespasian, a fold of his toga covering his head, wielded the knife. Its forelegs and shoulders began to shudder, blood flowing down them. Its tongue lolled from its mouth and it voided its bowels with a steaming splatter as the juddering limbs collapsed, bringing the victim to its knees in front of the Senate House. Standing arrayed on the steps in order of precedence, the five hundred senators currently residing in the city looked on with a solemn dignity as this ancient ceremony was enacted, as of time immemorial, in the very heart of Rome.

Vespasian had stepped back, keeping well away from the various discharges emitting from the bullock – it would be considered a bad omen for the presiding Consul to have his toga sullied and the whole ritual would have to be repeated. The Father of the House supervised the removal of the filled basin by two public slaves just before the animal slumped to the ground, its heartbeat fast diminishing as it made the transition from living flesh to inanimate carcass.

Vespasian repeated the formulaic words over the dead beast, entreating Jupiter Opitmus Maximus' blessing on his city, just as they had been intoned by incumbents of his office since the founding of the Republic. Four more public slaves rolled the body onto its back and stretched its four limbs in preparation for the belly incision.

The stench of steaming, fresh viscera assaulted Vespasian's nostrils as his honed blade slit open the gift to Rome's guardian god; the crowd, packing the Forum and beyond, held its collective breath. After a series of careful, expert incisions Vespasian lifted out the still warm heart and, having presented it to his fellow senators and then to the equites at the front of the huge throng, placed it to sizzle and hiss in the fire burning on Jupiter's altar before the open wood and iron doors of the Curia.

Two public slaves on either side pulled back the ribcage and Vespasian began the tricky task of detaching the liver without staining his toga. Having presided over many sacrifices he knew that the key to this was steady work; with methodical patience, the organ was soon removed intact and placed on the table next to the altar. Using a cloth put there for the purpose, Vespasian wiped the liver clean of blood and ran his hand over the surface. In an instant he froze and felt his heart attempt to leap into his mouth; his chest heaved with a couple of laboured breaths and his eyes stared fixedly at a blemish, almost purple on the red-brown flesh. But a blemish has no regular or specific shape and that was not true of the mark on the liver's surface caused, it seemed, by two veins coming almost to the surface together; it had a well-defined form, almost as if it had been branded on, in much the same way as a slave-owner would brand his possession: with a single letter. And it was the letter that had startled him; small but prominent, it was the letter with which his cognomen began. What he saw before him was the letter 'V'. But more than that, the mark was in almost the exact centre of the liver just to the left of the thin central lobe; in the area that the ancient Etruscan diviners considered sacred to Mars, his guardian god.

Knowing that an omen, found on a liver gifted to Jupiter in Rome's name, so blatantly referring to him, as the master of the sacrifice, could be open to many interpretations – most of them incurring the jealousy of those in power – Vespasian turned the liver over and examined a reassuringly unblemished underside. Then, taking care to place his thumb over the potentially treasonous mark, he lifted the organ and showed it to the Father of the House and declared the day propitious for the business of Rome. But the image of the mark played before his eyes.

'So be it,' the Father cried in an aged, reedy voice as Vespasian placed the liver on the altar fire. 'Bring out the prisoners!'

There was movement around the Tullianum, the prison at the foot of the Capitoline Hill, next to the Germonian Stairs, in the shadow of the Temple of Juno on the Arx above it. Soldiers of the Urban Cohorts cleared an area in front of the single door before a centurion, with the transverse white horsehair crest on his helmet fluttering in the light breeze, rapped on the door with his vine cane.

The crowd hushed in anticipation.

A few moments later the door opened and a line of manacled prisoners shuffled out and still the crowd stayed silent, waiting for the one man they had all come to see.

And then a bulky figure filled the open doorway to Rome's only public prison, his head bowed as he passed through into the open. There was a massed intake of breath; he was not miserably clad and beaten down like the wretches before him. Quite the contrary; he wore the clothes and held the demeanour of a king.

'Very clever,' Gaius murmured, 'the grander you dress him the higher you elevate him, and the greater Claudius looks when he tears him down and humbles him.'

Vespasian gazed at the prisoner standing there, his bronze winged helmet reflecting the weak sun, his hands manacled but his chest blown out and proud beneath a weighty chain mail tunic as the crowd's reaction grew into a cacophony of booing and hissing. There stood the man whom he had not seen since that night, five years before, when he had led his army out of the shadowed north and come within moments of catching the II Augusta manoeuvring into position. There stood the man who had almost destroyed a legion, Vespasian's legion.

There stood Caratacus.

CHAPTER II

THE PEOPLE OF Rome jeered and hurled abuse and missiles at the captives as they were driven across the Forum Romanum. Yet Caratacus feigned not to notice as he looked around like a tourist on his first visit to the greatest city on earth. However, it was not with an overawed countenance that he observed the arched facade of the Tabularium and the majestic columns of the Temple of Jupiter perched above it, nor did his round, ruddy face betray any wonder as he passed the Temples of Concordia and Saturn. And it was with grey eyes devoid of admiration that he arrived at the steps of the Senate House. His magnificent, drooping moustaches rippled in the breeze as he surveyed the grave faces of the five hundred leading citizens of Rome draped in their chalked-white togas edged with a thick purple stripe, shod in red leather and with all those eligible wearing military crowns or surrounded by lictors according to rank.

Vespasian stood at the top of the steps, at the very centre of the senatorial throng, as Caratacus was brought to a halt at their foot. He raised both hands for silence, which was slow in coming but eventually manifest as the people realised that the proceedings of the day would not progress unless there was order. 'Caratacus of the Catuvellauni,' Vespasian declaimed in a clear, high voice, pitched to carry over the expanse of faces looking at him. 'You have been defeated in arms and captured by Rome; now you have been brought here for the Senate to take you to your Emperor for sentence. Do you have anything to say?'

Caratacus drew himself up and looked Vespasian in the eye. 'Titus Flavius Vespasianus, Consul of Rome and erstwhile legate of the Second Augusta, whom I had the honour to face in battle, I greet you as a brother-in-arms and congratulate you on the skill that you showed in saving the lives of your men on the night I ambushed you. Consul, I salute you.'

To Vespasian's surprise and the surprise of all else present, the Britannic King snapped a Roman salute, slamming his fist onto his breast.

'I have two things to say to you before I go before the Emperor: firstly, although Rome did defeat me in arms, Rome did not capture me; I was betrayed by the witch-queen Cartimandua and her husband Venutius of the Brigantes, who broke the laws of hospitality in a way that would shame even the most primitive of peoples. And secondly, Claudius is not my Emperor; if he were so then I would not be here but, rather, at home where I once happily lived. However, I would be pleased to meet the man who desires to possess more than all this.' He gestured around the expanse of the Forum Romanum before turning back to Vespasian. 'So lead on, Consul, I am curious to meet your Emperor.'

Vespasian's twelve lictors led the procession along the Via Sacra, past the House of the Vestals and the Domus Publica and many other sights, to no more than a rumbling murmur from the crowd. Gone were the jeers and the insults and not even a crust of stale bread flew towards the Britannic King as he strode behind Vespasian and the other leading magistrates, erect and dignified, a full head taller than most of them and their lictors. News of his words had filtered through the crowd and it was with reverence that they watched him pass with the rest of the Senate following behind, out of the Forum and then left, up towards the Vicus Patricius where the buildings became less grand as the tenements of the Subura jostled against one another for mutual support and where prostitution was the main reason for the transferral of coinage.

But it was with unseeing eyes that Vespasian made the journey; his mind was not on this world.

Ever since, as a boy of fifteen, he had overheard his parents discussing the omens found at his naming ceremony, he had suspected that he was subject to the will of his guardian god, Mars; but no one would tell him what had been predicted as his mother had subjected all present to an oath never to reveal what signs they had seen on the sacrifices. Was what he had seen today similar? A 'V' stamped in the realm of Mars on the liver dedicated by him to Rome's greatest god, Jupiter. But there were many parts of this puzzle and as he tentatively pieced them together a picture emerged whose entirety he had already glimpsed.

The Oracle of Amphiariaos holding a centuries-old prophecy to be delivered only to him and Sabinus. Tiberius' astrologer advising the old Emperor that a senator who witnessed the Phoenix's rebirth in Egypt would father the next dynasty of emperors: Vespasian had witnessed the event in Siwa and thought nothing of it until Sabinus had told him that the oasis had once been a part of the Kingdom of Egypt. Then there was the Oracle of Amun and the dying gift of his patroness, the Lady Antonia: the sword of her father, Marcus Antonius, one of the greatest of all the Romans. There was also Myrddin, the immortal druid of Britannia; he had told Vespasian that he had seen the destiny that Mars held for him. That destiny had terrified Myrddin because he was convinced that Vespasian would one day have the power, but fail to use it, to halt a disease now germinated in the heart of Rome; a disease, Mryddin believed, that would eventually destroy the old and true religions. Twice, Myrddin had tried to kill him with his gods conjured to life; proof that the gods existed, proof that they had power. That he had survived, Vespasian knew, was proof that Mars held his hands over him; and because that was certain, what he had seen that morning should be taken seriously.

All this echoed around his head as he led the procession towards the heir to the Julio-Claudian bloodline: a twitching, limping, dribbling fool ruled by his wife and freedmen. A scholarly historian? Perhaps. A legal pedant of some note? Certainly. But a wise emperor who weighed his words or a vain fool, dismissive of the talents of others, resentful for years of humiliation and under the mistaken impression that he was one of the finest wits of the age?

On they went up the Viminal, along the Vicus Patricius, to barely a raised voice, past the more respectable brothels of both sexes and on towards the Viminal Gate, beyond which waited the fool who drooled. Vespasian put his thoughts to the back of his mind and wondered how the Emperor would deal with a man of such dignity and so worthy of respect as Caratacus.

Then Vespasian considered what he would do were he in Claudius' position.

The Praetorian Guard crunched to attention, shaking the ground as thousands of feet stamped down in absolute unison. Beyond the ranks and files of regimented cohorts, crows rose, in wing-beating chaos, from the rooftops of the Praetorian camp, protesting with shrill caws the interruption of their morning slumber. The sharp bellows of command and the resulting military thunder echoed between the camp's walls and the city's high, brick-built Servian defences for a few moments before fading abruptly to leave only the fluttering of massed banners and the faint hiss of the breeze blowing through thousands of horsehair crests, augmented occasionally by mournful bird-cry. Rigid, the men of Rome's élite unit held their eyes to the front, unblinking, as the Senate paraded through the Viminal Gate, Vespasian at their head, bearing the gift of a captured king and his retinue to their Emperor.

Claudius was seated on one of two daises to the left of the Guard's formation with the wives and children of the leading men in Rome to his other side. Flavia and their eight-year-old daughter, Domitilla, were seated in places of honour to the front of the women; her pride in Vespasian's position was very apparent as she sat, bolt upright, her head turning from side to side acknowledging the real or imagined compliments of her peers, her worries over wet nurses temporarily put to one side.

The Senate progressed without haste, giving every guardsman the chance of a glimpse of the rebel King before he met his inevitable death: garrotted and self-soiled at the feet of the Emperor. Even from a distance Claudius' nervous tic was apparent; his head jerked and his limbs shook with irregular frequency as the parade neared him.

It was with a shock of disgust that Vespasian saw the occupant of the second dais: Agrippina. Never had a woman been raised to the same level as the First Man in Rome. Not even Augustus' wife, Livia, had sought such an honour and not even Cleopatra had achieved it when she had visited her lover and father of her son, the dictator Gaius Julius Caesar, in Rome almost a century earlier. And now here was the direct female descendant of those two great men, well into her forties, acting as if she were their equal while her uncle-husband twitched and dribbled, dabbing the drool from his chin with the edge of his toga; incongruous in his laurel wreath and purple.

Arranged around the two daises were the men and women who benefitted from their close connections with either one – or both – of the occupants. Exactly between them was Pallas, his beard and hair now flecked with grey and his face and eyes, as ever, neutral; a mask that could not be read, a mask that Vespasian had only once ever seen drop.

Between Pallas and Agrippina stood Nero: fourteen years old and with the milky-skinned face of a young god, resplendently topped by lush curls, the golden-red hue of dawn. He stood, almost side-on with his left foot pointing forward, wearing the senatorial toga that the Senate had voted him, along with the rank of proconsul, when he had come of age a mere fifteen days ago. In sharp contrast, to Pallas' other side, stood Britannicus, ten years old and still wearing the toga praetexta of a child with its narrow purple stripe. That and his thin, lank brown hair, long face and deep-set eyes, all inherited from his father, placed him physically well in the shadow of the dazzling Prince of the Youth, as his stepbrother was now titled.

Behind Britannicus his sister, Claudia Octavia, evidently found the allure of her stepbrother hard to resist and her eyes wandered in Nero's direction with a frequency that could not be helped in a newly pubescent maiden.

Both in their early fifties and both running to fat, Lucius Annaeus Seneca and Sosibius, tutors of Nero and Britannicus respectively, hovered near their charges, anxious that their manners should be impeccable for fear of it reflecting badly upon themselves and the consequences that it would bring.

In the shadow of the tutors lurked Narcissus and Callistus; the first bearded and bejewelled with a full figure and face, the latter wiry and bald, wringing his hands and flicking his eyes here and there as if surrounded by enemies. Both still held positions of power but neither had the influence with the Emperor that they had once held; Pallas had seen to that. Narcissus caught Vespasian's eye and gave the faintest of nods, surprising Vespasian: it was unlike Narcissus to be so indiscreet; he looked away wondering if that was a sign of desperation on the freedman's part.

Vespasian's gaze then alighted on his lover of over twenty-five years now: Caenis, as beautiful as ever with her sapphire-blue eyes, smiling briefly at him as he came to a halt just five paces away from the dais. Having been Narcissus' secretary until Pallas had commandeered her services as he emerged victorious in the struggle to become the Master of Rome, she stood ready to record the speeches on wax tablets with a slave supporting a desk on his shoulders kneeling before her. Loved by Vespasian and tolerated by Flavia, she was the woman whom he could never marry as a result of the injunction on senators marrying freedwomen; she had been born a slave.

Vespasian's lictors and those of all the other magistrates moved away to the left, leaving a swathe of senators surrounding the prisoners.

There was a pause as Claudius endeavoured to collect himself, his mouth working hard as he tried to form his first word. With a spray of saliva it finally came: 'W-w-w-what does my loyal S-S-Senate bring before m-m-me?'

Vespasian took a couple of steps towards the Emperor. 'Princeps and colleague in the consulship, we have the honour to bring a gift from Publius Ostorius Scapula, the Governor of the province of Britannia, on behalf of all the Senate. We have the rebel King, Caratacus of the Catuvellauni, and the remainder of his followers here in chains.'

Despite the fact that the whole event had been choreographed for this moment, Claudius feigned surprise. 'Caratacus? I know of the name. What would you have me do with him?'

'We ask for your judgement upon him.'

'His c-c-crime?'

Vespasian struggled to keep his face dignified as he played out the farce with the fool. 'He is the man who refused to bow to you after your glorious pacification of the island.' This, Vespasian knew, was stretching the truth by a considerable margin. The island of Britannia was far from conquered but that could not be admitted publicly, seeing as the Emperor had already celebrated a Triumph for his victory there and then graciously allowed Aulus Plautius an Ovation upon his return. It was for this reason that Caratacus had been paraded from the Forum for execution outside the city walls rather than the other way around as in a Triumph. To imply that the military operations, involving four legions and the equivalent in auxiliaries, still raging in the infant province were anything more than local mopping-up operations against a handful of rebels would be to invalidate Claudius' victory and call into question his Triumph. Securing Claudius' position as emperor with the glory of conquest had been his freedmen's whole object when they had ordered the militarily ill-conceived venture.

Claudius pretended to consider the issue for a few moments, melodramatically rubbing his moist chin, while all those present did their best to conceal their embarrassment. 'It shall be d-d-death. Burrus!'

From behind Caenis, Sextus Afranius Burrus, Agrippina's choice as the new prefect of the Praetorian Guard, stepped forward and yelled to his men, 'The execution party will advance!'

Six men with garrottes marched from the ranks while a further dozen made their way to the prisoners and herded them forward. The females and some of the younger males fell to their knees before the embodiment of the Roman State, twitching on his curule chair, and issued pleas for their lives in broken Latin, tearing at their hair and rending their clothes as their executioners ranged in a line behind them.

Vespasian looked at Caratacus, hoping that the man who had been so worthy an adversary would not stoop to the level of some in his retinue; he was not disappointed. The Britannic King stood, erect and proud, disdaining to plead for his life; instead, he stared at the Emperor of Rome with no sign of incredulity at his unbecoming appearance and, when he caught Claudius' eye, he inclined his head fractionally as if greeting an equal.

Claudius frowned and then held up a hand for silence. 'B-b-before the reb-b-b-bel dies let him explain his actions.'

Caratacus lifted his hands so that all could see his chains. 'Had my restraint while I was prosperous matched, rather than fallen short of, my honour and noble birth, I would have entered Rome as your friend and not your captive. You would not have disdained to receive a king descended from such illustrious ancestors, the lord of many nations, and we would have signed a treaty of mutual friendship and peace. However, now my humiliation is as glorious to you as it is degrading to me; but I have brought myself to this pass. I had men, horses, arms and wealth. Who would blame me if I parted with them reluctantly? If you Romans, in your halls of marble, who have so much, choose to become masters of the world, does it follow that we, in our huts of mud, who have comparatively little, should accept slavery? I am here as your prisoner because my pride would not allow me to give you all that I had. But I say this to you, Emperor of the Romans, neither my fall nor your triumph will become famous; I shall be just another king crushed under your heel. My punishment will be followed by oblivion and your victory will be soon forgotten. Whereas, if you grant me my life, I shall be an everlasting memorial of your clemency and bring glory to your name.'

Claudius gawped at the Britannic King, his jaw moving as if masticating stubborn gristle, while weighing these words.

As he vacillated, Agrippina stood and held out her arms to Caratacus. 'Your eloquence has moved me.' A tear rolled down her cheek as if in confirmation of the veracity of the statement. She turned to her son. 'What does Nero Claudius Caesar Drusus Germanicus, the Prince of the Youth, think?'

Nero had taken his mother's lead and, with a mighty sob of raw emotion, had begun to weep. 'I believe, Mother dearest, that my father should show clemency in this one instance. A merciful ruler is a lauded ruler and his praise will be written and sung.' He looked towards Britannicus as his tutor, Seneca, nodded in sage agreement, the picture of self-satisfaction. 'I'm sure my brother would agree.'

Britannicus did not meet his stepbrother's eyes. 'A ruler who does not punish rebellion will encourage more.' Heads nodded in agreement with such wisdom from so young a source. 'I believe *Domitius* to be wrong.'

There was a hush around the daises and all eyes looked at the Emperor to see if he would reprimand his natural son for such an insult to his adoptive one. Sosibius visibly paled and stared at his charge, his mouth open in horror. Vespasian saw Titus, standing with the other youths of the imperial household, smile involuntarily before taking on the shocked expression of his fellows.

Claudius' head jerked and he shook as he felt the ice-glare of his wife biting into him. Nero fell to his knees as melodramatically as the wronged lover in a comedy, his tears now streaming down his face. He took the supplication pose with easy perfection as Seneca placed a sympathetic hand on his shoulder. 'Father, don't let my brother repudiate me.' Nero flung his head back, one hand running through his luxuriant flame curls and then rested the back of his other hand on his brow before addressing the heavens. 'As the gods are my witness, I ceased to be a member of the Domitii when you adopted me, Father.'

Claudius' throat spasmed as he tried to form a word; eventually it exploded from him: 'Britannicus!' It echoed around the walls. 'Apologise!'

Britannicus did not quail. 'The legitimate heir to the Purple apologises to no one. You should support your own blood, the pure blood of the Julio-Claudians, against that tainted by the Domitii. I say Caratacus should die.' He glared at his rival who was now catching tears on his fingertips and displaying them to the crowd.

Claudius held out his fist as if adjudicating at a gladiatorial fight and kept his thumb pressed close to it in imitation of a sheathed sword. 'C-C-Caratacus shall live! As shall his retinue.'

Burrus looked to the Empress; she glared at Britannicus and then nodded with a triumphant smile. The Praetorian prefect turned to his cohorts. 'All hail the Emperor's mercy!'

The roar of nine thousand voices rose to the sky, once again sending aloft the crows in fluttering spirals. The other captives fell to their knees at the foot of Claudius' dais and reached up with their hands to touch his feet as Caratacus strode forward and bowed first to the Emperor and then to the Empress and her son, who had now risen to his feet and taken a pose with one hand on his heart and slowly shaking his head while staring into the middle distance as if attempting to summon the words with which to describe such a majestic act of mercy.

Caratacus then presented his chains to Burrus.

'There is a very canny man,' Gaius observed in Vespasian's ear as Caratacus' manacles were unlocked to renewed cheering from the Guard.

'And there is a very unhappy boy and a very frightened tutor,' Vespasian said, watching Sosibius usher Britannicus back towards Titus and the rest of the youths. 'I wonder if he'll dare to beat him one last time before he finds himself looking for a new position.'

Sosibius glanced at Agrippina in terror and Britannicus looked over his shoulder at Claudius with undisguised hatred, as the Father of the House launched into the first of many sycophantic, senatorial speeches praising the mercy of the man who had executed more of their number and the equestrian class than had his predecessor, Caligula.

The sun was well past its zenith when Claudius, having exhausted the supply of snacks brought to him at regular intervals during the long succession of speeches, grew tired of being lauded on an empty stomach and called for his litter.

Vespasian brought proceedings to a close by proposing a full debate in the Senate the following day to vote his colleague in the consulship a double-life-sized bronze statue in the Temple of Concordia in praise of his magnanimity and his ability to bring concord to all peoples.

Suitably flattered, the Emperor left, having been helped into his litter by the latest addition to the equestrian class; Caratacus was also now the proud owner of a villa on the Esquiline Hill that had belonged to a senator who had forfeited his property having been falsely accused of treason by Agrippina and executed.

'I think you did very well out of that, dear boy,' Gaius observed as they watched the Empress give one final venomous glare in Britannicus' direction and then leave with Nero laying his head on her breast as the curtains of the litter were drawn. 'The Senate will vote for Claudius' statue and he'll thank you for it when you step down in three days.'

'He may thank me but he won't reward me, Uncle.'

'He might reward you,' a voice said from just behind them. 'In fact, he had plans to do so.' Vespasian and Gaius both felt a hand on their shoulder and turned to see Pallas; the Greek inclined his head. 'And in a way that you would, perhaps, have expected.'

'I'd expect to be given a province, and not a senatorial province but an imperial one with legions and the chance of some military glory; just as my brother has.'

'That is what you deserve but unfortunately—'

'Unfortunately I seem to have incurred the Empress's displeasure,' Vespasian interrupted, 'because my son is friends with her son's rival.'

'It does seem a little unreasonable, I'll admit, if you phrase it in those terms; however, there's more to it than that, much more. Walk with me, gentlemen.' Pallas guided them back towards the gates; Vespasian's lictors fell in behind, unable to precede him as they did not know where they were headed. 'Obviously we are talking in confidence as only old and trusted friends can?'

Vespasian glanced at his uncle, feeling a twinge of guilt. 'Of course, Pallas.'

'Then you'll spare me a denial when I say that I know that you have both agreed to meet with Narcissus tonight somewhere in secret.'

Vespasian met Pallas' eye and inclined his head while Gaius blustered something about coercion. All around horns rang out, centurions bellowed and men stamped feet and crashed weapons in unison as the Praetorian Guard turned to march, cohort by cohort, back into their camp to the voluble admiration of the watching women.

'I don't blame you for agreeing to meet him; the way that it was put to you made your options seem very limited: a faithful son of Rome cast out by a grudge-bearing woman; lost and friendless, and then Narcissus comes to his aid offering a chance of preferment once again. I'm not going to ask you not to go, quite the reverse as a matter of fact. I want you to go and agree to whatever it is that he wants you to do for him. No doubt he's moving to push me aside and reinstate himself as Claudius' most influential advisor. I'll be interested to know how he plans to go about it, so it should be a fascinating meeting.'

'How do you know about this, Pallas? I only decided to go this morning.'

'Then that should answer your question for you.'

'But Narcissus' messenger Agarpetus and my slave Hormus are the only people who know; other than my uncle and Magnus, of course.'

'Do you trust your slave?'

'Implicitly.' Vespasian paused and made the obvious assumption. 'So, Agarpetus must work for you, Pallas?'

'Not in a way that he would know it; I just have his movements tracked and when he goes somewhere that interests me, like your house this morning for example, I make closer enquiries. Agarpetus is extraordinarily fond of the young lad who shares his bed and discusses much with him. Unfortunately for him that young lad has a greater love of coinage than he has respect for his lover's privacy. One gold aureus bought me the fact that you were meeting with Narcissus, and when I noticed the look that passed between you both upon your arrival here I knew that I hadn't been cheated out of my money. As to the time and place: I could guess that it was not going to be in the palace, for obvious reasons, and therefore Narcissus would be wise to use the festivities planned for this evening as cover to help him slip unnoticed through the city. They will still go ahead despite the Emperor pardoning Caratacus. The feast will now be to celebrate Claudius' mercy in victory rather than his ability to vanquish all enemies.

'But where Narcissus would be heading through all this joyful celebration, I don't know for sure. However, if I were him I would choose Magnus' tavern because his loyalty to you would ensure Narcissus' complete safety.'

Vespasian could not help but smile. 'It's evidently quite pointless trying to have a secret from you; I suppose you know what we are going to discuss even though I have no idea?'

'That I don't know but I want you to tell Caenis after the meeting; she'll be expecting you. She will inform me in the morning.'

'And if I don't?'

'Then Agrippina will have her way and all that promise that you've shown in your career so far will most certainly be lost. Help me in this matter, spy on my enemy, and I will persuade the Emperor and Empress that you are the perfect man for a delicate task that could earn you much credit. Believe me when I say it's the only chance you'll get to serve Rome once you step down from the consulship. Agrippina's mistrust of you is such that this offer is the only thing that I'll have a chance of getting her to agree to.'

'What have I done?'

'It's what you didn't do. You didn't kill Messalina.'

'But Burrus did.' Vespasian recalled the night in the Gardens of Lucullus when he had accompanied the then tribune Burrus to execute the faithless Empress.

'He did, but only after you offered her the honour of suicide. Burrus is a very ambitious man and if he can do someone down at the same time as benefitting himself then he will grasp the opportunity. He has made much of your weakness in the Gardens of Lucullus that night, implying to Agrippina that you showed sympathy to Messalina to the extent that you might not have wished her death. Agrippina takes that as an indication that you would rather she were not empress. She does not forgive sentiments like that, even though I have tried to persuade her otherwise.'

Gaius was outraged. 'But he offered his sword to Messalina not out of pity but out of a desire to see her do something that she had forced so many others into through jealousy and spite.'

'Burrus does not frame it in those terms.'

Vespasian shook his head, sighing at the injustice of the matter. 'And Burrus has done very well out of doing me down to the Empress.'

Pallas inclined his head in agreement. 'He immediately became the obvious choice for Praetorian prefect.'

'Very well, Pallas, I will spy for you despite the fact that you have given me no firm guarantee of advancement, just a promise to try to persuade the Emperor and Empress to allow me to perform some vague task.'

'That is a very sensible decision; and you needn't worry, I'm sure the Empress will agree to my proposal.'

'Why, Pallas? If she distrusts me so much how can you manage to get her to agree to my benefit?'

Pallas cocked an eyebrow and gave a rare half-smile. 'When she hears what I propose you do for Rome, she'll be most enthusiastic. She will certainly support it because she will fully expect you to die.'

CHAPTER III

UNRECOGNISABLE IN A deep-hooded cloak, Vespasian walked in silence next to his uncle, escorted by four of Magnus' crossroads brothers who had been sent to see them through Rome's nocturnal streets. Even in the middle of the night the city teemed with activity as suppliers made their deliveries with carts and wagons banned from Rome's thoroughfares and lanes during daylight hours and the people feasted on the generous handouts made by the Emperor in thanks for the defeat of his persistent enemy, Caratacus. However, the presence of so many people abroad at this time did not make the journey to Magnus' tavern any safer; quite the contrary in a city where the vast majority lived a hand to mouth existence. Gangs of footpads roamed the streets hauling the unwary or the intoxicated into dark alleyways to relieve them of their property and sometimes of their lives. Those who bore witness to the muggings would, in general, prefer the safety of minding their own business to the mortal danger of coming to the aid of a stranger. Only the club-wielding Vigiles, Rome's nocturnal fire-watchers and keepers of the peace, offered any assistance to those in trouble and then, often, at the price of the contents of the victim's purse.

With four torch-bearing crossroads brothers, daggers and cudgels secreted under their cloaks, Vespasian felt safe as they made their way along the bustling Alta Semita bordered by three- or four-storey tenements to either side; thin light delineated an occasional upper window and gloom-filled alleys divided them, leading into a dark and completely lawless world between the more frequented thoroughfares. But it was not his present well-being that concerned Vespasian as he blocked out the drunken singing, the cries of the street vendors and carters, the rattle of iron-rimmed wheels, the bestial calls of beasts of burden and the countless other sounds that made sleep a rare commodity on Rome's busier streets; it was what the future held for him.

'If Agrippina expects me to be killed,' he said eventually to Gaius, 'doing whatever it is that Pallas suggests, then how would you explain the mark that I found on the sacrificial liver this morning?'

'I can't explain it and I certainly wouldn't make it public,' Gaius said after hearing the incident recounted.

'I'm not stupid!' Vespasian snapped more tersely than he had meant to. 'But that mark implies that Mars has a destiny set for me that is somehow involved in the greater affairs of state. I'm no auger, but when I put together a clear reference to me on a sacrifice to Jupiter Optimus Maximus, made in the very heart of Rome by my hand as a consul of Rome, with the fact that the auspices at my naming ceremony were of such a sensitive nature that my mother forced everyone present to take an oath never to talk of them, then I begin to wonder what that destiny is, seeing as I've already achieved the consulship.'

'Well, I wasn't at your naming ceremony, so I can't comment.'

'If you had been you would be sworn against commenting anyway. But I'm beginning to have a suspicion that is so outrageous that I might as well discuss it with you.'

'So that's what you were brooding about all through dinner; I was thinking that you and Flavia had had another dispute over your differing attitudes to expenditure. Try me.'

Vespasian took a deep breath and hoped that the cause of his last few hours of contemplation would not provoke ridicule. 'It was Sabinus who originally put it into my mind when Claudius came to Britannia. Claudius noticed that I had Marcus Antonius' sword that had been given to me by the Lady Antonia; only Pallas and Caenis knew that it had been a gift from her, as they had brought me the sword after she had used it to open her veins. Claudius asked me how I got it because it was well known in the imperial family that his mother would only give it to the person that she thought would make the best emperor. I lied and told him that Caligula had given it to me. Pallas told me never to let the truth be known because, if Claudius found out, my life could be in danger. Sabinus witnessed the incident and asked me about it; I laughed it off saying that it was a simple gift and, besides, I didn't have the blood of the Caesars. He then asked how long that bloodline would last.'

'That's a treasonous question.'

'But it's a pertinent one. If Claudius does die soon, Britannicus will be moved aside and Nero will become emperor having married his stepsister who is also his first cousin once removed; it's not quite Egyptian but it's getting close. How long can a bloodline like that last? Suppose it finishes with Nero, what then?'

'Then the Guard will proclaim an emperor.'

'That only works if there is a suitable candidate from the imperial family. But each province with legions will want their own generals, because if they support a man to the Purple they know they'll be very well rewarded.'

'Civil war, you mean?'

'Of course. And there're no rules about what blood a man needs running in his veins in order to win a civil war; he just needs to ensure that it stays in them.'

Gaius turned his hooded face towards Vespasian, his voice conveying his consternation. 'You, dear boy?'

'Why not? Sabinus was at my naming ceremony; he saw the auspices but has always refused to talk about it because of the oath. However, he asked me, after Claudius had taken back the sword, what if Antonia had not given it to me as a simple gift but had actually given it to the person that she thought would make the best emperor, as she had always said she would? And at that moment I thought: Why not? Why not me? Because someday it will be someone from a different family; it has to be if Rome is to survive. Tiberius, Caligula, Claudius? If Nero is like any one of them then …' Vespasian trailed off; the point did not need to be made.

'You think that Sabinus believes you could become …?' It was Gaius' turn to leave a question hanging.

'I'm not saying that; all I'm saying is that he put it into my mind. And I think that Pallas also has a suspicion; I think Antonia said something to both him and Caenis when she gave them her father's sword to pass on to me before she died, but I'm willing to bet that she swore them to secrecy. But I think that Pallas managing to help me to a position which is obviously so fraught with danger that Agrippina does not expect me to survive is his way of testing whether Antonia was right.'

'You mean if you survive you'll eventually become ... ?' Gaius tried but again failed to complete the sentence.

'I expect that if I survive Pallas might look at me in a different light.'

'You don't seriously think that you could be the ... ?'

'Why not, Uncle? Look at me: look at how far I've come since being brought to your house when I was sixteen with lofty ideals of serving Rome for the greater good. I'm now consul, admittedly only for two months, but I've reached that rank because of what I've achieved and not because of what blood flows in my veins. I've commanded a legion in the field for six years, four of those in Britannia against some very unpleasant tribes; I've spilt blood when necessary and sometimes when not. Here, in Rome, I know how the politics of the city and of the palace work because for years now I've been unwillingly wading through their mire; I've become just as ruthless as the practitioners whom I've learnt from and whom I've come to admire. I understand the power of money, fear and patronage and know that any man can be bought by a mixture of all three; it's just a question of finding the right levels of each ingredient. I'm ideally qualified.'

Gaius' jowls quivered with fear. 'You can't believe that you'll succeed to the ... ?'

'No, Uncle; but I may fight my way there one day. If the blood of the Caesars fails there'll be a scramble for the Purple and who better than someone like me? But if it's to be someone like me then *why not me*?'

'And you think all this just because of a mark that looks like a "V" on a liver?'

'Not just that. I think this because then many things, strange things, that have happened in my life start to make sense: the Phoenix, the prophecy of Amphiaraios, Myrddin, the Oracle of

Amun telling me that I had come before it too early to know the right question to ask; every weird thing that has happened to me would be explained by that.'

'This is something that you should keep to yourself, dear boy; it won't do to go about shouting that you're a potential ...' Gaius still could not bring himself to say the word.

'Oh, I will keep it to myself, Uncle. And I won't dare to believe that I'm right until it happens. However, because I know the possibility is now there I shall watch out for sensible opportunities and will not do anything rash in the meantime.'

'Like agreeing to secret meetings with scheming imperial freedmen in the middle of the night, for example?' Gaius suggested as they came to the acute junction of the Alta Semita and the Vicus Longus at the apex of which stood Magnus' tavern.

Vespasian smiled at his uncle. 'This may well be an opportunity; and besides,' he added as he pushed open the door, 'it's not a secret.'

Vespasian did not pull back his hood as he entered the crowded fug of the parlour; sweat, stale wine, cheap-whores' perfume and burnt pork fat assaulted his nose, his ears rang with drunken shouting and harsh laughter and his eyes immediately moistened with stinging charcoal fumes from the cooking fire behind the amphorae-lined bar at the wider, far end of the tavern. Gaius' girth caused some comment – not all of it good-humoured – as they followed their escort across a wine-sticky floor, through the shadowy crowd of drinkers and whores filling the widening room. To quizzical looks they passed through a leather-curtained doorway and then turned right into an unlit corridor. At the far end on the left, the leader of their escort, a huge bald man in his late fifties, knocked with a ham-sized fist on a substantial iron-reinforced door and opened it at the sound of a response from within.

'Well done, Sextus,' Magnus said, getting up from his seat behind the desk as the door swung open. 'Any trouble?'

'No, brother,' Sextus replied, stepping aside to allow Vespasian and Gaius into the room.

'Good. Now take your lads outside and keep an eye out for our two guests.'

Sextus hesitated for a moment and then rumbled slowly into a guttural laugh. 'Aw, very good, Magnus,' he managed between bursts of mirth. 'Keep an eye out! I like that.'

'Yes, yes, yes,' Magnus said, shaking his head, exasperated. 'It was almost funny the first time we had that joke, three years ago.' His one good eye looked at Vespasian apologetically while his glass replica glared at Sextus, adding to the man's enjoyment of the humour. 'Now get out and do what you've been told.'

'Keep an eye out,' Sextus chuckled as he left with his brothers, 'right you are, Magnus.'

'Sextus has got a new joke, I take it,' Vespasian said as he took the seat that Magnus had just vacated.

Magnus picked up the pitcher on the desk and poured three cups of wine. 'Each time he hears it he thinks it's for the first time.'

'Just like he used to when he was always offering to give one-armed Marius a helping hand.'

'Yes, it's the same thing and it keeps him amused for hours.'

Gaius sat in the chair next to his nephew, accepting a cup of wine. 'Still, he's a reliable solid lad, from what I know of him.'

'Solid being a good choice of word in more ways than one, sir,' Magnus observed, proffering a cup to Vespasian. 'He knows his limitations and didn't make a fuss when I promoted Tigran to my second in command when old Servius died.' Magnus walked across the room, opened a door on the far side and looked out into the darkness beyond. 'I do miss the old bugger,' he continued, closing the door and bolting it. 'Even though he was blind towards the end he could still see the right way through a problem.' Magnus paused to consider for a moment. 'I was thinking over what you were saying this morning about retiring now; it may not be such a bad idea. I promised Tigran that I would soon. Perhaps it'd be better to do it now rather than have it forced upon me by one of the other brotherhoods staging a takeover or Tigran slipping a knife between my ribs because he can't wait.'

Vespasian raised his eyebrows. 'He'd do that?'

'He's already thought about it; it was only my promise that stopped him. Anyway, that's how *I* got the job all those years ago.' Magnus closed and secured the shutters on the only window in the room, dulling the rumble of traffic and drunken shouts coming in from the street.

'Twenty-six, to be precise,' Gaius informed them. 'I should remember because it cost me a fortune in bribes and blood-money to save you from being condemned to the arena.'

'For which I've always been grateful, senator.'

'And you've repaid me many times over.' Gaius chuckled, holding his cup in both hands. 'I don't suppose I'll get quite as good service from the brotherhood if Tigran becomes the patronus.'

'It'll certainly cost you more; but I'm sure we can come to an accommodation as part of the transfer of power.' A knock on the door prevented him from elaboration on the point. 'Ah, your guests.' He opened it to find Sextus' massive form blocking the doorway; he moved to one side, his shoulders shaking slightly as if he was still controlling his amusement.

A moment later, Narcissus walked into the room, removing his hood; Agarpetus followed. Narcissus glanced at Magnus with languid, pale eyes. 'The redoubtable Magnus of the South Quirinal Crossroads Brotherhood,' he crooned, walking straight to a chair and sitting opposite Vespasian and Gaius; the scent of his pomade wafted through the room. 'Thank you for your hospitality. Losing your grip a bit recently, I hear, hmm?'

Magnus bristled. 'Not so as you'd notice.' He shot Narcissus a one-eyed glare and then pushed past Agarpetus and left the room.

Narcissus affected not to notice the slam of the door. 'Good evening, gentlemen.'

'Good evening, imperial secretary,' Vespasian and Gaius replied as Agarpetus stepped forward to stand at his patron's right shoulder.

'You had a safe journey, I trust,' Gaius asked at his most ingratiating.

'I came by carriage and the roads were terrible; clogged with scroungers and wastrels drunk on our merciful Emperor's wine.' The Greek examined one of the many bejewelled rings he wore on each of his chubby fingers and spoke as if addressing the ruby set in it: 'Which is exactly why I chose tonight for our meeting. So we will get directly to business and forgo the small talk.'

'We've always respected your penchant for straight-talking,' Vespasian replied while pouring another cup of wine.

Narcissus' mouth twitched into the nearest he ever came to smiling. He leant forward and placed his elbows on the table, steepling his fingers and pressing them to his lips above his trimmed and oiled black beard; weighty gold rings, dangling from each ear, glinted in the lamplight as they rocked to and fro. He considered Vespasian and Gaius for a few moments, his eyes slowly passing between them as if he was deciding whom to address first. Raucous laughter over a steadily increasing chanting and clapping filtered in from the tavern; a whore and her client were evidently being encouraged in their endeavours.

Vespasian pushed the filled cup across the desk, holding his visitor's gaze when it fell upon him, and was shocked by how lined Narcissus' well-filled-out face had become since the last time he had seen him at such close quarters. The strain of losing his position of influence with the Emperor – if not his title and function – to his colleague Pallas had evidently borne down hard on him; it was not easy living with the constant fear of execution. However, Vespasian felt no sympathy for him as he observed the black staining of dye on the pale skin around his hairline and beneath his beard. The threat of arbitrary death had been the lot of every Roman of the equestrian order and up from Tiberius' reign onwards; the closer one was to the centre of power the more acute that danger became. It was something that Pallas had admitted the one time he had let his mask slip in front of Vespasian.

'You both know very well the situation that I find myself in,' Narcissus began, half-closing his eyes. 'I am the Emperor's secretary, in charge of his appointments and therefore access to him; yet for the last couple of years my influence over him has been negligible. Since Pallas and Agrippina manoeuvred me into ordering Messalina's execution before Claudius had completely settled his mind upon it, I have been out of favour with my patron. Yes, I can still make a great deal of money charging for audiences but that is nothing compared to what Pallas makes charging for influence. I remain alive because Claudius cannot bring himself to order my execution as only I know the ins and outs of all his business affairs; I'm alive because he is too chaotic to survive without me. Agrippina has made a couple of attempts on my life but I'm too careful for her; but very soon she won't have to resort to murder. Once Claudius is dead I think it is very obvious to all what will happen.' He parted his hands a fraction and held them still, inviting Vespasian to fill in the gap.

'Nero will become emperor.'

'Yes, Claudius' attitude to Britannicus this afternoon showed us just how far he has estranged himself from his own flesh and blood. He even granted Agrippina's request and had Sosibius executed this evening as being responsible for Britannicus' carefully studied insult.'

Vespasian was shocked at the extreme result of Britannicus' revenge and wondered if either the boy or Titus had realised the possibility of that outcome. He found himself hoping that they had: it was sweet justice for the man whose lies had forced him to bear false witness. 'Of course, he was Messalina's appointment; I suppose it was only a matter of time before Agrippina got him.'

'She is not feted for her mercy; and she is ruthless in fighting for Nero's and therefore her own position. She couldn't have the boy executed so the tutor would have to do.' Narcissus inclined his head a fraction. 'Lucky that Titus wasn't standing next to Britannicus.'

Vespasian chilled but then felt a surge of hope. 'Perhaps with his tutor's death, I've got a good excuse to find an alternative for Titus.'

'I'm afraid not; Britannicus' education and that of his companions has now been entrusted to Seneca. Claudius has managed to put Britannicus in even more danger by giving him to the one man whom Agrippina respects and Nero actually listens to.

Because Seneca's as ruthless as the two of them in the pursuit of power he will share their view that Britannicus is an obstacle. Whatever you thought of Sosibius, at least he provided some sort of protection from those three.'

Vespasian took the point and began to wish that the odious tutor had not been so summarily dealt with.

'So, Claudius will condemn his own son to death by making Nero his heir and that poisonous little snake does everything his mother tells him to.' Narcissus re-steepled his fingers and looked meaningfully at each of them in turn. '*Everything*. And she gets him to do everything she asks because she in turn does *everything* that he asks of her; and I can tell you, gentlemen, that his requests are far removed from what a son should ask of his mother.'

Vespasian shuddered at the image but, having seen Nero snuggling up to Agrippina and resting his head on her breast that afternoon, it did not come as much of a shock to him. In fact, he reflected, after what he had seen with Tiberius and Caligula, that there was very little that the imperial family could now do to shock him. Caligula had made free with all his sisters, Agrippina amongst them; why should she not go further than him and do the same with her son? But then how would the Senate and people of Rome take to having such an unnatural couple rule over them? And if Nero felt free to bed his own mother, what depravity would not be beyond him?

From the bar the clapping and cheering had reached a crescendo; a successful conclusion to the business was clearly imminent.

Narcissus raised his voice, slightly, over the noise. 'One of the first conditions that she will extract from Nero for her acquiescence to his unhealthy demands once he becomes emperor will be my death; and that, gentlemen, is something that I intend to avoid.' Narcissus paused for a sip of wine, frowned his disapproval at the vintage, or lack of it, and then dabbed his lips with a handkerchief. 'Now, interestingly, you two find yourselves with a similar, if not quite so potentially fatal, problem.' Narcissus indicated to his freedman with a fractional head movement. 'Agarpetus came across some very interesting intelligence from the trierarchus of a trading ship just back from the Kingdom of Colchis on the eastern coast of the Euxine. It would seem a Parthian embassy passed through Phasis, the major port of Colchis, towards the end of September heading home by way of the Kingdoms of Iberia and Albania and then across the Caspian Sea, thus skirting very close to the north of our client kingdom of Armenia.

'Now, that may be nothing in itself: the Parthians are often sending embassies to the tribes and kingdoms around the Euxine and our traders are always reporting them; we pay well for the information. But what caught Agarpetus' eye was an earlier report intercepted from one of Agrippina's people that he had killed an agent, as he had been ordered, very soon after the man had informed the Governor of Moesia that a Parthian embassy to the tribes beyond the Danuvius had arrived in Tyra, just to the north of that province, and therefore this agent had been prevented from getting the news to his pay-master; unfortunately we don't know who that was. This happened, as I said, in September, at the end of which month, incidentally, our puppet king in Armenia was subject to an invasion led by his nephew. It's a reasonable assumption that this was the same embassy and it's also reasonable to assume from their route home that on their way to the Danuvius they passed through Iberia. Now, Iberia was the base for this invasion that has since managed to topple the Armenian King.' Narcissus raised an eyebrow at his audience and braved another sip of wine as a massive cheer broke out next door.

Vespasian saw Narcissus' implication immediately. 'Therefore the Parthians could have triggered the Armenian usurpation on their way through and Sabinus must have failed to kill or capture them, even though he had been warned about their presence.'

'It would seem that way; very careless, wouldn't you say?' Narcissus dabbed his lips again; the noise level from the tavern had dropped back down to laughter and boisterous conversation. 'If we had a chance to question them we would know the object of their mission to the northern tribes and, more importantly, we would know for sure if Parthia is once again trying to destabilise Armenia. Still, it's done now and one can only hope that the consequences aren't too ... er ... disastrous for Rome – or indeed, for Sabinus and perhaps even his family?'

'Are you threatening us, Narcissus?'

'My old friend,' Narcissus crooned without a trace of amicability, 'I am doing nothing of the sort; I don't need to. Agrippina has made sure that news of his failure has already reached Claudius and Pallas and she has insisted that after such a mistake your family cannot be trusted. Yesterday, at the Emperor's request, I personally crossed your name off the list of governors for next year; Titus Statilius Taurus will go to Africa in your place.'

'Africa?' Gaius blurted. 'The Emperor was going to reward Vespasian with Africa?'

'I'm afraid so, but it is not to be. A shame really, such a prestigious province.'

Gaius' jowls quivered with outrage. 'You took Africa away from our family?'

'Calm yourself, senator; I did nothing. I just amended the list at the Emperor's instructions after he had been advised by the Empress. She really doesn't like you, Vespasian.'

'I'm aware of that and of the real reason why; but she likes you even less.'

Narcissus parted his hands and exclaimed in feigned joy, 'Ah! Back to the subject I can never tire of: me. Yes, she would have me dead; and what's the best way to avoid that whilst at the same time doing yourselves a great service by removing the block to your family's career?'

Vespasian glanced at his uncle and realised immediately that he would not be furnishing the answer. 'Kill Agrippina?'

Narcissus tutted and raised his cup for another sip of wine before thinking better of it. 'Kill another empress? I don't think I'd survive that again, no matter how chaotic Claudius' affairs are. No, gentlemen, the answer is to expose her for what she is.'

It was Vespasian's turn to be dismissive. 'You and Pallas both tried to do that with Messalina but Claudius refused to believe you.'

'Precisely, but this time the emphasis has changed. Then we were trying to get Claudius to believe that Messalina had savoured most men of the equestrian and senatorial classes and gone through the Praetorian Guard century by century, which, despite the truth of it, is a huge claim and easily rebutted on the grounds of impossibility. This time I just have to convince Claudius that his wife is not only sleeping with his most trusted advisor but he's also being cuckolded by her son whom she has persuaded him to adopt as his own.' Narcissus leant forward on the desk, looking directly into Vespasian's eyes. 'It's all rather nasty, wouldn't you agree? And yet again our divine Emperor is looking less of a god and more of a fool. Of course, we're used to that, but he's not; I think that the shock will make him very vengeful and all three of his betrayers will, at the very least, live out the rest of their lives on a barren rock, rather like Agrippina's namesake, her mother, and her two older brothers.' He twitched the corners of his mouth once again into the closest he ever came to a smile. 'You could almost say that it runs in the family.'

Vespasian could not but admire the logic of it. 'With one move you rid yourself of both your rivals, remove Nero and restore Britannicus to the succession with you as the arbiter of the potential regent when the time comes. No doubt you would choose someone of little consequence who was also well in your debt and once more you would be the Master of Rome.'

'And you would be governing whichever province you wished for; Sabinus' error would be quietly forgotten and you, my dear Gaius, would have that long overdue consulship.'

Vespasian kept his face placid; he was tempted but he knew better than to trust this Greek. He remembered only too well how Narcissus had been prepared to go back on the promise never to reveal Sabinus' part in the assassination of Caligula when political expediency pressed.

Gaius, however, took the bait: his eyes glinted in the lamplight. 'What do you want us to do, my dear Narcissus?'

'The only people that Claudius would believe are Agrippina or Pallas themselves.'

'But neither of them is ever going to admit to the thing that'll bring them down.'

'Of course not, senator.' The Greek's irritation at a statement of the obvious was conveyed by a lowering of his voice.

Vespasian cocked an ear; the noise from the tavern had taken on a different timbre.

Gaius reddened. 'I apologise.'

Narcissus flourished a dismissive wave, half-closing his eyes. 'But they will confess to Claudius if the alternative is being accused of treason; palpable treason, for which they will most certainly be executed.'

'Treason?' Vespasian asked, his attention now back to the conversation. 'What've they done?'

'The timing and the source of these reports from the East and then the recent trouble in Armenia have led me to believe that Agrippina has precipitated a crisis that not even Pallas knows of. If my instincts are correct, it is connected to the Parthian embassy that your brother so carelessly lost; but as yet I have no proof. But both of you could help me with that. Now, if this treason comes to light, it will certainly be assumed that Pallas was a party to it and will be executed along with—' A woman's shriek from the tavern cut him off and he looked to the door in alarm.

Vespasian jumped to his feet; masculine shouts and bellows erupted, joined by the crashing of wooden furniture. Agarpetus pulled a sword from beneath his cloak, opened the door a fraction, looked out and then quickly stepped back.

Magnus came barrelling in. 'We're under attack!' he yelled as he raced across the room to a wooden chest. 'The bastards have used the celebrations to slip past our security.' Throwing open the lid he pulled out a sword and lobbed it over to Vespasian; another two followed for Gaius and Narcissus as Sextus crashed in. 'Take these into the tavern, brother,' Magnus said as he scooped out the remainder of the box's contents and jammed them into Sextus' arms, keeping one back for himself, 'and then pull back here with the lads. We'll stop them in the corridor.'

'Who's attacking you?' Vespasian asked, pulling the sword from its scabbard with a metallic ring.

Magnus rammed the tip of his blade between two floorboards. 'Fuck knows, but they're serious.' With a grunt he pulled back on the weapon and sprang a board up.

Vespasian realised just how serious they were as the first whiff of smoke came through the door.

'They're torching the place!' Narcissus shouted, drawing his sword and looking at the blade in disbelief.

'That's why we need to fight our way out of the back door,' Magnus said, hauling a strongbox out from under the floor.

The clash of iron against iron rang above the yells; then a wail added to the noise, rising in pitch and fearful realisation – someone had been hideously wounded.

'Uncle, help Magnus with that box.' Vespasian pushed past Narcissus and Agarpetus and stuck his head around the door to see a couple of whores burst through the leather curtain from the bar; smoke wafted in with them. They turned down the corridor and then caught sight of him, screamed, doubled back and disappeared up the staircase at the other end. Vespasian ran along to the curtain and carefully pulled it back a fraction. Flames raged behind the bar where the cooking fire had been fed some incendiary liquid; a body writhed on the counter, its wails weakening as its flesh charred. Dozens of figures struggled in the blaze's glow, in pairs or groups, wrestling hand to hand or stabbing at close quarters, screaming, cursing, growling as they fought for their lives. The bodies of the dying squirmed in agony on the floor, entangling the legs of friend and foe alike as men strove to keep their balance and their chances of survival. Over their heads and beneath the thickening pall of smoke Vespasian could see that the door at the narrow end was barred by two hulking shapes with staves – no one was leaving by that exit.

Sextus, bellowing like a goaded, chained bear, hacked and cut downwards onto a smaller opponent's upturned sword, forcing it ever lower as his brothers slowly gave ground around him, under pressure from weight of numbers and the growing strength of the flames. There was no way forward, only back.

'Sextus!' Vespasian yelled into the room. 'Now, before it's too late!'

Sextus roared and sliced his blade down again with a force that dislodged his opponent's from his grip. With a speed that belied his bulk, Sextus changed the stroke from vertical to horizontal, slicing through the exposed throat with an explosion of blood, black in the flicker of the flames, before backhanding the sword into the upraised arm of the intruder next to the dying man, taking the limb off at the elbow and sending it spinning, spiralling gore, over the heads of his comrades, weapon still in hand and glinting with firelight.

Vespasian backed away from the doorway as the South Quirinal Crossroads Brothers took advantage of the moment of extreme violence to retreat a few more steps. As he went back along the corridor the first of them pushed through the leather curtain.

'Are they coming?' Magnus asked as Vespasian ran back into the room.

'As fast as they can,' Vespasian replied.

Narcissus looked at him. For the first time Vespasian saw a genuine expression on the freedman's face; it was fear. 'I'm the imperial secretary; I can't be trapped here. I must get out!'

'We must all get out, but not that way.'

'This way,' Magnus said, unbolting the door on the far side of the room as Gaius struggled with the strongbox, 'there're two back doors, well, three actually.'

Narcissus and Agarpetus dashed past him into the darkness beyond.

The first few of the brothers scrambled into the room, wafting in thick smoke as they did. The noise of fighting in the corridor carried on, fierce and unremitting, as the rest of Magnus' brethren gave ground slowly with Sextus' voice booming above the rest.

'Whoever's attacking didn't just come for tonight's takings,' Vespasian observed as he took one end of the strongbox from Magnus.

Magnus shook his head, both eyes glaring, one sightlessly. 'No, and that makes me think that we're in the middle of a commercial takeover.' Sword in hand he headed back to the corridor door. 'We'll get all the lads in here first, secure the door and then make our break for it together; if this is a move by a rival brotherhood they may well know about the exits. Fall back, lads!' Pulling a few of the brothers out of his way he made it to the corridor as the smoke intensified. 'Sextus, get them all in here.' He turned to an easterner, complete with pointed beard and trousers, and an old Greek with an ugly scar on his left cheek where his beard grew rough. 'Tigran, take half the lads to the south exit and wait for me to give the go-ahead before you pull the bolts. Cassandros, take the rest to the northern one and don't forget the sledgehammers, just in case. We all go together. And get the lads to relieve the senators of that strongbox; what the fuck are they doing manual labour for?'

Tigran and Cassandros moved off, marshalling the brothers, two of whom took the strongbox from Vespasian and Gaius, as Magnus pulled more in from the corridor until there was just Sextus' thrashing bulk preventing him from securing the door. 'Now, Sextus!'

Sextus leapt backwards and, with a lightning thrust, rammed the tip of his blade into the shoulder of the nearest intruder; the man fell back into his comrades and Magnus heaved on the door, slamming it shut just as Sextus extracted his sword. He jammed the bolt into its socket as Vespasian ran forward and retrieved the iron bar that barricaded the door; within an instant it was firmly wedged in its housings.

'Time to go, sir. Well done, Sextus, my lad.' Magnus turned and crossed the room with his brother following as the rein-forced door started to shake with blows from the far side. 'They'll have to pull back soon because of the smoke.'

Vespasian went to the desk and blew out the last lamp left burning in the room, leaving it lit only by the dim light coming in from the escape route. Magnus was waiting for him and bolted the door behind him as he slipped into another corridor even longer than the last as the building widened in accordance with the diverging lines of the Alta Semita and the Vicus Longus. He followed Magnus across and into a small room. From beyond an open door at the far end came the sound of fighting.

'The stupid bastards have tried to go before we're all there,' Magnus hissed as they ran towards the sound.

An instant later they burst into a storeroom, the width of the building; a dozen or so of the brothers were struggling to heave shut a door leading out to the Vicus Longus. A honed-muscled giant with scars on his forearms stood in the narrow opening, one foot on the body blocking the door from closing, lashing out with a bloody sword at all who fell upon him, his movements a blur of fluid motion.

'Fucking ex-gladiator,' Magnus cursed as he too threw his weight against the door. 'Pull that body clear!'

As Tigran and another brother took it in turns to trade blows with the fighting machine trying to gain ingress, Vespasian bent down between the two brothers and caught hold of one of the dead man's wrists. He pulled, using all his strength, and the dead weight slowly shifted. A ringing clash above his head made him instinctively jump back; Tigran had blocked a downward blow meant for his neck. The easterner parried again and Vespasian held his breath and grabbed the arm once more. This time he pulled with the desperation of a doomed man; the corpse slid, lubricated by its own blood. As the impediment cleared the opening, Magnus' brethren slowly forced the door closed, compelling the ex-gladiator to retreat or risk losing an arm in the narrowing gap.

'Who the fuck gave the word, Tigran?' Magnus snarled as the door finally shut and the brothers slammed the bar across it.

'He did, brother,' Tigran shouted, pointing at the corner. 'He and his freedman opened the door.'

Narcissus stood, cowering, looking down at the dead man at Vespasian's feet. 'I have to get out! I can't die in a hole like this.'

'You could have killed us all!' Tigran shouted, lunging at Narcissus with his blade aimed at his throat.

Narcissus howled.

Vespasian grabbed Tigran's wrist and arrested the stroke a thumb's breadth from the Greek's quivering flesh. 'He stays alive!'

Tigran tried to force his arm forward but Vespasian held firm; with a nod and a shrug the easterner pulled back.

Narcissus spouted tears of relief.

Vespasian looked at the Greek who had ordered so many deaths; in disgust he kicked the corpse at his feet. Its head lolled into the light: Agarpetus.

Magnus wasted no time on recriminations. 'Tigran, stay here with a couple of lads and keep an eye on the door. The rest of you, come with me.' He ran to the other side of the room, but there was no exit to the Alta Semita, only a small window; he turned left up a further corridor.

Vespasian grabbed the sobbing Narcissus by the sleeve and hauled him away after Magnus.

At the far end of the corridor they came into a final room; there was one door to the Alta Semita but no other exit. It was crammed with at least a score of men.

'I thought I'd be safer down here,' Gaius told Vespasian as he pushed his way through to him. 'I could see that Narcissus ordering Agarpetus to open the door before we were ready was a bad idea.'

'What if they've blocked this exit too, Uncle?'

'The prognosis wouldn't look too favourable. There's no other way out except for going back.'

'I have to get out!' Narcissus bleated.

But it was not the door that Magnus headed to; it was the blank wall on the opposite side. 'We won't risk the obvious way. Cassandros, you got the hammers?'

The scarred Greek nodded and indicated to a brother who lifted two weighty tools and handed one to Cassandros.

'Get on with it then, lads.'

Magnus moved back and the brothers took their places next to the wall facing each other and hefted their hammers over their shoulders. In the dim light Vespasian could see a faint line, door-shaped, drawn upon it.

'We keep this for special occasions,' Magnus informed Vespasian and Gaius. 'Never had to use it so let's hope the bastards don't know about it.'

The first blow hit with a resounding crack; on the other side of the room the tell-tale glow of flame flickered in the narrow gap between the ground and the door.

'Soon as you like, boys,' Magnus said as Tigran and his two lads came pelting up the corridor. 'Don't even say it, Tigran, I can guess. Just bolt that door.'

Tension in the room escalated as smoke began to creep under the door to the street and the flames on the other side grew. The hammers worked with fast alternate blows, soon knocking away all the thick plaster.

Vespasian's heart sank as a solid wall of thin bricks was exposed; he looked over his shoulder to see that the fire was quickly gaining.

'All right, lads, a few good blows each at the very base should do it.'

Vespasian watched, ever mindful of the danger eating its way through the wooden door, as the hammers beat at the lower bricks. To his great surprise the blows sent them shooting out; they had not been mortared. After three or four strikes there was a foot-high gap; an instant later two of the lower bricks fell to the ground and then the rest followed, tumbling, chinking down in a cloud of dust.

'Clear it, lads,' Magnus ordered.

Half a dozen brothers stepped forward and began heaving and hurling the bricks out of the way. After less than fifty heartbeats the mound was low enough to scramble over and the brothers streamed out. Vespasian found himself in the corner of a delta-shaped courtyard, stinking of rotting refuse and faeces, sandwiched behind the last tenements on both the Alta Semita and the Vicus Longus; to his left flames from the tavern at the apex of the junction could be seen rising to the sky, to his right were the backs of another couple of tenements divided by a narrow alley.

'Quickly through there, lads, then split up and slow down; lose yourselves in the alleys on the other side.'

As the South Quirinal Brotherhood dispersed silently, Magnus had a quick word with Tigran and the brothers carrying the strongbox and then looked at Vespasian and Gaius. 'I'd say that I'm going to have to rely on one of you for hospitality tonight.'

'And maybe a few nights to come, my friend,' Gaius observed.

'I don't think so, sir. If that was organised by who I think it was, then I'm a dead man if I stay. I'm out of Rome as soon as I can.'

'What about me?' Narcissus asked, some of his haughty dignity returning to his voice. 'I can't risk going to find my carriage. You must protect me; this was meant to be a safe place for a meeting.'

Magnus frowned at that statement and then led the way across the courtyard.

Vespasian looked at the Greek and wondered whether he would feel gratitude for saving his life or the opposite because his latent cowardice had been exposed.

He decided he had nothing to lose and would probably have more to gain by aiding him. 'You'd better come with us.'

Speed was the issue, or, rather, lack of it, as Magnus guided Vespasian, Gaius and Narcissus through the unlit alleys and yards that separated the insalubrious dwellings, built with little thought of civic planning, between the two diverging major roads of the Quirinal. It was not Gaius' girth nor was it Narcissus' inability to run more than ten paces without gasping for breath that impaired their progress; it was the refuse, both solid and slimy, scattered on the dirt ground already laced with unseen potholes. Magnus cursed as he led them, single-file, stumbling forward, arms outstretched and feet taking unsure steps, through gloom that was only occasionally alleviated by guttering light from a candle burning in a window or a torch sputtering in a holder next to a door. From all around came shouts and cries, not the sounds of escape and pursuit but the noise of the inhabitants of this underbelly of the city arguing and fighting amongst themselves in an environment where contentment is a far-off dream.

Vespasian glanced over his shoulder; the end of the alley was faintly illuminated by the glow of the fire raging through the tavern, two hundred paces away. There were no signs of their attackers nor of Magnus' brethren who had split up into small groups and fanned out in different directions, blending into the neighbourhood and losing themselves. But that was easy for men dressed in the rough woollen tunics and cloaks favoured by the urban poor; their passing would cause no more notice amongst the footpads and cut-throats than that of one of the mangy dogs that infested these lawless lanes.

He pulled off his cloak and handed it to Narcissus in front of him. 'Cover your clothes with this; and keep your hands inside it so that your rings aren't visible.'

'Surely we're safe enough with Magnus; no one's going to rob us in his area when we're with him?'

'You may not have noticed,' Magnus said, stumbling over an unseen obstacle that squelched and then gave off the sickly scent of decomposition, 'but someone has just burnt down my cross-roads headquarters and tried to kill me. I'd say that my authority in the area is at quite a low ebb at the moment. And besides, if a gang of thieves catch a glimpse of your rings or fine clothes in a pool of light and they outnumber us, they ain't going to have a look to see who you're with until we're all lying down bleeding copiously from our slashed throats. I think that it'll be a bit late by then, don't you?'

Narcissus drew the cloak about him, breathing heavily after the exertion of talking and walking fast.

Gaius pulled his hood over his finely tonged hair. 'Who do you think that was, Magnus?'

Magnus turned right with the confidence of a man who knew his way. 'If it was one of the brotherhoods then it could be any number of them, but my guess is it was Sempronius' lads from the West Viminal; we share a border and have a few disputed streets. Sempronius and me have never got on personally since a dispute over whore-boys twenty-five years ago. We've had a few run ins and he holds a grudge better than a woman.'

'Do you want me to do something about him?' Vespasian asked.

'Oh, you'll never be able to touch him, even as consul.'

'Who protects him?'

'His brotherhood controls the Viminal Gate and so consequently has close ties with the Praetorian Guard who use the brothels along the Vicus Patricius; Sempronius and Burrus, the prefect, have a very good understanding, if you take my meaning?'

'So what will you do?'

'I ain't going to do anything, Tigran will. I spoke to him and told him to take the strongbox; he'll take over now. It's a younger man's game and I don't qualify any more, especially after losing the eye. He'll do nothing until he knows for certain who it was and who's behind them. If it was one of the brotherhoods, he'll have to hit them hard and quickly. A lot of blood needs to be spilt in order for the South Qurinal to reassert itself.'

'What do you mean "if"? Surely it was a rival brotherhood? You just said it was.'

'You'd think so, wouldn't you, sir? That is until you look at the timing. It might be just a coincidence but why did they choose to attack at precisely the moment that the Junior Consul and the imperial secretary were on the premises?'

CHAPTER IIII

'HE WANTS ME to help him force either Pallas or Agrippina into admitting to Claudius that she has cuckolded him not only with Pallas but also with her own son.' Vespasian ran his fingers through Caenis' raven hair, enjoying the musk scent rising from it. 'He says that he believes she is responsible for a treasonous crisis that Pallas is ignorant of but would be implicated in anyway.'

Caenis ran a hand across his broad chest, moist with the sweat of exceedingly active sex, and nuzzled her cheek on his shoulder. 'What treason?'

'He was about to tell me when the attack started and then, when we eventually managed to get to Gaius' house, he refused to elaborate and insisted on being escorted back to the palace by almost every one of Uncle's slaves; he left promising that he'll be in contact when he's made the necessary arrangements for what he wants us to do, warning us that it will involve leaving Rome for a while. He wouldn't give us any more details. However, he did say that it was connected with the Parthian embassy to the tribes north of the Danuvius and the timing of the toppling of the last Armenian King. And he says that Agrippina's using my brother's failure to intercept the embassy against me and has had my governorship of Africa revoked so that the only hope I have of preferment is to help him get rid of the bitch and in the process bring down Pallas.' Vespasian stared up into the dark of Caenis' bedroom slowly shaking his head in disbelief at the position he was being forced into.

Once again he had been sucked into the mire of high imperial politics, caught between two opposing forces who cared only for safeguarding their own positions. In the past he had learnt to make as much money as possible out of his enforced involvement in situations not to his liking. That had helped to wash away the inevitable bad taste that was left in his mouth as he acted in ways so contrary to his lofty, youthful ideals of service to his family and to Rome; those lost ideals had existed only in his imagination when he had first entered the city twenty-five years before as a naïve lad of sixteen. He had discovered over time that Rome was an entirely different place to his delusional juvenile picture of it; the only goals worth achieving were the twin gods of status and power, and access to these was only through the much worshipped deities of patronage and wealth. Nothing else mattered.

This time, however, he could see no way of benefitting financially from what he was being compelled to do and no way that he could extract himself without damage to the patronage that he enjoyed of Pallas and, to a lesser extent, Narcissus. He had betrayed Narcissus already by telling Caenis just what the imperial secretary required of him and Narcissus would be sure to find out at some point; if the imperial freedman ever rose to prominence again, Vespasian could expect no preferment from that quarter. Therefore it seemed to him that his best option was to work for Pallas; but even if he remained loyal to him, Agrippina would continue to block his career and Pallas' patronage would be worthless. And then there was also the question that Magnus had planted in his mind as they escaped from the tavern: the question of Pallas' loyalty to him. Only Pallas had known of the time and place of his meeting with Narcissus and he had made a special point of having Vespasian confirm the location; had he ordered that attack as a convenient way of getting rid of his rival as collateral damage in a supposed underworld feud? Was Vespasian's life the price paid for such an opportune demise? This thought he dared not share even with Caenis because he felt sure that if it were true she would either know about it, in which case her love was false and she was no more than a spy in his bed and that thought he could not endure; or, more likely, she was unaware of her master's duplicity and would be suitably outraged and feel obliged to take some form of vengeance on Pallas, thus exposing herself to his wrath should he suspect her of moving against him.

All in all, Vespasian could see no satisfactory way forward other than to retire from politics and live out the rest of his life farming his estates with the seasons marking the years and, as his brother had once said, the years being differentiated solely by the standard of the annual wine vintage. That was something he could not contemplate: how could his sons hope to thrive in Rome if their father had no influence to push them through the series of military and magisterial appointments that was the Cursus Honorum? How would they get the plum posts in the provinces and legions if he just disappeared? And then, more to the point, how would he ever manage to pursue and realise the destiny that he felt sure had been conceived for him as the sacrifice's liver had indicated only a few hours ago that morning?

No, he decided, somehow he had to navigate himself through this and try to come out of it with, if not some credit, then at least without too much damage.

'Pallas will always try to help you if it coincides with his interests,' Caenis murmured, kissing him.

'That's just the point: while he is, for whatever reason, Agrippina's lover then his and my interests will never coincide. I stand more to gain by Narcissus bringing down the Empress, but I've already jeopardised that by having this conversation with my lover who will report it back to Pallas.'

'I don't have to, my love.'

'Of course you have to; and, of course, I had to tell you because I'd promised Pallas I would. He'll be impatient for the full transcript first thing tomorrow and he'll be expecting me to keep him informed of all contacts that I have with Narcissus concerning this matter. You know and I know that trying to lie to him is not an option; to construct a lie that fits the facts as he knows them will be fine now but it'll be impossible to maintain as events take their inevitably unforeseen course.'

Caenis was quiet for a few moments and then looked up at him in the dark. 'There may be a way for you to play both sides but it involves patience.'

'I can be patient.'

'We need to find out exactly what Agrippina's done and get proof of it before Narcissus does.'

'We?'

'Of course "we", my love; who else can you trust to help you? I'll tell Pallas all that you've told me. He'll want to know what Agrippina's done and how he could be implicated and I'll be able to say, quite truthfully, that Narcissus didn't have time to tell you before the tavern was attacked. All he said was that he believed it was to do with the embassy. That will leave Pallas with a straight choice: demanding Agrippina tells him what she's done behind his back, which he'll be afraid of doing for fear of her refusing and their relationship being permanently damaged; or finding out himself and then making a judgement whether to betray her to the Emperor to save his skin.'

Vespasian stifled a yawn. 'Which, if I can help him achieve that, would free me of her and keep Pallas in a position where he could still be of use to me.'

'And you can help him achieve that: Pallas will see that the easiest way to find out what she has done is through you; he'll realise that Narcissus didn't come to you because he thought you would help him as Agrippina's blocking you. Narcissus doesn't care about things like that. He chose you because you, and only you, can help him. Narcissus can't accuse Agrippina and Pallas of treason without the proof. I know how his mind works because I was his secretary for six years; he feels that you and your uncle are the key to finding that proof, otherwise why else did he want to meet with you in secret? Now, why would that be? Why did he specifically choose you?'

Vespasian squeezed Caenis' shoulder. 'Of course! You're brilliant, my love; what's the common factor between Agrippina's supposed treason and me and Gaius? Sabinus. What she did has something to do with the embassy that Sabinus failed to capture. Narcissus suspects that, inadvertently, Sabinus knows something that can help.'

'Exactly; and my guess is that Narcissus wants you and your uncle to talk to your brother and find out; he will ask you both to travel to Moesia.'

'Both of us?'

'Yes, I assume so; it seems odd, but otherwise why meet with you both?'

'But what can Gaius do or say that I can't?'

'I'm sure that'll become clear. Now, when I present this to Pallas I can do it in a way that he comes to the same conclusion as you just did. He will think that it's his idea and his first reaction will be to have Claudius recall Sabinus to Rome and question him here.'

'Then Narcissus would know for sure that I've betrayed him.'

'And Pallas will lose any advantage he may have; far better for him to have Narcissus believe that he knows nothing. Far better for Pallas that Agrippina doesn't suspect that her lover is investigating her. Far better for us that you go to Moesia at Narcissus' request but with Pallas' secret blessing. And to convince Narcissus that you are working solely for him I shall have Pallas dismiss me from my post for plotting against him.'

Vespasian sat up as the full implication of what Caenis was suggesting hit him. 'And if I were to find out the proof of whatever it is that Agrippina has done, then when I return I can give it to whoever has the best chance of giving me the governorship of a province.'

'Precisely, because both will believe that you are working solely for them until the moment that you hand over the information to the other one. And I will be able to take my position back with whomever we choose because I will be seen to have done no wrong in their eyes.'

'That, my love, is cold, dispassionate politics worthy of Pallas or Narcissus themselves.'

Caenis cupped his face with her hands and kissed his lips. 'Thank you; but you must remember that I've lived and breathed their world all of my adult life and I know how they function better than anyone. But my loyalty is not to them, only to you, my love, and when they threaten you I will always help you defend yourself. I will always see you safe.'

Vespasian returned the kiss with full measure, feeling shame welling up inside. 'I'm sorry that I doubted you.'

'Doubted me? Why?'

He told her of the timing of the attack on the tavern and how only Pallas knew when he and Narcissus would be there.

'You think that if I knew of that then I might not have told you? Of course I would. But I can honestly say that Pallas had nothing to do with it; I would have known.'

'Then who did organise it? Callistus perhaps, trying to edge his way back into power by eliminating Narcissus?'

'No, he's just happy to keep his position as secretary to the Law Courts; it's very lucrative. He knows that Agrippina has her eye on him, firstly for being Messalina's creature and secondly for not supporting her becoming empress. He wouldn't do anything to attract her attention.'

'Who, then?'

'It was coincidence, my love; a brotherhood turf war that you got caught up in. Now put it from your mind and get some sleep.'

Vespasian kissed her again and lay back down. But sleep would not come; he found it very hard to believe in coincidences.

The summons from Claudius came as a surprise to Vespasian as he left the Senate House that afternoon preceded by his lictors. The immaculately presented Praetorian centurion, waiting at the foot of the steps, snapped a rigid salute, his right arm thumping his highly polished scale-armoured chest and causing his transverse white horsehair helmet crest to judder. With military brevity he begged leave to report that the Emperor wished Vespasian to accompany him back to the Palatine as soon as the trial, over which he was presiding at the far end of the Forum Romanum, concluded. Vespasian found himself with little option but to process slowly towards the open-air court, receiving petitions from the importunate and cursing Claudius for his inconsideration in keeping him from a reviving bath that he hoped would wash away the fatigue he felt at having had very little sleep.

'I can't imagine what good they think it'll do giving a petition to a consul who has only two days left in office,' a clipped voice observed as Vespasian dismissed a supplicant with platitudes about looking into his appeal concerning his right to contest his father's will.

'Corbulo!' Vespasian exclaimed, his expression turning from irritation to mild pleasure as he spied his old acquaintance watching him from beside the Rostrum. 'I didn't know that you were back in Rome.'

'I've just got back today,' Corbulo said, walking forward, looking down the long nose of his horse-like face at Vespasian and proffering his right arm for him to grasp. 'I'm here to pay my respects to the Emperor and thank him for giving me Asia.'

Vespasian took Corbulo's arm, astounded. 'But you're the Governor of Germania Inferior.'

'I was, Vespasian, was.' Corbulo drew himself up and adjusted his face into a picture of aristocratic smugness as they continued progressing towards Claudius' court. 'But I did such a fine job of dealing with the Cherusci and Chauci trying to take advantage of our weakened state on the Germanic frontier. I killed thousands of the bearded barbarians and taught them that just because we've taken three legions away from the Rhenus and one from the Danuvius to subdue some fog-drenched island that no one is interested in, that's no reason to stop paying tribute to Rome. The Emperor's very pleased with me – or at least his freedmen are.' Corbulo wrinkled his nose in patrician distaste. 'I've been summoned back to Rome to be presented with Triumphal Regalia.'

'That doesn't mean anything these days; Claudius gave every one of the hundred or so senators who accompanied him to Britannia the right to wear Triumphal Regalia. Even my uncle, who's never done anything more martial in his life than inspect the monthly payday parade, has that privilege; it's completely reduced the status of the award.'

'Yes, well, my status is not in question. I've been given Asia and the promise of another military command soon; there's a growing worry about the stability of our client kingdom of Armenia and with my experience I'm obviously the best man for the job.'

'I'm sure you are, Corbulo,' Vespasian agreed without much enthusiasm.

'You don't seem very pleased for me. Have you been given Bithynia or somewhere equally as unprestigious? Not that it would be surprising, your family being what they are; I was very surprised when I heard that Sabinus had been given Moesia, Macedonia and Thracia.'

Vespasian was used to Corbulo's snobbishness, having known him for twenty-five years since they served together as military tribunes in the IIII Scythica during the Thracian revolt; but that did not make it any easier to swallow. 'Yes, it was a surprise seeing as we *are* New Men and at the time our family could only boast one consulship; but it's even more surprising that, now we can boast two, I don't get given a province and yet you, whose family is far older than ours and yet has only achieved the consulship once, if I recall, get given a second province.' Vespasian hid his amusement as Corbulo harrumphed at the dig. 'But I am pleased for you, Corbulo; although I confess that I'm surprised that you've heard about trouble in Armenia. It hasn't been discussed in the Senate.'

Corbulo took Vespasian's elbow and pulled him closer, away from the lictors. 'That's because officially there isn't any trouble there and Mithridates, our client king, is still on the throne.'

'That's what I'm aware of officially. And unofficially I know that he's been deposed but I don't know the details.'

Corbulo's smug expression reached new heights as he revelled in being in the possession of superior knowledge. 'Unofficially, three months ago at the beginning of October, Mithridates was defeated by a young upstart with the uncouth name of Radamistus, the son of King Pharasmanes of neighbouring Iberia. Obviously we detect Parthian money behind Radamistus as nothing happens in Armenia without either their or our collusion.'

'And we wouldn't depose our own puppet.'

'Quite, not even ... well, I won't say who is that stupid. Anyway, I'm told that if diplomacy fails then an invasion may be required and my military experience makes me the obvious choice for leading it.'

'And what would happen if diplomacy failed and, the gods forbid, you didn't restore Mithridates by military force and Armenia became a Parthian client kingdom?'

Corbulo frowned, unable to comprehend something so outrageously implausible. 'I won't fail.'

'Yes, yes, of course you won't, Corbulo. But let's just say, for example, that the Emperor sent someone else, not of your calibre, who did fail, and Armenia came back under Parthian sway for the first time since Tiberius; what then?'

'Then the Emperor would have to send me out to redress the matter.' A loud bleating noise erupting from deep in Corbulo's gorge alerted Vespasian, who recognised the symptoms, to the fact that Corbulo had attempted levity. It soon passed. 'But seriously; if that were to happen then we would have a very serious situation. Parthia would soon have access to the Euxine and a Parthian fleet in that sea threatening the Bosphorus with the possibility of breaking out into Our Sea is not something that we would wish to contemplate.'

More than that, Vespasian thought as they arrived at the court, they would also have access to the Danuvius and therefore to the heart of Europa. He stopped close to the imperial litter awaiting Claudius and admired Narcissus' ability to construct a viable narrative out of so few facts and wondered briefly what connection Agrippina could have with Iberia, Armenia and a Parthian embassy to the trans-Danuvius.

'And as for you, you're a stupid old fool!'

Vespasian looked up in the direction whence the yelling came to see a lawyer hurl his stylus and wax tablets.

Claudius yelped and ducked as the missiles narrowly missed him.

'A curse on your idiotic, cruel judgements!' the lawyer continued with rising venom. 'How can you admit the evidence of a woman, a common prostitute at that, against a member of the equestrian class?' He pointed indignantly at the defendant standing in the well of the court; seated beyond him were the fifty jurists, all fellow equestrians, looking in outrage at their Emperor and the overly painted woman, dressed in the masculine toga that symbolised her profession, standing before him.

Vespasian sighed and shook his head, looking at Corbulo. 'It's been getting worse in the past couple of years. From all accounts he drinks himself senseless every evening and it seems to be making him more and more erratic.'

Claudius adjusted his toga in an attempt to restore some dignity but still managed to look shambolic. 'C-c-curse me if you like, b-b-but keep your hands off!'

'The trouble is,' Vespasian continued as he watched Claudius unroll and read a legal document, 'that because he has such respect for the ways of our ancestors and the law he believes that he should run the courts as if there was still a Republic. He allows all the mud-slinging and insults and generally gets made to look a complete fool and does nothing to punish people who abuse him.' Claudius rubbed his bloodshot eyes and then squinted at the small script. 'During the hearings, that is,' Vespasian added. 'Outside the courts anyone who mocks him is liable to find themselves on a capital charge and given one more opportunity to mock him in court before being executed.'

With shaking hands, Claudius rolled up the scroll. 'I w-w-will allow her evid-d-d-dence and I will also pronounce my judgement based upon it.'

The defence layer slammed a fist down on his desk. 'Her testimony is even less reliable than that of the lowliest citizen, you fool.' The scores of spectators, mostly ordinary citizens, surrounding the court took umbrage at this slur – as they saw it – on their honesty and began shouting abuse at the lawyer. Claudius again ignored the insult, handed the document to a clerk and then rummaged through a pile of scrolls and wax tablets in front of him.

'But then he forgets his Republican sentiments,' Vespasian continued, 'and decides that his opinion is the only one that counts and makes unilateral decisions bypassing the jury.'

'I find the d-d-defendant.' Claudius paused as he scanned another scroll. 'D-D-Didius Gaetullus, guilty of paying for services in this honest lady's establishment with forged coinage and I advise the jury to do likewise.'

There was a huge cheer from the spectators who had taken the lawyer's remark to heart and were now only too pleased to see a man of higher status convicted, whether it be on spurious evidence or not.

'So whose patronage do you have to thank for this new appointment?' Vespasian asked while the jury voted.

'Ah!' Corbulo looked around to make sure that no one was within earshot and lowered his voice. 'That is the strange thing and I was hoping that, as the sitting consul, you could help me understand it.'

'I doubt it, Corbulo, seeing as yesterday was the first time that I'd heard anything about this Armenia problem.'

'Well, try. All the correspondence has come to me using the imperial relay system. However, even though the despatches bear the imperial seal none has been signed by Claudius or by one of his freedmen in his name, as would be normal. I questioned all the couriers and they insisted that they had received the despatches from the palace but had always been given them by a low-ranking functionary.'

'That's not unusual.'

'I agree; but I've never received orders bearing the Emperor's seal without his signature or one of his freedmen's on them.'

'So why did you believe them to be genuine?'

'I wasn't sure until my replacement turned up with a mandate from the Emperor.'

'Guilty!' the lead juror replied to Claudius' question.

'You see,' Vespasian muttered, 'they'll condemn one of their own rather than go against the Emperor's will; even if the evidence is suspect.'

Corbulo looked at the whore in disgust; the smile on her face was one of pure vindictive pleasure as she glared at the defendant who held his head in his hands. 'It's a disgrace taking her word above that of a wealthy man.'

Claudius finished writing the verdict on the relevant scroll and then addressed the court. 'I shall now pronounce sentence. I—'

'He's a forger!' someone in the crowd shouted. 'He should have his hands cut off.'

Claudius' head jerked a couple of times as he tried to locate the source of the suggestion.

'It's the way of our ancestors!' a different voice reminded the Emperor, not untruthfully.

The defendant took his hands from his face, stared at them and then at Claudius in horror as he seemed to consider the unsolicited counsel. The horror on his face then blended with terror as Claudius began to nod, his mind evidently settled on the justice of the punishment. 'D-D-Didius Gaetullus, I condemn you to a life without hands to prevent you from putting them to ill-use again. S-seize him and s-s-summon the executioner.'

Uproar ensued as the hapless man was secured; the spectators, scenting pain and blood, cheering the Emperor for his wisdom while the jurors made known their rage at the barbarity of the punishment on the man whom they did not have the courage to acquit.

Vespasian turned away, unwilling to watch any more. 'So you think all this has been done without the Emperor's knowledge?'

'I'm not sure what to think, which is why I've come straight to the Forum to present myself to him before anyone else has a chance to tell him that I'm here. It'll be interesting to see his reaction.'

'More to the point, it'll be interesting to see the reaction of those surrounding him. I would say that whoever feigns the biggest surprise at the sight of you is your secret patron. And if it's who I suspect it is then I should watch my step.'

'What do you mean?'

'Let's just say that you don't want to be involved with *her*.'

Corbulo contemplated this as a heavily muscled man carrying a wooden block and a cleaver passed them, heading into the court, followed by two more men with a brazier full of red-hot coals. 'But surely Agrippina would never dare to meddle so obviously with imperial policy. She may be the Empress but she's still only a woman.'

'Perhaps, but yesterday she was seated next to the Emperor on a dais of equal height and then instigated imperial policy by recommending Caratacus' life be spared.'

'That's outrageous; sparing a rebel! If I'd done that in Germania, we wouldn't receive any tribute and would be in constant fear of invasion across the Rhenus.'

'For all Claudius' concern about "the ways of our ancestors" he's unable to control his wife as they did.'

There was a lull in the commotion coming from the court broken only by the pleading screams of one man.

'I'll not be beholden to a woman for my position,' Corbulo asserted.

'It's that or quiet retirement on your estate until she's gone; that's the choice we all face.'

The screams abruptly stopped, silenced by the dull thump of honed iron striking solid wood; then followed a howl of agony accompanied by a low gasp of appreciation from the crowd. A few moments later the crowd gasped again but the sound did not mask the desolate wail of a man freshly deprived of both his hands.

Vespasian tried to block the pitiful noise from his mind, standing in silence with a thoughtful Corbulo as the court slowly broke up and the spectators dispersed in search of new amusement, chattering happily together about the outcome.

'Ah! Th-th-there you are, Consul,' Claudius called cheerily, lurching behind his lictors as they cleared a path for him towards his litter. 'We have much to discuss.'

'Princeps,' Vespasian replied, acknowledging the Emperor with a slight bow of the head.

'Princeps,' Corbulo echoed.

'C-C-C-Corbulo? Did I summon you too?'

'You did, Princeps.'

'All the way from G-G-Germania Inferior?'

'Indeed, Princeps. You've replaced me there and have given me the province of Asia to govern.'

'H-h-have I now? Well, well, that is fortuitous. Join us; you might as well hear what I have to say to Vespasian as it may well affect you if you are going to Asia. After all, Asia is almost next door to Armenia.'

'So you see,' Claudius said, adjusting his position amongst the copious cushions in his litter, 'it's of vital importance to our eastern policy and to our dealings with Parthia that Armenia remains in our sphere of influence. Should we lose it, the client kingdom of Pontus would be open to Parthian meddling or even annexation and our provinces of Asia and Syria would both be under threat.'

He had surprised both Vespasian and Corbulo by the fluency of his speech; he had hardly stuttered at all as he explained the present crisis in the region while they progressed along the Via Sacra. His grip of the detail, however, was not a revelation to them; they were both well aware that this chaotic man had a sharp mind for facts, both legal and historical, having written many books that had been praised for their learning. It was a scholarly inner-self betrayed by the drooling, twitching, limping exterior that was compounded by his feeble wit, his blurted, inappropriate comments, his malleability in the hands of his wife and freedmen and, of course, his increasing drunkenness. Although Claudius could see through a problem, the solution, however, was normally placed in his mind by one of the schemers who parasitically sucked on his power. And this case was no exception.

'So Pallas has suggested that the best way to counter this is to send an embassy to Armenia and I agree with him, as does the Empress. She also believes that you, Vespasian, are the most suitable man for the job: as my junior colleague in the consulship this year you will still carry much authority when you step down. That should impress these petty easterners. I had been going to give you Africa to govern, but Agrippina persuaded me a couple of days ago that your family perhaps don't make the best administrators and that your talents would be wasted there and that I should wait to see if something more suitable came along for you. I'm so pleased she did; she must have had divine guidance as Pallas only made his suggestion this morning.'

'Most fortuitous, Princeps,' Vespasian lied through gritted teeth. 'What should I aim to achieve on this embassy?'

'Pallas is waiting to brief you at the palace.'

Vespasian was admitted without question to the freedman's apartments on the first floor of the section of the palace built by Augustus. Pallas was waiting for him in his formal reception room: a spacious chamber decorated with statues and frescoes of

Greek mythology and furnished in a plain style with much use of polished wood and a marked absence of lavish upholstery. The sun, westering over the Circus Maximus and Aventine beyond, bathed the room with thin, winter-evening light.

'Things have moved much faster than I anticipated,' Pallas said, surprising Vespasian by getting to his feet as the steward showed him into the room. 'Caenis' report this morning caused me some concern; however, the timing is most convenient. Narcissus can ask you to stop in Macedonia and speak to your brother on the way out to Armenia. No doubt he will do as soon as you leave these rooms; I imagine that he has a messenger stationed outside to fetch you to him. I was careful to let him find out that you're here being briefed for your mission to the East.'

They grasped forearms as equals although one was a consul of Rome and the other a mere freedman. Vespasian put the thought to one side knowing that there was nothing 'mere' about Pallas. 'You have no idea what Agrippina has done?'

Pallas waved his steward away. 'If, indeed, she's done anything. It may be just Narcissus' wishful thinking or a calculated lie contrived to seed mistrust between the Empress and me.'

Vespasian took the seat indicated by Pallas next to an already filled cup. 'If that's so then I'd say it's working.'

'Yes, well, Caenis' analysis was correct: I can't confront Agrippina with it so you have to find out for me; an admission or denial from her would put a strain on our relationship without doubt. However, if there is truth in the accusation and Narcissus is right and it does have something to do with the Parthian embassy, then I can make a shrewd guess as to what she has done.'

'She's the money behind Radamistus.'

Pallas' face twitched, betraying surprise. 'How did you get to that?'

Vespasian took a sip of his wine and closed his eyes as he savoured it; it was exquisite. 'It's the timing. The Parthian embassy arrived towards the beginning of September, stayed for a few days and then headed home, evading Sabinus on the way. According to Narcissus, the embassy went through the port of Phasis at the end of September. Also in September, Radamistus took his army from Iberia into Armenia and, in a very short campaign, deposed Mithridates by the beginning of October. Narcissus is certain that the embassy travelled to and from Parthia via Iberia. Now, one of Agrippina's agents murdered the man who informed Sabinus about the embassy; Agrippina not only ordered his death but also the timing of it so she evidently wanted Sabinus to know about the embassy. But how was Agrippina aware of the embassy in the first place in order to make that decision? I find it very hard to believe in coincidences.'

'Yes, as do I. If Narcissus is right and she is somehow connected to that embassy then that is the logical conclusion. And if that is the case, I can perfectly understand why she hasn't taken me into her confidence. But what concerns me more is why my agents knew nothing of this. I've been well aware of the events in Armenia for a couple of months now, but this embassy being the possible instigator of Mithridates' deposal is news to me. Agrippina evidently knew and Narcissus found out by inter-cepting Agrippina's messages; but being closer to her than he is I can normally get access to all the correspondence that arrives at the palace; but not in this case. When it comes to messages about the Parthian embassy only his people intercepted them, not mine. It's as if I've been purposely kept in the dark or, more worryingly, as if Narcissus has been purposely enlightened.'

'But now you *do* know, what do you think the objective of the embassy was?'

'Instability along the Danuvius to keep our eye off Armenia.'

'Has there been any?'

'No more than usual.'

Vespasian thought for a few moments, savouring his wine; somewhere in the gardens below a dove started cooing. 'What does Agrippina have to gain by deposing our client in Armenia and replacing him with someone loyal to Parthia?'

'I don't believe that he is completely loyal to Parthia; these slimy eastern Kings don't have any loyalty other than to them-selves and their family – those family members that they allow to live, of course. Radamistus is Tryphaena's nephew, she was the—'

'Queen of Thracia, I know, I met her when I was with the Fourth Scythica there.'

'Of course; so then you're aware that she has always been a friend of Rome's.'

'So why would the Parthians help Radamistus to seize the throne if his family is pro-Roman?'

'Assuming, again, that Narcissus is right and they did, with Agrippina somehow involved, that is what you have to find out while you help Mithridates back to his rightful place where we originally put him.'

'Me? Depose the usurper? I'll need an army for that.'

'That's what we're trying to avoid; if we send an army in we'll be at war with Parthia. It may come to that but where would we take the legions from?'

'Perhaps you shouldn't have invaded an irrelevant island like Britannia and then tied up four legions trying to keep hold of it.'

'What's done is done and it achieved the political aim at the time of giving Claudius a victory and securing his position.' Pallas paused and regarded Vespasian for a moment. 'But I will admit that the repercussions of that venture have gravely reduced our aggressive power. We can't strip any more legions from the Rhenus; we can't risk moving them from the Danuvius as, although nothing has happened as yet, we must assume that the embassy was to encourage the northern tribes to push south into Moesia. The two Egyptian legions and the single African one protect the grain supply from those provinces and so cannot be moved and the Hispanic ones are busy most of the time cowing the locals. And if we send the Syrian legions in, Parthia could sweep through the province to Our Sea, no doubt aided by those treacherous Jews, if they can manage to unite themselves; although my brother Felix, whom I persuaded the Emperor to make procurator of Judaea, tells me that they are still as argumentative as ever.'

'So we can't afford to go to war.'

'Not at the moment; we need a few years to prepare.'

'So you want me to achieve by intrigue what we're unable to do with force in order to remedy a situation that threatens the stability of the Empire that may have been instigated by the Empress herself for reasons that seem to escape everybody?'

Pallas' face remained unmoved. 'Yes.'

Vespasian laughed, loud and hollow. 'It'll cost you.'

'You could come back from this very well.'

'I'm not asking to be paid to come back, I'm asking to be paid to go.'

'What do you want?'

'Protection from Agrippina, a guarantee of a province when I return, my brother to be exonerated of all responsibility for losing this Parthian embassy and, just so I can get some financial gain from this situation, reinstatement into the equestrian class for a client of mine.'

'I could guarantee all but the first; the Empress's grudges are not easily forgotten.'

Vespasian thought for a moment. 'But my wife's are; in which case I also want the finest Gallic wet nurse available in the city. Make sure that Flavia knows just how much she costs.'

If Pallas felt surprise at that request he did not show it. 'Very well. You'll leave as soon as you step down from the consulship in a couple of days.'

'But it's still winter; the shipping lanes won't be open yet.'

'I'll give you enough gold to tempt a crew out of their hibernation. You can cross to Epirus and then take the Via Egnatia to Macedonia; there you can question your brother and find out what it is that Narcissus suspects he knows that proves Agrippina's treachery. As Caenis suggested, I've dismissed her from my service, ostensibly for disloyalty; Narcissus will assume that she refused to tell me what you talked about last night and think that he's safe in trusting you.'

'Caenis believes that Narcissus thinks my uncle is somehow important in that respect.'

'I can't see why but nevertheless you'll take him with you: he can come back to Rome and give me the information once you've seen Sabinus.'

Vespasian knew that he would not be sending Gaius back with any information until he knew which freedman to give it to.

'You, meantime, will carry on east in one of Sabinus' ships and then travel overland from the coast and be in Armenia by the spring.'

'Does Agrippina suspect that I have a dual mission?'

'No, she suspects nothing. She's just pleased that you're going. Whether she is behind Radamistus or not, she isn't concerned because she thinks that you will fail.'

'Then she does suspect one thing.'

'What?'

'She suspects that I'll never come back.'

Pallas regarded Vespasian with a shrewd eye. 'That's in the hands of the gods.'

PART II

❧ ❧

MACEDONIA AND THE ROMAN EAST,
FEBRUARY AD 52

CHAPTER V

Snow, driven by a harsh easterly wind, lashed into Vespasian's face. He pulled his hood lower and hunched his shoulders against the worsening conditions; his mount plodded next to a wagon creaking along the Via Egnatia pulled by a pair of rough-haired horses, their obvious reluctance to move forward into the wind punished by regular licks of Magnus' whip. Hormus sat on the bench next to Magnus rubbing his hands and looking miserable with chattering teeth. Despite the knitted woollen mittens and socks, Vespasian's fingers and toes were almost numb and he thought with envy of the relative comfort that Gaius must be enjoying in the covered rear of the vehicle and contemplated joining him.

'I would if I were you, sir,' Magnus said, giving his team another sharp reminder of their duty.

'What?'

'Get under cover. You've glanced over your shoulder three times since the last milestone.'

Vespasian looked up at the eleven lictors – the due of a man of proconsular rank on official business – marching in step in front of the wagon with their fasces on their shoulders and shook his head. 'They're having it far worse than I am; seeing as they're the only protection we've got I want them well disposed towards me should I require them to risk their lives. Besides, it can't be more than another four or five miles to Philippi.'

'If that's the case then we should be able to see a huge area of marshland to the south,' Gaius called from inside.

'We're having trouble seeing the horses' arseholes at the moment, sir,' Magnus informed him, not quite truthfully. Gaius pushed his head through the flap in the leather wagon cover.

'Oh, I see what you mean.' Although the snow had only just started to fall thickly and was yet to settle in depth on the ploughed fields on either side of the dead-straight road, visibility was very limited. 'Well, take it from me, Vespasian, that your grandfather on your father's side and great-grandfather on your mother's and my side were both here just over eighty-four years ago.'

Vespasian thought for a few moments and then remembered his history. 'Of course they were, but on opposite sides of the field.'

'Indeed, dear boy. My grandfather served with Augustus and Marcus Antonius in the Eighth Legion.'

'And my grandfather, Titus Flavius Petro, was, if I remember rightly what my grandmother told me, a centurion of the Thirty-sixth Legion under Marcus Brutus' command. She said that it was mainly made up of his old Pompeian comrades who had surrendered to Caesar after the Battle of Pharsalus.'

'It's a shame that we can't see that far; between the two armies they fielded almost a quarter of a million men, which must have been quite a sight.'

'On both occasions,' Vespasian reminded Gaius. 'Petro made it through the first battle and then his legion got badly mauled in the second, twenty days later when Brutus was crushed. He managed to escape and made it home to Cosa but he was amongst the couple of thousand equestrians that Augustus forced to commit suicide.'

'Whereas mine was rewarded with the land of one of those men.' Gaius chuckled. 'And now here we are, all those years later, the products of either side of the argument in the breakup of the Republic, trundling across the site of the greatest battle between Roman citizens that's ever been known, on our way to do the dirty work for two Greek freedmen who are the ultimate beneficiaries of that battle. It would seem that for all the cries of freedom issued by either side the end result has been domination of us all by a couple of ex-slaves. I wonder if Augustus, Marcus Antonius, Brutus or Cassius could have foreseen that and, if they could, would any of them have done things differently?' He rubbed flakes of snow off his ruddy face, looked around quickly, his mouth pursed ruefully, and then disappeared back inside.

'Course, it don't make any difference for most of us, though, does it?' Magnus stated with certainty. 'If you was just a common legionary, whether you was on the winning side or losing side in that battle didn't make a scrap of difference – if you survived, that is. Only a few legions were disbanded; the rest went back to business as usual. Whatever the political changes back in Rome, most of the legions just returned to their camps on the frontiers and guarded the Empire. The only change they noticed was that the oath was worded differently but everything else was the same: their centurions, their food, the discipline, everything was exactly as it was. So the whole exercise was purely for the benefit of a few vain men whose sense of honour meant that they had to be seen to have a say in how the Empire was run. If only they'd realised that most people couldn't give a fuck. They could have dispensed with the armies and just had a nice scrap amongst themselves; a couple of hundred dead and the whole affair would've been sorted out and everyone would've been happy.'

Vespasian laughed, despite his freezing lips. 'Much easier. But it didn't happen that way and the result of that struggle and all those deaths has been hijacked by two self-serving freedmen.'

'Ah! But at least they didn't force a quarter of a million men to fight each other so that they could grab power. In a way Pallas and Narcissus have got less blood on their hands than Augustus. You senators almost resent the fact that they've come to power without a good civil war in which thousands of common citizens die; that would legitimize them in your eyes. Their greatest crime is sneaking their way to power rather than bludgeoning their way there like all those upstanding families in the Republic used to.'

Vespasian found himself unable to rebut that statement and instead wondered at the truth of it. To follow that line of logic, Augustus was the only ruler for the last eighty years to be legitimate because he had fought his way to power.

He had thought that his resentment of Narcissus and Pallas was mainly based on the way that they had come to power and then held on to it; but was their way any more unjustified than

Caligula's? He too had come to power by trickery and subterfuge if the rumours were to be believed. But then neither of the freedmen's great-grandfathers had killed more of his enemies' soldiers than they had his on this plain so far from Rome.

So, therefore, it was to do with who the freedmen were, not how they got to where they were, that was the real cause of the growing resentment. The resentment that he had felt when Narcissus had – as Pallas had predicted – *ordered* him to a private room as he left Pallas' apartments had been bitter. The resentment had grown when the freedman had suggested that Vespasian's appointment as ambassador to Armenia was a very convenient cover for him to use to stop off in Macedonia and speak to his brother so that he could furnish Narcissus with the information *he* needed to defeat Pallas. When he thought of Pallas he remembered him as Antonia's steward. Then, he knew his place; now, he was forming imperial policy. He was a man who had risen way beyond his station and Vespasian realised, for the first time, that the real cause of his resentment for the pair of them was envy. Envy that people born so low should have risen so high. Ex-slaves had no right to such power. He came from a family far above them and yet they could order him to do things that he would rather not do. It began to seep into his mind that he was jealous of their power because he wanted it for himself, and if he were to have it he would have to take it in the old-fashioned manner: he would bludgeon – as Magnus had put it – his way there. Then the image of the 'V' on the sacrificial liver played in his mind and, much to his surprise, it seemed to calm him.

As the wind lessened and the snow thinned the wagon passed over the plain of Philippi and the walls of the city came into sight. Vespasian left his thoughts of power at the site of the battle that had decided so much and wondered, instead, how his brother would greet him after a three-year separation.

Before they reached the gates that granted access to the city of the living they passed through the city of the dead. Tombs lined the Via Egnatia for the last quarter of a mile or so; large and small and inscribed in both Latin and Greek attesting to the relative wealth and origin of the interred. But it was not just the dead in their cold and sombre dwellings that they passed; there were also the dying. Suspended between life and death, as they hung from crosses, a score or more of pain-wracked, newly crucified, naked men writhed above Vespasian and Magnus as they made their way. Groaning with agony, struggling for every breath, their flesh bluing in the bitter cold, some sobbed and some muttered what sounded to be prayers as their lives trickled away at a painfully sluggish pace.

'Looks like Sabinus has been very busy,' Magnus remarked as he cast a glance up at a youth who was staring in horror at the blood-crusted nail impaling his right wrist. Snow flurried around him.

Hormus flinched at the sight and lowered his head, keeping his eyes on the paved surface of the road as a wail of sheer agony rose from a man splayed out on a cross lying on the ground. The volume increased with every blow of the hammer, driving a nail through the base of his thumb, wielded by an auxiliary optio with the dexterity of one old in the way of crucifying men. The auxiliaries holding the victim down laughed at his torment and made jokes aimed at the last two shackled prisoners, eyes brimful of fear and tears, waiting their turn to be nailed to a cross, their breath misting from their mouths.

'It must have been a serious incident if he's been obliged to nail this many up,' Vespasian observed, counting the crosses. 'Twenty-two plus those last three.' The executions did not surprise Vespasian: they had been told by the prefect of Thessalonike, on arrival in the capital of Macedonia, that the Governor had been called away the previous day to quell a disturbance in Philippi. This had not been an inconvenience as Philippi lay on their route, straddling, as it did, the main road to the East. 'I'd guess that my brother has got the disorder in hand now; I can't imagine that there are too many more who would wish to join them.' He cast an eye over a bedraggled group of women, watching their menfolk's execution in miserable impotence, flinching with every hammer-fall as the last nail was driven home and the screams intensified.

'Well, whatever they've done they're learning their lesson,' Magnus said as he brought the wagon to a halt outside the city's western gate.

The sight of eleven lictors and the flash of the seal on Vespasian's imperial mandate were enough for the duty auxiliary centurion to allow the wagon through without searching it and to send a message on to Sabinus. Vespasian got down from his horse and, helped by Hormus, donned his senatorial toga before proceeding at a stately pace through the town, disdaining to notice its populace, to the Forum at the far end of which stood the residence used by the Governor. A crowd had gathered there, despite the snow, curious to see the high-status new arrival. With auxiliary soldiers smartly at attention lining the steps, Vespasian ascended with the dignity of a proconsul who would never for one moment question his authority or right to respect. Sabinus awaited him in front of the tall, bronze-plated double doors and took him into a formal embrace, to the cheers of the onlookers, before leading him into the building.

'What are you doing here?' Sabinus asked without much trace of fraternal affection.

'And it's lovely to see you too, Sabinus. Apart from finding out how you are and to bring news of our mother and your daughter and grandchildren, I'm here with Gaius to talk to you.'

Sabinus' eyes flicked nervously sideways at his brother. 'Are you here because of the Parthian embassy thing?'

'The Parthian embassy fiasco, you mean?' Vespasian enjoyed the pained look that shadowed Sabinus' face. 'Yes, but not to bring you any official reprimand. Despite the damage your failure did to our family, I've managed to strike a deal with Pallas to have you exonerated of all responsibility.'

'How did you manage to do that?'

'Say thank you and I'll tell you.'

Sabinus pursed his lips. 'Thank you.'

'Don't mention it.'

'But I think that the explanation will have to wait for dinner. I suspended a trial when I got the message that you'd arrived; I really should complete it.'

'It'll keep until dinner.' Vespasian broke from his Sabine country burr and assumed the clipped accent of the old aristocracy. 'I assume that you have dinner at the normal hour, even this far from Rome.'

Sabinus was forced to concede a smile. He clapped his younger brother on his back. 'Do you know, it really is quite good to see you, you little shit.'

Sabinus took his seat at the far end of the high-ceilinged audience chamber in the Governor's residence; braziers were placed to either side of him to supplement the heat rising from the hypercaust beneath the floor, which failed to fully warm the cavernous room. Vespasian, Gaius and Magnus slipped in through the double doors as Sabinus signalled to a waiting centurion to bring the accused back before him; a couple of clerks, seated at desks to one side, waited to record the proceedings. A woman in her late forties was led in by two auxiliaries; their hobnailed footsteps echoed around an otherwise empty hall, for Sabinus had decided to hold the trial inside in private because of the temperature in the Forum. As the accused was neither a Roman citizen nor male there could be no appeal against the Governor's decision.

'Where had we got to?' Sabinus asked one of the clerks.

The clerk consulted the tablet in front of him. 'The widow, Lydia of Thyatira, had admitted to giving the agitator, Paulus of Tarsus, lodgings during his stay here in Philippi two years ago.'

'Ah, yes.' Sabinus contemplated the well-dressed and evidently wealthy woman standing before him. Her hair was demurely covered and she stood with her hands clasped and her eyes lowered – the image of a respectable lady. 'Did you allow Paulus to spread his treasonous teachings under your roof?'

'We had prayer meetings most evenings,' Lydia replied in a quiet voice.

'She must be a follower of that nasty bow-legged bastard Paulus,' Vespasian whispered to Magnus.

'Who's he, dear boy?' Gaius asked.

'He's a preacher who's been travelling around the East stirring up trouble in the name of that Jew that Pontius Pilatus had Sabinus crucify when he was in Judaea.'

Magnus spat in disgust and then wiped it off the floor with his foot as he remembered where he was. 'We last saw him in Alexandria when he was busy stirring up trouble between the Greeks and the Jews – not that they needed much help.'

Sabinus was carrying on his questioning. 'And at these *meetings* did he tell his followers not to make sacrifices to the Emperor when they renew their oath to him and instead ordered them to claim that they have the right to make a sacrifice *on behalf of* the Emperor and not *to* him like the Jews do, even though most of his followers here are Macedonians?'

Lydia did not raise her eyes from the floor. 'There is only one god and Yeshua is his son.'

Gaius frowned. 'One god? Whoever heard such nonsense? Who's this Yeshua?'

'Yosef's kinsman, the Jewish trader; the one who helped us rescue Sabinus from the Vale of Sulis in Britannia we told you about?' Vespasian answered, remembering with a chill druids manifesting the goddess Sulis in the body of a sacrificed girl. 'Yosef revered Yeshua as a teacher but this Paulus has turned him into some kind of god, and a pretty exclusive god, just like that Jewish one from what I can make out.'

Sabinus glanced at Vespasian, evidently annoyed by hushed voices in the corner of his court, before turning back to the accused. 'Are you a Jew?'

'I am a Macedonian and before I met Paulus I was a god-fearer.'

'A god-fearer? What's that?'

'We are not Jews as such but worship their god. We do not follow the dietary rules of the Jews and the men do not subject themselves to circumcision. Paulus says that as followers of Yeshua we can honour their god without becoming Jews.'

Sabinus looked less than impressed. 'I questioned Yeshua.'

'You spoke with him?' Lydia asked, forgetting her position.

'Yes, before I executed him.'

Lydia's eyes widened at this revelation. 'You crucified the Christus?'

'No, I crucified a man called Yeshua who died like any other man. And I can tell you that he didn't like non-Jews; he called me a Gentile dog, in fact. So whatever nonsense this Paulus is telling you does not come from the teachings of Yeshua; Paulus is perverting them and in doing so has caused a lot of deaths. Do you know that he was the captain of the chief priest's guard and was sent to claim Yeshua's body after he'd been crucified so that he could bury it in secret? He persecuted Yeshua's followers and I asked him why. What was he so afraid of? And he said: "Because he would bring change." And yet now he seems to be doing the very thing that he feared. Do you really want to trust that man with your life? You can save yourself by telling me where he is, this man who tried to kill Yeshua's woman and his children.'

'I saved Yeshua's wife and children from Paulus in Cyrene when he was trying to expunge all trace of Yeshua's bloodline and teachings,' Vespasian informed Gaius as Lydia contemplated the question.

Gaius frowned, confused. 'But now he spreads them?'

'It seems that he had a complete change of heart; although Alexander, the Alabarch of the Alexandrian Jews, thinks that he's just discovered a way to make himself important.' Vespasian closed his eyes, thinking. 'I remember he said that he's found a way to turn the world upside down with himself finally on the top.'

Lydia lifted her gaze to Sabinus. 'I was the first person that Paulus baptised in Europa, here in Philippi in the River Gangites; I will not betray him.'

'You in turn were betrayed by one of his followers who did not fancy spending his last hours on the cross.'

'I will gladly suffer that fate rather than turn traitor.'

Sabinus paused, evidently less than willing to pronounce sentence on the woman. 'What was your husband's business before he died?'

'He dealt in purple, not porphrya but the cheaper vegetable dye that comes from my home town.'

'And you now run that business?'

'As a widow I'm entitled to in law.'

'And you are prepared to see all the hard work that your husband put in during his life to build up that business wasted, because, if I order your execution, I will confiscate your business. Are you that selfish as to think that Paulus is worth your dead husband's life's work?'

Lydia's silence answered the question.

Sabinus' fist slammed down on the arm of his curule chair. 'Very well!' he shouted. 'Take her to the cells and leave her there for a few days to consider her position.'

The auxiliaries hauled Lydia away.

'I will find him,' Sabinus shouted after her, 'whether you end your life in agony on a cross or in comfort from the spoils of your husband's business. I will find Paulus!'

'I had him,' Sabinus growled, heading for the chamber door. 'I had the arrogant little bastard.'

'You did what, dear boy?' Gaius asked, waddling hard to keep up with Sabinus' bad-tempered pace.

'I had him here, Uncle, locked up in prison.' Sabinus thumped at the door before the startled auxiliary guarding it had a chance to open it entirely.

'Here? Why didn't you crucify him? If there's one thing he needs it's crucifixion.'

Vespasian understood the reason for his brother's seeming omission. 'That may be but it's the one thing he can't have. He's a Roman citizen.'

'He's a what? Then why is he spreading such anti-Roman ideas like not making a sacrifice to the Emperor?'

'Is that what he was arrested for?' Magnus asked as they clattered down a cold, dimly lit corridor.

Sabinus slowed his pace. 'No, it was before we knew he was encouraging such things. He claimed to have cast an evil spirit out of a slave girl of one of the leading magistrates here; she was a well-known seer. Mithras only knows whether he did or not, but the end result was that her powers of divination were gone and the magistrate was incensed because he lost the income from her soothsaying. He had Paulus and his companion whipped and then thrown into prison for tampering with his property without permission and referred the case to me. I had to decide what to do with the odious little shit; I couldn't execute him because it was not a capital charge and his followers had not yet refused to take the oath to the Emperor. As he had the law on his side I was on the point of letting him go when there was an earthquake, not a big one, but big enough to break open the prison gates and Paulus and his companion were free. Of course, this was seen as divine intervention and proof that Paulus must be favoured by this god who is powerful enough to free him from gaol. However, he didn't run but stayed in the gaol and demanded that I acknowledge that he had been treated unlawfully. Unfortunately he was right and I had to have the magistrate apologise to him for having him whipped. Once that had happened he left and the gaoler became a follower of his as well as a few score others in the town, some of whom are presently languishing outside the gates. It was terrible. After that he disappeared and I've lost all trace of him, although I do know that he was in Thessalonike because I've had to nail a few of them up there too. He leaves a trail.'

Gaius' jowls wobbled with indignation. 'Then why haven't you followed it?'

'Because it's not continuous; you have to wait to see where the malignancy starts sprouting next and then hope that he hasn't moved on. He seems to have headed south into Achaea. I've warned the Governor, Gallio, about him.'

'Seneca's brother?'

'Yes, but he hasn't heard even a rumour of him; it looks like we've lost him for the time being.'

'You're good at losing things at the moment,' Gaius pointed out.

Sabinus stopped in front of a closed door, understanding exactly what his uncle was alluding to. 'I was seasick; I couldn't think straight.' He turned and barged through the door into a *triclinium* with a table and couches set for the evening meal. 'They sent out three ships as a diversion and whilst we were taking them the Parthians rowed by in a fast little liburnian. We didn't have a hope of catching them.'

Vespasian shrugged, dismissing the explanation as a steward bustled in with Hormus and four slave girls following. 'Well, it's got us into a lot of unnecessary trouble and the end result is that I've got to go to Armenia.' He launched into an account of the sequence of events that had followed Sabinus' failure to deal with the Parthians, as the slave girls took their togas and shoes and then provided them with slippers and washed their hands in preparation for the meal.

'So what could I possibly know that could prove that Agrippina is behind this?' Sabinus asked when his brother had finished his tale.

'Something that links the embassy to her. Something that Uncle and I will recognise. Tell us all you know about them.'

Sabinus scratched his thinning hair and accepted a cup of wine from his steward. 'Well, the agent said that there were three of them all richly attired as if kings in their own right in order to impress. They were men of influence, their leader was a cousin of Vologases, the Great King of Parthia. They brought gifts of gold, incense and spices for each of the Kings that they met.'

'What were their names?'

'There was the Dacian King, Coson, Spargapeithes of the Agathyrsi – they're Scythians who worship Thracian gods and seem to enjoy dying their hair blue. Then there was Oroles of the Getae and Wisimar of the Bastarnae who are Germanic. And countless chieftains of all the sub-tribes of each nation.'

Vespasian looked at his uncle as the *gustatio* of six varied dishes was carried in. 'Do any of the names mean anything to you?'

'My dear boy, they all sound positively barbarous.'

Magnus, unsurprisingly, looked equally uninspired.

'Did you ever find out just what was discussed?'

Sabinus shook his head with regret and helped himself to some of the leek and egg salad. 'No, I couldn't send the agent back because he insisted on reporting to his real pay-master.'

'But we don't know who that is.'

'Oh, but we do. His pay-master, or mistress actually, is our old friend the former Queen Tryphaena.'

'Tryphaena! You're in contact with her?'

'Not as such; but she does share information with me occasionally. She's instructed her agents to report things to me if they deem their information to be of interest to Rome. She is very helpful to me.'

'She is also Agrippina's cousin,' Gaius said slowly, his mouth full of semi-chewed sausage.

'I suppose it's a connection but it hardly proves that Agrippina set this embassy in motion, and anyway, why would Tryphaena draw it to your attention if she was in league with her cousin?'

'Because, dear boy, she doesn't know about the embassy; that must be it. She may be the great-granddaughter of Marcus Antonius but on the other side of her family she is a princess of Pontus.'

'I thought that she was Thracian.'

Gaius wagged the remains of his sausage at his nephew. 'She married a Thracian king but she has no Thracian blood; she's Greek. Her family have provided kings and queens for half the client kingdoms in the Empire and beyond. Her younger brother is King Polemon of Pontus and her elder brother Zenon was also known as King Artaxias, the third of that name, of Armenia.' Gaius let the last word hang for a few moments as everyone contemplated the significance and wondered if it was just a coincidence. 'When he died,' Gaius continued, 'the Parthians tried to place their own king on the Armenian throne but we wouldn't accept that so we compromised by having Mithridates, the brother of the Iberian King, crowned instead.'

'So why would Tryphaena want to replace the uncle with Radamistus the nephew?'

'Radamistus' mother is the daughter of Artaxias, Tryphaena's brother. Mithridates is no relation to her, but Radamistus is her nephew. She's ensuring that her blood-family remain in control of Armenia.'

'Then why alert us to the embassy that seems to have triggered this all off?'

'Because she didn't know about it. The embassy didn't trigger the crisis off, it's just been timed to seem that way. Tryphaena isn't being disloyal to Rome; if anything she's securing our position in Armenia by replacing a compromise puppet king with a controllable one. Radamistus will be loyal because Tryphaena will see to it that he is.'

'So, Narcissus is wrong,' Sabinus said. 'Agrippina hasn't committed treason.'

A smile slowly crept across Vespasian's face as the truth dawned on him. 'No, brother, he's not wrong; far from it. He's seen a pattern. Tryphaena's agent that came to you was murdered by an assassin of Agrippina's on the way to inform his mistress; Narcissus' freedman Argapetus intercepted the message from the killer. This tells us two things: first, that Agrippina didn't want Tryphaena to know about the embassy and, second, that Agrippina must have known about it. How else could she have given orders to her people to prevent news of it reaching Tryphaena's ears?'

Magnus drained his cup and held it out for more. 'And why didn't she want Tryphaena to know about it?'

Gaius had followed Vespasian's logic. 'Because, Magnus, it would have alerted her to the fact that Agrippina had used her. I would hazard that it was at Agrippina's suggestion that Tryphaena supported her nephew's usurpation of the Armenian throne, and I would guess that the timing of it was made to look as if it was sparked by the embassy travelling through Iberia so that we would blame the Parthians and therefore march an army in to restore Mithridates.'

Sabinus looked confused. 'But you said that Radamistus would be loyal to Rome; why would we want to get rid of him?'

'This is the clever bit of Agrippina's plan: Tryphaena suspects nothing, she readily agrees to placing her nephew on the throne; as she sees it, it's good for her family and good for Rome. But then we see that Radamistus invades from Iberia at exactly the moment that a Parthian embassy is in the kingdom and so we assume that the two things are linked and that it's a Parthian plot. Meantime, Agrippina manoeuvres Claudius into recalling

Rome's up and coming general, Corbulo, and has him posted to a province close to Armenia. Now play out the scenario, Sabinus.'

Sabinus sighed. 'We demand that Mithridates is restored but we're probably too late as he would have been murdered along with his family. Then we negotiate with Radamistus, who refuses to go. Parthia sees the new King as too pro-Roman because of his blood-tie with Tryphaena and demands that he is removed, which confuses us so we decide to let matters rest. This will then prompt a military response from Parthia that we will, in turn, have to counter with a proven general who just happens to be in the region, and before we know it we have a war with Parthia.'

Vespasian spread his hands to emphasise the simplicity of the scheme. 'Exactly; and at the same time the northern tribes swarm over the Danuvius as arranged by the embassy and the situation starts to look very bleak, and who will be blamed? The Emperor; old, drooling, drunk most of the time and not at all popular with the Senate; time for him to go and no one will look too closely if he just suddenly drops down dead. And if he does that soon then there'll be only one choice to succeed him: Nero. That's what this is all about: it's ensuring that Claudius is removed before Britannicus comes of age and blurs the inheritance issue. Nero comes to the throne, Corbulo wins a great victory and Nero, the grandson of the great and martial Germanicus who also famously prevailed in the East, takes the credit, celebrates a Triumph in the first year or so of his reign, making him very popular and securing his position. Brilliant.'

'So the evidence of Agrippina's treachery is with Tryphaena,' Gaius concluded.

'Yes, we need to talk to her.'

'She's at Cyzicus on the Asian coast of the Propontis,' Sabinus informed them glancing around at the window onto the court-yard; hobnailed boots clattered across at an urgent speed. 'I'll organise a ship for you.'

'Then we can pass by on the way to Armenia.'

'I'll come with you.'

'Why would you want to do that? You'll spend the whole voyage vomiting.'

'I need to talk to her about putting down all resistance in Thracia to Rome once and for all; if we're threatened by the northern tribes, I cannot afford to have disloyal nobles in the south. She will know who they are, their weaknesses and what to bribe or threaten them with. After we've spoken with her you can drop me at Byzantium; it's time I visited the city and gave it a taste of Roman justice. You can sail on up through the Bosphorus into the Euxine and then along the northern coast of Bithynia to Trapezus in Pontus. From there it's about two hundred miles over mountainous terrain to Armenia.'

Magnus held out his cup for yet another refill as a slave entered with a platter of grilled diced lamb on skewers. 'There is one thing that doesn't fit: for all this to have worked, Agrippina would have had to know the timing of the Parthian embassy; how could she have known that?'

'That's the fact that proves her treason: she couldn't have known about it unless she instigated it. It's what Narcissus suspected but couldn't prove: she's been in contact with the Par—' Vespasian was cut short by the auxiliary centurion who had allowed him into the city bursting into the room; Vespasian's senior lictor was close behind him.

'What's the meaning of this?' Sabinus almost shouted.

'I'm sorry, sir, excuse me,' the centurion puffed, his eyes darting around the occupants of the room, 'but you need to come to the western gate; there's been an attack.'

Vespasian and Sabinus walked at a dignified pace behind the centurion who was doing his best to restrain himself from breaking into a run. Vespasian's lictors carried torches to light the way through the city that was now muffled by a blanket of snow.

'I apologise for the meal; the cook is local,' Sabinus said, trying to keep an air of nonchalance in his voice. 'I left my cook behind in Thessalonike when I raced here a few days ago to round up those idiots who'd started a riot rather than make their annual sacrifice.'

'What makes them think that they have the right to change their oath of loyalty?' Gaius asked, gnawing on a skewer of lamb as he waddled along behind, evidently not sharing the same reservations as Sabinus about the local cook's ability; Hormus followed him with some reserve skewers.

Sabinus sighed. 'Paulus has convinced them that the highest power is not the Emperor – or his wife and freedmen – but this Yeshua and his father, who was the Jewish god but now seems to be everybody's god. Anyway, after things had come to a head I gave them the choice between obeying the law or opting out of society on a permanent basis.'

'And them that made the wrong decision are the ones hanging around outside the gates, if you take my meaning?' Magnus observed, pulling his cloak tighter around his shoulders as Gaius handed a finished skewer to Hormus, receiving a new one in return.

'Yes, about half of them made that choice. It's beyond me; perhaps they like the idea of dying in the same manner as their beloved Yeshua.' Sabinus shivered. 'He was a hard man; I don't think I've ever met somebody with such strong will. It was as if he could push you over with just one look from his piercing eyes. But somehow I couldn't dislike him. I had to order that his death be hastened so that his body wouldn't still be on the cross on what the Jews call the Sabbath, which is their sacred day every seven days; but rather than have his legs broken, I ordered merciful death and had him speared instead. I don't know why but I just didn't want him to suffer. Then I allowed his mother, wife and his kinsman Yosef to take his body even though the chief priest had sent his men for it, mainly just to annoy Paulus.'

'But it also put Yosef in your debt,' Vespasian pointed out as they approached the closed western gate, 'and without him you would have died at the hands of the druids.'

Sabinus blew on his hands, rubbing them. 'True, but now I wish that I'd given it to the priests to bury in secret; then we wouldn't be having all this rubbish about Yeshua coming back to life three days later, just as my Lord Mithras did, to show that death could be beaten.'

'It would be a potent message if you could believe it.'

Sabinus signalled for the gate to be opened. 'From what I've seen, it is a potent message for the poor who have nothing in this world.'

'We're promised all in the next.'

The gate swung opened but neither Vespasian, Sabinus, Gaius nor Magnus walked through; they just stared in shock at the source of the remark. Hormus lowered his eyes, his pallid face coloured.

'Are you one of these, Hormus?' Vespasian asked, recovering himself.

'I know of them, master; there are growing numbers amongst the slaves in the houses on the Quirinal but I have not joined their sect.'

'What do you know about the sect?'

Hormus held the lamb skewers close to his chest with both hands as if seeking protection from them. 'Only that God loves us all, even someone as irrelevant as me, and the way to him is by following the teachings of his son, Yeshua, the Christus, who died for us.'

'My Lord Mithras is the way to God,' Sabinus asserted dismissively, turning and walking through the gate. 'We follow his light and at the Lord's Supper we are cleansed by the blood of a bull and nourished by its flesh.'

'They are cleansed by the blood of Yeshua, the Lamb of God, and gain sustenance by eating his body.'

Gaius wrinkled his nose. 'That's disgusting.'

Vespasian shook his head as he followed his brother out through the gate. 'I don't think it's literal, seeing as he died nineteen years ago; it's symbolic. Magnus and I have seen it done.'

'We have?' Magnus looked puzzled.

'Yes, with Yosef in his house on the Tor in Britannia. He filled a cup with wine, remember? He said that the cup had belonged to Yeshua.' Vespasian looked up at the line of sillouhetted, occupied crosses. 'Then he shared a loaf of bread and made us drink and eat. I thought that it was strange at the time but then I remembered in Alexandria someone saying that Paulus claimed to turn bread and wine into Yeshua's body and blood, and I realised that Yosef had just done the same thing.'

'Well, he didn't do it too well, did he? I ate bread and drank wine.'

'I know, you drained the cup. But the point is it's symbolic.'

'So what happened here, centurion?' Sabinus asked, coming to a halt at a cross lying on the ground, its occupant missing; two bodies lay close to. He signalled to one of the lictors to come closer with a torch.

The centurion swallowed. 'I don't rightly know, sir. I had the gate closed at the sunset curfew as usual and left a couple of the lads outside just to keep an eye on the crosses.'

'Just a couple?'

The centurion winced. 'Well, what with the weather and all I didn't think—'

'No, you didn't, did you.' Sabinus bent down and looked at the bodies of the two dead auxiliaries. 'They've both had their throats cut, so I suppose they were taken by surprise from behind by whoever took down this cross.' He touched one of the wounds. 'The blood's drying so they've been dead for at least half an hour or so. When did you find them, centurion?'

'When their relief went out. I came straight to you to report it myself.'

'As if that would help excuse your slackness; a patrol of just two men outside the gates at night.' Sabinus shook his head in disbelief as he looked at the empty cross; the nails had been wrenched out but their positions were marked by blood glinting in the torchlight. 'Who did they take down?'

'The young lad, sir; I don't know his name.'

Sabinus took the torch from the lictor and walked along the line of crosses touching the flame to the torso of each victim; a few groaned but none showed any sign of strength, their breath was forced and shallow as the last of their life slipped away. 'Well, he won't survive the night and anyway he'd be a total cripple if he did.' He looked back down at the vacant cross. 'That seems to be wanting an occupant, centurion.'

'Er, yes, sir.'

'Get that woman Lydia and nail her up instead.'

'What, now?'

'Yes, now! I'll not have people interfere with Roman justice and I'll show them what happens if they try to.' Sabinus thrust the torch at the centurion and turned on his heel. 'Just who do these people think they are? You're the expert, Hormus, tell me, what do they really believe?'

'They believe that through Yeshua the meek will gain strength in the next life.'

'Who the fuck are the meek?' Magnus asked, taking one of Gaius' lamb skewers from Hormus. 'I've never heard of them. What have they got to do with it?'

Vespasian was thoughtful. 'I think that in the context of Paulus' religion the meek are just about everybody in the Empire who's not of magisterial rank, a merchant or in the army. Comparatively few other people have any wealth to speak of, so aiming a message promising more at the meek who want more is clever.'

'Fucking meek!'

Gaius pointed a half-finished skewer at Sabinus. 'The one thing that I can see from all this is that it's a very dangerous new movement. If you start having these meek people believe that everything is going to be far better in an afterlife so that they stop worrying about what they get up to in this life, thereby lies chaos, dear boys.' He waved his skewer at the crucified men. 'Look at those idiots you had to deal with yesterday: they practically nailed themselves to their crosses judging by what you said. Granted, it can't be a very pleasant way to die, not like lying in the bath with an open vein, but if they think that they're marching off to another world where they're not going to be meek any more then we'll be getting a whole underclass that has no fear of death, and then how will we control them and who will do the work? It'll be like another slave revolt; there aren't many people who don't shudder at the name of Spartacus. If this carries on, the names of Paulus and Yeshua will resonate just as nastily as his still does.'

'What would you recommend, Uncle?' Sabinus asked, heading back towards the gate.

'Kill the lot of them; get them off to their non-meek world as soon as you can before this thing starts to grow. Don't imprison them or send them down the mines because they'll just infect other unsuspecting meek people with their twaddle. But most of all you've got to find and execute this Paulus and put a stop to the filth that he's spreading.'

CHAPTER VI

VESPASIAN ADMIRED THE fortified walls of Abydos on the Asian shore, just half a mile off to starboard as the trireme rowed by, struggling against the current of the Hellespont and a contrary wind. For what was once such a strategic town positioned at the junction of Europa and Asia it was now a city of little importance, as Roman peace had negated the need to guard against invasion from one continent to the other. Looking to either bank of this mile-wide channel he tried to imagine the bridges that Alexander, Darius and Xerxes had used to transport their armies across and found himself recalling his one-time friend Caligula's bridge across the Bay of Neapolis; that had been three times the length needed to bridge the Hellespont. The brash young Emperor had ridden across it wearing Alexander's breastplate in an attempt to outshine those colossi of history. However, the bridge was to be a memorial to Caligula's folly rather than the proof of his military prowess. Vespasian smiled as he recalled his thoughts on seeing the Pharos in Alexandria for the first time: if you want to be remembered, build something that's of use to the people. Caligula's mistake had been to build something that was of no use to anyone – not even himself.

'You seem pleased with yourself,' Sabinus said, joining him at the rail looking very wan; he had spent the first two days of the voyage from the closest port to Philippi, another Neapolis, proving yet again just what a bad sailor he was.

'I was thinking about Caligula.'

'That's nothing to smile about; it's something that I try to avoid doing. I see Clementina's face as he dragged her off to rape her and then I see her as she lay dying in our house, flayed by a malevolent god.'

119

Vespasian shuddered and was silent for a few moments as he remembered the confrontation with the god, Heylel, conjured by druids in the garden of Sabinus' Aventine villa; Sabinus' wife had suffered a hideous death at its hands. 'Yes, I'm sorry.'

'Don't be; I've got used to it now. And it's a comfort having my son serving as a military tribune with the Fifth Macedonica. It means I get to see him three or four times a year.'

'Which reminds me, I need you to take the son of a client of mine on as a military tribune.'

'Whose son?'

'Laelius.'

'The chickpea contractor?'

'That's the one. I had Pallas get the Emperor to restore him to the equestrian order as part of the deal to come out here.'

'What's in it for me?'

'Call it repayment for having you exonerated of all blame for missing those Parthians.'

Sabinus leant heavily on the rail and breathed deeply to control his churning innards. 'I'm never going to live that down, am I?'

'So it's a deal?'

'Yes, it's a deal; I'll write to Laelius offering the lad a position as soon as I'm back in Thessalonike.'

'I'm sure his gratitude will be expressed in chickpeas.'

'As long as it's expressed I don't care.' With a sudden heave Sabinus lost the battle with his guts and shot a thin stream of pale liquid over the side.

Vespasian slapped his brother on the back. 'I just hope that whatever Tryphaena manages to tell you about the Thracian nobility is worth all this discomfort.'

'It will be,' Sabinus said in a high voice as he convulsed again. 'When we apprise her of the situation she'll be very anxious to convince us of her total loyalty to Rome so that we will vouch for her if Agrippina's ever exposed. That's got to be worth a few potential traitors' names and suggestions on how to deal with them.'

*

The arrival of two men of proconsular and one of propraetor rank caused a flurry of activity in the recently modernised port of Cyzicus the following day. The two customs officials who waited on the quay for the gangway to be lowered looked at each other in alarm at the sight of senatorial togas surrounded by so many lictors. After a brief enquiry as to the names of such distinguished visitors the paperwork was suddenly deemed to be unnecessary and all thought of searching the ship or charging the exorbitantly high mooring fees disappeared from the officials' minds, as they tried to outdo one another in their attempts to ingratiate themselves with their illustrious guests. Messages announcing their arrival were sent to Tryphaena and all the other worthies of the city, refreshments were called for as suitable transport was arranged, and flattery and obsequiousness oozed out of every sentence in the firm belief that one can never fawn too much to men of high rank.

Eventually two suitable carriages were procured and the brothers and their uncle were aided into one by many willing hands as Magnus and Hormus were obliged to climb the small gap between the ground and the other vehicle's step using nothing but their own exertion. The two officials then insisted on guiding the lictors through the town, which was situated on the south coast of an island in the Propontis and connected to the mainland by a causeway a third of a mile long. With expressions of sincere gratitude for having been allowed to be of service, and with heartfelt requests that the Cyzicus customs service should be spoken of in a positive tone should their excellencies ever find occasion to mention it in the high circles that they surely inhabit, the two officials delivered their precious charges to the impressive building that was Tryphaena's residence. They watched Vespasian, Sabinus and Gaius being received by the great lady herself without noticing Magnus and Hormus emerging from the second carriage, and therefore missed the chance of a purse of silver that Vespasian had instructed Hormus to give them should a tip be appropriate. In mutual agreement that they had done their finest crawling to persons of much importance, they walked away, convinced that they had shown the Cyzicus customs service in its best light, oblivious to the fact that they had totally failed in their duty to collect revenue for the province of Asia in the presence of three of Rome's élite.

It had been over twenty years since Vespasian had seen Tryphaena and she had aged like wine rather than milk. Born in the same year as both Magnus and Gaius, she was now in her early sixties and had weathered the years far better than they. Her hair, gloss raven, was definitely dyed, Vespasian decided, but in a far more subtle way than Gaius' tonged curls; indeed his use of rouge and kohl were made to seem extravagant next to her restrained application of cosmetics.

She smiled at Vespasian with dark eyes as he squeezed the fingers of her proffered right hand; her finely woven aquamarine stola accentuated, but did not flaunt, the curve of her hips and breasts – although what devices lay hidden beneath it to counter natural forces on that part of her anatomy, Vespasian could not guess. 'Welcome, proconsul and ambassador to my nephew Radamistus, the rightful King of Armenia.'

'You are well informed, Tryphaena.'

She inclined her head with a slight raising of her eyebrows in acknowledgement of Vespasian's use of the familiar: the last time they had met she had been a queen and he a mere military tribune; now he was a proconsul and she just a private citizen. 'My agents keep me up to date.'

'Do they, though? Do they really?' With a questioning look, he walked past her into the atrium where the city worthies waited and a steward had assembled slaves with trays of refreshments.

Half an hour later, Vespasian stood on a terrace overlooking the city of brightly painted public buildings and whitewashed, Greek-style houses. Sipping pomegranate juice from a blue glass goblet engraved with Bacchus – or more probably, Dionysus – enjoying the nectar of the vine, he rested one hand on the balustrade and looked in amazement at the huge amphitheatre that dominated the view even though it was outside the city walls.

'Some consider that it should be ranked amongst the wonders of the world,' Tryphaena's voice said softly in his ear. 'It's over a hundred and fifty paces across and its walls are taller than your Circus Maximus.'

'It's an impressive building.'

'It's more than that; it's a work of brilliance. It's built on top of a river that's covered over but can be dammed so that the arena floods and naval battles can be staged there.'

Vespasian was genuinely impressed but concealed the fact. 'Claudius is going to stage a naval battle on the Fucine Lake before it's drained.'

'But, my dear Vespasian, that's a one-off event and it's miles from Rome; here we can entertain the people without them having a two-day journey either way. I've suggested to my cousin Agrippina that when Nero succeeds his father it might be a project worthy of a great emperor to be remembered by: an amphitheatre that can be flooded, as large, or larger, than this, built in the centre of Rome for the people of Rome.'

'That could be a monument that stands forever,' Vespasian agreed. 'After all, who would want to destroy a place of public entertainment?'

Tryphaena took a fruit juice from a passing slave and said casually, 'But you believe Agrippina has other plans for her son?'

Vespasian stroked the smooth white marble of the balustrade in thought. 'So your agents do indeed keep you up to date.'

'Yes, they do and you are both right and wrong. Right in that Agrippina wants to secure her son's accession as soon as possible. But wrong in that you believe that she instigated the Parthian embassy and wanted to keep it secret from me.'

'You have very good agents, Tryphaena, and fast. They must have travelled at a great speed to bring that to your notice before we arrived; I only said it three days ago. And I spoke quite quietly at a private dinner.'

The former Queen was unapologetic. 'To survive one often needs to hear the quietly spoken private word.' She looked over to Sabinus deep in conversation with a city worthy whose name Vespasian had instantly forgotten upon being introduced. 'The man to whom Sabinus is talking is furnishing him with the names of the chieftains of my former kingdom whom I would consider to be less than happy with Rome's annexation of Thracia six years ago. You see, Vespasian, with what alacrity I press to prove my loyalty to Rome?'

'So you did have a hand in removing Mithridates and replacing him with your nephew? Otherwise you wouldn't feel induced to make such a swift protestation of loyalty before it's even been questioned.'

'Oh, but it has been questioned, quietly and in private. I had more than a hand in the coup: I got my brother-in-law to suggest it to my nephew and provide him with the army. It was easy to do: I just made him think that Radamistus was plotting to murder him and take his throne, which I did without difficulty as it was the truth.'

Vespasian shook his head in disapproval. 'Is this how eastern politics work?'

'It's much the same as Roman politics, proconsul: power and position. The only real difference is that we have fewer families fighting each other, which means that there's a much higher incidence of patricide, fratricide, infanticide and any other type of family "cide" that you can think of.'

'Charming.' Vespasian's gaze wandered over to the dun-brown mainland strewn with rugged formations of rock and copses of leafless trees housing hundreds of birds; the sun was weak and the land was still in winter's grip. Goats tore at rough grazing watched over by small boys wrapped in cloaks made from the skins of their charges. Here and there a slender spiral of smoke rose to the sky, marking the position of a mean dwelling where the boys' elder brothers and fathers worked with their hands, chopping wood, repairing tools, roofs and fencing, while sisters and mothers fetched, carried, cleaned, mended and cooked as the family struggled to survive the winter. It was a view, Vespasian surmised, that had not changed in centuries: the common man scraping a living. 'But I imagine that it was ever thus for the royal houses of the East just as it was ever thus for those farmers.'

'Do you disapprove?'

'Who am I to judge?' As he looked back to the mainland all the birds rose as one from the trees and flew off, out to sea. 'The rural poor have the same choice everywhere inside and outside the Empire: stay where they are and work the land or join the army and fight for the powerful. Whereas for the powerful families it's the opposite: fight to maintain your position or eventually become a part of the rural poor. If that means killing your father, son, uncle or whatever, so be it; but we try to do things differently in Rome.'

'Do you, though? Do you really?'

A trembling in Vespasian's legs distracted him; all conversation on the terrace died off as people looked around, startled. Vespasian felt the tremble grow, accompanied by a deep bass, distant rumble and the closer rattle of cups and plates shaking and clinking on vibrating tables; his drink formed concentric circles, the waves moving outwards with increasing rapidity.

Tryphaena put a reassuring hand on his forearm. 'It's just a tremor, nothing to worry about. We have them all the time in this area; the people believe that it's because we live close to an entrance to the underworld. I should have read the signs; the gods always warn the birds. I'll offer a sacrifice to Hades and Persephone; perhaps that will help to restore harmony between them before she returns to this world to bring spring and summer back to us.'

The sea seemed to shudder, waves breaking irregularly; beyond, on the mainland, the goats ran in fluid groups, changing direction at random, flowing hither and thither as their small minders huddled for safety beneath trees and boulders, terrified of the wrath of the gods that the tremor might well presage.

But the gods' anger did not boil over and calm soon returned; the conversation on the terrace picked up with the forced nonchalance of people wishing to mask their fear.

Tryphaena breathed a deep sigh as if she had been holding her breath; she looked over to her steward who had noticeably paled. 'Have a pair of the blackest bulls brought to the priests of the chthonic gods. They're to sacrifice them to Hades and Persephone in the name of the citizens of Cyzicus; but let it be known that it is at my expense.'

The steward bowed and went about his errand.

'Displays of piety have a twofold benefit if they are made publicly,' Tryphaena remarked, 'wouldn't you agree?'

'In that they gain the favour of the gods and the popularity of the people?' Vespasian was relieved to see that his pomegranate juice no longer vibrated.

'I may not be a queen any longer but the people of this city look to me for leadership and patronage; all the new building that you see was paid for out of my own coffers. That buys me influence just as it would in Rome. It's no different here.'

'We don't go around killing close family.'

'And you don't consider Tiberius' great-nephews or Caligula's cousin and great-uncle to be close family?'

Vespasian did not offer an opinion.

'You accepted my assertion that Nero will inherit?'

Vespasian saw where she was heading with her argument. 'Yes and he's bound to kill Britannicus; but Britannicus is only a step-brother.'

'Indeed; but although it will be Nero who orders the knife wielded or the poison poured, Britannicus will have actually been killed by his own father. Claudius committed infanticide the moment he adopted Nero. So don't try to pretend that you act in anyway different in Rome than we do in the East. Agrippina will kill her uncle and husband, Claudius, just as Caligula killed his great-uncle, Tiberius, just as Radamistus killed his uncle and father-in-law, Mithridates.'

'So Mithridates is dead then?'

'Smothered; and both his sons too.'

'Smothered?'

'Yes, Radamistus swore to his uncle that he would never harm him with blade or poison. Whatever may be said of my nephew, he's no oath-breaker, so he had Mithridates smothered under a pile of clothes and then smothered his sons for mourning their father openly. I'm sure that comes as no surprise.'

'Not really, no; it was the logical thing for Radamistus to do.'

'As you said quietly in private the other night.'

Vespasian could not help a half-smile. 'You're not as well informed as you think. It was Sabinus who actually said it; I just agreed with him.'

'I should have my agent strangled for that error,' Tryphaena said lightly.

'Then perhaps you will be able to tell me who it was?'

'That would be the act of a fool.'

'As would be having such a useful, active agent killed.' Vespasian noted that Tryphaena did not dispute the point and immediately changed the subject. 'So my embassy is a waste of time; I can't restore a dead man to the throne, and yet if I don't remove Radamistus Parthia will attempt to do so by force and we will be heading for war.'

'It is a conundrum, proconsul.'

'One which you helped to create.' Vespasian looked at her pointedly. 'Time to really press to prove your loyalty to Rome, I think. Persuade your nephew to step down.'

'You'll have to kill him because he won't relinquish the throne now.'

The suggestion came as no surprise to Vespasian. 'And will you help me do it?'

'What would I gain by it?'

'You would regain Rome's trust.'

Tryphaena pointed to Sabinus still deep in conversation with the worthy. 'I have just sold out at least a dozen of my former countrymen to do that. What would I really gain by helping you kill my nephew? Claudius will soon be dead, as you've worked out; my kinswoman Agrippina will see to that for the good of Rome before he completely loses our family's power to his freedmen. In his place will be our golden boy Nero, and my Roman family will once again be back in control. So I will retain Rome's favour and the favour of my brother in Pontus, my brother-in-law in Iberia and my nephew in Armenia; I am surrounded by friends.' She indicated again to an enthusiastic-looking Sabinus. 'What is more, the Governor of Thracia is now very well disposed towards me, and the new Governor of Asia, as you know, is my old friend Corbulo. So I ask you again: what would I gain?'

'So you do want war with Parthia?'

'Of course, proconsul; as you have already guessed – quietly and in private, but for many of the wrong reasons – that's what this is all about. I may not be a queen any more, Vespasian, but the blood of the royal houses of the East and the Emperors of the West still flows in my veins. I would have neither of those great houses return to the level of the rural poor, as you so astutely observed.'

It was as if curtains before Vespasian's eyes were drawn back and he suddenly saw Tryphaena for what she really was: another Antonia. But she was not fighting for one family's survival in power, but two. 'It's you who is behind this, not Agrippina. You knew of the Parthian embassy and you timed your nephew's invasion of Armenia to make it look as if they had instigated it in order to get a Roman embassy sent there; you wanted Parthia provoked. You know Corbulo, you had him recalled and given Asia so you could have Rome's best general awaiting in the region because you couldn't afford to have Rome lose the war that would secure both your families. If Rome beats Parthia in Armenia you gain even more than Agrippina.'

Tryphaena tutted with disappointment. 'I always had high hopes for you, Vespasian; you're close but you've missed one vital point. I knew that you had a keen mind and Antonia mentioned a few times in her letters just how impressed she was with your development; she evidently was being a little too generous. However, you did work out who my agent was when I carelessly as much as admitted that he was still with you; but you tried to take care not to let me know by changing the subject. Do you know which one?'

'By a process of deduction, if it is one of my lictors – and how else would my words travel as fast as me? – then it has to be the only one that could disappear for half an hour without the permission of the senior lictor so that he could brief you upon our arrival before you came up here. Therefore it has to be the senior one himself and that would be confirmed by the fact that

I saw him lurking outside the triclinium door the other night when it was opened suddenly and I had been talking quietly and in private.'

'Very good. Will you keep him? As a favour to me, that is.'

'So that he can spy on me?'

'No, so that he can keep you alive.'

'That's what lictors are meant to do, amongst other things.'

'Yes, but he will keep you alive for my sake because I chose him specifically to look after you.'

'How? I only knew that I was coming East three days before I left; you had no time to get that news here and then fiddle with the lictor appointments.'

'I'd already done it.'

'So you'd already decided who would lead our embassy?' Vespasian did not need an answer; now he truly understood and his eyes widened. 'Your agent knew of the Parthian embassy because he was with it when it arrived in Tyras; he was with it because ...' Vespasian paused in admiration.

'Go on; say it.'

'He was with it because it didn't come from Parthia, it came from here.' Vespasian's eyes widened as Tryphaena did nothing to deny his assertion. 'It was false. You set it up to seem as if the Parthians had negotiated with the northern tribes and had your agent tell Sabinus who, naturally, believed him; and then you made sure that his failure to capture it was brought to the notice of the people who count in Rome. Meanwhile, the fake embassy returned here and you paid a trierarchus heading back to Rome to give Agarpetus information that implied that the embassy had travelled via Iberia; this was enough for Narcissus' spy-master to bring the matter to his master's notice. You timed the Iberian attack on Armenia at the same moment as the embassy would have been in that country to make the whole thing look as if it were a Parthian plot. Finally, you made sure that Narcissus suspected his enemy, the Empress, of treason by having Agarpetus intercept a false message purporting to be from one of her agents that implied that Agrippina knew of the embassy and was trying to keep it a secret from you. Pallas was right: he had been purposely kept in the dark while Narcissus was purposely enlightened. You also rightly concluded that Narcissus would think that he had an ally in me because Agrippina hated me and would use any excuse to block me. He also guessed that my brother might have known more than he had let on so therefore my uncle and I would be the best people to talk to him. But most of all you knew that a consul, newly stepped down, is the most obvious candidate to lead an embassy to Armenia if the grandeur of Rome is to be taken seriously and Pallas, who would make the final choice, would see me as his ally in a delicate matter. You are why I'm here.'

'And all for the cost of three expendable ships.' Tryphaena looked genuinely pleased at the exposure of her duplicity and took Vespasian by the arm and led him inside. 'Antonia did train you well after all. Now I shall put all that training to good use.'

'And why should I serve your cause?'

'Because, proconsul, you would be foolish not to and I don't think you are a foolish person. Now, how are your powers of suggestion? Because the procurator of Cappadocia, Julius Paelignus, is the key to this.'

Grey clouds rolled in on a northeasterly wind, thickening over the trireme's masthead as if the incoming thunderstorm was aimed at that vessel alone and anything else that it hit was peripheral. Thunder rumbled with brooding menace across the Euxine and over the mountains of Pontus. The coastline showed the same threatening intent: high, dark cliffs rose from an unsettled sea, jagged teeth of rock at their base waiting to gnaw hungrily on any hull driven onto them by Poseidon's malice, Fortuna's whim or just plain bad seamanship.

Magnus pulled his cloak tight about his shoulders, his grey hair lank with spray as he looked with angst at the looming shore a quarter of a mile away to starboard and coming ever closer. Vespasian, standing next to Magnus at the starboard rail, glanced back at the trierarchus, positioned between the steering-oars; the deck bucked once more and all lurched in an effort to remain upright. The trierarchus scanned the endless procession of cliffs, his face set grim as the steersmen to either side battled to keep the two steering-oars' blades straight in order to prevent any more drift towards the sure death that lurked so close to them.

'He can't see anywhere safe to heave-to,' Vespasian said, his voice raised against the growing storm.

'Then we should run before the wind,' Magnus opined through clenched teeth.

'What makes you a nautical expert all of a sudden?'

'Logic: if you can't fight against something then go with it.'

At that moment the trierarchus evidently came to the same conclusion and screamed a stream of orders through his speaking trumpet that sent the cowering crew scuttling barefoot to all points of the deck. Ropes were unsheeted and hauled upon as the steersmen pushed their oars to starboard and, as the trireme came round, a small section of the bow sail was unfurled; the leather immediately ballooned, pumped by the wind that drove the ship before it faster than it had done for the last five days. Five days since they had dropped Sabinus and Gaius – along with the untrustworthy lictors, despite Tryphaena's request – at Byzantium and begun the long pull along the coast of Bithynia, Paphlagonia and then Pontus. Five days in which Vespasian had tried to get to grips with the magnitude of what Tryphaena had asked him to do; no, not asked, ordered. And it had been an order that he could not refuse because to have done so would have spelt disaster for him and his family. Gone had been the kindly Queen who had helped him when he had been a young military tribune in Thracia; now he could see that she had only been kindly because he had been working for Antonia's, and therefore her own, agenda. It had not been threats that had bent him to her will; it had been bald statements of fact.

Fact: his family were not well established and could revert to the status of the rural poor within two generations if Tryphaena's two families decided to make it so. Fact: however Tryphaena's scheme ended, either Pallas' or Narcissus' life would be forfeit, leaving the survivor in Tryphaena's debt and Vespasian would benefit from that. Fact: that what he was to do would ultimately benefit Rome and, although it could never be made public knowledge, his participation would eventually be whispered in the right people's ears and in the meantime he could console himself with the thought of service for the greater good. But there had been one other reason why he had finally decided to do Tryphaena's bidding and that was not a fact but, rather, a hunch; and it was a hunch that he kept to himself.

But he had not been fooled into feeling safe and that was why he had entrusted Gaius with a letter to Caenis. If something should go wrong with what he planned to do and he was exposed and killed, she would be able to make sure that his reasons for acting as he did would not remain secret as Tryphaena would wish. Gaius would wait out the year with Sabinus in his provinces before returning to Rome next spring with Vespasian, all being well, and if not, then with just the letter.

As the ship began to run fast with the gathering wind, carrying him swiftly towards his destination, Vespasian felt a strange relief; the gale was hastening what he must do. If his mission went well, Tryphaena would reward him and Corbulo would have the military command that he desired.

Because Vespasian was hastening towards Armenia to provoke Parthia into war.

CHAPTER VII

'DO YOU HAVE the Emperor's authority for this outrageous request?' Julius Paelignus, the procurator of Cappadocia, drew himself up to his full height, which was limited to five feet owing to a severe curvature of the spine. 'Because, I would remind you, I am a very good personal friend of Claudius and it would not do to cross me.'

'I am well aware of your relationship with the Emperor.' Vespasian looked down at the deformed little man and tried not to let the contempt that he felt for the procurator's self-importance play on his face. 'It is not a request; it's a suggestion. I have an imperial mandate to act in whichever way I see best in relation to the current crisis in Armenia and I suggest that your auxiliary cohorts secure its border with Parthia.'

'All of them?'

'All of them!' Vespasian's voice echoed around the marble columns and walls of the procurator's palace located in the eastern city of Melitene in the mountainous province on the edge of the Empire.

'I can't spare them all.'

'Are they doing anything else important at the moment?'

'They're guarding our border with Armenia.'

'That border is guarded by the Euphrates River; Armenia's border with Parthia is a vague line just to the south of Tigranocerta.'

Paelignus spluttered, looking up at Vespasian with protruding, bloodshot eyes; his thick, moist lips dominated the lower part of his gaunt face. 'But they are *my* troops.'

'And you shall command them, Paelignus, as is only right as, although I've made the suggestion, this will be *your* idea.'

Paelignus' thin nose twitched and he rubbed it with his thumb and forefinger; his fingernails were chewed almost to the cuticles. 'And I shall take the credit for any victory?'

'Procurator, I am not here. You have seen my imperial mandate and that should be enough for you. My presence should not be mentioned in any official papers or letters and should not be reported to your direct superior, Ummidius Quadratus, the Governor of Syria; so therefore the obvious conclusion is yes, you will not only be able to claim all the plunder but also take all the credit for any victory, worthy feat of arms or successful negotiation through force that *you* may achieve in *your* securing of the southern Armenian border during this period of instability in that client kingdom.' As well as any fiasco, dishonourable retreat or double-dealing agreement, Vespasian added in his head as he smiled ingratiatingly at this puffed-up little joke of a procurator whose eyes had narrowed as he contemplated riches and honour easily come by. He had only met Paelignus once previously, on the last day of the Secular games three years before when the man had been present in the imperial box almost begging Claudius to be given the post of procurator of Cappadocia to restore his finances; his friendship with the Emperor involved many games of dice and wagering on just about anything and his purse had been severely depleted by Claudius' passion for gambling. Why Claudius would associate himself with such a buffoon he could only ... but then he realised that, as a hunchback, Paelignus was exactly the sort of person that Claudius would enjoy having around him: he would make the drooling fool seem less of an oddity. Now that Paelignus had his wished-for position, Tryphaena had judged that his greed and venality would serve her purposes well. Vespasian was unsurprised as the procurator acquiesced.

'Very well, proconsul,' Paelignus affirmed, summoning as much dignity as he could in order to seem in command. 'I will leave in ten days.'

'Wrong, Paelignus; speed is of the essence and the Emperor will commend you for it. You will leave in three. In ten days you will be in Tigranocerta. Meanwhile, King Polemon of Pontus will bring an army in from the north and secure Artaxata.' Leaving the procurator speechless and gaping, Vespasian turned on his heel and marched quickly from the room. He was in no mood for more delay; now that he was close to his objective he wanted to achieve Tryphaena's dubious aims and then get back to Italia and watch the results from the relative safety of one of his estates. It had already taken over half a month to make the two-hundred-mile journey from the port of Sinope, the seat of King Polemon, Tryphaena's brother. Vespasian had not been surprised to find himself expected and treated with the utmost courtesy by the ageing King; he had been furnished with a unit of Polemon's personal guard cavalry for his protection overland. They were armed with lances in the image of Alexander the Great's companion cavalry; shieldless but with stout leather cuirasses and bronze helmets they looked like troops from days gone by, but Polemon had assured him that they had no equal when it came to horsemanship. Their mere presence deterred any banditry along the route and it had been with some regret that Vespasian had released them, upon their arrival in Cappadocia, having not seen them fight.

As he went in search of Magnus who was settling into the sparse comforts of the guest quarters of the draughty and seldom-used palace, Vespasian allowed himself a satisfied smile; he felt as if events had finally started to move. He had commandeered his army: five auxiliary cohorts of eight hundred heavy infantry each, all trained to fight in dispersed order; ideal for mountainous terrain. But fighting was not going to be their primary function and he was looking forward to seeing the expression on the ugly, drawn face of Paelignus when he found out just what really was required of them.

'This will be a glorious march of conquest!' Paelignus all but screeched as he raised his voice for the small army of over four thousand foot and horse to hear. 'The Emperor and the Senate look to us to restore Rome's rightful influence over Armenia. We will invade from the west and capture Tigranocerta whilst our Pontic allies come in from the north and take Artaxata. For us the hour has come when we can write Cappadocia into the annals of history as the province that saved Roman honour in the East.'

As Paelignus continued to harangue his troops with notions of grandeur far in excess of what was really being asked of them, the infantry stood beneath their banners, rigid, eyes front; weak sunlight glinted on their chain mail, javelin heads and unadorned helms, and the red of their tunics and breeches matched painted shields emblazoned with crossed burnished-iron lightning bolts, giving the impression of rank upon rank of blood and silver. Beside them the baggage train was formed up in surprisingly neatly dressed lines, their appearance less uniform as their clothing was not standard issue. However, they shared one common factor with their infantry comrades: a look of complete non-comprehension.

'I don't know why he bothers to waste his breath like that,' Magnus said, pulling back on the reins of his skittish horse. 'I don't suppose more than a dozen of them can speak Latin better than the average five year old.'

Vespasian chuckled as he too was forced to control his mount, which had been spooked by its neighbour. 'I don't suppose it's even occurred to him that he'd have a better chance of being understood in Greek; all he can think of is being seen as the equal of Caesar, Lucullus, Pompey and all the other generals who've campaigned in this region. There's no one so blind as a small man with no military experience who thinks that he's been given the chance to be a hero without actually doing anything.'

Vespasian steadied his horse, pulling it closer to the mule-drawn cart carrying their tent and personal effects, driven by Hormus, and caught his slave looking with admiration at one of the many young muleteers of the army's baggage train in which he would travel. The lad smiled back with the promise in his dusky eyes of all received coinage being delightfully rewarded.

'And so, soldiers of Rome,' Paelignus falsettoed, his normally pale cheeks almost matching the tunics of his audience, 'follow me to Armenia, follow me to Tigranocerta, follow me to victory and glory in the name of Rome.' He punched his sword into the air to little reaction and was forced to repeat the gesture another

couple of times before his audience realised that the end of a
rousing speech had come and began to react accordingly.
Paelignus addressed the five auxiliary prefects standing behind
him on the dais before descending the wooden steps to the
ragged cheering of his troops. After the bare minimum time that
could politely be allowed for an army hailing its commanding
officer the prefects signalled to their primus pilus centurions;
raucous bellows of command easily cut through the noise
followed by the blare of horns. Centuries snapped to attention in
unison and turned left, with thuds of massed hobnailed sandals,
converting them into eight-man-wide columns. With another
series of martial bellows and repeated *bucinae* fanfares the whole
formation began to move, century by century, cohort by cohort,
off the parade ground in front of the city's main gate to head, in
one long serpentine column, east towards the Euphrates beyond
which lay the snow-capped peaks of Armenia.

Vespasian was impressed by the speed at which the column was
able to travel along the Persian Royal Road, built by Darius the
Great to connect the heartland of his empire with the sea to the
west. Wide and well maintained, it was the equal of any road of
Roman construction and its even surface enabled the auxiliaries
to march at a good pace.

In fact, the speed with which the whole expedition had been
brought together reflected well on the command structure of the
province's military. It was with something approaching a guilty
conscience that, later that day, Vespasian watched the auxiliaries
traversing the seventy-pace-long bridge over the Euphrates. In
order for Tryphaena's plan to work, it was not to victory that they
were heading.

The bridge was narrower than the road, causing a bottleneck,
and it took the rest of the day and the best part of the following
one to get the whole force and its baggage across; it was as the
final carts trundled over that the first tiny silhouettes of horsemen
were spotted on the crest of a distant hill.

'It didn't take long for news of our march to spread,' Magnus
commented, climbing into the saddle.

Vespasian swung himself up onto his mount. 'I'm sure that King Polemon has taken the precaution of warning both Radamistus and the Parthians of our arrival by now.'

'Naturally,' Magnus agreed. 'You can't trust anyone in the East; they'd betray their own mothers for a goat if they thought that they could get more practical usage out of it. But you don't seem to be too concerned by it. I thought that the whole point of quick strikes like this was to keep the element of surprise.'

'That would be helpful if this were meant to be a quick strike.' Magnus shaded his eyes as he took another look southwest at the scouts. 'What do you mean?'

Vespasian turned his horse. 'Has it occurred to you that we don't really have anyone to strike at? Radamistus is meant to be loyal to Rome and the Parthians have not, as yet, as far as we're aware, invaded.'

'But I thought that you told Paelignus that the whole point of this mission was to secure Tigranocerta whilst King Polemon invaded from the north and took Artaxata on the basis that whoever controls the two royal capitals controls Armenia?'

'That is indeed what I told him; but it is far from the truth. Had I told him that, he would probably have tried to have me arrested for treason.' Vespasian enjoyed the surprise and confusion on Magnus' face as he kicked his horse forward in search of Paelignus.

'Probably just local brigands,' Paelignus announced as Vespasian drew up his mount. 'It's beneath the dignity of Rome to send scouts scurrying around the country investigating riff-raff.'

'If you're sure, Paelignus,' Vespasian replied, scanning the hilltop. 'Whoever they were, they've gone now.'

'That'll be the last we'll see of them.'

'What makes you so certain?'

'The Armenians would never dare to attack a Roman column.'

'Maybe, maybe not; but Parthians would.'

'The Parthians? What would they be doing in the country?'

'The same as us, procurator, staking their claim to it in a time of change. And, if they did come, I believe they would come from the southwest.' He pointed to the hill on which the horsemen had appeared. 'And judging by the sun, that is the southwest.'

The column followed the road east for three days until it turned and meandered south through the dun and dusty rough terrain of the uplands that preceded the Masius range. The horsemen were not seen again. By the time the auxiliaries approached Amida, on the banks of the young Tigris River, where the road struck east again towards Tigranocerta, across the hundred-mile passage in the gentle northern foothills of the Masius mountains, the horsemen had been forgotten by almost everyone. Paelignus led the march on at a hurried pace, imitating the Roman generals of old by disdaining to send out scouts on the spurious basis that looking out for ambushes set by barbarians was yet another thing that was beneath the dignity of Rome.

But what was not below Rome's dignity was greed and it was soon after noon on the fifth day that the column halted to the blare of bucinae, above the peaceful-looking little town of Amida, set astride the road. The high-pitched calls of the bucinae, used for signals in camp and on the march, soon gave way to the deep rumbles of the G-shaped cornu favoured for battlefield signals, and the column started to deploy into line.

'What is he doing?' Magnus asked as auxiliaries filed left and right and farmers, ploughing the freshly thawed fields, abandoned their ploughs and sprinted for the relative safety of the town's walls.

'Exactly what Tryphaena predicted he would: rape and plunder. He's never had this chance; being a cripple no one ever took him into their legion as a military tribune so he's never been on campaign and he's never felt the power of the sword.'

Magnus was confused. 'But this is an Armenian town; how does he think he'll forward our interests if he destroys everything he comes across?'

'He doesn't think, at least he doesn't think beyond schemes of personal gain, and that's his problem; that is why he's so suitable.'

'We want him to alienate the Armenians?'

'This is right on the border between Armenia and the Parthian Empire. Tigranocerta is a frontier town that guards the Sapphe Bezabde pass through these mountains into Parthia; what better way to provoke the Parthians than firstly to burn Amida close to the border and then to occupy and rebuild a fortified city actually looking out over their lands.'

Magnus turned to the south. 'You mean beyond those mountains is Parthia.'

Vespasian surveyed the peaks above them. 'Yes, if you climbed to the top then as far as you could see and miles, miles further than that is all Parthia. Tryphaena showed me a map and there was hardly anything on it after these mountains, just the Tigris and Euphrates that flow all the way to the sea from where you can sail to India. Almost all the cities are on one of those two rivers but between them is desert.' He pointed southwest. 'A hundred miles in that direction is Carrhae where we lost seven Eagles in one battle, and then fifty miles west of that is the frontier of the province of Syria. Across those mountains is where Rome's influence stops; if the Great King sees us on his border he'll send an army to try to dislodge us and take Armenia back.'

'And Paelignus will be responsible for starting a war and you might have some nasty questions to answer.'

'No, I'm not here officially; if I'm ever asked, King Polemon is prepared to vouch that I was in Pontus all summer using it as a base for my negotiations with Radamistus.'

'But he's invading Armenia from the north.'

'No, he's not; he's staying where he is on his sister's advice. I told Paelignus that to make him feel safe, to ensure that he would bring his forces in. Paelignus will get the blame for starting this war, but as he's an old friend of Claudius' he'll probably survive.'

With the long, low rumble of cornu two of the auxiliary cohorts moved forward as, from either side, the forty cart-mounted carroballistae of the army began to hail down missiles onto the scantily defended walls. From within the town came a great wailing as thousands of people despaired for their lives. The braver, steadier inhabitants shot arrows and slingshot towards the oncoming troops to little effect: many of them fell back, headless, in sprays of blood, decapitated by well-aimed artillery.

With their oval shields raised, the auxiliary soldiers of Rome came on at a steady, silent march as the practically defenceless town lay helpless before them.

Vespasian could see from Magnus' expression that he was totally confused by the reasoning behind this needless slaughter. 'We have to fight Parthia sooner or later, we always do, every thirty years or so. But rather than doing so on the defensive, trying to stop them from taking Syria and gaining access to Our Sea, it would be better to have the war on neutral territory as it were. We'll have less to lose and just as much to gain,' he explained.

'But it could take two years or so for Parthia to muster her armies.'

Vespasian watched as the first of the scaling ladders were raised against the walls and troops began to swarm up them. 'No, they'll be here in a couple of months; in fact we saw their scouts on that hill just three days ago. Tryphaena really did have King Polemon send a message to Ctesiphon telling the Great King exactly what we were going to do.'

As the first auxiliaries made it onto the wall, the gates opened in a futile attempt to surrender; but peace did not come to the town, only death, and showing it the way was a crooked little man with an unbloodied sword.

Paelignus was having his first taste of glory.

Vespasian and Magnus coaxed their horses past the gates and onwards into a town veiled in smoke and steeped in misery and death. Throughout the narrow streets auxiliaries rampaged, hunting booty, both live and inanimate. Bodies were strewn left and right, broken, pierced, blood-drenched and almost exclusively male. Their womenfolk shrieked and pleaded for mercy as they were tracked down and subjected to the brutal fate that always awaited females in a captured town. Those considered too old to stir carnal passions within the troops were despatched summarily; only babes and infants were considered too young and were likewise doomed.

Huddles of soldiery formed round screaming victims, ripping off their clothes, holding them down and cheering on their comrades as they mounted and rode the spoils of war. Each man hungrily awaited his turn to defile the thrashing wenches who cursed and spat at the persecutors pumping away at them, slapping their faces in vain attempts to quieten their hissing rage.

Those auxiliaries whose lust had been sated guzzled wine and roamed through the town with drawn swords and burning torches, raising fires with heedless recklessness and slaughtering the elderly and the young in the same casual manner.

'It'll take a lot to calm the lads down after this,' Magnus muttered as they passed a group of drunken soldiery urinating into the mouth of a barely conscious teenage girl whose hideous ordeal could be measured by the bruising and welts on her face and naked body, as well as by the pool of blood that had seeped from between her legs.

Vespasian forced himself to watch the final act in the girl's life as one of the auxiliaries shook the drops from his penis, adjusted his dress, then took his sword and thrust it into her mouth; blood sprayed, diluted by urine, and the soldiers laughed as they wandered off in search of similar sport. 'Just as long as enough of the populace survive to be able to spread the news of what this little Roman army is capable of doing,' he muttered, urging his horse on up the main street that bisected the town from the western gate to the eastern one. 'Now I need to find Paelignus and impress upon him the need to push on with all due haste in this glorious campaign of liberation that he has embarked upon.'

Magnus took one last look at the dead girl and then followed. 'Now he's got the taste for it, I imagine that it'll be hard to hold him back.'

'I'll rest my soldiers for two days,' Paelignus announced from behind a vulgarly large desk to his cohort prefects and their senior centurions as Vespasian and Magnus were shown into the grandiose chamber. The stooped general had commandeered the most impressive house in the town for himself. 'After such a gruelling victory they deserve rest and recuperation. There'll be no parades or drills, all fatigues are excused and all outstanding disciplinary charges dropped, double rations of both food and wine are to be issued for both days and sentry duty and patrols should be set at the bare minimum.' If Paelignus had expected his senior officers to applaud his sensitivity towards his rampaging troops he was much mistaken: his declaration was met with barely concealed disgust both for his orders and his appearance. Paelignus, however, seemed unaware of his staff's derision; he rose from his chair, placed his fists on the desk and thrust his face towards his subordinates. 'Any questions?'

'Yes, sir,' a balding prefect of auxiliary infantry barked, stepping forward and crashing to attention.

Paelignus sighed with irritation. 'What is it this time, Mammius?'

'How can my centurions and optiones keep discipline if you excuse all fatigues and drop all outstanding charges just because we've taken a town?'

'This was an outstanding victory, prefect.'

Mammius was unable to contain himself. 'No, procurator, it was not; my grandmother and four-score hags of equal age could have taken this place armed only with their distaffs. Where was the defending garrison? Where are their bodies now that we've scaled the walls and stormed through their gates? Surely we should be able to see dead men in some sort of uniform with armour and helmets?'

'We were shot at by arrows; men threw javelins at us!'

'Civic Militia!' Mammius bawled. 'A rabble incapable of doing anything more than hurling a few sticks before bravely running away only to be caught and butchered up alleyways. They even opened the gates for us; but you didn't call the troops back. And now you want to threaten the cohesion of our cohorts by rewarding them for rape and slaughter when the most danger any of them have been in is from getting a spear up the arse from the man behind them tripping over drunk. I've had a report of one single death in my cohort and that was some stupid bugger getting his cock bitten off and bleeding out.'

Paelignus' mouth opened and shut for a few moments in speechless outrage at the force of the prefect's diatribe. 'How dare you shout at me, prefect! I'm a friend of the Emperor.'

'No, Paelignus, you're the butt of the Emperor's jokes as you are the butt of ours.'

'I think, Paelignus,' Vespasian said in a conciliatory manner, walking further into the room, 'that we should sit down and consider the situation in a calm and logical fashion.'

Paelignus' outrage persisted. 'And what gives you the right to walk in here uninvited and tell me what to do?'

'Military experience, Paelignus; something that you evidently lack, as Mammius was only trying gently and politely to make clear to you. Now sit back down.' He glared at Paelignus until he sat with as much dignity as he could muster. 'Good; now listen to me: Mammius is right. There is no conceivable way that today's farce could be called a glorious victory, Paelignus; therefore the troops do not deserve two days' rest nor do they deserve all the other rubbish that you were suggesting, much to the amusement of all listening, no doubt. I suggest that you rein in the men immediately, get them out of the town, build a camp and give them the night to sober up before marching on to Tigranocerta in the morning. In the meantime, Paelignus, why don't you strip this house of all that's valuable and have it loaded onto the baggage train so that you can start to pay off the debts that your *friend* the Emperor saddled you with as you tried to ingratiate yourself with him, playing dice.'

Paelignus' sharp-featured face drew back into an ugly leer. 'That's already being done, Vespasian, as well as all the other houses of value; that's why I need two days.'

'You haven't got two days; I suggest you leave tomorrow.'

'I give the orders here!'

'No, Paelignus; you just take the credit and the plunder.' He turned to the assembled staff who were having difficulty in hiding their shock that a man whose presence they had been only vaguely aware of on the expedition should exercise such control over their commander. 'I believe that you gentlemen would also deem it wise to move first thing in the morning rather than let the men lose discipline over the next couple of days.'

'Yes, sir,' Mammius replied; his colleagues nodded dumbly.

Vespasian walked to an open door and passed through it onto the terrace beyond, looking north towards the heart of Armenia. 'Have patrols range out along the border keeping parallel with us as we move east. They're to keep their wits about them and not infringe upon Parthian territory.'

'Yes, sir,' Mammius said, frowning. 'But on whose authority do you take command?'

'I'm not taking command, prefect, in fact I'm not even here – officially. I'm just making suggestions that Paelignus will no doubt want to take up. Isn't that right, Paelignus?'

The procurator did not deny it.

'Good. See that the patrols go out and pull the men back into order; execute a few of them just to sober the others up. And we are going to need them sober, gentlemen; because when news of what happened here today gets to the Parthian army that is already marching towards us they are going to increase their pace. We need to be safely behind the walls of Tigranocerta when they arrive, otherwise we'll find ourselves outnumbered on a battlefield and, soon after, quite probably dead.' Vespasian smiled at the uncomprehending expressions that greeted that news. 'Yes, gentlemen, I know; the walls of Tigranocerta have not been rebuilt since the last Parthian war as a condition in the peace treaty. But the peace treaty also specified that Rome would not take any troops into Armenia; something that Paelignus neglected to think about in his haste to gain favour with the Emperor and restore Rome's influence here.'

'You told me to!' Paelignus shrieked, pointing an accusatory, shaking, chewed finger at Vespasian.

'No, Paelignus, all I did was to suggest that while there was a period of instability in our client kingdom of Armenia it might be wise to keep an eye on its southern border with Parthia. I'm not the procurator of Cappadocia, I had no authority to order an invasion, because that's what it is, isn't it? You commanded it, you assembled the troops and you've led them. Now I suggest that having broken the treaty with Parthia you garrison Tigranocerta to prevent it falling to our old enemy. It's either that or return to Cappadocia having prodded the Parthian beast and giving it a good reason to go into an undefended Armenia. Not even your close relationship with the Emperor would get you out of that mess.' Vespasian turned to leave. 'I suggest you get busy, Paelignus.'

'Are you ever going to explain to me just what you're trying to achieve?' Magnus hissed as he followed Vespasian out of the room.

'Yes,' Vespasian replied without venturing any further information.

'When?'

They walked in silence down the corridor past gangs of slaves stripping the building of anything valuable under the supervision of the auxiliary quartermasters. Vespasian tutted with regret that Paelignus was enriching himself with such ease but he knew that was the price to be paid for the procurator's folly that would advance Tryphaena's ambitions in Armenia. Besides, he would not possess his new wealth for long. What mattered was that Paelignus' greed and vanity had driven him to sack a peaceful town that was part of a kingdom allied to Rome in direct contravention of all treaties with both Armenia and Parthia. News of the outrage would spread and condemnation would come from all sides. With one rash act the procurator had given Parthia a just cause for war and also given Radamistus reason to appeal to the Emperor in protest at Rome's unprovoked attack.

'Tryphaena's objective is to secure her nephew Radamistus on the Armenian throne,' Vespasian informed Magnus.

'Then she's got a strange way of going about it, getting you to persuade the procurator of a Roman province to invade, even if it is with a piss-poor little army.'

'I didn't persuade Paelignus to do anything; I just suggested things. However, that piss-poor little army, as you term it, has just done more for Tryphaena's cause than if she had ten legions of her own. When Parthia invades and overruns Tigranocerta and then moves north to take Artaxata, Rome will be obliged to send in the legions, no doubt under Corbulo's command.'

'Great, so what?'

'So who will be leading the Armenian resistance and allied with our legions?'

Understanding began to spread over Magnus' face. 'Radamistus,' he said slowly. 'And then when it's all over in three or four years' time and Parthia has withdrawn, Radamistus stays as king because he was our ally and the fact that he murdered Mithridates will be conveniently forgotten.'

'Precisely.'

'And Nero, her other kinsman, will be emperor by that time and earn the glory of a Parthian defeat.'

'And will no doubt be voted the name Parthaticus by the Senate, myself amongst them, after celebrating his Triumph.'

'And meanwhile a whole lot more people like that girl we saw earlier are going to suffer.'

Vespasian shrugged as they clattered down a staircase of ancient oak. 'I don't like it any more than you, but what can I do? I'm trapped. I'm meant to be working for Pallas in order to help him protect himself from Agrippina and then I'm also meant to be working for Narcissus in order to help him bring down Agrippina; but I end up working for Tryphaena who's trying to secure Agrippina as the mother of the next emperor because she has persuaded me that whatever Agrippina might think of me, Nero is my best chance of advancement.'

'Nero?'

'Yes; and having listened to her arguments, I agreed with her, but not for all the reasons that she put forward, although some of them were very persuasive.'

'How would Nero becoming emperor possibly help you?'

Vespasian pushed open the main door that led out to the town's agora; smoke stung his eyes and caught in his throat. The carnage still continued, although with less vigour than before as most of the population had by now either fled or been despatched. 'That's hard to say in logical terms because it's really just a hunch

– but a very strong one based upon the auspices of a sacrifice that I made. Let me put it into your vernacular: judging by the way that he makes free with his own mother, I think that Nero's got more chance than Britannicus of fucking up on a fucking large scale.'

CHAPTER VIII

E VEN THOUGH ITS walls were not intact, Tigranocerta was impressive, cascading down a high foothill of the Masius range. Framed by snow-capped peaks soaring up behind it, the city was built in concentric squares, each one higher than the last until the hill's summit was crowned with a royal palace of Caligulan proportions. It had been founded by King Tigranes the Great, over a hundred years before when Armenia was at the height of its power. It lay on the western bank of the Tigris, opposite the river's confluence with one of its tributaries, the Kentrites. It had been built to guard the Royal Road as it followed the eastern bank of the Tigris through the narrow Sapphe Bezabde pass in the Masius range; the road then bridged the Kentrites and then swung west, carrying on its journey to the Aegean Sea. However, an army could leave the road before the bridge and follow the Kentrites north into the heartland of Armenia. To guard against incursions from his larger but more fractured neighbour, the Seleucid Kingdom, Tigranes had built two further bridges connecting Tigranocerta with the road, both across the Tigris: one to the east bank before the river reached its confluence with the Kentrites and making its ninety-degree turn to the west, and one after the bend to the north bank. Strategically this forced any invading Seleucid force to take both bridges and then the city itself if it wished to proceed without a constant threat to its one supply line through the Sapphe Bezabde pass. The inevitable lengthy process of the siege gave Tigranes time to assemble his army and march south to repel the Seleucid invaders. But that vestige of Alexander's empire had been ripped apart by Rome and Parthia, and since the rise of those two superpowers Tigranocerta had changed hands many times, occupied both by

Rome and Parthia until the most recent settlement, which had handed it back to Armenia on condition that its defences remained in ruins. That condition was now being broken, much to the relief of its reduced population.

'Paelignus complained to me this morning about his precious troops being used for what he terms "slaves' work",' Vespasian said as he and Magnus made a tour of the works on the fifth day after their arrival. Auxiliaries worked shoulder to shoulder with all able-bodied male citizens while the women and children kept their menfolk supplied with food and water.

'Just goes to show how little he knows about soldiering,' Magnus said through a half-chewed mouthful of onion. 'What did you say to him?'

'I suggested to him that he should address his complaint to the commanding officer and pointed out that of all people he was the person most likely to get a fair hearing.'

Magnus laughed, spraying onion over the calves of a kneeling auxiliary shaping stone with a hand-pick. The man turned round, invective ready on his lips, but it stayed there and died when he saw who was responsible. Since the sack of Amida, ten days previously, Vespasian and Magnus had become objects of curiosity to the auxiliaries. It was known that Vespasian had prevented Paelignus from giving the men two days' rest – one of the centurions gossiping, he assumed – and it was also known that he had recommended some executions to help bring the men back into line; over twenty had lost their lives. This had made Vespasian someone to fear: a man who ostensibly held no command and yet could order death and countermand their commander. Being auxiliaries raised in Cappadocia, none of them recognised Vespasian from Rome where his time as consul, admittedly for only two months, had made him a familiar face in the Forum Romanum, but not here in the southern foothills of the Masius mountains between the Tigris and the Euphrates. So the rank and file did not know Vespasian's identity and the officers, if they did, kept it to themselves, having been warned to do so.

However, the auxiliaries had more pressing concerns than the identity of the man in their midst with the power of life and death: why were they fortifying a city in order to wait behind its reconstructed walls for a Parthian army that was rumoured to be heading their way and would surely outnumber the small Roman force by tens of thousands? But that question was not answered as their centurions and optiones bullied them and their civilian co-workers into working harder, faster and longer, hauling stones, shaping stones, lifting stones, placing stones and doing just about anything with stones that could be conceived even by the most imaginative of centurions.

In five days the four thousand men of the five cohorts and roughly the equivalent number of citizens had repaired most of the large gaps in the two-mile wall to a tolerable standard and it once again stood twenty feet high continuously around the entire city. Now the men were working on the lesser damage in the hope that they could bring the defences up to a state of near-perfection so that the host coming up from the south would break upon the walls when it arrived.

'Then he said,' Vespasian continued, 'that we should at least reduce the number of hours spent repairing the defences every day from twelve to six.'

Magnus looked up to the royal palace that dominated the whole city. 'So Paelignus is still trying to make himself popular with the men? It's beyond me why he bothers. None of them is ever going to show that hunchback any respect more than is due to his rank. The way he tries to buy their favour is by slackening their discipline, which, of course, will make them into weaker, sloppier soldiers; and they're the sort that generally end up dead. Who wants to be popular with dead men?'

'Quite. I think that if I hadn't been here, Paelignus would have four thousand very drunk and surly men with which to defend Tigranocerta from the Parthians.'

Magnus knotted his brow, puzzled. 'From what I can make out, if you weren't here then none of us would be. And I'm still trying to work out why we're here anyway.'

Vespasian stopped and looked out to the south, shading his eyes from the midday sun, down the length of the Sapphe Bezabde pass with the Tigris glinting at its base, the Royal Road coupled to its eastern bank; at its far end, thirty or so miles away, the pass opened up into the Parthian satrapy of Adiabene in what had once been Assyria. 'We're here because we want the Parthians to attack us; whoever heard of a war without someone attacking someone else?'

'Yes, but why do we want the Parthians to attack us? And if we do then why didn't we bring enough men to make a decent fight out of it?'

'We don't want a decent fight. In a decent fight lots of men are liable to be killed.'

'Oh, so fewer of our lads will get killed if we're outnumbered ten to one than if we had even numbers; is that what you're saying?'

'It is indeed.'

'Then you evidently know less about soldiering than Paelignus.'

'That's about to be tested,' Vespasian said very slowly as his eyes narrowed.

Magnus followed his gaze south to the horizon and then after a few moments he too saw what had taken his friend's concentration. 'Fuck me!'

'I think that we're all going to be far too busy to take you up on that very kind offer.' Vespasian did not look away from the dust cloud smudging the horizon.

'I think you're probably right,' Magnus agreed, his eyes also fixed on the brown smear that stained the clear blue sky.

They both stood still staring into the distance because, even though it was thirty or forty miles away, they could tell that the cloud was not caused by a herd of cattle or a trading caravan; no, it was far too big for that, far too big for a legion or even two. This was the dust cloud caused by an army of magnitude.

The Parthians had come; and they had come in force.

'We should leave immediately!' Julius Paelignus squawked, recoiling, as if he had been punched, at the sight of the approaching horde.

'And go where?' Vespasian asked. 'Even though they're still two days away they would catch us out in the open if they were so minded. And I'm sure they would be; their cavalry can move a lot faster than our infantry. We're safer in here; heavy cavalry are useless in a siege no matter how many they've got and their light horse archers will only shoot arrows at us from a distance. As for their infantry, they'll be mainly conscripts who're treated not much better than slaves and would rather be anywhere but here.'

Paelignus looked up at Vespasian, his eyes blinking rapidly as if there were specks of dirt in both of them. 'But they'll swarm all over us.'

'How? We've got ample men to man the walls now that they're rebuilt. Their numbers mean little to us. In fact their numbers aid us.'

Paelignus scoffed. 'Aid us?'

'Of course, Paelignus. How are they going to feed that massive army, eh? The crops haven't even sprouted; they won't be able to stay here for more than half a moon. Now, I suggest you use the time before they arrive to send out foraging parties and get everything edible within a ten-mile radius and bring it within the walls. And also check that all the cisterns are full.'

'I still think we should leave.'

'And I suggest that you stay – if you want to live, that is.'

Paelignus' gaze flicked across the faces of his prefects, each with a wealth of experience of fighting in the East, and each nodded their agreement with Vespasian's assessment of the situation. 'Very well; we prepare for a siege. Prefects, send out foraging parties; as many men as we can spare from the final work on the walls. And have the city council round up anyone with suspect pro-Parthian or anti-Roman sentiments.'

'That's a very wise decision, procurator,' Vespasian said without any hint of irony.

Two days later the entire length of the Sapphe Bezabde pass was filled with men and horses; but this huge host was not a dark shadow on the landscape but, rather, a riot of gay colours. Vivid hues of every shade adorned both man and beast as if all were competing to be the most garish in an army where conspicuousness was equated with personal prowess. Banners of strange animal designs fluttered throughout the multitude adding yet more colour and giving Vespasian, who had seen the apparel of many different peoples' armies in his time, the impression that here was a culture totally alien to him.

The auxiliaries, drab in contrast to the arriving foe, lined the walls of Tigranocerta in regimented ranks of russet tunics and burnished chain mail, their expressions dour and fixed as they watched a party of a dozen or so horsemen cross the east–west bridge and then pick their way gently up the hill towards the main gate under a branch of truce. Each rider had a slave scrambling to keep up with him, holding a large parasol over his master's head even though the sun had yet to pierce the cloud cover.

Vespasian stood next to Magnus with Paelignus and his prefects on the wall above the gates as the delegation halted a stone's throw away: a line of bearded men, nobles, on fabulously caparisoned steeds, the richness of which was outdone by the dress of the riders. Brooches of great value, precious stones set in worked gold, fastened vibrant cloaks edged with silver thread over tunics decorated with rich embroidery that would have taken a skilled slave months to achieve. Trousers of contrasting colours were tucked into calf-length boots of red or dun leather that seemed as supple as the skin they protected. Dark eyes stared out solemnly from beneath dyed or hennaed brows that matched the curled and pointed beards protruding from each chin. The delegation's lavish appearance was topped, literally, with flamboyant headgear littered with pearls and amber and then laced with gold thread.

'He can't just rush out of bed every morning,' Magnus muttered as one man, even more elaborately dressed than his companions, his beard a bright red, kicked his horse forward to address the waiting garrison.

'I am Babak,' the noble called out in fluent Greek, 'the satrap of Nineveh; the eyes, ears and voice of King Izates bar Monobazus of Adiabene, loyal vassal of Vologases, Great King of all the Kings of the Parthian Empire. To whom do I address myself?'

Paelignus puffed up his pigeon chest and stepped forward and then glanced involuntarily at Vespasian, who nodded his assent.

'I, Julius Paelignus, Cappadocia procurator, commanding here,' Paelignus shouted in appalling Greek. 'What want you, Babak, Nineveh of satrap?'

If Babak was surprised by the standard of Paelignus' Greek he was far too well mannered to show it; Vespasian now understood why the procurator had addressed his troops in Latin.

Babak indicated the rebuilt walls. 'The tidings that were brought to me were not unfounded.'

Paelignus looked momentarily confused as he tried to translate in his head; then his eyes brightened. 'What news to bring found you?'

Babak frowned and then held up his hand for silence as his fellow nobles began muttering amongst themselves. 'I bring no news, Paelignus, just a request: dismantle what you have rebuilt and return to Cappadocia with your lives.'

This was evidently far too advanced for Paelignus and, as he struggled with the meaning, Vespasian walked forward to take over the negotiations before there was a calamitous error of translation. 'Honoured Babak, satrap of Nineveh, I can speak for all here without fear of misunderstanding. We are here to safeguard the border of the Emperor's client kingdom of Armenia while a state of uncertainty prevails.'

'You have rebuilt the walls of Tigranocerta; there is no uncertainty about that. Equally, there is no uncertainty that that is in direct contravention of the treaty that we have between us. I must ask you to undo what you have done and leave.'

'And if we do, Babak, will you too leave with your army or will you stay to impose your master's will on this country and bind it closer to Parthia?'

'Although my master Izates has recently embraced Judaism, I remain a follower of Assur, the rightful god of Assyria, and continue to fight *hitu*, the False, with *kettu*, the Truth. I will not dishonour either the Lord Assur, myself or you, Roman, with a lie; no, we will not leave. We will garrison Tigranocerta and then move on to Artaxata where we will remove this Radamistus and replace him with Tiridates, the younger brother of the King of Kings, Vologases, as he himself has commanded.'

Vespasian smiled inwardly, impressed by Tryphaena's accurate prediction of events. 'I thank you for your honesty, Babak. I am sure that you will understand our position: if you will not leave then we cannot do so either; not until honour has been satisfied. However, Babak, we will not cast the first javelin nor release the first arrow.'

Babak nodded to himself as if he were unsurprised by the answer he had received, his fingers twisting the point of his beard. 'So be it; we shall see honour satisfied. I shall dress for battle.' With a deft twitch of the reins he pulled his mount round and set off at a canter back down the hill; his entourage followed, leaving their parasol-bearing slaves scampering after their masters to the jeers of the auxiliaries lining the stone walls of Tigranocerta.

'Well, that told him,' Magnus observed as shrill horns blared out from the Parthian host. 'You had him pelting off with his tail between his legs to change his clothes, no doubt for the fourth time today.'

'Honour to be satisfied? What does that mean, Vespasian? What have you condemned us to?' Paelignus hissed, his Greek evidently just adequate enough to understand that phrase.

'Nothing that we can't cope with, procurator; I suggest you order your prefects to stand the men to and have the Civic Militia mustered and issued with bows and javelins.'

'You do it, seeing how all this seems to be your suggestion.' With a suspicious glare Paelignus stalked off.

Vespasian called the prefects over. 'Gentlemen, our esteemed procurator has left it to me to make the dispositions, which I think is, in the circumstances, a very wise and far-sighted decision.'

'In that he doesn't have a clue what to do?' the prefect Mannius asked.

'He is the best judge of his own abilities.' Vespasian suppressed a smile. 'Mannius, your First Bosporanorum cohort takes this southern wall.' He looked at the four other prefects. 'Scapula the east, Bassus the west, Cotta the north, and you, Fregallanus, will keep your lads in reserve. All of you will mount your ballistae on the walls; fix them well – we won't need to dismantle them for we'll not be taking them with us when we leave.'

'When we leave?' Mannius questioned.

'Yes, Mannius, when we leave.' Vespasian's tone precluded any further discussion on the subject. 'All of you divide up the Civic Militia equally between you until we get a clue as to which of the walls the Parthians will be favouring with their attentions.'

'With an army that size it'll be all of them at once,' Fregallanus, a battered-looking veteran whose nose seemed to take up half his face, commented sourly.

Vespasian gave him a benign smile. 'Then splitting them evenly between the walls now is the right decision.' He glanced south at the enemy; there was much movement within their ranks as units of both light and heavy cavalry peeled off to either side followed by scores of covered wagons. 'I suggest, gentlemen, that you keep one half of your men resting and the other half on watch and rotate them every four hours. Have the women set up kitchens every two hundred paces and tell them to keep the cooking fires going day and night; I don't want any of the lads to complain about fighting on an empty stomach. And also have teams of boys and older men ready with fire-fighting equipment, as I imagine that Babak will try and warm things up for us. It would be churlish not to return the favour, so have as much oil and sand heated as possible in case they should make an attempt to get over the walls.'

The five prefects saluted with various degrees of enthusiasm, although Vespasian judged that they would do their duty, and dispersed to carry out their orders. Vespasian joined Magnus who was watching the unfolding manoeuvres of the Parthian army. The cavalry were still splitting off left and right but were making no attempt to encircle the city. One column were crossing the bridge to the western bank and then dismounting and setting up tents and parking their covered wagons on a grassy hill half a mile to the south of the city while the other column headed north, past Tigranocerta, following the Kentrites towards the pass in the next mountain range, some fifty miles distant, leading to Lake Thospitis and the heartland of Armenia.

'Babak doesn't seem to be very interested in using his cavalry,' Magnus observed as yet more of the troopers disappeared north.

'I think we'll see why very soon,' Vespasian replied, straining his eyes further down the Sapphe Bezabde pass. 'In fact, I can see them now.'

Magnus shaded his eyes and squinted as the last of the cavalry left the pass leaving behind an infantry force that would easily outnumber the defenders of Tigranocerta by at least five or six to one and, behind them, as many slaves. 'Fuck me!'

Vespasian, once again, declined the offer.

For the remainder of the day the Parthian conscript infantry and slaves crossed the bridge to the western bank and swarmed like ants around the walls of Tigranocerta, just within bowshot and well within the range of the carroballistae, which by mid-afternoon were all rigged on the defences. Vespasian, however, kept his word and did not give the order to shoot; he knew it was vital for Tryphaena's scheme that Rome should not be seen as the aggressor, and the more he had thought about her plan, the more he had become determined to see it through to a successful conclusion.

When the last of the Parthian force had crossed the bridge the middle two arches were destroyed making retreat impossible.

'Well, that makes Babak's intentions quite clear,' Vespasian mused. 'He's not going to give his conscripts the chance to run. Excellent.'

Magnus looked gloomy. 'You should have held the bridge.'

Vespasian was unrepentant. 'I'm trying to do this with minimal loss of life. Their heavy cavalry would have forced a crossing sooner or later and then their light cavalry would have destroyed our retreating lads before they gained the city. What we have now is the same result: a siege, but without our first incurring casualties. And I'm very happy to watch them get into position.'

And so the Parthians laid out their siege lines unmolested. As night fell, thousands of torches were lit so that the great works could continue in the golden light encircling the town like a halo. Unrelenting in their exertion and goaded on by the bullying of their officers or the whips of their overseers, the silhouetted figures levelled ground, dug trenches and raised breastwork while the unsleeping sentinels on the walls watched, the torch-glow flickering on their faces set hard with the determination that all the enemy's work should be for nought.

Vespasian repaired to a room in the palace at the top of the city and slept, knowing that in the coming days he would have precious little time to do so. When Hormus brought him a steaming cup of hot wine the following dawn he rose and donned his armour, feeling refreshed and ready for the coming ordeal. Sipping his morning drink he pulled aside the gently billowing curtains and stepped out onto a terrace that commanded a view south; his gaze wandered down the slope of flat roofs punctuated by thoroughfares and alleyways, over the walls lined with artillery and sentries and on to the fruit of a day and night of unceasing Parthian labour. And the sight took his breath away: the city was encircled by a brown scar scored in the verdant upland grass of the Masian foothills; but it was not the scale of the works nor the speed with which they had been completed nor the thousands of waiting troops within them that astounded him, it was what was behind. Scores of siege engines that had been dismantled for the march were being reassembled by the slaves in the growing light. But these were not the light carrob-allistae that fitted onto mule-drawn carts that the auxiliaries travelled with; these were far heavier. Squat and powerful with a kick like the mules they were named after, the *onagers'* throwing arms were capable of hurling huge rocks to smash walls and, if Tryphaena's information was to be believed, of delivering a weapon of far greater terror; a weapon of the East that Vespasian had heard of but had never seen deployed. One look at the stacks of earthenware jars next to the piles of rounded stone projectiles behind the fearsome engines told him that he would soon witness the destructive power of that strange substance named after Apam Napat, the third and lesser of the trilogy of deities in the Parthians' Zoroastrian religion; Mithras and Ahura Mazda, the uncreated creator, being the other two.

'You're to keep everything packed, Hormus,' Vespasian said, taking a tentative sip of the scalding wine. 'With what they've got down there honour may be satisfied sooner than I thought.'

'Master?'

'We may be leaving in a hurry.' Vespasian raised his gaze and surveyed the mountains, towering with majesty up from the foothills to form the natural barrier between Armenia and the Parthian Empire. 'A shame really; it's beautiful country, don't you think so, Hormus?'

Hormus stroked the scraggy beard that tried but failed to disguise his undershot chin as he contemplated the scenery, uncertain how to respond having very rarely been asked his opinion by his master on anything more aesthetic than the order of precedence that clients should be received in. 'If you say so, master.'

Vespasian frowned at his slave. 'I do; but you should have your own opinion on the subject and not just take my word for it.' He gestured at the expanse of natural beauty that dominated the vista, dwarfing the relatively insignificant disfigurement that humanity's belligerence had scratched in its shadow. 'This should speak to you, Hormus; after all, it is somewhere around this area that your family came from – you told me Armenia, didn't you?'

Hormus' smile was wan beneath his equally feeble beard. 'Somewhere *near* Armenia, master, but I don't know where. My mother told me in her tongue but when she died I forgot that language as it was of no use any more, and with it I forgot the name of my land.'

'It'll come back if you hear it again,' Vespasian assured him but then hoping that he was wrong; a sense of belonging was not what he wanted for Hormus, preferring his slave to be compliant and meek – no, perhaps meekness was not something to be wished upon him either.

There was a scratching on the door and Hormus crossed the room, his footsteps muffled by the sumptuous rugs of deep reds, blues and umbers with which the floor was littered.

'You'd better come quick, sir,' Magnus said as the door opened; he was wearing the chain mail of an auxiliary. 'Paelignus has seen that the Parthians have got some serious artillery and he doesn't want to play any more, if you take my meaning?'

'I do. Where is he?'

'Mannius caught him trying to slip through the gate; he has him under arrest in the gatehouse.'

'You have no right to hold me!' Paelignus shrieked as Mannius showed Vespasian and Magnus into the small room where the nominal commander of the expedition was being held.

Without pausing, Vespasian slapped Paelignus' cheek as if he were punishing a recalcitrant slave girl. 'Now listen, you rapacious worm, I'll do anything I like to you if you try to go over to the enemy again. I may even hang you on a cross and see if that does anything to straighten out your back.'

'You can't do that; I'm a citizen.'

'Perhaps I'll forget that fact just as you seem to have forgotten where your loyalties lie. What were you trying to achieve?'

Paelignus rubbed his cheek, which was coming out in a reddish welt. 'I wanted to save us. There're thousands of them and they've got artillery.'

'Of course they've got artillery, but can they use it?' He grabbed the procurator by the arm and dragged him from the room, past the guards on the door, who were unable to conceal their amusement at the sight, and up the stone steps next to the gates that led to the walkway running along behind the crenellated parapet. Magnus and Mannius followed, the prefect putting the two guards on a charge as he passed for failing to show due respect for an officer.

Vespasian held Paelignus' chin in a cruel grasp and forced him to look through a crenel at the enemy lines. 'See there, procurator, thousands of them, just as you said, but they're conscripts. None of them have had any training beyond being shown which end of an arrow or a javelin to aim at the enemy. They look impressive but they're nothing compared to our lads; they're just cattle, human cattle, to be stampeded forward knowing that they cannot retreat because the bridge is down. Their best troops are their cavalry, half of whom have disappeared north and the other half are sitting on that hill and, apart from shooting arrows at us, will take no more part in the proceedings than the spectators at the Circus Maximus. As to the artillery; even if they make a breach in the walls, who's going to storm through it? The crack Parthian infantry? The Immortals and the apple-bearers are with their King of Kings; this Babak is just a satrap of a client king, we have nothing to fear from his infantry.'

As he finished the last word, a single arrow soared into the sky, trailing a thin furrow of smoke over the Parthian host. A mighty roar emanated from the siege lines followed by the massed release of thousands of archers and Vespasian knew that he was about to have the veracity of his words tested as the sky went dark with tens of thousands of arrows.

The Parthian assault on Tigranocerta had begun.

CHAPTER VIIII

ARROWS FELL, CLATTERING, in a relentless percussive roll, with showers of sparks off the stone wall, walkway and the paved streets below; a hail of iron and wood that was fatal only to the very few foolhardy enough to look up into it and then unlucky enough to receive a direct hit in the eye or throat. For the rest of the garrison on the wall the initial volleys were little more than an annoyance as, by the time they had flown through the dawn air to the city, they were spent and the sight and sound of them was far more fearsome than the reality; if they did pierce an exposed arm or leg, they hung limply from the limb and could be withdrawn with minimum pain and little blood. For the populace of the city they did not signify, as very few fell further than ten paces beyond the wall such was the excessive range.

But Babak had not intended the archery of his conscripts to cause death on a grand scale; he was using it to preserve lives – the conscripts' own – until he deemed it right to spend them. As they released their arrows, haphazardly in their own time, the conscripts were pushed forward, the few braver ones willingly but the majority with the whips and spear- and sword-points of their officers, jabbing and lashing them into action. And then the cavalry began to form up in long lines of horse archers and deep blocks of closer formation lancers. As Vespasian, safe within the lee of the parapet and still restraining Paelignus, peered through the crenel, he realised what the heavy cavalry had been doing since dismounting: they had, like Babak said he would, dressed for battle. Gone were the bright trousers, embroidered tunics, elaborate headdresses and gaudy caparisoning and in their place was burnished iron and bronze armour, both of laminated plate and chain mail that covered the riders entirely as well as the heads, necks and withers of their mounts. As they were unable to march more than a very short distance in their full battle gear before falling victim to complete exhaustion, their armour was transported in covered wagons. Vespasian had heard of these cataphract cavalrymen so weighed down by metal that they could only charge at the trot, knee to knee, needing no shield and driving all before them with their twelve-foot *kontoi*, but he had not expected to see them deployed here. What in Mars' name could they possibly achieve on a hill before a walled city?

But this question was soon to be answered as he watched the herd of conscripts come on across the two hundred paces of open ground between the siege lines and the walls. Arrows still spat from them in their thousands but despite the decreasing range their accuracy did not improve; in fact, quite the reverse as more and more flew high or slammed into the walls, hastily aimed as the advance accelerated from a walk to a jog. Their war cries increased commensurately with their speed, rising in note and apprehension as terror for what awaited them began to outweigh the fear of their officers driving them.

Vespasian raised his head and risked a quick look east and west before an arrow hissed past him in what was very nearly a lucky shot. Nothing was moving on either side; only the southern wall was under attack and he immediately understood why. 'Mannius!' he shouted at the prefect sheltering a few paces away. 'It's just us they're interested in. Send messengers to the other three walls and tell them not to come to our aid; that's what Babak will be hoping. They're to stay where they are under all circumstances. And tell Fregallanus to bring half his reserve cohort up to stand by here on the off-chance that we need a little help; they should have the heated oil and sand ready by now.'

Mannius saluted.

'Oh, and get us some shields, they might prove useful.'

Grinning at the understatement, the prefect despatched his runners before ordering his officers to ready their men.

Along the southern wall centurions and optiones shouted at their men hunched under shields to prepare to hurl the first of their three javelins; the auxiliaries hefted their throwing weapons, lighter than the *pila* issued to legionaries but capable of greater distance, and waited, grim in the face of combat. A paltry amount of the Civic Militia archers stationed amongst the auxiliaries on the southern wall shot at the oncoming mass through crenels, but so few were their number that they did less harm than the men goading on the attack from behind with swords, spears and whips.

As the horde reached one hundred paces out the cataphract cavalry started crossing the siege lines and fanning out behind the conscripts with the light cavalry forming up behind them. Vespasian comprehended with a jolt what they were to be used for and why. 'They're to prevent the infantry from retreating.'

Magnus squinted his one eye. 'What? Are they going to drive them into the wall and hope they push it over?'

'No, I can see ladders; they're going to try an escalade.'

Paelignus yelped and twisted from Vespasian's grip to hurtle back down the steps.

Magnus moved to fetch him back but then thought better of it. 'Just against this wall?'

'Yes; Babak is trying to draw away the troops on the other walls.'

'He must think you're stupid.'

Vespasian slipped his *gladius* from its scabbard, enjoying the weight of it in his hand. 'No, he thinks Paelignus is in command.'

A young auxiliary scuttled up with three shields. 'We only need two now, lad,' Magnus said, taking one for himself and handing another to Vespasian. 'The procurator has just remembered some urgent paperwork that needs his immediate attention.'

Vespasian looked out again as the speed of the advance, fifty paces out, increased to a run and the war cry was now more of a hysterical scream than a martial challenge; the ladders were now very much in evidence but the shooting had tailed off. He tensed, preparing for what he knew would follow, and offered a prayer to Mars that he would hold his hands over him and see him safely through his first combat since he left Britannia five years before. He had been sadly aware of the tightness of his back- and breastplates as he fastened them on that morning and fervently hoped that his extra weight would not slow him down too—

'Release!' Mannius' cry brought Vespasian out of his introspection. As the command was echoed each way along the wall by centurions and their optiones, the eight hundred auxiliaries of the I Bosporanorum rose to their feet and, in one fleet movement, hurled their first javelins towards the packed oncoming mass of unarmoured conscripts protected only by the flimsiest wicker shields. Sleek iron-tipped projectiles hurtled down into an unmissable target, slamming into the exposed chests and faces of men whom, just a couple of months earlier, had been forced from their farms and workshops to fight for a cause that they did not understand against a people they did not know. And down they went, their terrified war cries little different from the screams of pain and anguish that they became as the blood exploded from ghastly punctures punched through torsos, necks, limbs and heads by tearing iron. Arms were flung high over pierced bodies bent back as if attempting some macabre tumbling act; gore sprayed in mimicry of the movement and faces distorted with pain into wide-eyed, bared-toothed rictus snarls as they crumpled to the ground to disappear, trampled beneath the feet of those behind who, however much they would have wanted to, were unable to halt because of the momentum of the terrified horde jabbed and whipped into following them. Feet tangled with the thrashing, writhing limbs of the wounded or the shafts of the weapons impaling them, bringing down men so far unscathed to share the crushed death of their howling comrades as, an instant or so later, the auxiliaries of the I Bosporanorum pulled back their right arms for a second time, all brandishing a fresh javelin.

But it was not with impunity that they killed; feathered shafts appeared, as if conjured out of nothing, in eyes and throats of more than a score of auxiliaries as their arms powered forward again. More shafts juddered into shields, vibrating with the impact, as others rebounded off chain mail to leave vivid bruising on the unbroken skin beneath; the horse archers had entered the fray and, with a lifetime of experience with their beasts and weapons, their aim was good. But still well over seven hundred javelins hurtled into the human cattle now less than fifteen paces from the wall so that the terror in their eyes was visible for all the defenders to see. And see it they did and they took heart as more of their foes were pummelled to the ground into which their lives would seep away as they turned it to mud with their blood and urine. With the joy of battle rising within them, the men of the I Bosporanorum took up their third and final javelins.

However, the horse archers were fast and closer now and numerous auxiliaries flew back as if yanked from behind to crumple on the walkway or tumble to the street, their uncast weapons clattering to the ground. But most of their comrades drew their straight *spathae* from their sheaths having reaped the final long-range batch of lives before the close-quarters slaughter began. And then ladders, scores of them, swung up and slapped down onto the walls to be pushed back by the defenders; but each one that fell seemed to be replaced by two others, such was their number. The horse archers kept their aim, almost unerringly, at head height above the wall as the auxiliaries hacked and pushed at the ladder tops in attempts to topple as many as possible before the weight of bodies on them made the task impossible. More defenders went down screaming, dead, dying or wounded as the feathered shafts flicked amongst them. Vespasian and Magnus joined the frantic attempt to ward off the escalade, heaving at the ladders that kept on arcing up from below, for although the auxiliaries had hurled nigh on two thousand javelins into the mass, most of which had struck a target, thousands more of the human cattle came on, knotting at the foot of the walls, pushed on by a new terror behind them: the terror of a solid wall of mounted metal, punctuated by lance points. Those cattle closest to the cataphracts shoved and kicked their way forward to escape the deadly shafts and trampling hoofs so that those nearest the defences were forced to choose between a certain crushed death compressed against the wall, or a probable pierced death on the blades of the defenders, twenty feet above them.

And so the human cattle began to climb the ladders.

*

'Where's the oil and sand?' Vespasian shouted at Mannius as he tried to twist away a ladder that had slammed against the wall in front of him.

The prefect bellowed at a centurion, who sent a man scurrying down the steps.

Vespasian gave up trying to dislodge the ladder, now weighed down securely in place by three hapless conscripts who had no choice but to climb or fall; he looked down into their terrified eyes, gritted his teeth and, squeezing hard on his sword's hilt, brought it up behind his shield, ready. A brace of arrows slammed into the leather-covered wood, straining the muscles of his left arm with the abrupt impact; he rolled his shoulders, loosening them. Magnus growled next to him, working himself up to battle fever, his one good eye glaring down at the enemy with the same wild intensity as the inanimate glass copy. And on they came, forced inexorably upwards by the press of cattle below; struggling to hold on to the ladder as it bounced and bucked under the different pace of each man's ascent, the conscripts screamed in terror at the proximity of death either above them or below. But natural instinct took over: to fall into the crush beneath them was certain oblivion, but there was a small chance of survival up on the wall and so they took it and surged on up. All along the defences, to either side of Vespasian and Magnus, the Parthian swarm mounted countless ladders that rose from their massed formation like bristles on an angry hog's back.

'Stop the bastards here, lads!' Vespasian roared above screams and bellows to the men around him as another arrow punched his shield; he braced himself squarely on his feet, his left leg leading, and, hunching his shoulders down, kept his eyes focused on the ladder head just protruding above the base of a crenel. His world shrank as his concentration intensified and he saw the top of the headdress of the first man up the ladder. With an inchoate snarl he exploded forward, punching the tip of his blade, through shattering teeth, down the gullet of the bearded conscript at exactly the same moment as a bloodied arrowhead burst from the man's right eye socket in a spray of gore and jelly. The horse archers had not ceased their volleys as the conscripts reached the top of the ladders.

'The horse-fuckers are carrying on shooting!' Magnus spat in indignation as a shaft hissed past his sword arm, which was stabbing repeatedly forward. 'They're killing their own men.'

'And ours,' Vespasian shouted, looking to his left as he yanked his blade from the dead Parthian's mouth, releasing the corpse to drop, deadweight, onto his erstwhile comrades. To repulse the escalade the auxiliaries exposed themselves to the horse archers' continual onslaught and more than a few had fallen. 'They can afford to kill ten of theirs for each one of ours.'

And that was the bleak arithmetic upon which Babak had evidently based his plans: force the defenders into exposing themselves as they prevented the conscripts gaining the wall and keep the hailstorm of sharpened iron pouring down upon them; the human cattle were collateral damage in the greater objective of thinning out the resistance on the southern defences and forcing reinforcements to be called from the as yet unassailed walls.

Still the conscripts kept on climbing, forced up by the straining pressure below, and still the hail hammered into both Parthian and Roman auxiliary alike. Vespasian's shield thumped with hit after hit, the irregular, hollow thuds booming in his ears, as he held it rigid and punched and slashed with bloodied sword from behind it at those Parthians lucky enough to gain the wall without being shot by their own side. Twenty paces to Vespasian's right, along the defences, where the ladders were thickest, a pocket of conscripts had managed to gain a foothold, pushing back the auxiliaries, more by weight of numbers than by prowess. The cattle bellowed their fear and slashed, at the real soldiers hemming them in, with low-quality blades that buckled or snapped when parried by a standard-issue auxiliary spatha. The defenders pressed back at them with their shields, herding them into a tight knot that became tighter as more conscripts completed the ascent and were forced by pressure from behind to jump screaming into the fray. Blades flicked from between auxiliary shields, opening bellies and arteries as the penned-in cattle strove uselessly to defend themselves in such restrictive circumstances.

But still they swarmed up the ladders, adding to the pressure and widening the knot despite the culling to which they were being subjected. However, they died at a slower rate than they were replaced and so the foothold grew and the dead soon became the saviours of the living as they remained upright, jammed against the auxiliaries' shields so that their blades could no longer reach unpierced flesh. By some miracle the conscripts were making progress and the defenders directly facing them were now forced to jump from the walkway to a twisted-ankled, broken-legged landing on the paving stones below, leaving only their comrades to either side, four men wide across the walkway and two deep, hunched and straining against their shields, to hold back the growing herd.

'Stay here,' Vespasian ordered the auxiliaries to his left, satisfied that they should be able to hold the position. 'Magnus, with me!' They hurtled along the walkway, past a dozen or so private combats where the defenders were hurling the conscripts back through the crenels – or at least preventing them progressing forward – and came to the outer edge of the ever-expanding melee as it abutted the parapet through and over which the conscripts flowed. Arrows hissed higher overhead as the horse archers' commanders realised that progress, which should not be impeded by slaughtering the cattle making it, was being made on this section of the wall and they had their men raise their aim into the city beyond.

'Pull back!' Vespasian shouted at the auxiliaries and tugging on a couple of shoulders. 'Pull back four paces and give them space.'

The auxiliaries obeyed his command, even though it ran contrary to their martial instincts to press forward onto the enemy, and stepped backwards. The sudden release of pressure freed the lolling corpses jammed up against the shield wall and they slithered to the ground leaving blood smears marking their passage down the emblazoning of combined moons and stars. The conscripts revealed by them cheered at their enemy's retreat and then were pushed forward to trip over their slaughtered comrades, landing at the auxiliaries' feet and falling prey immediately to the razor points of spathae that ripped necks and backs, slicing through vertebrae and muscle with sprays and slops of blood and agonised screams.

'Now forward!' Vespasian yelled, barging into the front rank, his eyes slitted and his lips drawn back in a bloodied-lipped snarl. 'Magnus, follow us up with as many men as you can get and stop the gaps!'

Vespasian and his small command stepped over the dead and, with nothing between their blades and the living flesh of their foe penned as they were like the beasts they resembled, began to slaughter; this time taking care not to press forward so hard as to form an upright cadaver-barricade. Vespasian felt the joy once more of working his blade; reaping lives with every combined thrust, twist and pull, stamping his feet forward and punching with his shield boss as liquids and semi-solids splattered down his legs and onto his feet, warm and glutinous between his toes, emanating foul stenches and creating a dangerously slimy surface underfoot. On they pressed, forcing many of the Parthians to jump from the walkway and take their chances with fractured limbs in the street below rather than face the four blades that leapt, at groin height or at chest or belly, from between the solid, short wall of shields, blood-slicked and deadly. Magnus and the auxiliaries following up dealt with each of the crenels as they were cleared, throwing men back with ripped throats and eyeless sockets, howling their last down to a shattered death on the growing mounds of mortally wounded and lifeless bodies.

From the opposing direction the other auxiliaries took heart from the progress of their comrades and held their shields firm, eviscerated corpses pressed hard against them, making a solid barrier through which there was no retreat for the doomed conscripts who screamed to gods deaf to their plight as their lives were ripped from slashed bodies.

Vespasian's breaths became ragged with exertion but he forced his muscles to power on, unwilling to forgo the joy of slaughter that had not been felt for so long as he had wallowed through the mire of imperial politics populated by men who could never live as intensely as he did at this moment. Iron-tanged blood, urine, faeces, sweat and fear cloyed his nose and the clash of weapons, the cries of the wounded and dying of both the victors and the vanquished alike rang shrill in his ears. But then a new odour penetrated his focused mind and a different sound accompanied it: acrid fumes and shattering impacts. Vespasian stepped back to let a second ranker take his place and glanced above to see an earthenware pot trailing fire and black smoke flash across the sky. He followed its trajectory and watched it smash onto the corner of a roof in the second level of the city, exploding into a maelstrom of flames that stuck to the tiles and walls as if they themselves were burning. He turned to see an auxiliary stare, transfixed in horror at the sky for an instant before the man's head disintegrated with a puff of blood, flesh, brain and splintered bone, leaving his body standing, rigid, for a couple of gore-spouting heartbeats before crumpling to the ground still disgorging its contents.

The Parthian artillery had entered the fray and they were hurling both fire and stone.

'What the fuck is that?' Magnus puffed as yet another burning streak hissed overhead.

'Naphtha!' Vespasian shouted back, slamming the tip of his sword into the face of one of the last wounded conscripts left alive on the walkway; in each direction along the wall the fight to keep the cattle out continued in a brutal fashion that now seemed commonplace to Vespasian after so much violence. 'Tryphaena warned me about it; she said it's the spawn of an eastern god of fresh water.'

'Bollocks, spawn can't burn; it's laid in water.' Magnus ducked involuntarily as the wind of a solid shot passed overhead.

Vespasian finally saw the sight that he had been waiting for and turned to his friend; a grin split his blood-splattered face. 'It's a fire god that lives in water which doesn't quench his flames so of course his spawn can burn.'

'Oh, River-god fire,' Magnus said, watching another smoking missile shoot by. 'I know it; useful stuff it is too.'

Vespasian's surprise at Magnus having heard of this weapon was tempered by a welcome sight. 'But we're now going to fight their fire with heat of our own.' As he spoke, teams of auxiliaries from Fregallanus' cohort, led by a centurion, jogged down the street with iron cauldrons on solid wooden stretchers insulated by soaked leather. They double-timed up the steps and the centurion saluted.

Vespasian did not wait for his report. 'Is this all?' he asked, counting a dozen pots.

'No, sir, just the first batch; there're at least six more batches of this size to come.'

'Very good, centurion; we'll start on this section.' He pointed to a crenel at which two auxiliaries were crouching taking it in turns to repel a seemingly endless stream of conscripts; all along the wall similar scenarios were being played out as the defenders kept low through fear of losing their heads to well-aimed solid artillery shots. 'Take that crenel, then every fifth one; that should give them pause for thought.'

With a perfunctory salute the centurion led his men off at a crouching lope as streaks of flame and black smoke passed overhead to explode as fireballs in the city beyond; heavy stones crashed into the parapet and skimmed through crenels with eruptions of human meat, of both attackers and defenders alike, spattering over the walkway.

Wishing to set an example, Vespasian stood erect, open to the artillery, and watched the first team lay down its stretcher; with dampened leather gloves two of them lifted the cauldron by a chain, attached to either side, onto the crenel as the auxiliaries defending it fell back after a flurry of lightning sword thrusts. They pushed the iron cauldron across the stone, steam issuing from their gloves, until it reached the lip and then the other two men lifted a wooden pole from the stretcher, placed it on the cauldron's rim and pushed, tipping it forward as their comrades held the chains fast. The heated oil within it began to dribble down and then pour slowly out as the cauldron toppled forward until, with a sudden surge as it crashed onto its side, the oil gushed down onto the skin and into the eyes of those unfortunate enough to be on the ladder below.

The screams of freshly blinded men pierced the battle's rage as the sirens' calls cut through the wrath of a storm. The cauldron was dragged back and an auxiliary leant through the crenel to pull in the vacated ladder; below, the enemy were too intent on scraping the searing gelatinous fluid from their melting skin to notice. A torch was then flung down to ignite the oil; it flashed in an instant, raging with an intensity that almost matched the Naphtha conflagrations blazing within the city, but outdid them for murderous effect in the cramped conditions beneath the wall as men, already in torment, burst into flame. Another clutch of desolate shrieks tore through the din and then more and more as the rest of the cauldrons were emptied of their oil or super-heated sand whose scalding grains inveigled their way into clothing and orifices to agonising effect. One cauldron, struck by a direct hit from a fist-sized stone projectile that shattered it, exploded its contents backwards, spattering the auxiliaries around it so that they shared the fate that was being meted out to so many of the human cattle threatening the southern wall.

And then the second load of steaming cauldrons arrived, followed by a third and then a fourth. With each delivery of broiling agony the pressure on Vespasian's section of the wall eased as ladders were drawn up and not replaced from below, so that the defenders could concentrate on fewer escalade points with more brutal efficiency.

With the sixth and penultimate downpouring of blistering death the will of the Parthians snapped and their terror of immolation exceeded that for their tormentors behind them. They turned and ran, as if by common consent, leaving their dead and dying stacked and smouldering against the base of the wall and littered across the field as they tried to break through the formation of cataphract cavalry, four deep, knee to knee, that hemmed them in.

The auxiliaries, too exhausted to do much more than give a cursory cheer, hunkered back down behind the parapet as the artillery continued shooting stone at the walls and lobbing fire into the city.

But that too was soon to cease as, from the north, a new threat appeared; horns blared in the Parthian ranks and cornu repeated the four-note refrain warning of approaching troops.

Both sides paused as they tried to ascertain to whose aid this new force had come.

'They're the Parthians who followed the tributary north,' Magnus opined, surveying the long column of cavalry tracing the line of the eastern bank of the Kentrites a mile or so north of its meeting with the Tigris. Dust partially obscured them so that their number was impossible to tell, but, through the cloud roused up by hundreds of hoofs, the banners and the dress of the vanguard could be discerned.

'Babak must have recalled them once he'd witnessed the strength of our defence,' Mannius reasoned, pride in his men's performance registering in his voice.

Vespasian shook his head and leant forward through the crenel, at the junction of the southern and eastern walls, as if the extra couple of feet would make a difference in his ability to identify the newcomers. If Queen Tryphaena had kept her promise then he knew who they were; but he needed to be sure. As his eyes penetrated the dust he allowed himself a small smile; these cavalry were slightly different. 'No, it can't be them; look at the colour of the clothes their light cavalry are wearing: the Parthian cavalry were all garish tunics and trousers and fancy headdresses, but these light horse are dull by comparison, undyed wool and linen, poor stuff.'

Magnus squinted his one good eye and rubbed his neck. 'I suppose you're right; but then whoever that is must have passed the Parthians.' He turned to Vespasian and Mannius, raising his brows. All three of them were crusted in dried gore as if they had spent the day sacrificing to every conceivable god who demanded blood but none of them affected to notice. 'There ain't enough room in that valley for two forces to pass each other without at least saying good morning.'

Mannius pointed to a group of horsemen traversing the bridge to the northern bank of the Tigris. 'There's movement over there.'

Vespasian watched the dozen or so Parthian light cavalry; having crossed the second bridge to the eastern bank of the Kentrites, they approached the column under a branch of truce. 'This should confirm who I think they are.'

'Confirm?' Mannius asked.

'Yes, prefect; I'm hoping that they're who I've been waiting for.' He looked around at the conscript infantry, dug in, surrounding the city and then focused on the three or four thousand manning the siege lines to the north, opposite the only other gate. The Tigris came to within a hundred paces of their rear with the bridge spanning it before it made its curve to the south.

Vespasian turned his attention back to the approaching cavalry. They had now halted at the confluence of the Tigris and its tributary, with the Parthian emissaries a little distance ahead of them; what was being negotiated and how those talks were going was impossible to tell from this distance. He watched the parley for another hundred or so heartbeats, each one feeling quicker than the last, until finally the Parthians turned their mounts and pelted back the way they came without a messenger from the newcomers accompanying them. 'Good, it is them.'

Magnus looked confused. 'Who are they?'

'They, Magnus, are the rest of our army and all that stands between them linking up with us are three or four thousand conscripts, so we need to get the north gate open and herd some cattle into the river.' He turned to Mannius' primus pilus waiting at a respectful distance from his superiors. 'Get messages to all the other prefects and have them stand by to leave the city through the north gate; Cotta's cohort will lead and will break through the siege lines; Fregallanus and Mannius' cohorts will follow up and form up to the west and east respectively to protect the rest of the force and the baggage while they cross the Tigris.'

The centurion gave a crisp salute and turned to relay the orders to a series of runners and Vespasian grinned at Mannius. 'Time to get your lads off the wall, prefect.'

Vespasian and Magnus strode purposefully around the narrow streets that circled the great hill of the city past many Naphtha fires being tackled by citizens, old and young, too busy to notice the Roman troops pulling back from the battlements and the baggage train assembling in the agora near the north gate.

'You travel with Hormus,' Vespasian ordered Magnus as they pushed through the chaos of the wagons and mules gathering at short notice. Hormus was close to the front, seeing to his team's harness; Vespasian was unsurprised to see the young muleteer he had noticed smile so enticingly at his slave just behind him. He was sure that was no coincidence. 'And find out the name of that lad and where he comes from; Hormus seems to have taken a fancy to him. We should make sure that his motives are purely financial.'

'You mean make sure that he's not pumping your slave for information, if you take my meaning?'

'I'm sure I do,' Vespasian said with a smile as he pushed on to Cotta's cohort forming up in a column at the north gate. Now all he had to do was clear the way for the new arrivals to link up with the Romans, then together they would abandon Tigranocerta and stage a fighting retreat, leading the Parthians further and further into the Roman client kingdom of Armenia and creating a just cause for war between the two empires. This was the war that Tryphaena had planned. A war that would secure her nephew the Armenian crown, a war that could be used to destabilise the drunken, drooling fool ruling in Rome and ensure that Nero, the son of her kinswoman Agrippina, would take the Purple before Claudius' natural son, Britannicus, came of age. And this is what Vespasian now considered to be the best course of events for him and his family: he had seen Nero and he had seen Britannicus and of the two of them it was obvious, even surely to a drooling fool, that Britannicus was the better choice. But it was not the better choice that would suit Vespasian's purposes if the destiny that he suspected had been laid out for him really was to come to pass; that better choice would stabilise the Julio-Claudians and perhaps secure their line for decades to come. No, it was the weaker, vainer, more arrogant candidate that Vespasian needed to succeed Claudius: Nero, whose suitability to rule was only superficial. The dazzling Prince of the Youth in the image of a young god; but underneath that appealing exterior lay what Vespasian believed could be the madness that would make Tiberius' behaviour in his latter years seem like mild eccentricity. He had recognised it in the moment he had seen Nero resting his head on Agrippina's breast and then had had it confirmed by Narcissus: an incestuous relationship with his mother. Giving absolute power to a man who saw nothing wrong in bedding his own mother was, to Vespasian's mind, a sure way to release within him the madness of unrestrainable self-indulgence. A madness that would exceed Caligula's and make his public sexual displays with his sister Drusilla be remembered as a mere foible. A madness that, in conjunction with the dominating presence of his mother and lover, Agrippina, insisting on recognition never before given to a woman, would be capable of bringing down the Julio-Claudian line because neither the Senate, the people nor even the Praetorian Guard would be able to countenance another emperor from that family that had deteriorated so dismally. And if the Julio-Claudians were to fail, who could guess what would follow? Perhaps it would be the time of New Men. Perhaps.

But that was still a long way off and first he had to help implement Tryphaena's plan; the initial stage had been accomplished: he had a Parthian army on Armenian soil. Now the second phase was coming to fruition because, as Tryphaena had promised he would, the usurper had come to fight alongside Rome.

Radamistus had brought his army to Tigranocerta.

CHAPTER X

THE SPEED WITH which Vespasian led Cotta's II Cappadocia Auxiliary Cohort out of the north gate, had it form up in two ranks, each of five centuries, and then advance towards the siege lines unnerved the conscripts manning them as he hoped it would. Once the centurions' bellowed commands had died away the eight hundred men marched in silence, their uniform footsteps more threatening than any battle cry, their inexorable progress across the field more ominous than any charge, and their precision drill as their shields came up and their right arms went back in preparation to release their javelins more crushing to the conscripts' morale than the impact of the volley itself. Before the first sleek point hissed into the Parthian lines the human cattle had stampeded despite the summary slaughter of many of their number by their pitiless officers who soon became overwhelmed by the herd's terror. They surged north, through the artillery, sweeping away the crews and on towards the Tigris, towards the bridge.

But the bridge was wide enough for only eight men at a time.

Barely pausing to jab the tips of their swords into the throats of those trampled in the panic, the men of the II Cappadocia Auxiliary Cohort crossed the siege lines in good order and drove the conscripts on to the river as behind them the other four cohorts began to march in column out of the north gate. The Romans were abandoning Tigranocerta, leaving it aflame and the citizens defenceless.

The arithmetic of getting more than three thousand terrified men across a bridge just eight paces wide did not work in the conscripts' favour and many suffocated in the crush. Many more drowned in the deep waters of the Tigris into which they threw themselves in desperation, praying that Apam Napat, the fire god of fresh water, would save them. But the god's eyes were elsewhere, focused on the Naphtha-stoked fires raging in the city; hundreds were swept away and hundreds were trampled underfoot. Yet hundreds more were shot down on the north bank by the Iberian and Armenian horse and foot archers of Radamistus' army as they traversed the bridge on the River Kentrites, the remainder of the army, its heavy cavalry, conscript infantry and baggage, following slowly behind.

'Have your lads cross the bridge and form up on the other side, Cotta,' Vespasian ordered the auxiliary prefect, 'and hold it while the other cohorts cross.'

'Cross?'

'Yes, prefect, cross; we're going north and leaving Tigranocerta to the Parthians.'

'But—'

'But nothing, Cotta; just hold the bridge so that we can link up with Radamistus.'

Cotta snapped a puzzled salute as Vespasian turned back to see, glinting in the strengthening sun, a wall of iron and bronze appear from around the eastern wall of Tigranocerta; the Parthian cataphracts had come to do battle with the enemy rather than with their own. To the rear of the metallic wall massed the supporting horse archers. At the head of the advance was a rider more sumptuously apparelled than the rest; Vespasian knew that to survive this day he had to talk with him and keep him talking for a while, because if that cavalry charged his auxiliaries, their weight could well sweep them from the field.

Walking fast against the tide of centuries streaming out of the city Vespasian quickly found Mannius at the head of his cohort shielding the evacuation, facing to the east. 'Have your centurions deploy your men in deep formation facing the heavy cavalry, prefect; and then join me in front of them. Get Fregallanus to join us as well.' As the centuries manoeuvred into a line eight deep and took up position side by side across the complete width of the field from the gate to the newly abandoned siege lines, Vespasian picked up a dead branch and stood alone in front of them waiting for the advancing Parthian cataphracts with Babak at their head.

Mannius and Fregallanus soon joined him as he watched the slow advance of the heavily armoured cavalry, conserving their energy in order to be able to accelerate to a trot. Behind him Mannius' cohort had finished forming up and waited in silence. Fregallanus' cohort faced to the west creating a path between the two units along which the rest of their comrades doubled out of the city, followed by the baggage. They crossed the bridge with all possible haste to the northern bank of the Tigris to the accompanying bellows of centurions who had one eye on the iron-clad menace advancing from the east.

'Where's Paelignus?' Vespasian asked, without taking his eyes from the wall of metal and horse-flesh.

Fregallanus also kept his gaze on the advancing threat. 'I haven't seen him since the assault ended. He was by the north gate screaming at his slaves to get the wagon holding all his plunder harnessed up; it looked like he was going to try and buy his way out.'

Vespasian laughed and raised the branch of truce in the air. 'I would have loved to have seen him try. Well, he's out now but I don't suppose he'll be joining us in negotiating our safe passage; someone like him has no idea of when honour has been satisfied.' He put all thought of the cowardly little procurator to the back of his mind as Babak, just fifty paces away, raised his right hand in the air. Trumpets sounded along the Parthian line and five paces later the cataphracts came to a halt in unison.

After a short pause Babak urged his armoured mount forward and halted a kontos-length away from Vespasian; he raised his silver-plated facemask inlaid with a bronze beard, eyebrows and lashes. 'We are in an interesting situation, I think you'll agree?'

Vespasian shrugged. 'We have put up a defence of the city against far greater odds and I now consider that honour has been satisfied. Tigranocerta is yours.'

'And I should just let you walk away with your troops?'

'If you massacre the Roman garrison after it has surrendered the city in accordance with the rules of war, then Rome will follow you for vengeance, even into Parthia itself. Whereas if you let us pass, the war between our empires will stay confined to a struggle for the mastery of Armenia and your people will not suffer. That is something that your King will appreciate as would his master, the King of Kings, in Ctesiphon.'

Babak smiled, sweat dripping down his face despite the cool temperature. 'If I kill you now the war will effectively be over.'

'Wrong, Babak.' Vespasian pointed north to the bridge over which auxiliaries were marching double pace; beyond it Cotta's cohort were formed up in a defensive position. 'I've already got enough of my men across to add substantially to Radamistus' army. By the time you break through this cohort I'll have extricated most of them. You can expect no help from the north as Radamistus must have defeated the troops you sent up the river on his way down here.'

'You parley to gain time; I do not consider that to be the act of an honourable man.'

'No, Babak, I parley to try to save as many of my men as possible.' He indicated to the city now overshadowed by a pall of smoke. 'Take your prize, Babak, and let me take my men.'

Babak looked down at Vespasian almost sorrowfully. 'I can't do that; now that Radamistus is here I must confront him and beat him and to do that he must have as few troops as possible.' He closed his mask with a clang and turned his huge horse.

Mannius looked at Vespasian, determination in his eyes. 'My lads will hold them for as long as possible, sir.'

Vespasian placed a hand on the prefect's shoulder. 'I'm sorry, Mannius, but I'm afraid that is exactly what you're going to have to do.' He turned to walk back to the line of ill-fated auxiliaries with the two prefects following. The last of the three cohorts was now passing behind with the baggage in close accompaniment. 'Fregallanus, get your men across as soon as the baggage is clear and then, Mannius, follow as best you can. I'll have Cotta hold the bridge for as long as he's able to.' As they passed through the ranks he looked over his shoulder; Babak had almost rejoined his cavalry; a horn sounded. 'Best of luck, prefect.' He grasped Mannius' proffered forearm with a firm grip. 'Your lads fought well this morning, you have a chance.'

'We always have a chance; Fortuna's watching.'

Vespasian nodded and walked briskly away into the traffic hastening to the bridge with ever-increasing urgency. He had sent men to their deaths many times and could do so with a clear conscience if the sacrifice would enable more to live; he remembered the young military tribune Bassius' suicidal cavalry charge into the rear of the Britannic army with which Caratacus had surprised Vespasian in the dead of night and had come close to being in a position to annihilate the II Augusta. That order had not been easy to give but he had done so without regret: it had been a desperate situation in a continuing war and the loss of a legion would have been a serious reversal for Rome – not to mention the end of Vespasian's career had he been unlucky enough to survive. This time, however, it weighed heavy upon him. He had engineered this situation and these men would be sacrificing themselves not only to save the rest of the cohorts, but also to further his personal ambition. There had been no military reason to defend Tigranocerta in the first place; they should have retreated in the face of such overwhelming odds. But he had defended it because he had to ensure that there was a clash with Parthia and a war initiated. Now he had abandoned it in order to join with Radamistus and fight a delaying retreat north into the heart of Armenia, leading the Parthians ever on to threaten the balance of power in the East, causing outrage back in Rome and questions to be thought and then whispered about the competence of an emperor who would allow this to happen. He felt that he had become little different from the men he had always struggled against: a man who spent others' lives to further the richness of his own. And yet that was the way in which they held on to power, so why should it be any different for him trying to achieve it?

'Are you just going to let them stand and die?'

Vespasian snapped out of his gloom-ridden introspection to see Magnus seated next to Hormus, driving the wagon at a quick trot. He broke into a run and caught up with them. 'What choice do I have?' he asked, vaulting up onto the vehicle. From this vantage point he could see over the heads of Mannius' cohort to

Babak raising his right arm; more horns sounded loud enough to penetrate the squealing cacophony of scores of carts and wagons being driven at speed, and from behind the cataphracts rose a great shadow as the horse archers loosed a massed volley. 'I could die with them; but would that make it better?'

Magnus looked with regret at the backs of the auxiliaries as they raised their shields over their heads, the front rank kneeling; they then hefted their javelins, preparing to use them as stabbing weapons to aim at the small round bronze grilles protecting the horses' eyes or to jab them at their unprotected mouths or lower legs and hoofs. 'They were good lads.'

Down came the first wave of arrows thumping into the upturned shields with a multitude of sudden staccato reports, causing little damage to the well-disciplined auxiliaries, as the second was launched. Some missiles fell long, landing amongst the baggage train, stirring up panic.

'But I ain't going to hang around and share their fate neither,' Magnus said, cracking his whip so that the wagon kept its pace as it approached the siege works.

A single pounding of a deep drum boomed over the field, followed a couple of heartbeats later by a second and then a third; the Parthian cataphracts moved forward at a walk, driven gradually on by the deliberate beat. The slow but inexorable charge had begun and the auxiliaries stood, waiting to receive it, knowing that the momentum of such heavily armoured troops would break them very soon after the first contact. But they stood nonetheless. Behind them the baggage scrambled to safety across the abandoned siege lines as the third cohort cleared the bridge.

Magnus whipped the mules continuously as they struggled across one of the two northern gaps in the trench- and breast-work left by the Parthians for the passage of their cavalry; Vespasian held on tightly as the vehicle rocked on the uneven ground. Smoke from cooking fires wafted about carrying the burnt odours of the conscripts' hastily abandoned midday meals still in pots over the glowing wood. The booming of the Parthian war drum continued, increasing fractionally with every few beats as the massive horses accelerated slowly under their enormous burdens, their great hearts working at almost full capacity even though they were travelling at little faster than a quick walk; soon they would break into a trot for the very last dozen or so paces.

As the horse archers continued their massed but ineffectual volleys, Vespasian looked across at the advancing cataphracts, hundreds of them in two ranks, their armour shining in the sun and their banners fluttering over their heads, and marvelled that such a beauteous sight could be so deadly. The sun blazing down on them made the slow-moving wall of burnished metal seem that it was crowned in golden flame.

Flame? Fire?

Vespasian started; the wagon had cleared the earthworks and was now passing through the few artillery pieces on this side of the town. He glanced along the line of machines; there were at least two onagers. 'Magnus! Pull over. Now!'

Magnus steered the wagon off the track and slowed, just ten paces from the bridge; the centurion in charge of the detail manning it signalled at them to press on but was ignored. Vespasian jumped off and ran to the nearest onager; and there he saw them: stacks of earthenware pots, one foot in diameter, with rags protruding from their wax-sealed tops.

Naphtha.

The war drum's tempo increased. He looked back; hard up against the breastwork protecting the front of the abandoned trenches, the auxiliaries' extreme left flank was just fifty paces away; the arrows had stopped beating down on their feathered shields for the cataphracts were finally at the trot and almost upon them.

'Magnus! Hormus! Help me with these and bring the lads on the bridge with you.' He picked up two pots and held one underneath each arm; he had expected to struggle but, surprisingly, they were not too heavy.

Magnus came barrelling over with the auxiliary centurion and his eight men.

'Two each!' Vespasian shouted at the men. 'And then follow me as fast as you can. Hormus, bring burning branches from the cooking fires in the trenches.'

A mighty shout rose to the sky drowning even the pounding of the war drum; Vespasian did not need to look to know that the Parthian cavalry had collided with Mannius' cohort. It was now just a matter of time.

Vespasian led his scratch incendiary unit at a lung-burning pace back across the siege lines directly to where the uneven cataphract-versus-infantry battle abutted them. He scrambled up the edge of the final earthwork, his arms cradling the Naphtha pots, struggling for balance and dislodging loose soil that tumbled down into Magnus' face behind him. His head cleared the top of the defence and he looked along the length of Mannius' cohort's line, all the way to the city walls, a bowshot distant. And it was ragged, beset by armoured killers mounted upon beasts almost impervious to the weapons being wielded against them. With their horses pressing their huge bulk against the cohort's front rank, pushing them down and back with cracked skulls and broken limbs, the Parthian troopers used their far-reaching kontoi to stab razor-edged points down into the faces of desperate auxiliaries in the second and third ranks, preventing them from using their weight in support of their comrades before them. Screams rent the air as eyes were pierced and throats were gouged; dying men dispersed sprays and mists of blood with their final explosive breaths as the juggernaut of cataphract cavalry pushed into the Roman infantry with the ease of a voyage-weary sailor penetrating a dockside whore. Javelins, swords and knives could not halt them, but Vespasian held in his hands the only weapon that would: fire.

Kneeling, he set down one of his pots. 'Hormus! Bring the brands.'

The slave clambered up the bank with three thick sticks with red-glowing ends.

Without thinking of the dangers or whether he was doing it correctly, Vespasian proffered the Naphtha. 'Light it!'

Hormus touched the glowing end of the brand to the trailing rag; it smouldered for a moment and then flashed alight as if impregnated by some accelerant, shocking Vespasian. Panicked by the rapidity of the fuse's burning, Vespasian leapt to his feet and brought the pot, two-handed, behind his head, bending his back and legs, and then levered it forward with the pressure of his whole body unfurling behind it. The pot soared along the Parthian line to crash down onto the unarmoured rump of a front rank horse, twenty paces away, splintering into jagged shards and spilling a viscous brown liquid over the beasts and troopers close by; but it was virtually unnoticed in the chaos of battle as it did no more than that.

Vespasian dropped back to his knees. 'Shit! Nothing happened.'

Magnus stuck his fingers into the wax seal of one of his pots, breaking it. 'That should help. Hormus!'

The slave had more life in his eyes than Vespasian had ever seen before; he touched the glowing brand to the rag and, as it flared up, Magnus jumped to his feet with his right arm stretched behind him and his left arm crooked in front, balancing, and, with one fluid motion, he hurled the pot, with as straight an arm as an onager's, so that it outdistanced Vespasian's throw by a few paces. It ignited an instant before it crashed onto the helm of a second rank rider, immediately engulfing him and his mount in flame and splattering his comrades close by with sticky, burning slops. With a sudden detonation, the contents of Vespasian's pot exploded with the deathly fury of the fire god. The agonised, terri-fied shrieks of both man and beast drowned the clash of weaponry and for a few moments all conflict ceased as the combatants watched the immolating horses buck and rear, dislodging writhing riders as both were roasted alive within the metal ovens that were supposed to make them almost invulnerable.

'Centurion!' Vespasian shouted above the continuous screams. 'Now that you've seen how these things work, take your men along the rear of our line and throw as many pots at those armoured bastards as you've got.'

With a grin the veteran saluted and, grabbing a couple of the brands from Hormus, loped off with his men following to cause burning mayhem. Magnus lit his second pot and tossed it at the cataphracts nearest the earthworks who had resumed beating down the lessening resistance of the overwhelmed auxiliaries. As they too were engulfed by the fire god's wrath, howling their pain to their own uncaring deities, the Parthians closest to the two conflagrations began to disengage, unwilling to risk sharing in the skin-shrivelling, fat-sizzling, baking deaths that were being meted out seemingly from the heavens.

And then clumps of flames burst forth from the Parthian line, one by one, at irregular intervals, marking the progress of the centurion and his men along the rear of the auxiliaries. With the exception of one poorly aimed shot that was bringing a searing death to a dozen or so screaming Romans, the centurion's men had managed to lob their deadly incendiary missiles over the infantry to cause their enemy's cohesion to fracture in many places as the animal instinct to run from fire became the cataphracts' overriding motivation.

And those that could turned and fled. Some with patches of sticky fire clinging to them, adding urgency to their retreat; others with armour heated by close contact with blazing comrades and steeds; and then others, the majority, untouched by fire but not untainted by the fear of it. Within a few heartbeats the surviving cataphracts had turned their tails and were heading back towards the horse archers who, in turn, withdrew to facilitate their comrades' withdrawal.

But it was not the fleet and nimble flight of the fresh and unencumbered; quite the reverse. Despite their powerful fear, the great beasts were unable to generate much speed, having been armoured for a few hours now, plus having charged and fought. All they could muster was a lumbering walk that left their exposed rumps open to the unthrown javelins of the jeering Romans; and, as Mannius realised the opportunity was there, they were used without pity. To the bellowed, succinct commands of their centurions each century hurled their primary weapons at the slowly retreating cavalry, adding to their panic as their hindquarters were riddled with deep wounds, causing many to collapse from stress and over-exertion.

Mannius, however, was a commander of experience and he kept a tight hold on his men, forbidding them to follow up their retreating foe and, instead, held them steady as Fregallanus' cohort began to follow the baggage train across the Tigris. The extreme right of his cohort abutting the city walls had started to peel back, century by century, to follow their comrades heading for the bridge.

Vespasian, Magnus and Hormus stood on the top of the earthen embankment surveying the field in astonishment, now littered with heaps of flaming metal that flared and sizzled as the bodies encased within them gave up their fat; smears of dark smoke, stinking of burnt man- and horse-flesh, drifted between the line of auxiliaries and the beaten, retreating Parthians. The cries of the wounded were surprisingly few and mainly confined to the Roman side, for neither cavalryman nor his mount could survive the broiling temperatures of the weapon given to man by the god of fire, Apam Napat.

'That's how to do eastern bastards who like to cover themselves with cooking pots,' Magnus observed, his blood-encrusted face now blackened with the smoke's residue. 'I'd say they were well done, if you take my meaning?'

Vespasian did but was in no mood for levity. 'You seemed to know something about that stuff.'

'I might have come across it in Rome,' Magnus muttered evasively. 'You wouldn't want to know the details.'

'I'm sure. Come on, we've still got work to do.' He turned and slid back down the slope as the centurion and his eight lads returned from their inflammatory rampage. Behind them Fregallanus' cohort had begun to cross the bridge. 'That was good work, centurion; now follow me.' He scrambled out of the other side of the trench and made his way as fast as possible back to the artillery; there were still a couple of dozen Naphtha pots piled next to the onager. 'Get these onto the wagon,' he ordered, pointing at Hormus' vehicle, which remained where Magnus had abandoned it.

As Fregallanus' men cleared the bridge and Mannius' battle-weary cohort began tramping across, carrying their wounded, the wagon was loaded. Vespasian rested, watching the men whom he would have condemned to certain death make their way across to the relative safety of the northern bank of the

Tigris, relieved that he did not have to bear the responsibility of their violent demise on his conscience. He offered up a prayer to the fire god of these lands in thanks for the inspiration that he had blessed him with and also for the gift of Naphtha.

There was no sign of the Parthians returning in force as the last century of Mannius' cohort crossed the bridge with the wagon loaded with pots following close behind.

Mannius was waiting for Vespasian on the other side; he gave a tired salute. Vespasian returned it. 'Well done, prefect. I thought you would all die.'

'I know; we've all had to give those orders in our time and I sympathised with you; what else could you have done? Fortuna, however, had other ideas.'

Vespasian smiled faintly. 'There've been a few gods at work here today and we shall thank them with the appropriate sacrifices once we unite with Radamistus' army. But first I want as many of the abandoned wagons, dead animals and as much other detritus as possible piled onto the bridge; we'll cover it with the rest of the Naphtha and make a fire that will burn for a day to slow Babak down while we head north. Let's make the bastard angry enough to really want to catch us.'

CHAPTER XI

'THE KING OF Armenia runs from no man no matter what my aunt Tryphaena expects me to do.' Radamistus did not look at Vespasian as he made this pronouncement but, rather, stared straight ahead at a bust of himself posing as Hercules that was placed next to the tent's entrance. Sitting bolt upright on a weighty throne, the one concession he made to Vespasian's presence was a dismissive, languid wave of the royal right hand in his direction. He had, with ostentatious magnanimity, deigned to grant Vespasian an audience in his camp guarding the east west bridge over the Kentrites while the Romans built their camp to protect the north–south bridge across the Tigris.

'You are not the King of Armenia, Radamistus,' Vespasian reminded him, keeping his voice in check despite his growing anger. 'Not until Rome says you are. And if you want Rome to confirm you on the throne then you will do what Rome tells you to do, and Rome says that you will retreat inland.'

'Does she? I've heard Rome say otherwise.' Radamistus turned his eyes, dark as a wolf's on a moonless night, on Vespasian and stroked his beard, twisting the pointed end as if in deep thought. 'Why should I retreat from an army that has already been beaten once? I was prepared to make the strategic withdrawal that Tryphaena had advised in order to draw a stronger army inland where we could starve them to defeat; but now things have changed: I've already defeated the force they sent to hold the northern road; the rest of the Parthians can be stopped here. Rome has requested it; I heard her voice just as I've heard her say that I am king.' The sickly sweet perfume with which his tightly plaited hair, like so many black rats' tails, was liberally doused turned Vespasian's stomach and he took a step back. Radamistus misread the move. 'That's right; you should fear the King.'

'You are not king, Radamistus,' Vespasian repeated.

'I am! And I will not have some second son of a low-ranking family insult me by suggesting otherwise. Your insolence in refusing to bow your head to me was insupportable and if you carry on with your impudence I shall have that head removed.'

Vespasian wondered how Radamistus was so familiar with his background. 'Don't try to threaten me, Radamistus, especially with something that you know only too well is not within your power.'

'His Majesty is well within his rights to issue such a threat, Vespasian,' a nastily familiar voice said from behind him.

Vespasian spun round to see a hunched little man entering the tent. 'Paelignus! What are you still doing here? The Parthian army is just a mile away and there's only one river between it and you.'

The procurator smiled malevolently and then made a great show of bowing to Radamistus, further upsetting Vespasian's stomach with the sight of a Roman paying homage to an eastern upstart. 'Your Majesty.'

Radamistus acknowledged the abasement with barely a nod. 'Explain the situation to this deluded man, procurator.'

'My pleasure, Your Majesty.' Paelignus bowed again quite unnecessarily, his curved back forcing his head almost vertical, before turning to Vespasian. 'As procurator of Cappadocia, the Roman province nearest to Armenia, I have confirmed His Majesty in his position of king. I will write to the Emperor informing him of the move, which I know he will support because it's in Rome's interest to have a strong king in this kingdom that's so vital to our security in the East.'

'And what has this *king* given Rome in return, Paelignus?'

'He has pledged to drive the Parthians out of the country, which, since my victories over their infantry and then their cataphracts, will be easily achievable.'

'Your victories? I can't remember seeing you since the Parthians first appeared.'

'I command the army therefore I take the credit, remember?' Paelignus leered, baring buckled teeth. 'Tomorrow our combined armies will cross back over the Tigris and defeat Babak's severely mauled rabble in front of the gates of Tigranocerta.'

'You won't defeat Babak; most of his cataphracts survived – as you would know if you'd actually been there.'

'King Radamistus has brought two thousand Armenian and Iberian heavy horse with him as well as four thousand horse archers and half as many again on foot; with that force combined with my auxiliaries we'll be undefeatable. I will tell the Emperor of this famous victory, the third in two days, in my letter informing him of my actions concerning the Armenian throne. I fully expect him to award me an Ovation as he did Aulus Plautius for his similar service in Britannia.'

Vespasian stared at the little man in mute amazement having never been in the presence of such a delusional fantasist before – with the possible exception of Caligula on a bad day. With a knotted-browed shake of his head he turned on his heel and, without even a glance at Radamistus, strode from the tent.

'The trouble is that technically he's doing the right thing: confirming Radamistus in return for his quick action in repelling the Parthians,' Vespasian informed Magnus not long later, over a glass of wine in their own tent. 'So I can't criticise him for it without it looking suspicious.'

'So what's wrong with what he's doing?'

Vespasian sighed, feeling that he was no longer fully in control of the situation. 'Well, I suppose nothing really, apart from risking and then probably losing the lives of a good many of his auxiliaries. If he does attack Babak tomorrow he'll be badly mauled as he crosses the bridge; the Parthian horse archers will disrupt his manoeuvring and he won't have time to form up into battle order before the cataphracts hit him; as he would know if he had the slightest bit of military experience.'

'What about Radamistus?'

'What about him? He's evidently a glory-seeking idiot with as much sense as his little friend.'

Magnus contemplated the contents of his cup as he digested this. 'Sounds like it'll be a shambles.'

'It'll be a deadly shambles, but it'll produce the same result. Radamistus will fall back north with whatever remains of his army and, having garrisoned Tigranocerta and securing his supply lines, Babak will follow, making war unavoidable. I was just trying to achieve the same thing with minimum loss of life.'

Magnus drained his cup as Hormus came in with a steaming pot containing their supper. 'I hope you've got the amount of lovage in that correct this time, Hormus.'

Smiling, Hormus almost met Magnus' eye. 'I think so, Magnus.' He put the pot down on the table. 'Half a handful for every four handfuls of chickpeas and pork.'

Magnus sniffed the contents of the pot then looked approvingly at Vespasian's slave. 'That's smelling quite good, well done, son.'

Hormus' smile became even broader. 'Thank you, Magnus,' he said, going back to attend to the rest of the dinner on the cooking fire outside.

Vespasian was surprised. 'Since when has he started calling you by your name?'

'Since I told him to. He's a good lad. It turned out that the boy he's bedding is a little too inquisitive and has evidently been sent to penetrate our little circle, if you take my meanings?'

Vespasian chose to take only one of them. 'By Paelignus I would assume, seeing as he appeared when we left Melitene.'

'Yes, apparently he's boasted to Hormus of friends in high places in Cappadocia.'

'How did you find all that out?'

'By questioning Hormus about their pillow talk as we were waiting to cross the bridge this morning.'

'And?'

'And Hormus admitted that the boy was very keen on asking if he'd overheard any interesting conversations and he'd always ask with his mouth full, if you further take my meaning?'

'You should never speak with your mouth full.'

'That's what I said to Hormus and I think he was quite upset when he realised that his lover had such bad manners; so to get back at him he's agreed to slip him whatever lies we like.'

'That could be a great help.' Vespasian looked thoughtful as Hormus re-entered with a smaller pot and some flat bread.

The slave placed the rest of the dinner next to the pork and chickpea stew and then laid out plates, knives and spoons; in the absence of couches Vespasian and Magnus sat up to eat.

'What's your boy's name, Hormus?' Vespasian asked as he spooned food onto his plate.

'Mindos, master.'

'Mindos?' Vespasian broke a flat loaf in half and scooped a mouthful of the stew onto it. 'Well, tell Mindos that you overheard a conversation between me and the prefects of the five auxiliary cohorts this evening. Say you couldn't hear very well but it seemed that I was telling them that I would lead their men home to Cappadocia in the morning and leave Paelignus with Radamistus. Tell Mindos that you think that they all agreed to come.'

'Yes, master.'

Vespasian took a bite and chewed thoughtfully before swallowing. 'That really is very good, Hormus.'

'I told you I'd get him cooking to a decent standard, didn't I?' Magnus said through a mouthful. 'That was just the right amount of lovage.'

'I thought you said that you considered it ill-mannered to talk with your mouth full.'

'It depends on the meat that you're chewing on.' Magnus grinned and masticated noisily.

Vespasian nodded to the open tent flaps. 'You get off, Hormus, and give Mindos his supper; hopefully he'll be as ill-mannered as Magnus.'

Hormus looked confused as he left.

'Do you think he'll do it?' Vespasian asked.

'Of course.'

'I think you're right. He seems to have got a lot more confidence since we came out East. He could, eventually, even become useful.'

'I'd say he already is. What do you expect will happen when Paelignus hears your little lie?'

'I expect it to suddenly become the truth.'

Vespasian was woken by bucinae, not sounding the reveille but, rather, the alarm.

Jumping from his low camp bed in his tunic as Hormus came rushing into the sleeping quarters, he began buckling on his back- and breastplates as his slave dealt with his belt and sandals; with his sash of rank secured around his midriff and his sword belt slung over his shoulder he crashed through the tent, tying the chinstrap of his helmet in a secure knot, to find Magnus waiting for him eating a bowl of cold pork and chickpea stew for breakfast, seemingly unconcerned.

'What's happening?' Vespasian asked, not pausing on his way out into the night.

'Fuck knows; jumpy sentries?'

The Roman camp to the untrained eye would have looked like chaos, but as Vespasian glanced around the torch-washed lines of tents he saw only the orderly assembling of the almost four thousand soldiers of the five auxiliary cohorts as each man made his way to his muster station, having dressed in double-quick time. Bucinae carried on unnecessarily blaring out the alarm as centurions and optiones bellowed at their men to form up on their standard-bearers; slaves scuttled about lighting more torches so that soon the square half-mile encompassed by a wooden palisade was ablaze with flickering light. By the time that Vespasian and Magnus arrived at the *praetorium*, the command post at the centre of the camp, they could see that most centuries in the two cohorts forming up along the Via Praetoria were at full strength with only the final few laggards being beaten into place by the vine sticks of their centurions. Whether the Armenian and Iberian troops in their camp just to the east of the Romans' were in the same state of readiness he did not know, although he hoped that, for their own sake, they were, as Radamistus had eschewed building a stockaded camp on the basis that the King of Armenia hides from no man.

And then, just as he was about to enter the praetorium, above the roars of the officers and the shrill notes of the horns came an even shriller sound; a sound that Vespasian recognised immediately and he knew with certainty that Hormus' loyalty was absolute.

'Don't you try and deny it, you traitors! You renegades! Deserters! Cowards! You're relieved of your commands. Guards, seize them and then bring Titus Flavius Vespasianus before me in chains!' Paelignus panted, his protruding eyes bulging more than usual; he stared at each of his auxiliary prefects in turn as Vespasian walked into the tent leaving Magnus to wait outside. The soldiers on guard had made no move to obey Paelignus' screeched order.

'I heard that you were asking to see me, procurator,' Vespasian said, as if Paelignus' demand had been the most polite and well mannered of invitations.

Paelignus glared at Vespasian, his eyes bulging even more, his chest heaving and his tongue hanging out like a dog's, as he drew a series of quick, ragged breaths. 'Seize him!' he eventually managed to ejaculate, his throat evidently constricted with rage. A trembling, hooked finger was levelled at Vespasian to help the guards identify the miscreant deserving of arrest. Once again they did nothing. 'Seize him! I order you!'

'Whatever is the matter, procurator?' Vespasian asked in the tone of one trying to ascertain the cause of a recalcitrant child's unruly behaviour.

'You've been plotting behind my back, all of you; now that I've relieved you of your commands I shall have you all executed.'

'Will you? Perhaps you would like to tell us why you feel such an extreme move to be necessary?'

'You're going to take my soldiers away.'

'Who told you that?'

'I know; you had a meeting in your tent earlier this evening, Vespasian. The prefects agreed to follow you back to Cappadocia and desert me, your rightful commander.'

Vespasian looked at the prefects, who all seemed equally as puzzled by the ravings of their slavering procurator as he was. 'Do any of you recall such a meeting, gentlemen?'

Fregallanus looked at Paelignus in disgust. 'I don't recall such a meeting, Paelignus, because there wasn't one. We are men of honour and would consider conspiring against our commander, whatever we may think of him, as a conspiracy against the Emperor himself.'

Mannius spat on the ground. 'If there had been such a meeting I would not have agreed to disobey your orders and take my cohort back to Cappadocia, despite my personal feelings about your military ability and even though you were planning to risk all our lives in the morning in an ill-advised attack. But now? I resent being called a coward by a man who I didn't see once on the wall whilst we were under attack yesterday. I have never served under a man who is so unfit to command; a man who, given a choice, will invariably make the wrong decision. You have relieved us all of our commands, runt; now we reinstate ourselves. Guards, seize him!'

This time the men responded to the order and strode forward.

Paelignus yelped and darted away from the desk. Vespasian watched in fascinated disbelief, as the little man ducked and dived, dodged and weaved around the tent while the two guards attempted to apprehend him as if it were a chase in a theatrical comedy; despite his abnormality he was as quick as a lithe rodent and soon outsmarted his pursuers and nipped out of the tent.

'Let him go!' Vespasian ordered the two embarrassed guards; he turned to the prefects. 'He'll no doubt run to Radamistus.'

'That arrogant piece of eastern shit is welcome to him,' Cotta said, speaking for all present judging by the murmurs of agreement. 'So what do we do now?'

The question was directed at his fellow prefects but it was to Vespasian that they all looked for an answer.

'It seems that you have a choice between withdrawing to Cappadocia or withdrawing north into Armenia with Radamistus; unless, of course, you would rather fight a battle here that you can't win.'

Mannius asked the question that they were all wondering about: 'So why did we come in the first place? You can't possibly hold a country like Armenia with five auxiliary cohorts.'

Vespasian shrugged. 'You'll have to ask Paelignus that; it was his idea. I just came along to offer suggestions if they were needed.' It was not a nice lie but a convincing one in the light of the procurator's behaviour. However, now that the auxiliary cohorts had served their purpose he was anxious that they should return to their bases without further loss of life. 'Personally, I think that you're well out of it now that your former commander has revealed himself to be an unstable imbecile. If you're going to have to withdraw in the face of a superior force, then, rather than go north into unknown territory, I would return home and send a message to the Governor of Syria and hope that he comes with one or two of his legions to help remove the Parthians.'

As the prefects began to talk amongst themselves, discussing their options, the bucinae began a fresh bout of blaring; again it was the alarm. Vespasian headed out of the tent with the prefects following. 'What is it, Magnus?'

'I've no idea, sir; but if it really is trouble it's just as well that the lads are all up and dressed and standing in those lovely ranks and files that the centurions are so keen on.'

Vespasian looked up and down the Via Praetoria, lined with soldiery, no doubt all wondering, as he was, what was going on. A horseman appeared galloping fast completely against the standing orders in any camp; in fact, riding horses in a camp was frowned upon as unlucky.

'Where's the procurator?' the man shouted as he pulled his mount up to a skidding halt.

'Disappeared,' Vespasian said. 'What's the alarm for?'

'The Parthians have surprised the garrison on the bridge. They're now in control of it and are crossing in force.'

'That's impossible, there was half a cohort guarding it.'

'Not our bridge, sir; the other one guarded by the Armenians. They made the broken bridge passable again and crossed the river to come behind Radamistus' army.'

Vespasian struggled to contain the shock on his face and looked at the assembled prefects. 'Well, gentlemen, I suggest that you deploy a holding force to the east, in case the Parthians break through Radamistus, to protect us whilst we strike camp as quickly as possible. It looks like the decision has been made for you; the route north is now blocked.'

Vespasian pushed his horse as fast as he dared in the growing dawn half-light; ahead, Radamistus' unfortified encampment was in uproar, drowning out the sound of the auxiliaries striking their camp and the horns of the cohort deploying as a screen. But although there were hundreds or thousands of raised voices, as yet he had not heard the clash of arms or the screams of the maimed and the dying.

He was unchallenged as he passed through the perimeter of the Armenian camp, which was a mess of cavalrymen mounting and forming up without any clear sense of order. He negotiated his way through the chaos as fast as possible without causing injury to one of the many who seemed to be running about in circles for no good reason other than just to be seen to be doing something. He eventually came to Radamistus' tent to find the King, resplendent in the tall crown of Armenia and a tunic of scale armour, stepping into a ceremonial four-horse chariot.

'What are you doing, Radamistus?' Vespasian shouted, pulling up next to the usurper.

Radamistus ignored the question as his mounted guards closed around him pushing Vespasian away. Then Radamistus paused for a moment and looked at Vespasian, frowning as if in thought; he called out in his own language into the shadows and received a reply that sounded affirmative to Vespasian. The chariot's driver cracked his whip over the team's withers and the vehicle moved off, surrounded by bodyguards, towards the bridge that Radamistus' army had been supposed to hold.

'The King is going to negotiate,' Paelignus said, stepping from the shadows leading a horse and accompanied by half a dozen royal bodyguards. 'Now that my men have deserted me we only have half the numbers that we thought we had and we're surrounded.'

Vespasian looked down at the procurator. 'What's he going to do? Surrender?'

Paelignus scoffed. 'The King of Armenia surrenders to no man; he'll fight if necessary.'

'He's not the King.'

'He is; you may have noticed that crown he was wearing on his head. I placed it there in Rome's name just now to confirm him in his position. That'll give him authority in his negotiations with the barbarians.'

'You little idiot. He needs to earn that from us, not be given it without conditions attached.'

One of Paelignus' guards knitted his hands; the procurator stepped on them and struggled up into the saddle in an ungainly manner. He looked at Vespasian as his guards mounted. 'Come and join me to see the result of the negotiations; in fact, Radamistus has asked that you should come. I think you'll be impressed by the wording of his oath of loyalty to Parthia. Of course, the King of Armenia is under no compunction to keep his oath to a man as lowly as the satrap of Nineveh. Parthia will retire, Radamistus will renounce the oath and stay on the throne with a crown presented by Rome, and I will have scored the greatest diplomatic and military victory since Augustus negoti-ated the return of the Eagles lost by Crassus at Carrhae. I look forward to being amply rewarded by a grateful emperor.'

'Parthia will never tolerate the breaking of that oath; they'll be back within a month of Radamistus repudiating it,' Vespasian replied and turned his horse, happy in the knowledge that if Radamistus were to swear loyalty to Parthia and break the oath then war would be unavoidable and his mission complete. 'But no thank you; I won't join you despite Radamistus' kind invita-tion. I'm going back to Cappadocia; I've seen enough of how things are done in the East.'

'Oh, but you haven't, Vespasian; there's one more thing that you should see.' Paelignus pulled his gaunt face into what was meant to be a pleasant smile but looked to Vespasian as if he was in an advanced stage of rigor mortis. 'It wasn't an invitation from the King to come with me.' He signalled to his guards. 'It was an order.'

Six spear heads immediately pointed at him; he was surrounded.

'Take his sword,' Paelignus ordered, riding off after Radamistus, 'and tie his hands.'

*

Vespasian sat on his mount, his wrists bound tight and then secured to the horns of his saddle so that he had no possibility of riding off. Paelignus took regular gloating, sidelong glances at him as if he were anticipating a sweet moment. Ten paces ahead of them, Radamistus stood in his chariot, facing Babak, having a long conversation which had been punctuated with many polite gestures, in what Vespasian assumed was very flowery language as each sentence in the unintelligible tongue seemed to go on for an age. Although Paelignus too had no idea of what was being discussed, Vespasian saw him nodding in agreement occasionally and then noticed that the bodyguard to his other side was whispering a translation into his ear. Behind him the Armenian army had formed up for battle, while behind Babak a small force of dismounted Parthian cavalry held the bridge. They were not enough to attack and defeat the Armenian host but were certainly enough to impede their passage.

Vespasian felt confident that Babak would cede to Radamistus' terms and let him pass so that he could head north. Babak would remain in Tigranocerta until news of Radamistus' treachery travelled down to him; then he would lead his army into the heart of Armenia and Tryphaena would have her war.

The negotiations seemed to be coming to some conclusion; Vespasian pulled on his bindings. 'Untie me, Paelignus.'

'You'll be released soon enough.'

As the procurator finished speaking, Radamistus turned around and signalled to the guard holding Vespasian's horse's reins; he led the beast forward. However, he did not stop when he was level with his master, but, rather, carried on to Babak who signalled to one of his entourage to take the reins.

'What's the meaning of this?' Vespasian demanded.

Babak signalled to his men on the bridge who began pulling back to let the Armenian army cross.

As he crossed the bridge with Babak at his side, Vespasian repeated the question.

'It's custom to conclude business with a surety in my country,' Babak informed him. 'And you are just such a thing. If Radamistus breaks his word and Rome sends her armies in to support him, then, until they are removed, you will spend the rest of your life in the darkest dungeon in Adiabene.'

'But you know that he'll break his word.'

'Do I? He swore on Ahura Mazda; for him there is no more powerful a god.'

'But he swore to you and he considers you to be too far below him in status to be able to hold him to his oath.'

Babak bridled at the implied insult. 'Then it would seem that things are not going to go well for you as a hostage of Parthia.'

PART III

✿ ✿

THE PARTHIAN EMPIRE, AD 52

CHAPTER XII

'WHAT WOULD YOU recommend that I do with him, Ananias?'

Vespasian knelt on the floor with his hands tied behind his back. The iron tang of blood filled his battered mouth; blood dripped onto the marble from a cut above his swollen, closed right eye. His tormentor, a massively muscled, bearded mute, wearing only a loincloth, stood before him, massaging his knuckles, raw from the beating he had just administered.

'He seems to turn the other cheek.'

If it would not have hurt so much, Vespasian would have smiled at this description of the way he had dealt with the punishment that had been meted out to him. He looked up at the speaker; he was seated on a wooden throne with gold and silver inlays of strangely foreign animalistic design. In his early fifties, with a long grey beard, his hair wrapped in a white cloth head-dress wound around his head, and with a black and white patterned mantle over his shoulders, he did not look as if he was the King of Adiabene. Yet he was; and more than that, as Vespasian now knew only too well, he was a Jewish convert. But it was not to the mainstream religion that the King adhered, but rather to the new cult promoted by Paulus' rivals in Jerusalem.

'King Izates, our master Yeshua,' the man named Ananias replied, 'did indeed preach that to be righteous we should turn the other cheek; but this man is not a Jew and Yeshua's teachings apply only to Jews, not Gentile dogs like this faithless scum.' Ananias consulted a scroll, his rheumy eyes squinting and his age-spotted hands shaking as they unfurled the parchment. 'I have a record of much of what he said here, left by his disciple, Thomas, on his way to preach to the Jews and god-fearers of the East; and it is clear that the Righteous are only those who fear God, whether as full Jews or as god-fearers who adhere to much of the religion. This man, Vespasian, cannot be one of the Righteous.'

'Very well, if you say so.' King Izates studied Vespasian for a few moments before turning to a woman sitting on a lesser throne next to his own. 'Tell me, with the heart of a woman, Symacho, my love: what would you do with this hostage to the honour of Radamistus, King of Armenia? Now that that Iberian liar has foresworn his oath of loyalty to my master, the Great King Vologases, the first of that name, and also now that Ummidius Quadratus, the Governor of Roman Syria, has sent a legion into Armenia, this man's life should be forfeit.' He pointed at Vespasian. 'And yet Babak told him that he would only be cast into the deepest dungeon for the rest of his life should the treaty be broken.'

'Then do that, my King.' She looked at Vespasian and smiled. In the two months that he had been held hostage in Arbela, the royal capital of Adiabene, Vespasian had shared many meals with the royal couple and had found the ageing Queen's company far more entertaining than that of her religion-obsessed husband or any of his twenty-four children from sundry wives. Izates showed all the tunnel-visioned fanaticism of a convert, always pontificating about his new religion and trying to apply it in all aspects of his rule, much to the obvious displeasure, Vespasian had noticed, of a fair number of his courtiers who clung, like Babak, to the old gods of Assyria. Symacho, on the other hand, did not flaunt her new beliefs and consequently was far more relaxed and convivial because of it. Vespasian almost forgave her for encouraging her husband to incarcerate him for the rest of his life; he would have preferred a quick death.

Another blow to the head stunned him momentarily; Izates had evidently ordered the beating to continue while he contemplated the issue from a religious angle.

This was a situation far removed from what he had encountered upon his arrival in Arbela; then he had been not exactly welcomed, but treated with a reasonable amount of courtesy.

'I'm pleased that the Lord has sent you to me,' Izates had said to him on the day of Vespasian's arrival.

They were standing on the immense battlements that crowned the oval hill of four hundred and fifty by three hundred and fifty paces upon which Arbela stood and had been standing for over six thousand years. The hill rose steeply, one hundred feet on all sides, to an almost flat top so that it stood like a huge base waiting for a mighty column to be raised upon it by the gods; a column that would reach the heavens and prop up the sky.

For longer than memory Arbela had dominated the Assyrian plain that stretched out in all directions, irrigated and fertile, a farmland that had given power to the ancient Assyrian Kings before they had been subjugated by first the Medes and then the Persians and then by Alexander. His victory over Darius III at Guagamela, just eighty miles away, had heralded almost three hundred years of Hellenic rule during which time Adiabene had managed to become an autonomous kingdom. Now this city, one of the oldest on earth, was subject to Parthia and it was over Parthia that Vespasian had been gazing, only half-listening to his royal host who seemed to have very little conversation other than theological.

'He has presented me with a way to solve a problem,' Izates had carried on.

'If I can be of service then I'd be only too pleased,' Vespasian had replied absently. He had been led to think that his status was somewhat more than a hostage by the way that he had been greeted after his month-long journey south with the main force of Babak's army. He had not been confined nor had he been guarded and the King had invited him on a tour of the battlements. Very soon he had bored Vespasian rigid with his talk of the Jewish god and rambling on about the prophet he had sent to save the Jews and those who feared their god by freeing them from the priests and all vestiges of human control on the most pure of religions – or something like that. Vespasian had not quite got to grips with the detail.

'You can, Vespasian, by God's grace you can.'

'How?'

'Do you think that Radamistus will keep his word? After all, he swore his oath by Ahura Mazda who obviously does not exist.'

Vespasian had carried on gazing at the vastness of the Parthian Empire. 'What makes you say that?'

'There is only one god, so it follows that the rest do not exist.'

'I've seen gods manifest. I've seen the goddess Sulis and the god Heylel take over the bodies of the dead and live.'

'Heylel? He who was cast from God's grace for his arrogance? He was not a god but an angel.'

Vespasian had been bored by this continual theological discussion to which the King was subjecting him. 'It's the same thing: a supernatural being that has more power than a human obviously demands worship. Call Heylel what you like but I call him a god and I should know because I met him.'

Izates had tutted and smiled benevolently as would a patient grammaticus at a talented but sadly misguided pupil.

Vespasian had ignored the patronising gesture, aware that he had probably been a little sharper in his remarks than was good for a hostage; he tempered his voice. 'The point is that Radamistus has no intention whatsoever of keeping his oath. It's not about whether he believes in Ahura Mazda or not; it's because he feels that the King of Armenia isn't beholden to any agreement reached with a mere satrap of Nineveh.'

'Ah! So we agree on what Radamistus will do?'

'Yes, but not why he'll do it.' He had bitten his lip, striving to keep control of his growing annoyance.

'So my lord has given me a way to show the world how righteous I am, a way to show the nobles like Babak who cling to the old gods of Assyria that I can be merciful but strong in my religion. By him giving you to me I can show my nobles that they should stop plotting against me and join me in the worship of the one true god and his prophet Yeshua.'

Vespasian was now all attention; he did not like the direction that the conversation had just taken. 'How can you do that with me?' His voice was low and the words slow as he had looked into the King's eyes, which shone with the happiness of an innocent child.

'When Radamistus breaks his word your life is forfeit. I can make a public show of my displeasure and devise some very nasty and long way to have you executed and then halfway through I can offer you mercy if you receive baptism into the faith. Which of course you'll accept because, after all, who wouldn't? When my nobles hear about that, they will be flocking to the river for submersion in Yeshua's name. You see? Simple.'

Vespasian gawped at the King, realising that the royal grip on reality was not as firm as it could be. 'I am a proconsul of Rome; you can't threaten me with execution and then try and force me to repudiate the religion of my ancestors without causing a serious incident.'

Izates slapped Vespasian on the shoulder genially. 'Nonsense, Vespasian; when Radamistus reneges on his oath I can do what I like with you.'

'Babak told me that when that happens I'll be thrown into a dungeon and kept there until Rome withdraws.'

Izates looked startled. 'He said that?'

'Yes.'

'He didn't say that you would be executed?'

'No.'

'But that's terrible.'

'Is it?'

'Of course it is. If he told you that you would live then live you must; God would never approve of me making a point to my nobles based on dishonour. And the nobles in turn would point to me not keeping a promise like a follower of Assur, the old god of Assyria, who claims to continue to fight for *kettu*, the Truth. They would say that the one true god represents *hitu*, the False. That's most aggrieving, terrible; he really did say that you would live?'

By now Vespasian's mouth gaped open in astonishment. 'Yes, I'm afraid he did.'

Izates rested his hand on Vespasian's shoulder and gave him an understanding look. 'Don't apologise, it's not your fault. Nothing *you* can do about it. How aggravating, most vexing, provoking in the extreme.' He went off muttering to himself, leaving Vespasian looking after him, dumbstruck by his behaviour. A searing pain struck Vespasian and white light flashed across his inner vision; he felt himself slump down to the floor and hoped he would be allowed to stay there while the clearly bewildered King wrestled internally with what he could do to make Vespasian's predicament spurious proof of some sort of bond with his god and tempt his courtiers away from Assur. He was disappointed; keeping his eyes shut, he felt himself being hauled up for a rapid series of blows to his stomach and ribs, knocking the wind from him. His knees collapsed again and as he fell he was vaguely aware of the King's voice shouting. The beating stopped and Vespasian was left to contemplate his growing pain from cracked ribs and a bruised and swollen face.

'I will gain nothing in the sight of God by giving him the choice between a prison cell and baptism,' Izates announced. 'How can I give him his life if I'm not going to take it? What will the nobles who refuse to join me in the one true faith think? They will not see magnanimity on my part nor will they see the power of God's love but, rather, my own weakness as well as the desperation of a man who would do anything to regain his freedom. Take him away and send a message to the Emperor Claudius that Titus Flavius Vespasianus will stay excluded from the world until the lying usurper Radamistus is removed from the Armenian throne and Ummidius Quadratus, the Governor of Roman Syria, recalls his legions from that land. Until that happens he shall stay locked away and an Adiabene army will defend the Great King of Parthia's honour against Roman aggression; there will be war in Armenia.'

So Tryphaena finally has her wish, Vespasian thought, as he was dragged away across the smooth marble floor, and she will not press for peace to save him even if she did have the power to do so. He could well imagine that nobody in Rome would care much about his situation: Agrippina would revel in it as a by-product of securing her son on the imperial throne; Pallas would do nothing to jeopardise that succession; and Narcissus would most probably not spot the subtle danger of a Parthian war to his position until it was too late and Nero was emperor and he was executed.

No, Vespasian found himself thinking, calmly, I am going to be here for some time; I can't expect to be rescued so therefore don't hope for it and I won't be disappointed. Hope for nothing because from hopes dashed comes despair.

And, as his gaolers dragged him down into the foundations of the ancient capital of Adiabene, deep into dark places excavated millennia before, deep into a realm where time has a different meaning, Vespasian fell back into his mind so that his thoughts and memories would cocoon him. Deep in the bowels of Arbela, Vespasian was locked into a cell that had seen countless years of suffering; a place where rats and nameless things held sway and time did nothing but gnaw. A realm of despair; and despair was the emotion that Vespasian knew he must protect himself from.

There was little point in keeping his eyes open as there was rarely any light to see by. Every so often Vespasian heard a grating of a key in a lock and then the creak and crash of a heavy door opening and closing that would presage the arrival of the golden glow of a black-smoking torch held aloft by a gaoler to guide him and his mate down slime-slick steps. Vespasian knew this because he had a grille in his door and could see at an oblique angle along the narrow corridor. How often the gaolers visited, he did not know; it might have been twice a day, once a day or once every few days. It made no difference because he had lost the concept of days, nights, hours or months. In the depths of Arbela there was only a moment and that moment was now.

The arrival of the gaolers would bring not only light but also sound. Low moans or cries for forgiveness, groans of pain or just plain mad gibbering always accompanied the gaolers' progress down the corridor, attesting to what sort of condition the inmate, behind each of the many locked doors punctuating it, was in. Vespasian, however, never made a sound, not even when the grille in his door was unbolted and swung open. He knew the routine after the first couple of visits and thereafter did not need to communicate. He passed his refuse bowl out and its contents were slopped into the open sewer that ran the length of the corridor to drain away who knew where. The bowl was returned, unsluiced and stinking. He then had to pass two of his other three possessions through the grille in turn: the first, a wooden jug, was returned filled with water that, by its taste, Vespasian knew would have been far from clear had he troubled to examine it. Second was his wooden food bowl, which came back containing a gruel of grains with the occasional morsel of gristle or bone floating in it. A stale loaf was then chucked through the grille as it was closed. With his sustenance safely grasped in each hand he would retire to his only other possession: a blanket that contained more life than the matted hair that clung to his groin, chest, face and head. Every so often some damp straw would be shoved through the hole to supplement the rotting heap upon which his fourth possession rested, but that was the only difference in the routine; he had no way of telling but he assumed that the straw arrived once a month as the second delivery was long enough after the first one for him to be surprised, having forgotten about it. He was unclear but he thought that he could remember at least a few more such deliveries; but what did it matter? What was sure was that even in this subterranean pit shielded from the sun by so much ancient stone it had got colder and Vespasian guessed that winter was approaching outside – if outside still existed.

And that was just one of the many things with which he kept his mind busy at the slowest pace possible. It was not thoughts of escape or life after release that preoccupied him, but memories of life enjoyed and abstract questions to which there could be no answer or a multitude of answers. Slowly he dipped small hunks of bread into the gruel, stirring them with infinite care in the chasm-dark as he replayed scenes from his life, chewing his food methodically and at the speed of some drugged bovine; his expression, if it could have been seen, changing in accordance with the mood of each episode. Wincing, he recalled at great length the hideous bullying and beating that Sabinus had subjected him to as a child. A tender smile as he remembered the loving tutelage of his paternal grandmother, Tertulla, the woman who had raised him on her estate in Cosa, while his parents had been in Asia for seven years. Regret while the decline of his friend Caligula from a vibrant youth to crazed despot flickered in degenerating episodes across his inner eye. As his three children flashed through his mind he felt growing pride that culminated with Titus' face, so much like his own, smiling at him, only to be dashed as Flavia appeared to make another demand. Contentment came in pulses as his passion for Caenis fired within him, although he was aware that he had to ration those thoughts as he sensed that masturbation in these circumstances could become addictive and sap what little strength remained to him.

However, he could review without ardour the lessons he had learnt from Caenis in her privileged position at the heart of imperial politics. As secretary to the Lady Antonia, his benefactress before her disappointment with her grandson Caligula had led her to take her own life, Caenis had acquired the political skill to negotiate her way adroitly through the tangle of self-interest that prevailed within the ruling élite. She understood the importance of attaching oneself to one faction without distancing others. With her it was never personal, only business, and thus she had retained a position of influence after she had been freed in Antonia's will. She had survived the remainder of Caligula's reign and the turmoil following his assassination and Claudius' elevation. During the subsequent years her ability to remain of use to both Pallas and Narcissus had enabled her to ride the infighting between them and, as secretary to first Narcissus and then Pallas, she had made a fortune by selling access to them; no one got to the seat of power other than through her. Vespasian might have smiled in the darkness as he remembered the shock that he felt when Caenis told him how she used her position to enrich herself; he might then have laughed as he recounted the ways that he had put that lesson to use since. Money was all important to him and through Caenis he had learnt how ... the light again; how long had it been since the last visit that he remembered?

This time there were more of them; how many he did not bother to count. Screams raged in one of the cells as his grille was opened. He went through the routine of the bowls and jug and was vaguely aware of a loud, wet thump as if a butcher's cleaver had rent a joint. The wail and then piercing shrieks that followed it did a little more to impinge on his consciousness; the smell of burning flesh that accompanied them he barely noticed as he focused on the straw being thrust through the grille. So more time had passed in the world outside … if it still existed, that was.

He refrained from burying his face in the straw because, although it was damp and old it was the freshest thing he could smell and reminded him of … no, he would not make that mistake again. The last and only time he had, despair had smiled at him, cold and grim, a false friend looming above him in his void of a cell, and he had felt the tears rise that, had they not been checked, would have driven him into the grasping arms of that fraud.

He stirred the gruel to soften the bread; the shrieks had subsided into mournful groans but seemed now to be coming from the other end of the corridor, Vespasian noticed dully. He took a bite and chewed with deliberation. A different inmate in a different cell? A different moment, perhaps? Possibly, for the last delivery of straw seemed distant; but it was certainly not a different place as it was still dark and the gruel still tasted the same. But the air did feel warmer as if there was heat in the world outside … if that still existed.

He nodded slowly to himself as he remembered that when the gruel had arrived he had been contemplating his uncle's reaction to his wild theory concerning what had been predicted for him. He was aware that this was not the first time since he had been confined to this moment that he had been over that conversation and had mulled through the meaning of every sign, portent or auspicious happening concerned with what once may have been his destiny. That word meant nothing; where was destiny in a single moment? What room could there be for it? He was almost sure that when he had thought about these things during another part of this moment that he inhabited he had put all the clues together, but then he had discarded the conclusion because it had meant reaching forward; and that he would and could not do. But the memory of his uncle being unable to finish his sentences, to say 'emperor' or 'purple', because he felt the words would automatically make him too conspicuous, even though no one could hear them, pleased him as he stirred his gruel and took bites of bread without haste, immersed in thought.

And thought threaded through his mind as his only sensation until, with a shock, he was tapped on the right shoulder. He opened his eyes and stared ahead, unseeing in the gloom, mystified as to how such contact could have come about. Then there it was again; but this time it was a double tap. He turned his head slowly but saw nothing; instead, he heard a distant sound, a sound that seemed to come from the world outside ... if it really was still there. Then it died away, as if it had never been. But it had forced Vespasian to listen, to be aware of the world, to climb out from his inner tranquillity. He tensed in the dark, feeling a strange calmness as in the moments just before a storm breaking. Then he was tapped again but this time he realised that it was him doing the tapping: his right shoulder was knocking against the wall and it was knocking against the wall because the ground was moving. The sound from beyond rose again but this time it did not recede but grew, and it grew commensurately with the shaking of the earth until his senses were filled with only sound and movement. And then things started to clatter down from above, crashing onto the stone floor all around him, but he remained squatting where he was, squatting on his blanket on its pile of rancid straw; squatting where he always squatted as cries came from the cells down the corridor and the whole world shook with the anger of the gods below as they bellowed their wrath.

The stillness was abrupt and for a moment all was quiet, even the wails of despair from the other cells. But the lull did not last for long and the next sound surprised Vespasian: it was a shout of exhilaration, a shout from close by. And then he remembered the story that Sabinus had told him, the one about the earthquake tumbling down the gates of the prison in which Paulus of Tarsus had been incarcerated, and he wondered vaguely if his guardian god, Mars, had come to his aid in the same way that it had been said that Paulus' god had come to his. With that thought he looked around and saw a sight that he had not seen since he had been placed in the moment in which he lived: he saw a dark grey rectangle in the otherwise Stygian black, he saw the dim outline of an open door. He stared at it incredulously until he was able to form a prayer in his head to Mars for his deliverance.

Vespasian got to his unsteady feet and, with his hands outstretched before him, moved towards what to him seemed like a beacon of light. Through the doorway he went, stepping over the fallen door, and out into the corridor in which a few dim figures scampered towards the steps at the far end. The shouts of those not fortunate enough to have had their confinement ended by the earthquake were ignored by the lucky few fleeing up the steps and on through the broken door at the top and out into the dark beyond.

Vespasian shuffled as fast as he could down a dark, debris-strewn corridor, not knowing in which direction the outside world lay but aware where he had come from and wary of returning there.

Dust stung his eyes and fallen masonry threatened his ankles but the earth's convulsions had stilled and he felt a glimmer of hope, a thing that he had denied himself for so long, grow within him and he dared to think beyond the moment. He dared to think of escape.

Suspecting that his fellow escapees had as little knowledge of the subterranean geography of Arbela as he, he decided not to follow them up a narrow spiral staircase and, instead, to use his own instincts. On he went turning left and then right, using his nose as a guide, sniffing for the cleaner air, always taking flights of steps up if they presented themselves and were not blocked.

And then there was other life, other people and Vespasian realised that he must avoid them for he was vaguely aware that his appearance and stench would mark him for what he was. He pressed on with caution, ensuring that he never got too close to anyone, through what was evidently chaos in the aftermath of a massive shock, all the time heading up towards lighter, sweeter-smelling levels.

With gut-wrenching realisation as he strained weakened muscles pulling at a door-ring there was, suddenly, nowhere to go; suddenly he was trapped. The corridor ended in a locked door and he had no key; he began to panic, he had allowed himself to think of escape and now he was trapped. He knew that he must calm himself; it was only one locked door. He must think, yes, think; and it was obvious: he must turn around. And so he began to retrace his steps to find another corridor that did not have a locked door at its end. Now he seemed to be going against the tide of people but he did not care for he knew that he was going away from the locked door and they were going towards it. He took another left turn and shuffled along a passage in which a guttering torch burned; he passed through its glow, shielding his eyes as he did, and then on to the end to meet only with another door: it too was locked. Panic welled ever higher within him and he turned and began to jog back through the torch's glow, back the way he had come. He tried to think but he could not; every thought he had seemed to end in a locked door. He tried another and then another; all seemed to be locked. He became increasingly frantic as he dashed from door to door up and down corridors that all seemed familiar and then, as the shout of 'There he is!' pierced his panic, followed moments later by a fist flying towards him, he realised that they were, indeed, all familiar because they were all one of the same two corridors.

Vespasian opened his eyes unsure of whether he had just been addressed as 'proconsul' or whether it had been a dream.

He was lying face down on a marble floor.

'Proconsul?'

There it was again and it seemed to be real enough. He looked up, squinting against the light.

'Ah, proconsul, you are back with us.'

Vespasian focused slowly and the architect of his torment, King Izates, materialised, smiling cheerfully despite the fallen columns around him.

'This is a most fortuitous occurrence,' the King carried on, beaming happily around the heavily damaged room. 'I expect that you thought the earthquake was a part of your supposed gods' plan to free you?'

Vespasian had but he was not about to admit as such to this man; he did not want his first conversation for however long to be a religious discussion. So he did not respond.

'But you didn't escape, did you? According to the gaoler he found you running backwards and forwards up and down two corridors. But the one true God does have the power to help those who worship him and follow his laws. Tell him, Ananias, tell him of Paulus, the man you baptised in Damascus.'

A man appeared in the corner of Vespasian's vision; he groaned as Ananias started to tell the same story that Sabinus had told about the earthquake breaking open Paulus' gaol, but with much embellishment and exaggeration. Vespasian was in no mood for it.

'So you see, proconsul,' Izates said with annoying cheerfulness once the tale was over, 'just how fortuitous this earthquake has been for you and for me. All you have to do is accept baptism into the Way of Yeshua and I can say to my nobles that God sent this earthquake to spring you from the deepest dungeon in order that you could follow him. Just think of it: my nobles would flock to the baptismal river if they knew that they could have a power like that on their side. And you would be free, free to live here as a permanent witness to the power of the one true God and his son, Yeshua. Free, proconsul, free and saved.'

Vespasian closed his eyes; he wanted none of the bewildered old King's freedom at the price of rejecting Mars. If Mars indeed had a destiny for him then it would be Mars who eventually would lead him to it, not some jealous god who would brook no other and insisted on men mutilating their penises. He heard the King shouting at him but took no notice as he slipped back into his tranquillity that had been so disturbed by the anger of the gods below. Soon he felt himself being dragged away and he knew with certainty what he would see when he next opened his eyes: it would be the same thing that he always saw in the moment.

And it was so as the hammering on the door to his cell, fixing it back into place, disturbed his peace and forced him to open his eyes. He was back in the moment; his brief surge of hope dashed. He pushed away the offer of consolation from despair, the would-be companion who had been locked out of his cell with the repairing of the door, left in the corridor to whisper through the grille. Back he went to his blanket and his gruel, forbidding all images of his brief foray into the outer world; more and more he played scenes from the past with his inner eye, chewing slowly on his bread and sucking on bones, occasionally nodding in the dark when certain images pleased him.

Straw came, then more straw came and then, perhaps, more straw had come. The last grains of his gruel were lapped up by his tongue as it methodically pursued them around the bottom of his food bowl. Satisfied with his accomplishment of so far ingesting every morsel of nourishment from his meal he began to suck on the bone that he had saved for last. His children again – or was it for the first time? – paraded before his closed eyes. He had planned to do something that may well endanger Titus, he was sure; it had been to do with Tryphaena. Yes, it was Nero; somehow he was helping Nero's cause, that's why he was here. Yes, that was it. It was because of Titus' friendship with Britannicus that he would be in danger if ... but he was sure that he had thought of the way to protect him before he had embarked on the road that led to this moment.

The light again.

But he had not quite finished.

He opened his eyes and placed the inedible remnants of the bone onto a heap of similar fragments in the corner, now just visible in the dim but growing light of the approaching torch; he noted with half-felt curiosity that it was quite big. Had the pile always been like that? No, it could not have been; it must have grown and he must have fed it with other bones.

He stared at the pile; so many bones.

A wave of panic hit him.

How many?

He did not want to count.

He felt his chest tighten as he stared at the physical evidence of the length of this one moment. He lashed out at the pile with both hands, smashing it apart, spreading the bones all across the floor of the cell; scattering them amongst the muck so that they could not be counted.

He needed to breathe; he tried to inhale but could not.

And then he heard himself: he was screaming.

It was uncontrolled and from his very core; from deep within a consciousness that had been buried deep within the deepest bowels of the first foundations made by man. It was fuelled by the millennia of misery that shrouded this pit and sucked what life was left in the barely living incarcerated within it.

It was raw.

But it was also fed by shouts from outside his cell; shouts of anger. The gaoler was shouting at him and he was screaming back. He had not had communication with anyone in the whole moment that he had been in this darkness; in the time that it had taken that pile of bones to appear. No one had spoken to him since Izates and even then he had not responded because he had shut the world off to preserve his peace. But now he was being shouted at and now he was screaming back. Now he was having a conversation, he was interacting with another human being, he was screaming and the gaoler was shouting at him for doing so: the gaoler was acknowledging his existence.

So Vespasian screamed some more.

And as he screamed he laughed. He lifted his face to the ceiling and screamed and laughed and he did not want to stop because he knew that when he did there would be only one friend to comfort him.

And that friend was false because his name was despair.

And so he carried on screaming; even as the door opened; even as his arms were pinioned; even as the first blows slammed into his shrunken stomach and rough hands pulled back his hair. He screamed as vomit surged in his gorge and then screamed again once it had sprayed all over his interlocutors – for they were still shouting at him and he was still pleased with the attention. He wanted this conversation to go on, even as his head filled with agony as his slop bucket crunched down on it, the contents drenching him. And then he screamed as he saw the floor rushing towards him as if it were a friend anxious to hold him in its embrace after a long absence. He screamed as he kissed it and felt the friend's arms about him and then he screamed a scream that he knew could be heard by nobody else; it was a scream that echoed around his head alone. It was a scream that could be part of no conversation because it was a scream that was reserved only for solitary use.

It was the scream of despair.

CHAPTER XIII

D ESPITE ALL HIS care to keep the door to the world outside locked, Vespasian now found himself with an unwelcome companion who resisted all attempts at eviction. No longer could Vespasian deny to himself the existence of the outside world and no longer could he not yearn to see it, feel it, exist in it. After all, he had almost escaped back to it after the earth-quake; yet then he had said not a word to anyone but now, with the gaolers, he had tried to communicate; now he could no longer keep himself hidden lost in an inner tranquillity.

And so his mind turned to the only two subjects that had any relevance: escape and revenge.

And yet, the second could not happen without the first and escape seemed impossible; there would be no more fortuitous earthquakes. He was never let out of his cell, which had no window, only a door and that was solid apart from the grille. Only the grille was ever opened and although it was big enough for him to squeeze through, the time it would take him to do it would be more than ample for the gaolers to incapacitate him; there could be no surprise rush through the grille. Therefore it had to be the door; the gaolers had opened it when he had had his screaming fit, so could he replicate that and overpower them as they came in to restrain him? His new companion provided the answer to that and showed him his weakened limbs and shrunken belly. But Vespasian refused to be driven down by despair, so, rather than retreat into a corner, cowed by his false friend, he fell to exercise, working his muscles that had been unused for who knew how long and planning the hideous ways in which he would inflict injury on Paelignus and Radamistus. Rather than sit or squat on his blanket he began to pace the cell

like a wild beast before release into the arena; he would inter-
sperse his walking with bouts of gymnastics, stretching and
working his neck, arms and legs, doing his best to ignore the
mockery of the companion who watched his every move.

Gradually his body began to harden but his belly remained
shrunken as the rigours of his regime far exceeded the nutrition
of his diet and he realised that he would not be able to gain sufficient strength to overpower two so obviously well-fed men. And
for a while he fell back into the arms of despair.

For a whole period between two straw deliveries he gave up
the fight, lying on the blanket with his friend, until he remembered that he possessed one thing that the gaolers did not:
intelligence.

And so he began to study them every time they came down
the green-slimed steps. The one who held the torch was bald and
bearded with a bull neck and hands the size of a loaf of bread. His
mate was slighter with unkempt hair and beard and looked as if
he was struggling under the weight of the sack of loaves and the
pail of gruel; Vespasian concluded that he must be a slave as
otherwise it made no sense that the smaller, weaker man should
be doing the hardest work. That gave him his first reason to allow
himself a morsel of hope: if the smaller man was a slave, he might
hate his master and would perhaps do nothing to defend him if
he were to be attacked. But then he remembered how the smaller
man had pinioned his arms; the grip had been that of a man
enthusiastic about committing violence. The hope died but he
carried on studying their routine and it was always the same –
until one visit, when everything changed.

It took Vespasian a while to realise that the slave was different
as the new man had the same build as the last and similarly
unkempt hair and beard. But, as the pair progressed down the
corridor, emptying slop buckets and distributing food, Vespasian
noticed that the slave was doing something that he did not
normally do: he was looking closely through the grille at each
inmate; it was then that Vespasian saw that he was new. As they
came closer, Vespasian studied the new man for signs that he
might be weaker than the previous slave and he looked for clues

as to the man's relationship with his master. But the slave gave nothing away. At each door he would put down his sack and pail of gruel, then, once the gaoler had unbolted the grille and opened it, he would take the slop bucket, empty it into the open sewer and hand it back. It was as he passed the bucket back through the grille that the man bent and looked closely at the occupant. Then he took the jug and walked back to the butt of water at the foot of the steps to fill it. Having passed the jug back he received the wooden bowl, ladled gruel into it, gave it back and passed a loaf through before his master swung back the grille and bolted it.

It was Vespasian's turn next and he passed out the slop bucket; as he received it back he locked eyes with the slave and after a moment the recognition hit him like a Titan's punch and he just managed to prevent himself from exclaiming out loud. It was with shaking hands that he went through the remainder of the routine and as he grasped the loaf of bread he felt an addition to it. As the grille closed he glanced down in his hand and saw a scrap of paper. He opened it quickly before the torch moved on too far and read: 'We're both here, be ready.' He screwed it up and breathed a long sigh of relief that turned into a series of sobs that he could barely contain and then gave up trying to. Tears streamed down his face and they were not tears of sadness as his false friend, despair, left the cell forever; they were tears of relief and hope. He cried freely as he wondered just where Magnus was and how Hormus had become the gaoler's slave.

Vespasian now doubled his efforts to toughen up his body, pushing it hard, forcing it through tiredness. When he was too exhausted to carry on, he slept, deep and peacefully, knowing that each sleep could be the last in this subterranean nightmare. Each time he heard the key clunk in the door at the top of the steps his heart leapt with hope and he put his eyes to the grille to make sure that it was indeed Hormus coming down the steps with the gaoler.

Each time it was and each time nothing happened; no shared look between them nor hand signal to notice, no note, nothing, not even a surreptitious nod until one time, as Hormus put his hand into the sack of loaves, he pulled out a knife. The first the gaoler saw of the weapon was as it plunged into his right eye, and then it was but the briefest of glimpses; his howl drowned the sound of misery in the corridor as Hormus twisted and turned the blade so that it made a mush of his brain. Vespasian looked on, almost panting with desire to wield the blade himself as the gaoler weakened and fell to his knees. Hormus withdrew the knife from the pulped wound and, as the light was dying in the gaoler's other eye, he thrust it in so that the man died blind. Working his wrist left and right, he howled with hatred and Vespasian realised that Hormus must have been put through an exceeding amount of misery by the gaoler in a comparatively short time for that hatred to manifest itself so strongly.

Hyperventilating with released tension, Hormus let the body slump back, threw the bolt on the door and pulled it open. 'We must hurry, master.'

Vespasian croaked; his mind had formed a reply but nothing came from his mouth and he realised that he could not remember the last time he had spoken. He stepped forward and took his slave in his arms and for the first time in the whole long dark moment that he had endured he felt the comfort of another human, one who was not trying to harm him. Hormus gently prised his master's arms from around his shoulders as all around a cacophony arose from the other inmates who had realised just what had happened and were now clamouring for release; but Hormus ignored them and led his filthy, naked master by the hand, up the steps. 'If we are to get out of here alive, we must do it quietly,' he said. 'We cannot afford to release the others because of the noise they'd make.'

Vespasian did not care one way or the other; all he knew was that he was mounting the steps that, apart from his brief foray beyond them, had been for the course of his incarceration the horizon of his world. With each step the weight of his misery seemed to lighten until he came to the door to the world beyond. As Hormus opened that door to a long dim corridor Vespasian saw that the world outside really did still exist and, with a ragged half-sob, he stepped back into it.

*

Hormus began to run and Vespasian, still holding onto his hand, kept pace. At the end of the corridor they came to a narrow, spiral staircase; it was not familiar to Vespasian from the dim memories of his failed escape. Up they ran taking the steps two at a time, but as they approached the top, Hormus slowed, then stopped. With caution he stuck his head around the corner and, after a few moments, signalled with his hand, before leading Vespasian, at a walk, out into another corridor. A light shone from an open door on the right, twenty paces away, and beyond it a silhouetted figure was walking towards them. Vespasian still grasped his slave's hand, his brain struggling to make the transition from a dark, enclosed world to this place of space and light. The figure walking towards them stopped just before the open door; voices emanated from it.

Vespasian felt Hormus' hand tense and became aware that the slave was still brandishing his knife in the other. The silhouetted figure had a sword, its blade shone dim in the light, and Vespasian realised that they had to kill the men in the room before they could progress for fear of being spotted as they crossed the doorway. Hormus let go of his hand; Vespasian stopped, feeling as if he had been cast adrift. Hormus and the man with the sword were now either side of the door with their backs against the wall; Hormus held up three fingers to indicate the number of guards in the room and then with a mutual nod of heads they whipped through into the light to surprised shouts that turned into agonised screams. Vespasian ran forward, suddenly clear in his mind as to what he needed to do. He hurtled through the door and into the light, a thing of filth and matted hair, and, with an animal growl that came from the bestial core of his being, he launched himself on the third guard, his lips peeled back, his hands like claws. Releasing the rage that had built up within him in all that time in a dark cell, he sank his teeth into the throat of the man as his hands tore at his victim's eyes. Feeling blood spurt into his mouth, he clamped his jaw tight and shook his head, ripping the flesh, while he forced thumbs into eye sockets. The guard flailed his arms, trying to fight back, but against such animal fury a mere human was powerless and Vespasian drove him down onto the floor. A red mist covered Vespasian's eyes as he savaged the guard with teeth and nails; he could see nothing, hear nothing, but he felt everything; he felt life so powerful, coursing through him as he ripped and clawed the body beneath him in a frenzy of death.

'That'll do you, sir,' a voice said, intruding on his bliss. 'If he ain't dead yet then I doubt that he can be killed and it'd be pointless to keep on trying, if you take my meaning?'

Vespasian felt a hand, firm, on his shoulder, pulling him up and prising him away from the tattered corpse beneath him. He loosened his jaw and released his teeth from the gaping throat; blood gushed from his mouth, slopping onto the eyeless face of the guard. He turned and looked to see who was talking to him; after a few moments he managed to focus and Magnus came into view. He tried to greet him and thank him but it came out as a series of grunts.

Magnus lifted him gently to his feet. 'We'd best get you dressed, sir; we can't have you walking around like that, you'll frighten the horses.'

Vespasian looked down at himself; he was smeared in muck and blood. He tried to apologise for the stink but again it came out as inarticulate drivel.

'Don't you worry, it'll come back,' Magnus reassured him as Hormus stripped the guard nearest to Vespasian's size.

Within a few moments Vespasian was slipping on the tunic, trousers and boots that Hormus had acquired and then they set off down the corridor. Being clothed again, even though it was in the eastern style, gave Vespasian a feeling of security and he no longer needed to hold Hormus' hand as all three of them broke into a jog as they veered to the left into a wider passage. Halfway down they made a right turn, Hormus somehow navigating his way through the labyrinthine building, took another right turn, then a left and then mounted a further set of steps. All the while the air was becoming fresher and warmer and for the first time for a very long time Vespasian allowed himself to imagine the sun in a blue sky because he knew that soon he would see it.

And suddenly, as another door opened, there it was and he had to close his eyes because of the brightness of it but he did not mind for he could feel it on his face and that alone was the most beautiful sensation he had ever experienced. Keeping his eyes shaded, he followed Hormus and Magnus out into a street and then, sticking close together, they blended into the crowd and Vespasian finally felt like a free man.

The city was far more crowded than he remembered but then, after so long alone, he assumed that it was just his mind playing tricks on him. They threaded their way through streets both wide and narrow and still filled with rubble from the earthquake, always heading south, moving at a good pace, fast enough to get away quickly but not so fast as to draw attention to themselves. Vespasian managed to frame a question in his head asking how they had found him but then was unable to transfer that into coherent sound.

Magnus, however, seemed to understand what he wanted to know. 'It was simple, really: when you didn't come back from Radamistus' camp as his army started crossing the bridge I assumed that he'd kidnapped you. So me and Hormus followed, attaching ourselves to the baggage train. Anyway, after a few days I managed to get Paelignus by himself for a nice quiet chat.'

Vespasian raised his eyebrows at the sound of the procurator's name.

'He'd gone with Radamistus because he felt safer there than with his prefects after they had relieved him of command,' Magnus explained. 'Also he seemed to enjoy playing the king-maker. Anyway, I happened to catch him on his own one night and after not too much persuasion he told me that Radamistus had given you to Babak as surety against him keeping his word. Well, as it was obvious that Radamistus had as much intention of keeping his word as a Vestal has of not opening her legs as soon as her thirty-year vow is up, I asked Paelignus why he, as the Roman procurator of Cappadocia, had allowed such a thing to happen.' Magnus paused for a grin. 'Even after his second finger had slopped to the floor he couldn't come up with a decent explanation and continued to insist that he had tried to prevent it. I let him go eventually. I thought that if he had betrayed you then you would enjoy killing him and I wouldn't want to intrude on your pleasure; and if he hadn't, well, two fingers was a fair price for doing nothing to stop Radamistus.'

Vespasian nodded, grateful that Magnus had left the cowardly runt alive for him; it would be a sweet day when they met again.

They stopped outside a three-storey house that showed little signs of damage, right next to the south wall; Hormus knocked thrice and then repeated the signal. After a few moments the door was opened by a youth of considerable beauty. Hormus embraced him and then spoke to him in a language that Vespasian did not understand. He shot Magnus a questioning look.

'That's Mindos' replacement, as it were; we disposed of Mindos when he tried to warn Paelignus that we were travelling with Radamistus' army. Hormus met this one soon after we arrived here a couple of months ago.'

Vespasian shook his head and pointed to his mouth as the youth stepped back and opened the door for them.

'Oh, I see; the language? It's Aramaic.' Magnus informed him, stepping into the house; Vespasian followed. 'It turns out that it was Hormus' mother tongue that he had forgotten after his mother's death. Remember he said he came from somewhere around Armenia? Well, it must have been here or close by. Anyway, it's very useful because we can get around without anyone noticing us. That's how we managed to rent this house and that's how we managed to sell Hormus to the gaoler after his previous slave met with rather an unfortunate end on his way to the market.'

Vespasian looked around the entrance hall; it was well appointed and light. At the far end was a rickety staircase. Magnus headed upstairs. 'Come on, sir, we need to get you cleaned up; there's a cistern of rainwater up on the roof. Once you've washed all the shit off and tidied up a bit, we'll think about getting out of this city, if we still can.'

Vespasian wondered why Magnus seemed to think that leaving was so difficult as he followed him up two flights of stairs and then up a ladder to the flat roof. As he eased himself out of the hole and stood up, he looked to the south; the roof was higher than the wall, just five paces away, and Vespasian had a clear view over it. Out on the plain he could see the reason for Magnus' misgivings: an army was camped before the gates of Arbela.

The city was under siege.

'Shit!' Vespasian exclaimed, surprising both himself and Magnus.

'They arrived a couple of days ago,' Magnus explained as Hormus scrubbed Vespasian's skin with a wet cloth. 'It's Vologases' army.'

'The Great King of Parthia?' Vespasian's voice felt raw and it sounded strange to him having not heard it in a long while.

'The very same.'

'What's he doing besieging one of his vassals?'

'Well, two years ago, after Radamistus went back on his oath to Babak and declared for Rome ...'

Vespasian put his hand up to stop him. 'Say that again.'

'Which bit? Two years?'

'Yes, that bit.'

'It's been two years, sir. That's how long you've been here; didn't you know?'

Vespasian stared at his friend, incredulous. 'Two?'

Magnus nodded.

Vespasian tried to think; he could certainly remember it starting to feel colder and then warm up again, but those were the only changes he could remember. Anything up to a year would not have surprised him; but two? 'They're going to think that I'm dead back home.'

'No, Hormus wrote to your brother when we found out where you were. After we got the information out of Paelignus, we had to go back to Cappadocia because Babak had blocked the pass into Adiabene; and then Vologases arrived with the main Parthian force. He defeated Radamistus, took Artaxata and put his brother Tiridates on the throne. There was no way through so we waited and then winter came and we were stuck in Cappadocia. When spring arrived, Paelignus turned up again so we decided to make ourselves scarce. The passes were still blocked so I reckoned that the best way into Adiabene was through our province of Syria.

And that's what we did, but once we got there we had to wait for winter before we could safely cross the desert to the Euphrates and then get across that to the Tigris and then over that to get here, only to arrive in the chaos of the aftermath of an earthquake. So here we are, two years later.'

'Two years?' Vespasian was having difficulty letting the information sink in. He took the wet cloth from Hormus, dipped it in the water and began to rub at his groin. He looked out at the army before the city. 'So Vologases has put his brother on the Armenian throne?'

'It would seem that way; but last winter was very harsh and he was forced to withdraw his army from Armenia, so how long Tiridates will stay on is anyone's guess.'

Vespasian allowed himself a small smile; his first for a long time – two years. 'That's excellent news; either Radamistus or a Roman army will have to come in to remove him; the war will rumble on. So what's Vologases doing camped out there?'

Magnus shrugged. 'Fucked if I know or care; perhaps King Izates has been a naughty boy. The point is that he is there and isn't allowing anyone in or out except emissaries.'

Vespasian looked over the Parthian lines. 'He doesn't seem to be doing much.'

'They're negotiating and I think it would be best for us to slip away before they fall out with each other. There's a river about ten miles to the south; it's a tributary of the Tigris. Once we're on that river we can head south.'

'South?'

'Yes, sir, south. There's no way that we can cross the desert in summer by ourselves so I thought we'd head south and get some help.'

'Help?'

'Yes, sir, help.'

'From whom? We're in the Parthian Empire; who's going to help us?'

'That's what I wondered and then I remembered that business in Alexandria fifteen years ago and realised that actually there is a Parthian family that could be in your debt.'

Vespasian puzzled for a few moments before that door in his memory reopened. 'Ataphanes' family?'

'Exactly. You sent all his gold back to his family in Ctesiphon.'

Vespasian remembered the effort he had gone to to send his father's freedman's life savings back to his family. He had Alexander, the Alabarch of the Alexandrian Jews, send the gold in one of his cousin's caravans. 'I don't even know if it got there.'

'Well, there's only one way to find out.'

'His family might not be that well disposed towards me; after all, my family did own their son as a slave for fifteen years before giving him his freedom.'

'Should make for an interesting meeting then.'

Vespasian was doubtful.

Magnus sighed and then pointed to the huge army. 'If they attack, this city will fall and each one of those bastards is going to want to kill us. If they don't attack, Izates is going to be combing the city for you so that he can tuck you up all nice and comfy back in your cell. So we've got to get out of here and, unless we all fancy a parched death under the desert sun to the west, then the one sensible thing to do is ask the only people we know in this whole fucking empire to help us. I don't know if they got the gold and I don't know if they would like to see you enslaved in revenge for what happened to their son; I don't know any of that. What I do know is that the only way back to Rome is across the desert and this family are traders and, therefore, they have caravans; I would reckon that it's worth asking them very nicely if they would mind us hitching a ride on one of them.'

Vespasian laughed; a strange sound in his head but a welcome one. 'You're right, of course, Magnus; it's the only sensible thing to do. I don't suppose Ataphanes' father is still alive but I remember him saying that he was the youngest of five brothers, so there's a fair chance of one of them still living. The question is: will they help us?'

'No, the question is: how do we find them?'

'His family are spice merchants so I suppose we could see if there's a guild or some such thing in Ctesiphon and then ask if any of them know of a family that does business with the Jews of Alexandria whose fifth son became a slave in the Roman Empire.'

'That's not the sort of thing you publicise.'

'Well then, how about looking for a family whose youngest son died in the service of the Great King forty years ago?'

'Hmm, it's a start, I suppose; but we've got to get there first. Hormus, trim your master's beard and cut his hair so that it's just off his shoulders; we're all going to look like eastern merchants so that we have no problems walking right through that army.'

The moon set shortly after the sixth hour of the night and Magnus led them back up onto the roof. They were dressed eastern style with long tunics over trousers, leather boots, headdresses, cloaks and a sword and dagger hanging from their belts; they were the image, Hormus' young chum had assured him, of mercantile respectability. The fires and torches in the surrounding host burned brighter and in more profusion than the stars as if the heavens had fallen to earth to encircle Arbela.

'Down,' Magnus hissed.

They lay low as a patrol passed along the wall.

'There're five an hour during the night,' Magnus whispered to Vespasian as the patrol disappeared towards the south gate. 'We've got plenty of time to get out.' Magnus and Hormus pulled up the ladder from below and then, having checked that there were no unscheduled patrols in sight, fed it out towards the wall, bridging the gap.

Vespasian and Magnus admired the beautiful sight surrounding them, pointedly not looking back to where Hormus was saying goodbye to his lover; the youth was in tears.

'He's not coming with us, I take it?' Vespasian asked.

'Hormus wanted to bring him but he felt, to quote him directly, that you wouldn't want your slave's bum-boy cluttering up the boat.'

'He said that?'

'Yes, he's quite perceptive.'

'I wouldn't have minded.'

'Well, it's done now; mind you, I think Hormus had his more selfish reasons. As everyone knows, the best bum-boys come from Mesopotamia; they're renowned for being very accommodating, in more ways than one, if you take my meaning?'

Vespasian did, only too well, especially having witnessed Caligula's public usage of one such youth. 'So you think he's planning on testing the truth of that assertion?'

'I'd have thought so; definitely. I've been with him almost all the time these last couple of years and I have to say that I really like the lad. However, he's got one weakness: he does love a boy or two; mad for them he is. It'll get him into trouble one day.'

Hormus disentangled himself from his latest passion and joined Vespasian and Magnus by the temporary bridge. The youth, with tears glinting in his eyes from the speckled light of the thousands of fires out on the plain, held the ladder firm as Hormus crossed first, with care, balancing a sack on his shoulders. Magnus followed and then Vespasian, trying his hardest not to look down into the dark void of the street below. Once they were all over, the youth withdrew the ladder and watched his lover disappear along the wall. Vespasian noticed that Hormus did not look back once.

They scuttled along, keeping low for about twenty paces before Hormus stopped next to an iron ring set in the wall and rummaged in the bag. Bringing out a long length of rope, he quickly knotted it around the ring and threw the end over the wall. Vespasian was finding it hard to believe that this was the same timid man who was rarely able to look anyone in the eye. With a testing pull on the knot he stepped back and indicated to Vespasian to go first.

As he heaved himself over the parapet, clinging onto the rope, voices came from further along the wall, near the south gate.

'Fast as you like, sir,' Magnus hissed, 'that's the next patrol on the way; they're early.'

With a muttered profanity, Vespasian braced his feet against the outside of the wall and pushed, throwing his body out while letting the rope slip through his hands so that he descended the fifty feet in a series of jumps with his cloak flapping up and down behind him like a bird's broken wing. Hormus was already on the rope when Vespasian landed at the base of the wall, jolting his knees, but thankful that he had built his body up to reasonable fitness during the last stretch of his incarceration. He was standing on a narrow ridge looking down the exceedingly steep slope of the hill that the city sat upon, one hundred feet down to the plain.

Shouts from above rang out and, looking up, Vespasian saw Magnus fling himself over the wall while Hormus was still only halfway down. The rope swung alarmingly from the extra weight on it and Hormus was having difficulty clinging on as Magnus came tearing down; but suddenly clinging on was academic: the rope was no longer attached. Hormus fell the last ten feet, managing to land upright and then roll with the impact; but Magnus had further to fall, much further.

Vespasian positioned himself directly underneath him; as Magnus hurtled to the ground he stretched out his arms, not in an attempt to catch him but to break his fall. The impact sent him crunching down onto his buttocks as Magnus bounced off him, hitting the ground with a lung-emptying thump before disappearing over the edge. Down he rolled, sending up clouds of dust and obscenities. With a quick check to see if Hormus was in one piece, Vespasian leapt after him as the first javelin quivered in the ground, just to his right.

The slope was loose scree and Vespasian found himself once again grateful for the trousers as his legs were spared much of the grazing and tearing from the sharp stones; his momentum increased. He could hear Hormus just behind him but could see very little, enveloped as he was in a cloud of dust on a moonless night. The slope gradually levelled out towards its base and his speed decreased until he stopped, jolting as he thudded into an object that groaned in pain as he hit it. Hormus then tumbled on top of him in a flurry of gravel.

'Jupiter's cock,' Magnus grumbled, his teeth clenched as he gingerly touched his left arm, 'you've got the whole fucking hillside to break your fall with and you both choose to do it on me instead.'

An arrow slamming into the ground next to them caused Magnus to cut short his complaint and in an instant they were on their feet sprinting towards the Parthian lines, two hundred paces away. Arrows whipped about them and shouts followed them. Vespasian glanced over his left shoulder and saw that the south gate remained shut; perhaps there would be no pursuit.

Magnus groaned with effort and pain as he ran, cradling his left arm and limping badly on the same foot. Vespasian slowed and put his arm around Magnus' shoulders, taking some of the weight as they ploughed on through the darkness. The arrows trailed off as the gloom swallowed them and soon they felt safe enough to stop and assess the damage. Magnus slumped down on the ground and Hormus examined his arm.

Vespasian did not need to be told that it was broken; the angle of the wrist attested to the fact.

'We need to get that set properly,' Hormus said as Magnus shoved him away and nursed his injury protectively.

'Oh yes? And where are we going to do that?' he hissed.

'He's right, Magnus,' Vespasian said. 'If we don't, you might never be able to use that hand again. We're just about to walk through an army and if there is one profession that clings to armies almost as much as whores do, it's doctors.'

Vespasian peered forward; the three men seated around the fire seemed to be dozing with their chins on their chests. It was the fourth such fire that they had checked but the first where the sentries seemed to be less fastidious about their duties.

Magnus tutted, in spite of his pain. 'Asleep on duty; they'd be beaten to death by their mates in our army.'

'Yes, well, let's be thankful that the Parthians seem to have a more lax view of discipline,' Vespasian said. 'Hormus, you go first; if you're challenged, give them your best Aramaic.' He looked at Magnus in the gloom. 'Just remember if you're going to moan, groan, mutter or mumble to do it in Greek; there're plenty of Greek speakers in the Great King's army but precious few Latin ones.'

Magnus grumbled something in Greek as Hormus stood and walked forward, skirting the fire.

None of the guards stirred as Hormus approached. Vespasian and Magnus followed close behind, hardly daring to breathe, keeping as much in the shadows as possible. The noise from the camp, even at this time of night, was enough to drown their footsteps. Just as they were level with the fire, one of the guards snorted in his sleep, causing him to splutter and shocking him awake. He opened his eyes and looked directly at Magnus. Hormus shouted in Aramaic and the guard turned to see where the noise had come from. Again Hormus shouted a sentence and then the guard started to laugh; he nudged his fellows awake and said something to them which made them smile, bleary eyed. The guard shouted something back at Hormus and waved them on and then added, with a grin, what sounded to be a quip; Vespasian and Magnus did not need a second invitation and, grinning back at the guard, they moved on.

'What did you tell them?' Vespasian asked once they were well within the camp perimeter and feeling less conspicuous.

Hormus looked shyly at his master. 'I said that my friend had broken his arm getting too close to the rear of a mule and we were looking for a doctor. They got the inference immediately and said that some doctors could be found towards the rear of the camp if we headed straight through. Then he asked if the mule needed a doctor too.'

Vespasian suppressed a laugh; Magnus mumbled something about jokes at his expense while he was in agony.

They walked slowly and with confidence through the camp as if they had every right to be there. After so long by himself in a sealed tomb, Vespasian found the variety of new sights, sounds and smells overwhelming and he had to fight the urge to take his slave's hand again, telling himself that it would soon pass as he readjusted to being part of the world.

In the short time that it took them to traverse the Parthian camp Vespasian heard more than a dozen different languages, saw as many, if not more, styles of dress and smelt so many different and new spices and herbs on the steam and smoke wafting from the cooking fires that his head would have spun even if he had not just been released from a solitary cell earlier that day.

Having asked for directions a couple of times, Hormus eventually guided them to an area of the camp, near the horse-lines at the very back, that was populated with larger, plusher tents.

'This looks to be the right sort of place,' Vespasian said, noticing the ostentatious displays of wealth in the form of silver lamps and elegantly carved camp furniture laid out around each tent, guarded by expensive-looking slaves, bulked with muscle. 'Giving false hope to the dying seems to be just as profitable here as it is at home. Go and make some enquiries, Hormus.'

The slave approached one of the huge guards and after a short discussion returned. 'For two drachmae, he'll allow us through; the best man for what we need is in the tent with the red and blue facings.'

'Drachmae?' Vespasian questioned.

'Yes, I was surprised too,' Magnus said, grimacing as he cradled his arm. 'Apparently they've used the drachma ever since Alexander's conquest.'

Vespasian nodded to Hormus to pay the man.

They followed Hormus to the appropriate tent and waited outside while the slave entered and tried to gain admittance for them.

'Twenty-five drachmae,' he said upon his eventual return. 'Plus an extra ten due to the lateness of the hour.'

Despite the exorbitant fee, far more even that the most avaricious doctor would have charged back in Rome, Vespasian led Magnus and Hormus into the tent. A waiting slave bowed to them as he took the purse that Hormus proffered; having satisfied himself that it contained the correct coinage, he said something in Aramaic to which Hormus replied, causing the slave to switch languages to Greek. 'Follow me; my master Lindos is waiting.'

Like so many doctors, Lindos was a Greek and, like so many Greeks, he treated those not of Attic blood and speaking serviceable but accented Greek with contempt. 'Where are you from?' he asked after Magnus had told him some rubbish about how he had broken his arm. 'Your Greek is ghastly.'

'We're from …' Magnus stopped and groaned with pain to cover his inability to answer the question truthfully.

'Colchis,' Vespasian answered after a couple of nervous heartbeats thinking.

Lindos' expression made it quite clear what he thought of the morals and sexual proclivities of those who hailed from that far-flung kingdom on the eastern coast of the Euxine. Having made his displeasure clear at having to come into physical contact with lowlife hardly better than barbarians, Lindos went to work at setting the bone and splinting the arm with remarkable professionalism. Biting down on a strip of wood, Magnus fought the pain, which, judging by the way Lindos pulled on the broken limb and also by the variety of Magnus's facial expressions, must have been considerable.

Within a quarter of an hour Lindos was finished and Magnus, with his arm set straight and protected by two splints, was covered in sweat, his eyes screwed shut. 'Jupiter's cock, that hurt,' he blurted as the slave removed the wooden bit from his mouth. He opened his eyes to see Vespasian staring at him aghast and dawning suspicion on Lindos' face.

He had spoken in Latin and had invoked Rome's best and greatest god.

Hormus was the first to react, grabbing the slave, and with both hands clamped to his head, twisted it, violent and sudden, breaking the neck with a snap.

Vespasian's shock at his previously timid slave's new murderous abilities was the instant that Lindos needed to flee and scream for help and quickly and loudly he did so, retreating back into the depths of the tent.

'This way,' Vespasian said, gathering his mind and drawing his sword. He ran to the side of the tent and slashed a long rend in it as burly bodies bundled through the entrance. He pushed the loose material aside and ran out into the night with Magnus and Hormus following. At speed they sprinted away, dodging a couple of guards whose agility was not helped by their bulk. Behind them cries of warning rang out. After they had covered fifty paces or so Vespasian slowed down so as not to draw attention to themselves; as he did so he caught the sweet animal scent of the horse-lines and, following his nose, walked swiftly towards them.

The horses were tethered in long lines and tended by slaves who groomed, fed and exercised them; hundreds of horses meant scores of slaves and Vespasian knew that any pursuit would soon think to look at the horse-lines. 'There's no time for niceties,' he said, striding forward with purpose towards the horses nearest them, his sword still naked in his hand. With a swift, military jab he rammed the point into the throat of an enquiring slave and within a few moments had unhitched the first three horses in the line. 'It'll have to be bareback,' he said, hauling himself up onto the unsaddled beast.

Hormus gave Magnus a leg up before mounting his horse as slaves came running towards them, their shouts alerting the guards, coming from the opposite direction in pursuit, as to the whereabouts of their quarry.

Pulling his mount round, Vespasian kicked it into action, followed by Magnus gamely hanging on with one hand, as Hormus slashed down at a slave attempting to grab his leg, opening up his face with a spurt of blood; the iron tang caused his horse's nostrils to flare and with flattened ears it sped away after his master.

Vespasian did not slow his mount as it clattered through the arriving guards, sending them diving to either side and leaving the escape into the empty south clear. They thundered their horses out into the night, leaving uproar behind them, and headed, with as much haste as possible in the black night, for the tributary of the Tigris that would take them down to the great river itself. Then they would follow it south, drawn by its current, into the beating heart of the Parthian Empire.

CHAPTER XIIII

THE TIGRIS WAS being kind to them, flowing at a steady pace, its surface smooth, gliding them south at the speed of a trotting horse. Vespasian lay in their boat's bow, looking up past the triangular sail at the cloudless sky and wondering how he could have lived for two years without seeing such beauteous colour; the intensity of the blue transfixed his eyes and it was as much as he could do to check the tears that he could feel welling up within him. Now that he had time to think, relief coursed through his whole being; relief that the dark ordeal was now over; relief at once again feeling the companionship of a fellow human being.

For the two days since they had come across the boat pulled up on the riverbank and covered with vegetation, Vespasian had lain prone in the bow as they sailed down the tributary river to its confluence with the Tigris. He had joined in some conversation with Magnus and Hormus but it had been an effort and he found that he preferred just to let his thoughts wander free and enjoy the exhilaration of having nothing over his head preventing him from seeing the sky.

He had listened to his companions' account of how Magnus, having befriended the gaoler, had sold Hormus to him at a reasonable discount after they had murdered his original slave and the sexual ordeals that Hormus went through at the hands of that man for the six days that he had served him before their escape. Vespasian's gratitude to his slave for sacrificing himself so that he could rescue his master was profound and he understood that Hormus was completely devoted to him, serving him in such a way that he could be trusted with anything. Hormus sat in the stern of the boat, holding the steering-oar as the current and the small sail, full bellied with wind, pushed them on towards Ctesiphon; his eyes fixed on the river ahead and his mouth set firm in concentration beneath the beard that masked his undershot chin. Vespasian studied the man and wondered what he had done to deserve such unquestioning, animal loyalty; he swore to himself that he would repay that loyalty by freeing Hormus at the earliest legal time: when he reached the age of thirty in a few years.

Magnus sat beneath the mast, his head on his chest, snoring; his splinted arm lay across his lap. Vespasian smiled at the sight. He had never dared give rein to the hope that his friend would find and rescue him in all those dark days; but there had always been a little flicker in the deeper recesses of his mind that it was a possibility. Now he was free he could afford to admit to himself that the reason he had survived relatively unscathed was because he had clung on to that tiny morsel of hope, nurturing it but not relying on it. He knew that he was extremely fortunate with his companions and, as they sailed on south, he said a prayer of thanks to Mars for holding his hands over him and promised the finest bull as soon as he was back within the Empire.

They kept to the middle of the river, a hundred and fifty paces from either bank, both of which were dotted with farms, small settlements and larger towns. The land was lush, most of it under cultivation and the communities that they passed seemed prosperous. Occasionally they would land just downstream from one and Hormus would walk back to buy food; they aroused no suspicion and other craft that they passed on the water would hail them cheerfully and sail on without incident.

Days melted into one another, the river widened and the temperature grew hotter. Gradually Vespasian began to feel the weight of his incarceration lift; he could sleep without fear of waking up to find himself back in his cell so that for the first time in two years he began to feel rested and strong and capable of an arduous caravan journey across the desert to either Judaea or Syria. As his strength returned so did his ambition: somehow he had survived an ordeal that would have left most people gibbering wrecks; he had done it with his will and, he was well aware, with the help of the gods. He was now sure that there was substance behind all the omens of his birth and the subsequent prophesies and signs. Mars was preserving him: how else had his mind been kept from cracking?

'We should be getting there soon,' Magnus observed, shading his eyes and peering forward. 'When I looked at a map back in Syria, from what I could make out, it seemed to be about two to three hundred miles from Arbela to Ctesiphon. This is our fifth day on the river.'

'How will we know that we're at Ctesiphon?' Hormus asked.

Vespasian sat up and looked south. 'Because it will be the biggest city that you've ever seen outside Rome or Alexandria. It's even bigger if you count the Greek city of Seleucia on the western bank of the Tigris.'

Magnus was surprised. 'You mean there's a whole city full of Greeks in the middle of the Parthian Empire?'

'Yes, and most cities have a sizable Greek or Macedonian minority. Thousands of colonists came out in the wake of Alexander and most of them stayed. There are Greek speakers all the way to India. Parthia is not an empire just comprising Persians, Medes and Assyrians; there are many different peoples and all owe allegiance to the King of Kings, who, incidentally, is the son of the previous incumbent, Vorones, and a Greek concubine.'

'They get everywhere, the Greeks,' Magnus said, shaking his head in disapproval.

'What have you got against the Greeks?'

'What, apart from being liars and cheats with an uncommon desire to be buggered and a penchant for sleeping with close relatives?'

'Yes, apart from all that.'

'Well, nothing, I suppose, other than the fact that Pallas and Narcissus are both Greek and look at how much trouble they've piled upon us in their lives. Tryphaena turns out to be Greek and it would seem that she's responsible for us being, without any obvious allies, in the middle of the Parthian Empire, which is ruled by some bastard who happens to be half-Greek. Do you want me to go on?'

'No, no, fair enough; fucking Greeks, eh? Anyway, what we have to remember is that most Greeks are completely loyal to the regime ...'

'As loyal as any Greek can be, you mean?'

'Yes, and as such it would be best not to let on that we're Romans even to a Greek.'

'Especially to a Greek; he'd sell that information faster than his sister once he'd taken her virginity. Did you hear about the Greek who took his new bride back to her family because he found out on their wedding night that she was a virgin?'

Vespasian frowned. 'No.'

'Well, he did, telling them that if she wasn't good enough for her brothers then she wasn't good enough for him.'

Vespasian laughed, long and loud; at first it was at the joke but then it became much more about the joy of freedom.

It was truly magnificent. Walls of stone, painted blue and yellow, decorated with animal motifs and studded with towers soaring to the sky, encasing a city almost the size of Rome; and that was just on the east bank of the Tigris. On the west bank, just before the river split in two to pass either side of a fortified island, there was another city, less old, set out in a grid pattern: Seleucia, the former capital of the Macedonian Seleucid Kingdom, built just over three centuries before. Equally as impressive in scale but without the painted walls, Seleucia's ordered streets made it feel like it was purpose built; whereas the higgledy-piggledy maze of Ctesiphon's layout showed a city that had grown slowly from nothing over the centuries. These two monuments to human achievement sat half a mile apart, either side of the Tigris, swarming with life, feeding off the great river that at the same time joined and separated them. Crafts of all sizes ploughed through the gently flowing water, browned by sewage, back and forth between the two cities as they supported each other in a symbiotic relationship of trade.

And it was because of trade that Vespasian, Magnus and Hormus had come, or, at least, to follow a lead based upon trade, and, as they steered their boat into the harbour just to the south of Ctesiphon's walls, Vespasian realised that it would be a daunting task to find Ataphanes' family: not even in Ostia had he ever seen so many mercantile ships. The quay was a mass of merchants and slaves; the merchants haggling and bargaining, the slaves lifting and humping. Sacks, bags, crates, baskets, amphorae and bales, all containing the produce of scores of exotic lands, were loaded onto and off-loaded from the traders in an endless cycle of commerce fuelled by greed and coinage.

'Where are we going to start looking amongst all this?' Vespasian said as Hormus slipped the boat into a free berth.

'Spice merchants must congregate somewhere,' Magnus observed, throwing a painter up to a young lad of thirteen or fourteen who seemed to have taken it upon himself to assist with their mooring.

'Smell the air, it's drenched with spices; there must be thousands of spice merchants here.'

'Ah, but how many deal with the Jews of Alexandria?' Magnus studied the activity for a few moments, watching a trail of slaves lug wicker baskets from a ship straight into one of the scores of warehouses lining the harbour. 'I imagine all this is coming in from the East because I know from looking at that map that the Tigris flows out into the sea and then that sea will take you all the way to India. What we need to do is find the merchants who trade the other way; the merchants who take the goods out of the warehouses and then send them on caravans west.'

It seemed to Vespasian, as he clambered out of the boat, to be a decent point and as good a starting place as any. Hormus followed him out, eagerly accepting the help of the boy, who did not seem to mind the slave's hands resting on parts of his anatomy that were not strictly in the way nor of much use for helping people out of boats.

'Does he speak Aramaic?' Vespasian asked as the boy looked with goggle-eyes at a silver coin that Hormus had extracted from the purse on his belt.

After a brief, unintelligible conversation, Hormus confirmed that his new friend did indeed speak Aramaic, which, judging from his expression, pleased the slave immensely.

'Ask him whether the spice merchants who deal with exporting goods to the West have any guild or regular meeting place or whatever.'

A short conversation ensued, during which Hormus seemed to find it necessary to emphasise a point by gently stroking the Persian boy's arm; the slave looked back at his master. 'Bagoas here says that there are many associations of traders throughout the city and over in Seleucia as well.'

Vespasian thought for a few moments. 'Ataphanes was Persian, I believe; not Median, Babylonian or Assyrian or any of the other sorts. Ask him where I should start to look for a Persian spice merchant.'

Another conversation followed involving a lot of eye contact, some shy smiles and, it seemed to Vespasian and Magnus, an unnecessary amount of stroking. 'We need to go to the agora near to the royal palace,' Hormus said, briefly dragging his eyes away from his informant.

'Good, tell him there is a drachma in it for him to show us the way there and then act as our guide for the rest of the day.' Vespasian paused before adding with a smile, 'And night.'

'You shouldn't encourage him,' Magnus grumbled as Hormus translated Vespasian's wishes. 'This is what I meant; he just can't help himself. Everywhere we went it was the same thing; I wouldn't have minded so much had all the grunting and groaning not kept me awake on so many nights.'

Bagoas whistled and another couple of boys emerged from the crowds on the quay; both were a year or two younger than him and, judging by their looks, were either his brothers or cousins.

Hormus eyed the boys with interest as Bagoas pointed to them and explained their presence. 'He says that they will look after the boat for a drachma each now and another on your return in the morning.'

Vespasian shook his head. 'Tell Bagoas that if he helps us find the people we're looking for we won't need the boat and he and the boys can keep it.'

After they had settled their account with the inevitable harbour official demanding mooring fees as well as a small donation directly into his own purse based on the number of people arriving in the boat which seemed to be in lieu of any goods in their possession worth stealing, Bagoas led them towards the city.

One look at the buildings lining the wide thoroughfare that dived, straight as an arrow's flight, from the harbour gate, bisecting the maze of streets, into the heart of the city was enough for anyone to realise that Ctesiphon was the heart of power. Only the dwellings of the noble or the immortal were allowed in such a prime position; consequently it was a succession of brightly painted palaces and temples interspersed with paradises – areas of manicured cultivation whose beauty exceeded the Gardens of Lucullus. Wide, splendid and rich and lined with many varieties of trees and flowering shrubs, the thoroughfare had been designed to mask the haphazard planning and the non-existent sewage system of the rest of the ancient city so that the Great King saw only beauty and grandeur and breathed nothing but sweet air as he made his way to his main palace at Ctesiphon's centre. But today the Great King was not using his way in and out of the city so the population were graciously allowed to promenade up and down and stare at its wonders.

Inured though they were to the glories of great civilisations – coming from Rome and having visited Alexandria – Vespasian and Magnus still found themselves staring in admiration at the architecture, the scale and the human endeavour that it had taken to create this avenue.

'That's a stable!' Magnus exclaimed, looking at a three-storey palace built around three sides of a courtyard in which horses were being exercised. A ramp led up to a wide balcony that ran around the first floor giving access to scores of individual stalls; a further ramp ran up to the second floor, which replicated the first. The stalls in the ground floor, however, were twice the size of those above. 'Those horses have more room than most families back in Rome, or anywhere else for that matter.'

'Easterners have always loved their horses,' Vespasian pointed out, 'and having seen the way that they whip their conscript infantry to almost certain death, does it really surprise you that the Great King's horses are more valuable to him than his people?'

'I suppose not; he seems to have plenty to replace the ones he loses and lots of different sorts.'

'That's an understatement,' Vespasian said as Bagoas steered them through the crowds, mostly attired in the Persian and Median manner but many other styles of dress were on display reflecting the diversity of the huge empire of which this was the hub: the flowing robes and headdresses of the desert dwellers to the south, the leather of the horsemen from the northern seas of grass, dark-skinned Indians from the East in long-sleeved tunics and baggy trousers, Bactrians and Sogdians in leather caps, sheepskin jackets and embroidered trousers, Greek, Jewish, Scythian, Albanian, everything that could be imagined; but amongst them all there was not one toga. Although he knew that with their eastern clothes they blended in well, Vespasian felt conspicuous, foreign, and he wondered what Caratacus must have thought when the Britannic chieftain had been brought in chains to Rome, seeing such an alien place and alien people for the first time. Here he saw what he realised was the Rome of the East: the empire that had subjugated as many, if not more, races. He recalled Caratacus' words to Claudius: *'If you Romans, in your halls of marble, who have so much, choose to become masters of the world, does it follow that we, in our huts of mud, who have comparatively little, should accept slavery?'* That was evidently as true for the peoples of the East as it was for those in the West. Here, therefore, was the balance to Rome; here was the empire that would always rival her, fight her but never dominate her because no empire could comprise both East and West. Both would stay strong through fear of the other; both needed war to take their conquered peoples' minds off their subjugation; both knew that to destroy the other would mean death because a super-empire with nothing to fear would break apart under its own weight.

And Armenia was the natural battleground on which Rome and Parthia could flex their martial muscles every generation or so, safe in the knowledge that it would prove fatal for neither side; Tryphaena had chosen her war well. He smiled to himself; Parthia was not a threat but, rather, a thing to be embraced. Conflict with this empire was a natural state of affairs; the skill was to know how to benefit from it.

He began to relax and feel less alien now that he had understood that this empire was a necessary part of Rome's existence; entwined in a symbiotic dance of war – much like Ctesiphon and Seleucia with their trade – both empires strengthened each other.

His mind wandered and he barely noticed the royal palace, set in a paradise surrounded by high walls, as they turned to the right off the thoroughfare and twisted through some narrower, sewage-reeking streets, one of which opened into an agora that made the Forum Romanum look like a provincial marketplace in a backwater of the Empire. At least twice the size of its Roman counterpart it was equally as crowded; thousands of merchants thriving on commerce, bought, sold, bartered and haggled in a tooth and claw contest to extract the largest possible amount of profit from even the smallest item of trade.

Vespasian took one look and any last hope of success withered. 'How are we going to find anyone in amongst that lot?'

Magnus looked equally as gloomy. 'I've a feeling that an offering to Fortuna would be appropriate.'

Hormus set down his sack and laughed and then said something to Bagoas, who did not seem to share his amusement but looked puzzled instead.

'Well?' Vespasian asked. 'Does he know where to start looking, Hormus?'

Another conversation in Aramaic ended with Hormus shaking his head. 'He says that the only way to find these people is to go around the agora in one circle and ask people at random; but if the people that we're looking for send caravans west then this is where they trade.'

Vespasian sniffed the air. 'Well, at least the smell of spices is fending off the stench of sewage.'

*

But it was a hopeless task.

They sweated and cursed as they pushed their way through the swirling mercantile mass with Hormus asking the same question about a family with a youngest son named Ataphanes every few paces. And always, once the interviewee saw that Hormus wished neither to buy nor sell, he was met by uninterested looks and treated to dismissive words and hand gestures.

The sun westered, trade dropped off and the crowds thinned, but even so people were not interested in helping three foreigners and a boy find a family with only the clue of a long-dead youngest son, and by the time the light began to fade remaining in the agora was pointless.

'Ask Bagoas if he knows of a clean inn nearby,' Vespasian ordered Hormus.

The slave's eyes brightened at the prospect of bed and dutifully asked the question. 'He says that a cousin of his has a place a few streets away; we can find rooms and a meal there. He says that we'll get a special price.'

'I'm sure we will,' Magnus muttered, 'specially high.'

'That can't be helped,' Vespasian said, nodding to the Persian boy to lead on. 'It's better than walking around, not knowing where to look. At least if it's a member of Bagoas' family they may well prove more trustworthy than a complete stranger.'

'What? In that they'll only charge us double and give us the smallest rooms and the toughest gristle in the thinnest of soups?'

Vespasian had a nasty feeling that his friend was close to the mark.

The clatter of boots on stairs and the splintering of wood jerked Vespasian from an uneasy sleep; he sat up, looking around in the dark, wondering for a moment where he was. Hormus' shouts from the room next door instantly reminded him that they were in Bagoas' cousin's inn where their welcome had been falsely friendly and all of Magnus' predictions had come true. He reached for his sword and then remembered that it remained hidden in Hormus' sack; with a curse he jumped out of bed as the door to his room crashed open and three silhouetted figures rushed in.

With nowhere to retreat to, Vespasian barrelled forward into the lead man with his shoulder, flooring him and knocking the wind from his lungs while ramming his fist into the groin of the attacker to his left, doubling him over with a strangled grunt. The surprise at the ferocity of the counter-attack by quarry that should have been, if not asleep, then at least off-guard caused the third assailant, to the right, to step back and shout for help; it was the moment of indecision that Vespasian needed. With the flat of his hand he struck up into the man's chin, cracking his jaw closed and his head back with a slop of blood as his teeth severed the tip of his tongue mid-shout. He fell to the ground gurgling in agony, clasping his hands to his damaged mouth as Vespasian barged past him out to an ill-lit landing.

He had a brief glimpse of Hormus being dragged down the stairs to his left as, to his right, Magnus was hauled out of his room, his splinted arm impeding his ability to defend himself. Without pausing, Vespasian crunched his knee into the thigh of the nearest of Magnus' assailants, deadening the muscle so that the man half stumbled, loosening his grip. Magnus used his freed right hand to grab the throat of his other detainer as Vespasian pounced on the limping man with an anger that expressed itself as a guttural animal roar. With his limbs working as fast as an athlete's in a foot race, he pounded his prey into screaming submission as Magnus deprived air from his victim's lungs with a merciless grip around his neck. His clamp-like fingers ever tightening, he cursed and spat into the dying man's purpling face as urine trickled down his legs and the stench of voided bowels clouded the air.

'That's enough!' Vespasian shouted, leaping towards the stairs.

Magnus heard the urgency in his friend's voice and bounded after him, leaving his man gasping and soiled.

Taking the stairs three at a time they clattered down to the common room on the ground floor. The innkeeper cowered behind the bar but there was no sign of Hormus or Bagoas. Caring not whether the man had had anything to do with the surprise attack, Vespasian ran straight for the door, pushing tables and chairs aside. With the one objective of freeing his slave before he disappeared into a city that could swallow a legion whole, he pulled back the door and ran out into a semicircle of club-wielding men.

He was dimly aware of Magnus screaming as a dark shape surged towards his head, heralding a splitting pain and a flash of light, closely followed by oblivion.

His head throbbed with every thundering beat of his heart as consciousness returned to Vespasian.

He felt himself lying on cold stone.

He opened his eyes and at first saw nothing; the room was dark. Then, as he grew accustomed to the gloom, he could make out a dim light not more than two paces away. It was seeping through a small, square window.

He peered harder and saw that the window was in fact a viewing hole in a door; a viewing hole with bars in it.

He was in a cell.

He was back in a cell.

Vespasian drew his knees up to his chest and clutched them; tight.

The wail started at the pit of his stomach and grew until it seemed to shake his entire being; it was long, hollow and full of emptiness and despair.

How long he had lain there, Vespasian did not know, but eventually the door opened and he was hauled to his feet; he moaned, it was more of a whimper. Unresisting, he was dragged through a series of dim corridors, passing the occasional flaming torch, and then up some steps; finally, a stout door was unbolted and he was thrown through to collapse onto some foul-smelling straw.

'It's good of you to join us, sir; although I'm sure we all wish for less limited circumstances, if you take my meaning?'

Vespasian looked up to see Magnus and Hormus sitting with their backs against the wall; above them daylight flooded in through a barred window. 'How long have we been here?'

'Two days,' Magnus replied.

'What happened?'

Hormus' whole body suddenly wracked with sobs.

Magnus looked accusingly at the slave and then turned back to Vespasian. 'I'm going to treat myself to an "I told you so".'

Vespasian understood. 'Bagoas?'

'It would seem that way. I said his passion for boys would get him into trouble one day; I didn't think that it would have us all wallowing in fucked-arse turds.'

'I'm so sorry, master,' Hormus cried, getting onto his knees and holding his hands out, pleading. 'I beg you to forgive me.'

'What did you do?'

Hormus sobbed a couple of times before managing to get himself under control. 'After we had … well, I fell asleep. The next thing I knew they were breaking down my door and Bagoas wasn't there; neither was our sack.'

Magnus shook his head. 'I reckon he stole the sack and then finding our swords and other stuff that's obviously Roman he made the right deduction, and him and his cousin must have decided to make a little extra on top of the boat and our cash and reported us to the civic authorities.'

Hormus wrung his hands. 'It's all my fault, master. I translated Magnus' comment about Fortuna to Bagoas.'

Vespasian could see it all. 'And he would have become suspicious about us as soon as he learnt that we worshipped a Roman goddess; especially as only you spoke Aramaic. That was a foolish mistake, Hormus.'

The slave nodded mournfully, his eyes never leaving the floor.

'What's done is done.' Vespasian patted Hormus' arm in a comforting manner and looked at Magnus. 'So, what do they plan for us?'

'I was hoping they might have told you that, sir.'

'I'm afraid not.' He got to his feet and walked to the door. 'However, since they know we're Roman I might as well tell them that they have a man of consular rank in their custody; hopefully that will make our lives slightly more valuable.'

'It might make us more of an embarrassment and therefore make our hosts decide on a speedy disposal, if you take my meaning?'

'I do, but have you got any better suggestions?'

Magnus shook his head. 'I believe they're very keen on impaling people here.'

Vespasian began to pound on the door and shout for the gaolers.

Eventually the viewing slat opened and a surprisingly elegantly barbered face peered in enquiringly and then astonished Vespasian by asking in fluent Latin, 'You have a problem?'

'Yes, I am a man of proconsular rank and you will cause a diplomatic incident by holding me here.'

'We know exactly who you are, Titus Flavius Vespasianus. We found your imperial mandate amongst your other possessions in the bag along with the swords with which you were planning on attempting to assassinate our Great King.'

Vespasian looked at the man, aghast. 'Assassinate the Great King?'

'Of course. Why else would you arrive in disguise in Ctesiphon the day before Vologases returned here?'

'We had business of our own to conduct.'

'We shall see; that is up to the Great King himself to decide.'

'What do you mean?'

'I mean that he will decide what you were here to do and he will decide your fate when you appear before him to be judged tomorrow.'

CHAPTER XV

THE BARREL-VAULTED ceiling towering over the great audience chamber in the royal palace was partially veiled by a thin haze of fumes. Despite the bright shafts of sunlight flooding through a long line of identically shaped arched windows, high in the walls, slashing through the heavy atmosphere alive with motes, the cavernous, long interior burned with thousands of lamps. It was a hall of light, both natural and artificial, the like of which Vespasian had never seen before. And the light illumined the colours in the marbles of the floor and columns, in the paintwork of the statuary, in the dyes of the occupants' clothes and beards and in the fired, glossy tiles of the walls and ceiling, each individually crafted to fit together, depicting scenes of hunting and warfare and other heroic acts of the Arsacid dynasty of Parthian kings.

So much colour and so much decoration in one magnificent chamber; but it was not that which struck Vespasian as he, Magnus and Hormus were led through the highly polished, dwarfing, cedar doors: it was the power that emanated from the seated figure on a dais at the far end of the room.

There sat Vologases, the first of that name, King of all the Kings of the Parthian Empire, and attending him were hundreds of courtiers, the élite of many lands, all of whom professed allegiance to the man who held the power of life and death over millions of subjects; the man who was now to judge Vespasian.

In contrast to the abundance of light and colour was the absence of sound, and once Vespasian and his companions had been thrown to the floor and hissed at to remain still, flat on their stomachs, there was a complete hush in the great hall. No one moved or whispered a word and through the stillness Vespasian could feel the enmity radiating from hundreds of pairs of eyes as they stared at the three prone forms, so small in the midst of such vastness.

For what seemed like an age he lay there, oppressed by the weight of the silence; it was not calm, it menaced.

The shouted order in Greek to crawl forward cracked through the quiet, shocking Vespasian with its abruptness.

Keeping his eyes to the floor he slithered towards the Great King, humiliated but still alive. With each foot of progress his rage at such treatment for an ex-consul of Rome grew and by the time he was ordered to stop he was seething with fury.

'What are you doing in my domain, Titus Flavius Vespasianus? Answer only with the truth: to tell a falsehood to the King of Kings is not only an insult to him but an affront to Ahura Mazda.'

Vespasian realised that this was the voice of Vologases himself speaking in the tongue of the Greek concubine who bore him. Struggling to control his anger, keeping his words to the minimum, he answered with the truth, understanding how much weight the Parthians place on honesty. He told the King of Kings briefly everything that had happened to him from the point when Radamistus gave him to Babak as surety for his false oath to his reason for looking for Ataphanes' family here in Ctesiphon.

'So your intention was not to assassinate me?'

'What gave you that idea, Great King?'

There was a yelp from the far end of the hall and Vespasian heard the sound of someone being dragged forward.

'This boy swore when he reported you that he had overheard you and your companions planning my assassination as I entered the city yesterday.'

Vespasian kept his eyes to the floor but guessed that Bagoas had been dragged in. 'How could he? He speaks no Greek and only one of my companions speaks Aramaic. I can only imagine that he made up that falsehood in order to make himself seem more important so as to get a greater reward.'

There was a pause as the Great King considered Vespasian's words.

'Can anyone here vouch for this Roman?' Vologases' voice echoed around the hall and faded into silence.

That silence held, still and clear.

And then, from the far end of the chamber, it was shattered.

'I can, Light of the Sun.'

Vespasian did not recognise the voice nor could he see the speaker as he was still lying with his face down. He heard footsteps walk the length of the hall and was aware of the whimpering of Bagoas somewhere behind him; a sharp slap silenced the boy.

The footsteps stopped next to him; in the corner of his vision, he saw a man, dressed in the Persian manner. He began to bow and then carried on until he was on his knees with his forehead touching the floor; but he did not stop there and, with remarkable elegance, the movement continued until he was flat on his belly, his lips kissing the floor before his Great King and his hands palms down either side of his face.

'Your name?' Vologases' voice betrayed a hint of surprise.

'Gobryas, Light of the Sun.'

'You may get to your knees and speak, Gobryas.'

Gobryas raised himself gracefully. 'I'm honoured, Light of the Sun.' He paused to compose himself, taking a couple of breaths as if calming galloping nervousness. 'Just over fourteen years ago a caravan came in from Alexandria; it carried the normal goods that you would expect coming from the Roman province of Egypt. However, there was one item that had been entrusted to the caravan's owner by his cousin, the Alabarch of the Alexandrian Jews. It was for my father, whose name I bear; it was a box and inside this box there was gold, a lot of gold. There was also a letter telling my father of the life of his youngest son, my brother, Ataphanes. Fifteen years a slave with a Roman family and then subsequently a freedman in their service for nearly the same duration. During that time he amassed a small fortune. When he died, in the service of the family who had owned him and freed him, he asked his patrons to send his fortune back to his family here in Ctesiphon. The Roman family must be truth-speakers because, despite the very obvious temptation to keep a dead man's gold to themselves, they did return it.'

There were murmurs of agreement from all sides of the hall.

Vespasian lay, hardly daring to breathe as he listened to the voice of the stranger who was saving his life.

'Yesterday morning a rumour came to my ears that there had been some people, foreigners, looking around the great market for a family of spice traders whose youngest son, Ataphanes, had been killed in the service of one of your predecessors. At first I thought that these people couldn't be looking for me because my brother was enslaved, not killed. However, I then realised that until the letter arrived we had no idea that Ataphanes had been in captivity, we had thought him dead; we had not told our acquaintances the shameful truth once we found out – who would admit to having a slave in the family? I admit it now only to defend a man in whose debt I find myself. These foreigners were being considerate; they didn't bandy about the word "slave", they understood our sensitivity. When I heard that some foreigners had been apprehended in an attempt to do harm to your person and that one of them was a Roman by the name of Titus Flavius Vespasianus I knew that they were the same people; and so I decided to exercise my right as head of the Ctesiphon Guild of Spice Merchants to attend your court and fight the Lie with Truth.'

Vespasian's mind was filled with prayers of thanks to his guardian god Mars and the chief god of the Zoroastrian religion, Ahura Mazda, who abjures the Lie.

'You speak forcefully for this man, Gobryas,' Vologases said after a few moments in thought. 'How can we be sure that there is no mistake or confusion after all this time?'

'Because, Light of the Sun, I still have the letter that came with my brother's gold. I have it here and it is signed by Titus Flavius Vespasianus.'

Vespasian saw from the corner of his eye a man walking forward from the dais, take the folded letter that Gobryas proffered and with great reverence hand it to Vologases.

There was absolute silence apart from the rustle of Vologases perusing the letter.

'Titus Flavius Vespasianus,' the Great King said after a short while, 'you may rise but your companions will stay where they are.'

Vespasian slowly got to his feet and raised his eyes to the Great King seated on his elevated throne. Vologases was a young man, early thirties, with solemn, dark eyes and a thin beak of a nose. On his head he wore a bejewelled gold diadem that held the shoulder-length, tight black ringlets of his hair in place. His beard was of a matching style and each ringlet was oiled and sheened like a raven's feathers setting into sharp contrast his pale skin that had had very little contact with the direct rays of the sun.

Vologases surveyed Vespasian, sitting bolt upright and perfectly still. 'Was it indeed you that sent the gold to Gobryas' family?'

Now that he was able to stand, the rage at being humiliated on his belly faded. 'It was, Light of the Sun.'

A flicker of amusement passed across the Great King's face at the Roman's use of his title. 'Then you are a follower of the Truth.' He looked beyond Vespasian. 'Bring them here!'

Vespasian turned and saw not only Bagoas but also his cousin, the innkeeper, their eyes watering in terror, being brought forward by two guards each. They were thrown to the ground and grovelled in their fear.

Vologases looked at the pair in distaste. 'Which one told the Lie?'

One of the guards answered the question by pulling Bagoas' head up by the hair.

'Take his tongue, nose, ears and one eye; the other I shall allow him to keep so that he can always see his mutilation in reflection.'

Bagoas had not understood the Greek and it was more in startled surprise rather than agony that he screamed as the guard flashed his knife from his sheath and severed his left ear. His right ear quickly followed, slapping onto the marble as Bagoas' screams intensified. The guard brought his knife to the base of the boy's nose and with a savage heave sliced through flesh and cartilage to leave a blood-spurting orifice in the middle of Bagoas' face. A second guard then squeezed Bagoas' mouth, forcing it open with one hand and, brandishing a knife in the other, pierced the tip of his tongue and pulled it out; his mate's wrist flicked down and with a gurgling wail Bagoas watched his tongue, quivering on the point of the knife, being taken away from him by a maniacally grinning guard. As Bagoas stared in catatonic horror at the macabre sight half his vision disappeared; but he barely registered the pain of his left eye being gouged out as his body and mind became rigid with shock.

'Take him away and let it be known that they who give the Lie to the Great King will receive no mercy.' As the bleeding, hyperventilating, mutilated boy was dragged away, leaving a trail of blood, Vologases turned his attention to the innkeeper shaking on the floor, his face rubbing in a pool of his own vomit. 'To him I will give death; impale him.'

Writhing and shrieking, the innkeeper was hauled off and Vologases graced Vespasian with the slightest of smiles. 'What was your purpose in seeking out Gobryas?'

'I had hoped that if he'd received the gold he would repay the favour by helping me and my companions back to Judaea or Syria with one of his caravans.'

'Would you have done this, Gobryas?'

'Light of the Sun, I am in this man's debt for, although his family kept my younger brother as a slave for such a long time, that was not by design. We all have slaves and those slaves all have families. It was not the fault of the purchaser that they came to own Ataphanes; it was the will of Ahura Mazda that he was spared death and enslaved. In all respects this man's family have acted properly. I shall repay him and, if you would sanction it, give him passage west on my next caravan that leaves at the full moon.'

'I do sanction it. Gobryas, you may take them and show them all hospitality until they leave.'

'It shall be as you command, Light of the Sun.' Gobryas bowed and backed away.

Vologases inclined his head a fraction. 'Take your companions, Titus Flavius Vespasianus, and go with the light of Ahura Mazda shining upon you.'

'My thanks, Light of the Sun,' Vespasian said; and he meant it with all his heart. He found himself bowing to the Great King and then backed away in imitation of his new host. Magnus and

Hormus got to their feet and also backed off, out through the door, past the writhing body of the innkeeper, his hands bound, struggling on his tip-toes to stop the pointed stake upon which he was perched intruding further up his rectum. As the doors to the audience chamber closed they turned and looked at each other and then at the man who had betrayed them, suffering so painfully.

'Jupiter's arse, cock and balls, that was close,' Magnus whispered.

'Yes,' Gobryas agreed, 'I have never known the Great King to be so merciful.'

Gobryas' garden was cool and peaceful, its atmosphere calmed by the gentle patter of fountains and the trilling of songbirds. It was a garden in bloom; some of the plants were exotic to Vespasian's eye and some familiar, but all shared a sweetness of scent that infused him with a sense of wellbeing. Over the last ten days since the interview with Vologases, Vespasian had sought refuge in this little paradise, healing the wounds of the long months of darkness that had been reopened by his brief reincarceration.

During this time he had had many conversations with his host and the two other surviving brothers of his late freedman; the family had proved courteous and surprisingly free from rancour and he answered their questions about Ataphanes' life at Aquae Cutillae, the Flavian estate near Reate, fifty miles up the Via Salaria to the northeast of Rome. He told them of Ataphanes' great friendship with his fellow freedman, Baseos the Scythian, who had also been a master of the bow; he spoke of their shooting competitions and their deadly accuracy with the weapon when it came to defending the estate from mule-thieves and runaway slaves. He also told the family of Baseos' lack of interest in gold and how he had given all that he earned to Ataphanes. He confirmed that, as far as he knew, Baseos was still alive and he promised that he would extend an invitation to the old Scythian to visit the family and receive the honour due to such a good friend of the dead youngest son.

The talk of Aquae Cutillae and the doings of the freedmen there made him long to return home and enjoy the rural life for a while, a life of mule breeding, wine making and olive pressing. He began to yearn for the peace of the estate and also of his other one at Cosa that had been left to him by his grandmother, Tertulla. He was sure that his lot was not to retire to the country life, at least not yet, not until he had done all that he could to follow the path set out for him; however, he was weary and he promised himself six months to a year of tranquillity upon his return to Rome. It would be time to rest while he watched from a distance the battle to succeed Claudius unfold and to see whether Tryphaena's grandiose scheme to secure both sides of her family in power would work. And then, if it did, how best to exploit the inevitable mayhem and misery that the incestuous reign of Nero and his mother Agrippina would bring. As he contemplated the realities of that, he began to think that perhaps he would be best served by remaining inconspicuous during that time; perhaps he would spend a few years on the estates after all.

It was as he was mulling these things over in the shade of a mature almond tree on the last afternoon before the caravan departed that a worried-looking Gobryas approached him accompanied by another man, grey of beard and with dewy eyes.

'Vespasian, this is Phraotes,' Gobryas said, showing courteous deference to the stranger.

Phraotes stepped forward and gave him the Parthian greeting-kiss of an equal, on the lips. 'Titus Flavius Vespasianus, the Light of the Sun, Vologases, the King of Kings, commands that you join him to enjoy the sport provided by the game in his paradise.'

Vespasian clung onto the side of the two-horse chariot with his left hand as its driver steered around a majestic Cedar of Lebanon; in his right hand he hefted a light hunting spear over his shoulder as he gauged the ever-changing distance between him and the Persian Fallow Deer doe that both he and Vologases were chasing. Both chariots were driven with prodigious skill over the smoothly manicured lawns of the royal hunting paradise; the speed at which they travelled was exhilarating and

Vespasian managed to forget the two horse archers following him with their bows ready to take him down should he threaten the Great King with his weapon. Vespasian had no intention of doing harm to Vologases but he understood the precaution; Vologases was showing him, as a Roman, a great deal of trust to allow him to bear both a bow and a spear in his presence.

The doe twisted to her left and Vespasian braced his knees as his vehicle swerved accordingly to keep the quarry to his right. He felt the wind pulling at his long beard and he smiled involuntarily at the thrill of the high-speed chase. As the chariot straightened up he glanced ahead to Vologases; the Great King stood tall on the platform of his chariot, ready to cast his spear; however, he looked back to Vespasian and with a small head gesture invited him to throw first.

Vespasian pulled his right arm back, his eyes fixed upon his prey, just thirty paces away, and hurled the spear with a mighty grunt, aiming a fraction in front of the doe. It flew true and the deer ran straight but the instant before impact it bucked and the spear just grazed under the beast's belly and entangled in its hind legs, bringing it tumbling down in a flurry of thrashing limbs. Vologases' driver hauled on his reins, slowing his team up, so that the Great King could jump clear. Vespasian joined him kneeling by the stunned creature; the doe breathed in fast, regular breaths as it lay on its side.

Vologases ran his hands over all four limbs. 'None appear to be broken; she should be fine once she's got over the fall. I shall hunt this pretty thing on another day and give her the death she deserves and not just skewer her as she lies helpless on the ground.' Vologases got to his feet; he stood a full head taller than Vespasian. 'Come, we shall eat.'

The main dish of rice with raisins, almonds, chicken and saffron had been exquisite and the accompanying platters of roasted meats and spiced vegetables had been equally pleasing. Vespasian sipped a chilled wine and settled back in his couch in the cool of the pavilion set on a lawn that sloped gently down to a reed-fringed lake alive with waterfowl.

Vespasian and Vologases were the only people dining; the rest of the party sat on blankets a respectful distance from the pavilion. Shadows lengthened as the sun disappeared into the west, torches were lit and Vespasian found it hard to comprehend that they were at the heart of one of the great cities of the East and not on some remote country estate.

Conversation had been polite and had not strayed onto any contentious subjects. It came, therefore, as no surprise to Vespasian when Vologases dismissed the two serving eunuchs and broached the real reason behind the invitation. 'My enforced withdrawal from Armenia because of a lack of supplies after two frozen winters and then a rebellion in the east that needs my attention this summer have had the obvious consequence.'

Vespasian placed his goblet down; he did not need long to gather what that consequence was. 'I assume that Radamistus has reinvaded?'

'Of course; but it's been unexpectedly fortunate.' Vologases raised his brow. 'Young pups like him don't know how to rule: he's executed every noble that he could catch, accusing them of betraying him. I think you'll agree that's very good for both of us.'

Vespasian stared in surprise at Vologases.

The Great King chuckled softly and sipped his wine. 'Do you think that I cannot see that this crisis in Armenia has been manufactured? We have been provoked into an unnecessary war; but why? One look at Claudius' age and health and the battle to succeed him tells me the real reason for this distraction. I do not know exactly who is behind it but I believe that you do, seeing that you just happen to have been in the right place at the right time. You, an ex-consul with an imperial mandate to act as ambassador to Armenia, come in from Cappadocia with an army led by a crippled idiot with no military experience, sack a peaceful town and then break the treaty between us by rebuilding Tigranocerta's walls? Only the most obtuse of rulers would not see that there is far more behind this than meets the eye; especially as King Polemon of Pontus and his sister, the former Queen of Thracia, both sent Babak of Nineveh messages informing him exactly what was going to happen. How did they know?'

Vespasian retreated to the safety of his goblet.

Vologases inclined his head in recognition of his guest's decision to remain silent rather than give the Lie. 'The interesting thing was that Babak told his king but Izates never passed those messages on to me; it was almost as if Izates thought that Babak's campaign in Armenia was about removing Radamistus for his own ends. Perhaps he felt that he could become king of that land as well? Fortunately Tryphaena sent me a very informative letter about my client king and I was able to have the royal army campaigning against Radamistus within two months of Babak's arrival; the former satrap of Nineveh spent his final hours in much discomfort.'

Vespasian shuddered, knowing exactly what that entailed. 'And Izates?' he asked, hoping that the man who had robbed him of two years of his life had also ended up on the wrong end of a pointed stake.

'He cringed and crawled and kissed the ground beneath my feet but I left him on his throne; I just didn't leave him with the means to see it. Still, he has twenty-four sons and twenty-four daughters so I'm sure one of them will hold his hand and guide him about.'

Vespasian felt a surge of bitter joy at the justice of Izates' fate. 'That is very pleasing.'

'I thought that would be your reaction.' Vologases contemplated Vespasian for a few moments. 'I will not ask you to tell me who you have been working for but I can guess. What I will ask you, Titus Flavius Vespasianus, is that, when you return to Rome to inform whomsoever, this unnecessary war of mutual convenience will be pursued with a modicum of vigour.'

'Mutual convenience?'

'Indeed. Tell them that the circumstances that have forced me to withdraw temporarily from Armenia will soon be dealt with; and next year I will return and we shall resume our sparring. I, like they, have political need of the distraction.'

'To keep your subject races from contemplating too deeply their position?'

'Amongst other things, yes; it also makes me look as if I'm defending my peoples' honour and keeps my army sharp. War with Rome is a necessity, not a luxury.'

'Yes, I've come to see that too, but from the opposite position.'

'No wonder the powers behind the Roman throne only allowed you the bare minimum time as consul: too much insight into high politics is a threat.'

Vespasian made no comment; if the Great King of Parthia could make inferences from his two-month term of office, then he knew he had been right to read it as an insult.

'So, my friend,' Vologases continued, 'I may call you that, mayn't I?'

'I am honoured.'

'Because of Radamistus' behaviour, when I go back to Armenia next year I will have the nobility on my side and I will sweep Radamistus from the country and reinstall my younger brother as king. It will take quite an army a few campaigning seasons to prise him out again once I've put him back. It will provide a very good distraction in Rome during the change of regime and will no doubt give young Nero his first victory in the Purple and thus secure him in power. From what my agents tell me he has the potential to make Caligula seem a sane and reasonable man. A man who gets pleasure from sleeping with his own mother on a regular basis will undoubtedly descend into unrestrained excess and depravity in search of new thrills.'

Vespasian nodded, smiling thinly. 'And you think what I think?'

'I think he will be the last of the line, which is why Parthia will do everything in her power to ensure that he inherits. We'll let the war rumble on in Armenia, then come to some diplomatic solution, after which Nero will concentrate on glorifying himself and financially ruin Rome. His subsequent assassination will spark a civil war that will further deplete Rome's coffers and whoever comes out on top will have such a financial crisis to deal with that he will find it hard to defend his borders. Then, if Ahura Mazda has spared me, I can decide how to treat with the new Emperor from a position of power.'

'Why do you tell me this?'

'I was just curious as to why you support Nero with its inevitable consequences.'

'To rid Rome of the Julio-Claudians once and for all.'

Vologases got to his feet. 'And with whom would you replace them? I tell you, my friend, if you were my subject there would be very few extremities still attached to your body.' He gave a friendly smile as Vespasian, too, rose. 'I wish you a safe journey tomorrow. I have ordered a troop of royal camel archers to accompany the caravan; not too many so as not to draw undue attention to it but enough to see you safely back to your empire. I wish you luck; I doubt that our paths will cross again.'

CHAPTER XVI

'YOU'VE GOT TO be joking with me.' Magnus stared in horror at the saddled camel, kneeling, waiting to be mounted; a grinning camel-wrangler held its bridle.

'How else do you plan to travel across the desert?' Vespasian asked, sizing up the beast that he was supposed to ride; it eyed him back with a haughty look, chewing methodically.

'We had horses when we crossed from Syria.'

'That's further north and it wasn't such a long journey. Mehbazu tells me that horses only stand a chance of making it across to Judaea in winter.'

'Mehbazu should know; he's made the journey at least a dozen times,' Gobryas said. 'It can take up to fifteen days to make the crossing once you've taken the ferry over the Euphrates.'

They were on the west bank of the Tigris having taken one of Gobryas' boats across at dawn. The caravan had been ready, waiting for them along with the eighty royal camel archers that Vologases had promised. Mehbazu, the caravan leader, had greeted Vespasian with a degree of awe as the man to whom the Great King of Parthia had shown such honour in providing him with men from his personal guard.

The seven other merchants travelling in the caravan had touched their foreheads and bowed to Vespasian as a man in high favour with their monarch, and so it was with a fervent desire not to make a fool of himself in public that he approached the waiting mount that seemed to have the entire fly population on this side of the Tigris feasting in its nostrils.

A loud, bestial bellow announced Hormus' successful mounting as his camel rose, hind legs first, almost unseating its novice rider. Hormus' camel-wrangler then mounted his own beast, showed him how to hold his legs to one side of the neck and then demonstrated how to use the goad to persuade the animal to move.

Vespasian and Magnus watched the lesson, which Hormus seemed to digest well.

'His confidence has returned now that he feels you've forgiven him for our arrest,' Magnus observed as Hormus managed to make his mount turn to the left.

Vespasian raised an eyebrow at Magnus. 'But I did warn him that he would end up like Bagoas if he ever again jeopardised my safety with his desire to interfere with young lads' bottoms.'

'That should keep his mind focused and his cock in his loin-cloth.'

The lesson came to an end, Vespasian and Magnus looked at each other and shrugged and then, with differing degrees of confidence, climbed onto the saddles perched atop their camels' humps.

Vespasian feared for his neck as his body was violently jerked by his camel rising to all four feet. The merchants and the eighty royal camel archers waited patiently as Vespasian, Magnus and Hormus practised starting, steering and stopping their novel mounts until they felt confident enough to embark on the five-hundred-mile journey to the Roman frontier.

'May Ahura Mazda watch over you, Vespasian,' Gobryas said in farewell.

Vespasian looked down from his high perch. 'Thank you, my friend. And thank you for my life.'

'It was given in payment of a debt; we are now equal.'

With a smile and a nod, Vespasian acknowledged the truth of the statement and urged his beast forward, giving a last wave to his saviour.

'What did the Great King have to say?' Magnus asked, drawing his mount level with Vespasian as behind them, with much bellowing, roaring and snorting, the hundred or so heavily laden pack camels were urged to their feet and into motion by their handlers.

'Oh, he just proved what a good mind-reader he is,' Vespasian replied, trying to settle into the rhythm of his camel's gait.

'What do you mean?'

'He told me that if I had been one of his subjects, he would have me executed or mutilated for having treasonous intent.'

'And have you?'

'Not directly, Magnus, but Vologases taught me two things yesterday: first, that a ruler must be able to show mercy, otherwise his punishments mean nothing. And second, that nothing should ever be taken at face value, especially when you're dealing with the motivation of an enemy; always ask yourself the question "why?".'

'Like: why am I on this camel?'

Vespasian laughed. 'No, that was not what I meant. The real question in this case is: why did you let yourself be persuaded into mounting the camel?'

The riders had appeared from the south, shimmering wraiths in the heat haze, and had shadowed the caravan for the last few hours. Every time the officer commanding the camel archers sent out a patrol to investigate them, the riders fled; once the patrol had been recalled they would return and take up station again, always two or three miles distant. Like the caravan, they were mounted on camels, but unlike the caravan they were not hampered by heavily laden beasts of burden.

Vespasian gazed south, shading his eyes against the glare of the sun that burned down on the wasted land. 'I can still only count twenty or so; they'd be foolish to try and take on four times their number.' He looked back down the caravan; it was a quarter of a mile long. It comprised almost one hundred camels, loaded either with goods or water-skins, strung together in groups of five, each led by a mounted slave. Mehbazu and the seven merchants to whom the camels and goods belonged rode, along with Vespasian, Magnus and Hormus, at the head, while to either side it was guarded by Vologases' archers. It was not a large force but a formidable one in this parched desert that could barely support life and certainly could not support a large body of men and beasts, unless they brought their own water and knew the locations of the very few wells and oases that were scattered about this unwanted buffer zone between the Parthian and the Roman Empires. Nobody lived here except the riders. 'So the gods alone know what they think they're doing.'

'Fucking Arabs!' Magnus opined, trying to adjust his position on his camel's saddle; he had not been comfortable for eleven days now.

'Nabataeans,' Vespasian corrected.

'You told me that they were called Nabataean Arabs.'

'Yes, that's right.'

'Well, I ain't going to waste my breath saying all that, so, fucking Arabs.'

'Have it your own way.' Vespasian pushed his white linen headdress away from his eyes and looked back out at the riders. 'I'd still like to know what they want.'

'Perhaps they want to trade?' Vahumisa, one of the merchants, suggested hopefully; as Gobryas' representative in the caravan its success was a matter of acute financial interest to him.

'Then why don't they just come close and ask us?'

'Perhaps they don't like the idea of coming so close to eighty archers,' Magnus said, his head going back and forth out of time to his beast's lumbering gait; he had not got the knack of riding camels and it was not looking hopeful that he ever would, even with the splint off his now mended arm.

'That's a fair point, I suppose. What do you think, Mehbazu?'

Mehbazu looked south to the riders and shook his head as if they were of little import. 'They want what everyone wants: money. They're just trying to work out the best way of extracting some from us.'

'Will they?'

'Inevitably; the Nabataeans are notorious thieves, black-mailers, extortionists and murderers. Somehow they'll leave here richer and there's nothing we can do about it.'

Vespasian decided not to concern himself any more about the Nabataeans until they posed a less distant threat; instead he turned his mind back to the question that had occupied him for the last eleven days since leaving Ctesiphon: how would he get Pallas to protect him from Agrippina? Could he even guarantee that Pallas could still be in a position to protect him from Agrippina? A lot would have changed in politics during his absence and Pallas may well now be out of favour with the Empress. What he did know was that just before he had left for the East, Pallas had managed to secure his younger brother Felix the procuratorship of Judaea. Marcus Antonius Felix had been Antonia's steward for her considerable property in Alexandria; she had freed him in her will and he had remained in the city after her death, looking after her affairs for her son, Claudius. It had been Felix who had helped Vespasian and Magnus steal Alexander the Great's breastplate from his mummified corpse in his mausoleum. If anyone knew the current situation back in Rome it would be Felix, the one-time slave who now ruled a Roman province. Vespasian decided that once they crossed the border, in a couple of days, he would head straight for Caesarea, the administrative capital of Judaea. There he could consult with Felix; indeed, if he found him still in position as procurator that in itself would tell him much about Pallas' standing back in Rome.

If Felix was not still the procurator and Pallas had fallen from favour, Vespasian would find out from his replacement whether Narcissus had now been reinstated as Claudius' preferred freedman. As long as one of them was in a position of power, Vespasian hoped that he could use his knowledge either to protect himself from Agrippina if he imparted it to Pallas, or to help bring her down if he imparted it to Narcissus

What Vespasian was sure about was that if Pallas or Narcissus still remained unaware of what Tryphaena was trying to achieve and how she was going about it, then his information would be of great value to one of them. What was more was that the conversation that he had had with Vologases on the day before his departure from Ctesiphon would be of much interest to either of the Greek freedmen; at least the part about being willing to continue a manufactured war to help secure Nero in power would be – he would not be mentioning anything about the Great King's real motivation for doing so, the motivation that was identical to his own: the end of the Julio-Claudians.

It was with these thoughts going round his head that the sun faded and the caravan halted for the night on a stony knoll, a barren island in the midst of a flat sea of desolation.

Vespasian lay with his hands behind his head just gazing up at the stars. Although it was their eleventh night sleeping out in the open he was still in awe of the vastness of the sky and the multitude of tiny points of light; the heavens seemed far bigger and fuller here, out in the desert, than they had anywhere else. 'How many people have lain on their backs, gazing up at the night sky and been overwhelmed by its splendour, do you think, Magnus?'

Magnus, lying next to him, contemplated the question for a few moments. 'Not as many as will do.'

Vespasian frowned to himself. 'That's remarkably philosophical for you.'

'What do you mean "for me"? And anyway, why are you accusing me of being philosophical? I'm just being logical.'

'Logical?'

'Yes, taking the facts as we know them and following them through to a conclusion based solely upon those facts without the influence of sentiment, wishful thinking or exaggeration.'

'Oh, I really have caught you on an evening of deep thinking. So, give me the benefit of your logic, if you will.'

'Well, it stands to reason, don't it, sir. If, despite all the efforts we make to the contrary, people are continually being born and then survive infancy, it follows that no matter how many people have already been born, that number will be topped by those yet to be born.'

Vespasian was surprised by his friend's insight. 'Provided that the world doesn't end, of course.'

'I can't see how it will.'

'The Jews believe that it will; and those who follow Paulus or his rival sect that worship Yeshua believe that it will end very soon. Remember him going on about the End of Days which is at hand, or some such thing; so if he's right, your theory, however deeply thought, is wrong.'

'Yes, but who can believe him? He also believes that Yeshua's mother was a virgin.' Magnus chuckled. 'Really? A virgin in Judaea after our lads had been marching up and down it for a few decades since Pompey conquered Jerusalem?'

'It had reverted to being a client kingdom at the time when Yeshua would have been born so there would've been hardly any of our boys stationed there.'

'Yeah, well, the only virgins I've ever heard getting pregnant were Vestal ones and they ended up being buried alive with a jug of water and a loaf of bread.'

Vespasian sat up and looked over to Hormus who was roasting slices of meat over a smoky, camel-dung fire. 'You're our expert on this, Hormus; have you heard people say that Yeshua's mother was a virgin?'

Hormus looked up from his cooking and grinned. 'No, master; no one would say that if they wanted people to believe the rest of the things that are spoken about Yeshua.'

Vespasian smiled back at his slave. 'I can see that we're all thinking deeply this evening; it must be the scale of the sky inspiring us to greater things.' He lay back down and returned to his contemplation of the vastness above him and was about to make an observation concerning the whereabouts of the gods amongst all those stars when a series of shouts disturbed the peace of the camp. Men, clustered around other cooking fires, sprang to their feet and grabbed their weapons. But there were no sounds of conflict. Vespasian unsheathed his sword and stood cautiously, looking towards the direction of the disturbance. From out of the blackness of the desert a darker shadow emerged; none of the Royal Guards made any attempt to stop it – in fact, quite the reverse: they backed away from it. As the shadow came within range of the glow of the fires it resolved into a group of men, almost two dozen, Vespasian estimated. They came unarmed and made no threat to any man. In their midst were a couple of the royal archers who had been on sentry duty out in the darkness; they were unharmed and released in full view of everyone to show that the newcomers came in peace.

The party then stopped and one man stepped forward and looked around. Eventually his eyes rested on Vespasian and he smiled the smile of a man who had just had his suspicions confirmed. 'Greetings, Titus Flavius Vespasianus, former Consul of Rome. My name is Malichus; I am the second of that name to rule the Kingdom of the Nabataeans. I have come to inform you that you are trespassing on my land.' He hefted a full goat skin, his smile growing ever broader beneath his bush of a beard. 'However, I am willing to overlook that for a little while and share my wine with you.'

'The truth of the matter is that I need a favour,' Malichus told Vespasian through a mouthful of roasted meat.

'And how did you know that I would be out here in the middle of nowhere?' Vespasian asked, warming to the man despite his better instincts.

Malichus waved a dismissive hand as if he bumped into ex-consuls every day in his vast but empty domain. 'Caravans cross my kingdom regularly, Vespasian; if I come across them they pay a toll whether it be in coinage, goods or information.' He paused to spit out a well-chewed lump of gristle, wiped the grease from his beard and then grinned at Vespasian, his teeth glowing in the firelight. 'When I heard that you would be passing through in a few days I praised the gods of my ancestors and sacrificed two camels and a slave in thanks for them hearing my prayers and answering them so swiftly.'

'I'm pleased that you have such a close relationship with your gods.'

Malichus looked hard at Vespasian, unsure whether he had heard sarcasm in the last remark. Vespasian kept his face neutral, masking his thoughts on human sacrifice.

Malichus burst into laughter and leant over to slap Vespasian's knee. 'All great men have close relationships with their gods; how could it be otherwise?'

'Indeed, Malichus. So what is this favour that your gods have brought me here to grant for you?'

Malichus became suddenly pensive, shaking his head at the remembrance of the weight of his problem. 'I'm a powerful man; a great man, you understand, Vespasian. I am independent from both Parthia and Rome. I rule my kingdom justly and with thought for my neighbours. But do my neighbours have the same consideration for me? Pah! They treat me worse than I treat my women!'

'I'm sorry to hear that,' Vespasian said as he realised that Malichus' expression was inviting comment. 'What is it that Rome has done to make you feel of less worth than one of your women?'

Again Malichus stared hard at Vespasian, looking for signs of sarcasm as again Vespasian's expression betrayed none; just genuine concern. With another laugh and slap on Vespasian's knee Malichus continued. 'Seventeen years ago, in my father's time, the Emperor Gaius Caligula transferred the sovereignty of Damascus to the Kingdom of Nabataea as a gift of friendship to a mighty neighbour in the first year of his rule.'

It was something that Vespasian was unaware of but he made sounds of approval nonetheless.

'And my father presented him with four magnificent Arab stallions.'

'Yes, I remember now; Caligula was very fond of one of them in particular, Incitatus was its name. I had the pleasure of dining with the beast on a number of occasions,' Vespasian said, recalling Caligula's habit of inviting his favourite horse to dinner.

Malichus evidently did not find an equine presence at the dinner table unusual. 'Then, when my father died three years later, Caligula confirmed the gift of Damascus to me upon my coronation.'

'And very right and proper for him to do so,' Vespasian commented solemnly, amused by how the brash young Emperor had managed to use the same gift again.

'Indeed, my friend; a gift from one equal to another.'

'Quite so.'

'And in return I sent him another four stallions. However, he, er ... died in the spring of the following year, before my gift arrived.'

'But Claudius accepted them instead?'

'Yes, he did, and then confirmed Damascus on me as a gift commemorating his elevation to the Purple.'

Vespasian hid his admiration for such an economical use of a single gift. 'Again the correct thing to do.'

'Yes, my friend, and now that I've been given the same gift three times over you would have thought that it really was mine to keep.'

'But it's not?'

'No! Two months ago that poisonous ex-slave Felix, the procurator of Judaea, a man so beneath my rank that it offends me even to look at a letter written in his name, wrote to inform me that Claudius has decided to take Damascus back under Roman rule as part of the province of Syria. Pah! Pah!'

Vespasian inclined his head in lieu of expressing an opinion.

'Damascus is my main income! The taxes from there alone are more than those of Petra and Bostra combined. My brethren in the desert, naturally, do not pay taxes, so I have to rely on the settled population of Jews and Greeks and suchlike in my three main cities for income. If Claudius takes Damascus from me, how will I be able to distribute wealth to my desert brethren and afford all the finest things for my horses and sons?'

'Cut back on what you spend on your wives and daughters?' Vespasian suggested, instantly regretting his flippancy.

Fortunately Malichus considered the suggestion worthy of deliberation. 'I have thought about that but it would not save enough. I have to provide respectable dowries for my daughters as befits a man of great position; this year alone I've married four of them off at the cost of many horses, camels and goats as well as much gold. As to my wives and lesser women, I already provide them with the bare minimum to keep them quiet and prevent too much friction in their living quarters. No, my friend, my budget is tight as it is; I need to keep Damascus.'

'Then appeal to Caesar.'

Malichus gleamed at Vespasian, his eyes twinkling in the firelight. 'My friend, you understand my predicament so well; that is indeed what I must do. However, I am not a Roman citizen so therefore I do not have the automatic right to make such an appeal.'

Vespasian thought he understood where the conversation was heading. 'So your favour is to ask me to appeal in your name as an ex-consul?'

'No, Vespasian; the favour that I would ask of you is to get me citizenship.'

'Citizenship?'

Malichus nodded enthusiastically. 'Yes, my friend; as a citizen I can go to Rome knowing that my person is safe and there I can appeal to Caesar face to face, man to man; a conversation between rulers. And also if I were a citizen Claudius would have less right to take my property away from me.'

And so therefore he would be hardly likely to grant the request that would prejudice his case, Vespasian deemed, though he did not share the thought with Malichus. 'As an ex-consul, I do have a certain amount of influence with the Emperor; I shall see what I can do. Tell me, do you know why he has decided to take Damascus back?'

'To finance the invasion of Armenia. Pah! Gaius Ummidius Quadratus, the Governor of Syria, and Gaius Domitius Corbulo, the Governor of Asia, have been ordered to retake that kingdom; however, they haven't been given sufficient finances so Quadratus suggested that if Damascus were to be added to his province it would go some way to covering the shortfall. The Emperor agreed and so I am expected to finance the war against the Parthians in Armenia. Pah!'

Vespasian mused for a few moments on how wide and varied were the consequences of Tryphaena's self-serving scheme to secure both sides of her family in power and then dismissed the thoughts as irrelevant. Power and fortune could never be spread evenly and if it was not Malichus who was suffering, it would only be someone else; as long as it was not himself or his family then Vespasian did not much care who it was. 'So if I try to get you citizenship, what favour will you do me in return?'

'Apart from not charging a toll on this caravan?'

'Yes, apart from that; this is not my caravan.'

Malichus grinned again. 'I shall send you a gift before you depart for Rome.'

Marcus Antonius Felix embraced Vespasian formally at the top of the steps leading up to Herod the Great's palace in the modern port-city of Caesarea. A fanfare of horns greeted the distinguished visitor. As the music died away Felix declaimed the ritual welcoming in the Emperor's name to a man of consular rank. Vespasian replied, equally as ceremoniously, thanking the procurator for his words and avowing his loyalty to the Emperor. With a thunderous crash, the cohort of chain-mailed auxiliaries, formed up in the agora before the palace with their standards fluttering above them in the sultry sea breeze, came to attention and then hailed the Emperor, the procurator and then finally Vespasian. The formalities over, Felix led Vespasian into the kingly palace that was now the residence for Rome's representative in the province.

'You come in troubled times, my friend,' Felix said as they entered the cool of the interior.

'I would think so, judging by the amount of occupied crosses I saw outside the city's gates,' Vespasian replied, easing his hastily borrowed toga away from his left shoulder to allow some of the trapped heat to escape; it was not the ideal garment for high summer in Judaea.

'There are even more outside Jerusalem.'

'We avoided that city; Sabinus' description of it from when he served as quaestor there didn't enamour me of it.'

'A sensible decision. I hate going there; I just get swamped by the bigoted self-interest of all the various religious factions. It's impossible to make a judgement without mortally offending at least half of the population. I've found that the best policy is to show no mercy; any offence against the rule of Rome is punished by death and I'll only repeal the sentence for a large financial consideration.'

Vespasian looked sidelong at the procurator; it was the first time he had seen him without a beard. Felix, unlike his older brother Pallas, had evidently decided to Romanise his appearance now that he had achieved such exalted rank. 'You must be doing very well out of it then, Felix?'

Felix smiled; it was a pleasant smile that reached his eyes. 'I need to have some reward for dealing with these people. But I mustn't complain too much; this was the best that my brother could do for me. No freedman has ever been made a procurator before so I suppose it's no surprise that I was given a shit-hole that nobody else wanted.'

'And how is Pallas?'

'He's well; he's still in favour with both Claudius and Agrippina and has been able to perform some substantial services for Nero. I think he's very well set.'

'Set for what?'

'Suffice it to say that Nero married Julia Octavia, Claudius' daughter, at the beginning of this month.'

Vespasian immediately understood the implication; Agrippina and Pallas had finally got their way. 'That would make Nero's claim to the Purple over Britannicus very hard to refute. Pallas must be very pleased.'

'Yes, he is. He wrote to ask me to emphasise to you the importance of seeing him before you see Narcissus or anyone else, including Caenis, upon your return.'

Vespasian was astounded. 'How did he know that I'd be coming here? I've been imprisoned in Parthia for the last two years.'

Felix shrugged. 'You'll have to ask him; all I know is that I've been looking out for you for the last two moons.'

'The whole of the East seems to be seething with insurrection but no place more than here in Judaea,' Felix told Vespasian as they looked out over the magnificent harbour of Caesarea; a trireme, its oars spread wide and dipping in time to the faint whistle of the oar-master's flute, manoeuvred with swan-like grace through the channel between the two great man-made moles that protected the port from the ravages of the open sea beyond. But this evening that sea was placid and the only thing to disturb its surface was the golden reflection of the setting sun, which caused

Vespasian to squint as it glowed warm on the bellies of the cawing gulls circling above him, riding gentle, salt-tanged breezes.

It seemed to Vespasian that nothing could seethe with insurrection in the face of such harmony between man and nature. 'How long before we have to fight to contain it, would you estimate, Felix?'

'A few years, perhaps. This war in Armenia won't help; if that drags on, things will speed up.'

'What do you mean?'

'Well, the way that I understand it is that if Parthia resumes her hostilities next year then the following year we will organise a full-scale invasion. Quadratus will threaten Parthia's borders whilst Corbulo will take at least two legions into Armenia plus the equivalent amount of auxiliaries. Where are those troops going to come from?'

'Oh, I see.'

'Exactly. I've got seven auxiliary cohorts here and I'll probably lose three of them at least. What do I do? I can't ease up on these people as they take kindness and understanding for weakness and then double their demands for exemptions for their filthy religion. Do you know that they are exempted from providing any auxiliary cohorts?'

'Yes, I did.'

'So my only option will be to make up for my paucity of troops by using those that I do have harder.'

'Which will add to the resentment and provoke the locals into rebellion.'

'As surely as if I'm nice to them and they perceive Rome as weakening her grip on Judaea.'

'I see the dilemma.'

'The only man who can rule the Jews is their messiah and the last man who claimed to be that was Herod Agrippa.'

'Did he? I thought he was just their king.'

'No, he tried to claim more than that; it was the year after you went to Britannia.' Felix gestured to the terrace that they were standing on. 'It was right here. He appeared wearing a silver cloak at about this time of day. The sun burned golden on it, just as it's doing now; he shone like a god and the crowd hailed him as such despite the blasphemy in Jewish eyes. They wanted him to be their messiah and lead them away from Rome and he didn't deny it. He betrayed his friend, Claudius. Anyway, as he proclaimed his divinity an owl, the bird of death, perched above his head and he immediately felt ill; five days later he was dead, eaten from the inside by worms, so they say. Claudius then returned Judaea to direct Roman rule so the Jews, instead of gaining their messiah, got a Roman procurator in his place. The majority of them are still awaiting their messiah; the King of the Jews who will defeat Rome as some believe or, as others say, the King of Judaea who will rule in Rome. It doesn't really make any difference as it's all palpable nonsense.'

'I thought that this Yeshua was their messiah?'

'Only to a handful of fanatics who used not to be able to agree with one another and spent the whole time stirring one part of the populace up against another; but now their influence is growing. Just before I was appointed they apparently had a meeting in Jerusalem; have you heard of Paulus of Tarsus?'

'I've met the bastard.'

'Well, you should have killed him.'

'I know.'

'Anyway, he'd been in Corinth in Achaea spreading his poison and offending the local Jews, who apprehended him in a scuffle and asked the Governor to deal with him.'

'Gallio?'

'Yes; but he couldn't find anything wrong with upsetting the Jewish population so ruled in favour of Paulus and let him go.'

'The idiot.'

'I know. Paulus has arrived here in Judaea and has met with the other supporters of Yeshua and they seem to have sorted out their differences to a certain extent; at least that's what my agents within the movement tell me. Apparently Yeshua's brothers and nearly all of his closest associates have agreed that Paulus can take Yeshua's message to the uncircumcised, as they call them; although they haven't been able to agree on whether they should eat with non-Jews or at least with people who do not keep their dietary laws.'

'If you've got agents within the movement, why don't you use them to arrest the ringleaders? At least get Paulus.'

Felix looked at Vespasian with wistful regret. 'I've got close to him once and I'll keep trying. The trouble is that they move around and are very secretive but we have had a couple of successes; you passed one of them as you entered the city. But they're still gaining strength all the time and now they've started to spread their poison further afield; it's becoming clear that it's wider than just the Jews.'

'Yes, I know. Sabinus is having trouble with it in Macedonia and Thracia and it would seem that Izates, the King of Adiabene, is also a convert.'

Felix did not seem surprised by this news. 'I'm sure; it's spreading all the time and we haven't the power to stop it because they can whisper their lies and convert people faster than we can kill them.'

'It's already reached Rome; my slave has heard it spoken of by fellow slaves. In such a crowded city, it will spread like fire.'

'It is, according to my agents. Paulus has written to his growing number of Roman followers saying that he plans to visit them on his way to Hispania.'

'Hispania?'

'I know; throughout the Empire. That's how grand their ambitions are.' Felix grabbed Vespasian's forearm and looked him right in the eye. 'I've tried to warn my brother in my letters to him of the seriousness of their threat and their blind fanaticism. For example, a couple of years ago they cut down a condemned man from his cross in Philippi.'

'Yes, I remember, I was there when it happened; he must have been almost dead.'

'Then it might surprise you to know that Paulus' followers claim that not only is the man alive but he has made a full recovery.'

'That's impossible.'

'Is it? These people believe it isn't.'

'What proof do they have?'

Felix tightened his grip on Vespasian's arm. 'Proof? Who needs proof when you've got faith? If this does spread throughout the Empire, it would have the potential to destroy all that is good. I know these people, having tried and condemned hundreds of them; they don't care for their lives and people who don't care for their lives are dangerous fanatics. When you see Pallas, impress upon him the need to take this threat seriously before it's too late.'

Vespasian was surprised by the vehemence of Felix's appeal and the look of worried concern in his eyes. 'Yes, I will, Felix. I've seen enough of it to share your concerns; I'll make sure that he understands the danger.'

'Thank you, my friend; it's for all our sakes. The sooner we act the better.'

'And the sooner I get back to Rome the better.' Vespasian looked out over the variety of vessels moored in the port as the sun touched the surface of the sea. 'When do you think I'll be able to take a ship?'

'I've already given orders to look for a suitable one.'

'Oh, I don't need anything fancy; just a seaworthy ship that will get me back swiftly.'

'It's not you that I was thinking of; I was assuming that you wanted to take the gift that Malichus, that rogue out in the desert, sent you.'

Vespasian had half-forgotten about the promised gift in return for Vespasian's help with his citizenship. 'Well, I suppose so; but why does it need a special ship?'

'Because you wouldn't want to damage them; I've never seen more beautiful Arab stallions.'

PART IIII

❧ ❧

ROME, OCTOBER AD 54

CHAPTER XVII

'So where are you going to keep them?' Magnus asked as he and Vespasian watched the five stallions being led at dawn down the gangplank of the wide-bellied trader in which they had made the journey from Caesarea to Claudius' new port on the northern bank of the Tiber estuary. Built around a central, man-made peninsula, supporting the biggest lighthouse in the world after the Pharos in Alexandria, the modern port could hold double the amount of ships than its older, fouler-smelling rival, Ostia, on the southern bank of the estuary. Equipped with tall cranes and lined with warehouses, the quay bustled with activity as trading ships from all over the Empire were offloaded of the essentials that would keep the Roman mob fed and docile and the luxuries that kept Rome's élite contented.

They had hauled-to just up the coast overnight and had entered the magnificent, circular construction in the half-light before dawn. But despite it being his first time in the new port, as the sun rose, Vespasian only had eyes for his horses. 'You keep on asking me that,' he replied, admiring the beasts' condition after twenty days at sea.

'And you keep on avoiding giving an answer.'

'That's because you keep on trying to persuade me to give them to your beloved Greens.'

'Not give them but loan them. What else are they for other than racing? Look at them, they're magnificent.'

And they were magnificent; Vespasian could not deny that, nor, for that matter, could anyone with an eye for horse-flesh. Five Arabian Greys: dished profiles, arched necks, level croups and high carried tails; they were beautiful and drew looks and comments of admiration from everyone on the crowded quayside watching

288

them disembark. The stallions, for their part, seemed to realise that they were the objects of much attention and responded by tossing their heads and snorting while regarding the onlookers with their intelligent dark eyes, their high-stepping hoofs clattering down onto the stone quay lined with recently built brick warehouses.

'Malichus even gave you five,' Magnus went on, his expression increasingly anxious, 'so that you've always got a spare.'

'I don't gamble, Magnus.'

Magnus winced in frustration, clenching his fists by his side. 'How many times must I tell you: it's not gambling! You don't have to bet on them; all you have to do is watch them win.'

'And what do I get from that?'

'I've told you, we can work something out with the Greens. My mate Lucius, one of your clients, well, he's quite high up with the Greens now. You can get him to organise a meeting with the faction-master and come to some financial arrangement. Then the horses can live at the Greens' stables on the Campus Martius, you can visit them whenever you like, take them for a spin around the Circus Flaminius now and again if you want, and meanwhile the faction pays for their very expensive upkeep and you share the profits of their prize money when they win. Not to mention the stud price of five champions; you'll make a fortune from that. I can't see what the problem is.' Magnus threw his arms in the air in frustration as he had done many times during the voyage; it had been a daily subject of conversation as they spent their time watching the two slaves who had come with the gift taking care of their charges.

Vespasian kept his face solemn although inwardly he was laughing; he had already decided to have a conversation with Lucius the following day, at his first morning *salutio* upon his return. Ever since Magnus had suggested the idea of loaning the horses to the Greens, Vespasian had been in favour of the notion, if only because the expense of looking after five such valuable creatures would be met by someone else. However, to help pass the time he had not shared his agreement with Magnus and his friend's attempts at convincing him had grown more desperate by the day. When Vespasian had suggested, innocently, that

Magnus should perhaps make enquiries of the Whites, Reds and Blues to see if they would be interested and so have a bargaining point to get a better deal – should he eventually decide to race them – his friend had almost screamed in horror and his good eye had stared at him with almost the same blank, uncomprehending expression as his glass one. 'I'll think about it,' Vespasian said, using his stock conversation closer that had served him well over the voyage. 'I'll see you later.' He pulled up the hood of his travel cloak partially concealing his face, and followed the horses down the gangplank, leaving Magnus looking with yearning at the five stallions, shaking his head incredulously; no doubt, Vespasian thought, calculating how much money he could win by betting on them the first time they raced.

Keeping his head bowed so as to be unrecognisable, Vespasian slipped into the crowd, leaving Magnus and Hormus to bring the luggage and the horses while he went ahead, incognito, so that news of his arrival back in Rome would not be generally known until after he had spoken to his uncle.

'Vespasian!' Flavia blurted in shock as her husband walked into the atrium of their house in Pomegranate Street on the Quirinal Hill, halfway through the third hour of the day. She covered her open mouth with both hands before running and flinging herself, in a very un-Roman-like fashion, at the man she had not seen for almost three years. 'I thought that you were dead, we all did, until Pallas told us a couple of months ago that you were in Ctesiphon.'

Vespasian held his wife close, marvelling at just how pleased he was to see her. He signalled with his head that the two waiting slaves should leave the room. 'There was a time when I thought I was dead too. How are you, Flavia?'

Flavia pulled away and looked up at him, her eyes brimming with tears; suddenly they hardened and she brought her right palm across his face in a brutal slap. 'How do you think I am after you go missing for such a long time? You didn't even write!' Another slap stung his cheek and Vespasian was forced to grab both his wife's arms to restrain her.

'Calm yourself, woman. Of course I didn't write; I was in a cell for two years that wasn't equipped with letter-writing materials.' He pulled her back to him and felt the sobs shuddering up from deep within her. He stroked her hair and murmured soothing words in her ear as Flavia let out the anguish of the past few years, drenching his tunic with her tears.

'Are you going to leave me on my own for years on end again, husband?' Flavia asked as she began to pull herself together.

Not being possessed of foresight, Vespasian could not say, although he rather thought that the answer was affirmative. 'How are the children?' he asked to change the subject.

Flavia wiped her eyes on his damp tunic, leaving black smudges of kohl, and attempted a smile. 'Little Domitilla is as all small girls should be: mischievous and dutiful in equal measure. She'll just want to hold your hand all the time. Domitian may notice you but only if you give him something; but make sure it's just for him as he's a three year old with no concept of sharing. It's Titus, though, who's going to be so pleased to see you; for the last year when he gave up all hope of you being alive he ... well, he wasn't good. Britannicus was a great comfort to him and he spent most of the time with him at the palace; he's there now, I'll send him a message telling him to come here.'

'Tell him that I'll be at my uncle's house.'

Flavia kissed him on the mouth, biting his bottom lip. 'Are you going to stay here tonight?'

'I'll be back later, my dear; but I need to have a long conversation with him before I do anything.' He smiled down at Flavia. 'But I don't have to go for an hour or so, not until Magnus has arrived.' Returning the kiss with a suggestion of more passionate ones to come, Vespasian led his wife by the hand towards their bedroom.

'I've sent a message to my mate Lucius at the Greens' stables telling him that you're back,' Magnus said matter-of-factly, as if it was the most natural thing to do.

'Oh yes?' Vespasian kept his voice disinterested as they walked the couple of hundred paces to Gaius' house at the commencement of the fifth hour of the day.

'Yeah, I thought he should know that his patron was back so that he didn't miss the salutio tomorrow morning.'

'That was very thoughtful of you, Magnus; although it was unnecessary as my clients have been attending my uncle whilst I've been away.'

Magnus looked sidelong at Vespasian, grunted and then walked on in silence. 'There was hardly enough room in the stables behind your house,' he suddenly blurted out after a few more paces. 'Not for all five of them anyway, the slaves told me.'

Vespasian was well aware of this as he had visited the stables when the stallions had arrived, once he had finished attending to Flavia. 'I'm sure they'll be fine in there. If it is a bit cramped I could always move a couple into my uncle's stables, or Caenis' for that matter.'

Magnus gave another sidelong glance, this time more nervous. Vespasian pretended that he had not noticed it as they arrived at Gaius' front door. He gave it a loud knock; the viewing slat slipped back, followed a moment later by the door being opened by a youth of outstanding beauty with long blond hair and a very short tunic.

Having never seen this young slave of Gaius' before, Vespasian named himself and sent the lad off to fetch his master. 'Uncle Gaius must be doing rather well for himself if he can afford something that good-looking,' Vespasian mused as they followed the door-boy through the vestibule and on into the atrium.

'He's always had a good eye for a boy,' Magnus affirmed, watching the retreating boy's buttocks move beneath the tunic that only occasionally concealed their entirety. 'Just as well Hormus isn't in his household otherwise he'd have to be sharing them.'

The boy knocked on Gaius' study door, then opened it and announced Vespasian's arrival.

'Dear boy,' Gaius boomed, waddling out from his study and into the atrium, 'I'm so pleased to see you; we had all but given up hope.' He turned to the door-boy. 'Tell the cook that there'll be two more guests for lunch; and have wine and honeyed cakes brought out to the garden.'

'Two more guests, Uncle?' Vespasian said as he subjected himself to Gaius' flabby embrace. 'Who else is here?'

'Just me,' Pallas said, walking out from Gaius' study. 'When I heard that you'd arrived in Rome I guessed that this would be the first place you would come, despite my brother writing to me to say that he'd given you my message.'

'I confess that I'm very pleased to see you alive, Vespasian,' Pallas said once the four of them were seated in the last remaining patch of shade in the courtyard garden.

'I don't suppose Agrippina shares your enthusiasm,' Vespasian replied, still angered by Pallas' presence, which prevented him from gaining an advance insight from his uncle into the state of Rome's politics; neither the gentle patter of the fountain in Gaius' lamprey pond nor the sound of birdsong floating on the warm air did anything to soothe him.

Pallas helped himself to a cake. 'She has yet to hear the news; but I doubt she will care one way or the other as she feels, at the moment, that her position is absolutely secure.'

'I've never known anything to be absolutely secure in Rome,' Gaius observed through a mouthful of cake, 'least of all one's position.'

'Claudius is due to address the Senate this afternoon after he's finished celebrating the Meditrinalia in honour of this year's new wine vintage. Agrippina and I fully expect him to confirm Nero as his sole heir as, since he married his stepsister, he is much more than just the Emperor's adopted son. It may not have pleasant consequences for his natural son as Nero will remain the only possible heir to Claudius until the day before the Ides of February next year.'

Vespasian frowned. 'How can you be so specific?'

'Because that is the day when Britannicus turns fourteen, the earliest possible time that he can come of age and therefore be a real threat to Agrippina's ambitions.'

'And your ambitions too, surely, Pallas?'

Pallas inclined his head to concede the point. 'So, obviously she ... we have a timetable.'

'Does that mean what I think it means?'

'I don't think that we want to know exactly what that means,' Gaius put in quickly, giving Vespasian a worried look; he fortified his nerves with another cake.

Pallas studied Vespasian over the rim of his cup as he took a sip of wine. 'I believe it does,' he said eventually, placing the cup back down on the table.

Pallas looked at Magnus and raised his eyebrows.

'I'll just, er ... go and wait inside,' Magnus said, getting to his feet.

'Thank you, Magnus.' Pallas waited until Magnus had left the garden, which he did at speed. 'What we're doing is for the good of Rome.'

'Believe what you like, Pallas,' Vespasian said, somewhat more tersely than he meant to, mainly because he knew that in supporting the Nero faction he was giving tacit consent to murder.

'I do believe it.'

'But assassination is still murder.'

'And who are you to condemn murder?'

Vespasian smiled wryly. 'I'll never be allowed to forget killing Poppaeus.'

'Murder stays with you for life; but it wasn't Poppaeus I was alluding to, it was Caligula's and your brother's part in it that you helped to cover up. You didn't condemn him for killing an emperor, why should you condemn me? Especially when the emperor in question is now so constantly drunk that it's almost impossible to get any sense out of him at any time of the day.'

With a jolt, Vespasian suddenly understood that it was not Britannicus that Pallas and Agrippina planned to murder, but the Emperor.

Gaius too made the connection and got to his feet in a state of alarm. 'I think there is some urgent correspondence that needs my attention in my study.'

'Sit down, Senator Pollo, you are already involved.' Pallas' voice, normally so level and measured, was harsh and Gaius sat back down sharply, causing his wickerwork chair to creak in protest. 'I apologise for my tone, Gaius; my nerves are very stretched at present.'

Vespasian could see the tension in the freedman's expression; his face had always been a mask, betraying nothing of his thoughts, but now that mask was slipping. 'So how are you going to achieve this?'

'Agrippina will be responsible for doing it.'

'Poison, then?'

Pallas nodded and drained his cup; his mask had returned and he showed nothing of his thoughts for or against the woman's weapon of poison. 'It will be done over a period of time with small doses and will be complete before Britannicus comes of age. It will appear as if it were a natural death; no one will suspect a thing. What I need of you two gentlemen is to ensure that the Senate doesn't dawdle this time in proclaiming Nero the new emperor. As soon as you hear the news of Claudius' death you must insist upon a full meeting of the Senate and both speak for Nero.'

Gaius did not look enamoured of the prospect. 'That will make us very conspicuous.'

'It will also serve to draw the venom that Agrippina harbours for Vespasian, Gaius. I made him a promise, when he went to the East at my bidding, to help protect him from her; this is me making good that promise. I'm trusting you both with advance knowledge of an emperor's death so that you can be the first to hail his successor; that should be the sort of conspicuousness that is a benefit not a curse.'

Gaius mumbled thanks and apologies at the same time and then tried to cover his embarrassment by tucking into the last cake.

Pallas took a deep breath to calm himself. 'But before I give my full and unequivocal support to Agrippina and Nero I need to know if she has committed any treason by colluding with Rome's enemies that could be used against her and therefore against me.' He turned to Vespasian and waited for him to speak.

Vespasian spoke for almost an hour recounting his conversations with Sabinus, Tryphaena, Paelignus, Vologases and Felix.

When he was finished Pallas sat in thoughtful silence. 'Tryphaena?' he said after a while. 'So the embassy wasn't Parthian after all but her people masquerading as such. I suppose that the leaders of the northern tribes wouldn't know the difference between a real and a fake Parthian. In reality they probably just spent a few days of meaningless conversation with the embassy, having no idea that they were being deceived; but it was enough to make us suspicious. It was just all about timing; that explains it.' He gave a rare smile. 'Narcissus was wrong; Agrippina had nothing to do with it.' His smile broadened. 'That's a great weight cleared from my mind. If she's not vulnerable to the accusation of treason then I can feel safe enough to press ahead with our arrangements. Tryphaena has prepared the ground for us very well indeed; there is even an Armenian delegation just arrived in the city to plead with the Emperor to send in more troops. Luring Parthia into a war with Rome has done everything that she hoped. People are now openly blaming Claudius for the instability in the East; only a couple of days ago a series of senators spoke against him in the Senate – in guarded terms, admittedly, but still against him.'

Gaius nodded, licking crumbs from his fingers. 'I was there; it made me rather uneasy. Can you imagine anyone doing that with Caligula?'

'Or, for that matter, in the early days of Claudius' reign?' Pallas contemplated that for a few moments. 'No, it has weakened him; that and his drinking as well as all the stories whispered by Seneca and Burrus, exaggerating Nero's capabilities and intelligence; people are now ready for a change. Especially since Paelignus came back to Rome boasting of how he lost a couple of fingers while he bloodied the Parthian nose but was then forced to withdraw because of lack of reinforcements.'

'Paelignus is back?' Vespasian felt a surge of hatred for the odious little procurator who had cost him two years of his life.

'Yes, and foolishly he's let it be known that he was very wealthy again with what he brought back and then what he inherited on the death of his father last year. Claudius made him a senator now that he's passed the financial threshold and has since, when sober, been systematically stripping him of his new wealth at the gaming table.'

'I'd like to strip him of a lot more than that. He betrayed me to the Parthians in Armenia.'

'Did he now? That's not how Paelignus tells it.' Pallas held Vespasian's gaze. 'You'll have the perfect opportunity for revenge for what he did to you in Armenia in the blood-letting that will follow Nero's ascension.'

'And will there be much?'

'I hope not. If, between Seneca, Burrus and myself, we can keep Nero in line then he could make a fine emperor; at least at the beginning.'

That was not Vespasian's reading of Nero's character. 'And after the beginning?'

'We'll see what happens once power ceases to be a novelty. The important thing is for him not to think that the Senate are against him, as Claudius did at the start of his reign; and that will be down to you two. Emphasise in your speeches that Nero will show strength from the very start by prosecuting the war in Armenia that Vologases is so considerately continuing for both our sakes.'

Vespasian had a moment of clarity. 'If it's strength that he wants to portray then he should also do something here, something tangible that both the Senate and the people will respect.'

Pallas was interested. 'What are you suggesting?'

'Your brother's warning about this Jewish cult; have Nero take a personal interest in stamping them out in Rome.'

'A couple of years ago, while you were away, Claudius expelled a whole load of people, Jews and otherwise, for worshipping somebody called Chrestus; is that the same thing?'

'Probably; but does it matter? The important thing is to unite the majority of the people behind the new Emperor by vilifying a dangerous minority and exterminating them.'

Pallas got to his feet. 'Yes, that should bring about a communal sense of wellbeing; especially if we can find a couple of higher profile members of this cult. Gaius, I'm afraid that I have to decline your kind offer to stay for lunch; I need to get back to the Palatine to escort Claudius to the Senate. No need to get up, gentlemen; I trust that you will be present to hear the Emperor speak at the seventh hour?' Without waiting for a reply he walked out of the garden, leaving Gaius sweating with fear of knowledge that he would rather not have possessed and Vespasian contemplating his revenge on Paelignus.

'Father!' Titus called as he entered the garden with Magnus shortly after Pallas had left. With a distinct lack of decorum he ran to Vespasian, who stood and returned his son's embrace with equal measure.

Making a conscious effort not to comment on how much Titus had grown or coming out with any of the other stock phrases that always seem to accompany a reunion with a child after some considerable time, Vespasian took his son by the shoulders and held him at arm's length, admiring him.

'I nearly choked when he was let in,' Magnus said. 'I thought it was you at the age when we first met.'

'There's no denying your paternity, Vespasian,' Gaius added, pleased to have a pleasant family observation to make to take his mind off what Pallas had revealed.

Titus was indeed the younger image of his father, stocky, round-faced with a prominent nose and humorous eyes; the one difference was that he lacked the permanent strained expression, as if he was having difficulty at stool, which Vespasian had developed during his time commanding the II Augusta.

'I thought we'd lost you, Father,' Titus said after a few moments of staring at each other.

Vespasian fingered Titus' toga praetexta, the purple-bordered toga worn by magistrates as well as boys who had not yet come of age. 'You'll be fifteen in December, won't you, Titus?'

'Yes, Father.'

'Then we'd better do something about this. Tomorrow I shall declare you to be a man.'

Titus beamed at Vespasian. 'Thank you, Father. May I ask Britannicus to come and witness it?'

'Lunch is ready, master,' Gaius' steward announced from the door.

Gaius' face lit up. 'At last, Ewald; I'm famished.'

Vespasian put his arm around Titus' shoulder and led him towards the house. 'I must insist upon you not seeing Britannicus for a while, Titus.'

'But what about our lessons together and our riding and sword play?'

'They're going to have to be suspended.'

Titus stopped and looked at his father as Magnus and Gaius walked on. 'Are you telling me that Nero is about to become emperor?'

'What makes you say that?'

'Because I know what will happen; Britannicus told me. Claudius will be assassinated, Nero will become emperor and Britannicus' life will be over. He's no fool, Britannicus. He knows that Claudius must die before he comes of age in order for Nero to become emperor unopposed; it's obvious, therefore, that he'll be assassinated sometime in the New Year. I assume that you telling me that I've got to break my ties with Britannicus is because you've found out about the assassination. Pallas' presence here means that he's told you so that you can be prepared to work for him in the Senate, supporting Nero.'

Vespasian was astounded. 'Did you work all that out yourself?'

'The part about the reason for Pallas being here, yes, but all the rest was with Britannicus.'

'Has he told his father?'

Titus was dismissive. 'Of course; but Claudius won't listen and just laughs it off and says "good luck to you, my boy" as if Fortuna can postpone the inevitable. He's told Britannicus that once he reaches his fourteenth birthday he'll change his will and make Britannicus his heir instead of Nero.' Titus gave a grim chuckle. 'Claudius is as stupid as Britannicus is clever and if Claudius chooses to do nothing then both their deaths will be inevitable. Britannicus does get some comfort from the fact that his idiot father will die before him; but I'll get no comfort from losing my friend who helped me keep my mind off you when we thought you were ...' Titus trailed off, evidently embarrassed to display such sentiments.

'You mustn't say a word of this to anyone, Titus.'

'Of course not, Father; unlike Claudius, I'm blessed with a brain.'

Vespasian looked into his son's eyes, assessing him for the first time as an adult and not a child any more. 'Yes, I can see that, and so I will trust you. You're right: Pallas is planning Claudius' death and Nero's ascension. I will aid him for two reasons: firstly, I have no choice, and secondly, even if I did have a choice, I believe that this is the best for our family. So your friend's life is over, I'm afraid.'

Anger flared for a brief moment in Titus' eyes and the muscles in his jaw pulsed; he took a deep breath. 'Now do you see how important it is for Britannicus to be present at my coming of age ceremony, Father? He's never going to have his own so he would dearly love to see mine.'

Vespasian thought about it for a few moments and then sentimentality, for once, got the better of cold reason. 'Very well, Titus, you can invite him; tell him to be at our house tomorrow at the second hour of the day, after I've finished greeting my clients.'

'Of course, not all your clients have remained loyal,' Gaius said, wiping his lips, moist with the juice of a pear that had rounded off the light lunch of bread, cold meats and fruit. 'They all attended me for the first six months or so, once I got back, but then after you hadn't been heard of for a while a few started to cultivate other senators.'

Vespasian swung his feet off his couch for one of Gaius' boys to slip on his red, senatorial shoes. 'Who, Uncle?'

'Generally, the sitting consuls and praetors.'

'No, I meant which of my clients?'

'Oh, I see. I don't have their names to hand but I know that Ewald has a list. He'll give it to you before you leave.'

The steward acknowledged his master's wish and went in search of the document.

Vespasian stood and allowed the boy to begin draping his toga around him. 'Thank you, Uncle; if there is one thing that I can't abide, it's ingratitude.'

'My feelings exactly, dear boy; that's why I had Ewald make up the list,' Gaius said as he patted his tonged curls into place with the help of a bronze mirror held up by another of his slave boys. 'We should hurry if we want to be at the Senate House before Claudius starts his address; assuming, of course, that he hasn't imbibed too much of this year's vintage in his enthusiasm for the Meditrinalia. If Pallas is right then the Emperor's going to set himself up for the most enormous, and fatal, piece of ingratitude.'

CHAPTER XVIII

THE PEOPLE OF Rome interrupted their business and cheered their Emperor as he passed, borne in a litter preceded by twelve lictors, down the Via Sacra from the Palatine to the Forum Romanum. They cheered and waved and applauded and then, as soon as the rearmost litter-bearer had passed, they immediately returned to their more pressing affairs, leaving the cheering to those further down the route so that the praise rippled down the street, desultory and conspicuously lacking the enthusiasm with which they had lauded Claudius at the beginning of his reign.

Claudius, for his part, either did not, or affected not to notice the lack of fervour with which he was received by his people; he reclined on his litter, hailing the crowd with a shaking arm – as much due to excessive drink as it was to his afflictions – while his head twitched erratically and his slack mouth oozed drool that he occasionally dabbed at with a handkerchief.

Two centuries of German Imperial Guardsmen surrounded the Emperor, tall and muscled, their hair and beards long but well groomed; their right hands gripped their sword hilts, ready for immediate action. They loped by with long strides, their barbarian trousers and strange tattoos reminding the people of Rome just how removed the Emperor was from them. But still they cheered, if only the bare minimum to ensure that Claudius was not insulted and would not decide to spend less money on the Ludi Augustales, the ten days of games that cumulated in the Augustalia, the celebration of the first Emperor's achievements, due to be marked on the following day, three days before the Ides of October.

Vespasian stood next to Gaius amongst the other five hundred or so senators currently present in the city on the steps of the

Curia, ready to welcome their Emperor. It had clouded over and a light rain now fell from the dull sky, dampening the wool of their togas and bringing out the scent of the urine in which they were washed.

The procession turned into the Forum and transactions along the arcades and the damp, open-air trial came to a brief halt, for politeness' sake, until, with the Emperor's passing, they could continue.

'He does look his age,' Vespasian commented out of the corner of his mouth as Claudius' litter was set down at the foot of the steps. Pallas and Narcissus both accompanied it; the latter, with swollen ankles and making heavy use of a walking stick.

'He looks eighty-four, not sixty-four,' Gaius muttered. 'He's the same age as me and Magnus yet he looks as if he could be our father; his trouble is that he doesn't abstain enough.'

Vespasian looked pointedly at his uncle's corpulence. 'Whereas you do, Uncle?'

Gaius rubbed his ample belly with affection, obscured not in the slightest by the copious folds of his toga. 'A well-rounded physique is not necessarily the sign of reckless overindulgence; whereas bloodshot, baggy eyes that lack focus and a florid, to say the least, complexion does hint of excessive consumption of the fruit of Bacchus. And that, along with his almost complete baldness, his sagging arse and breasts, makes him look twenty years older than me and helps me to feel remarkably good about myself.'

Vespasian could not argue, for his uncle's description of the ageing Emperor was very accurate; he looked even more ravaged than Tiberius had at the age of seventy-three, when Vespasian had been brought before him on his island hideaway of Capreae, twenty-four years before.

'Moreover,' Gaius continued in a whisper as the litter came to a halt in front of the Senate House, 'it's affected his mind; his grasp on detail has faded and his literary endeavours are so rambling now as to be barely intelligible.'

Pallas helped Claudius to his unsteady feet; he had evidently taken the Meditrinalia very seriously that morning. Claudius looked around at the senators, his eyes red and dewy and slightly downturned like his mouth, before shambling up the steps in a series of weak-kneed lurches, forcing his lictors to ascend faster than dignity dictated.

As Claudius passed, wreathed in a mist of wine fumes, Vespasian's eye caught that of Narcissus as he followed his patron up the steps next to Pallas. The Greek showed a rare hint of surprise as he registered that the man whom he had sent out East to investigate his suspicions about the Parthian embassy was indeed back in Rome and had failed to inform him of the fact.

'Senator?' Narcissus crooned as he paused next to Vespasian. 'You will, of course, come and see me at your earliest convenience?'

'Of course, imperial secretary,' Vespasian replied, unable to envisage a time of any convenience.

Narcissus nodded and then hobbled on after Claudius as the senators crowded up the steps in his wake, talking loudly of their eagerness to hear the Emperor's speech while thinking quietly about how they were going to stay awake during what was normally an hour or two of eye-wateringly pedantic tedium.

'The auspices from the sacrifice are good for the business of Rome. The Senate calls on our beloved Emperor, Tiberius Claudius Caesar Augustus Germanicus, to address the House,' the Junior Consul, Marcus Asinius Marcellus, declaimed, standing next to the seated Claudius; behind him, in what was an outrage that had now become so commonplace that nobody remarked on it any more, sat Pallas and Narcissus.

'I'm g-g-grateful, Conshul,' Claudius said, remaining in his curule chair and unrolling what looked to be an unusually thick scroll; even the most ardent sycophants' morale plummeted at the sight of it, for a long, stuttering speech from Claudius was not for the faint-hearted, especially when he was so obviously drunk. 'C-c-consh-script Fathers, I am here t-t-t-to speak t-t-t-to you on the shub-b-bject of inheritansh.'

Vespasian kept his most attentive expression activated as his mind began to filter out the stream of legal precedent, rambling pedantry and patronisingly self-satisfied references to the ways of the ancestors, punctuated only by brief pauses for dabbing at the excess drool issuing from both corners of his mouth and the constant stream of slimy mucus oozing from his left nostril.

Vespasian's eyes roved the four rows of senators, sitting on their folding stools on the opposite side of the Curia. There were more than a few new faces as a result of Claudius' perpetual tinkering with the senatorial rolls but there were many whom he recognised: Sabinus' son-in-law, Lucius Junius Paetus, was seated next to Vespasian's former thick-stripe military tribune in the II Augusta, Gaius Licinius Mucianus; both men inclined their heads towards him as they became aware of his gaze. That they should be sitting together was no surprise to Vespasian; what was surprising was who was sitting on Paetus' other side: Marcus Valerius Messalla Corvinus, the brother of the late Empress Messalina. Corvinus assiduously kept his eyes away from Vespasian; his old enemy was still keeping his promise to conduct himself as a dead man in Vespasian's presence in return for Vespasian saving his life during the downfall of his sister. Vespasian, murmuring agreement and nodding in time with the rest of the Senate as they endured Claudius' speech, wondered what could have possibly brought two senators, both indebted to him, so close to his sworn enemy. One thing was sure: a man was judged by whom he sat next to in the Senate. As he contemplated the question his eye wandered to another unlikely threesome: Servius Sulpicius Galba seated between the two Vitellius brothers, Lucius and Aulus. Aulus acknowledged Vespasian with studied noncommittal written on his face; their paths had first crossed on Capreae when Aulus' father had pandered his son to Tiberius who much prized him for his oral favours. There was no sign of the svelte young teenager now; Aulus had run to fat in the last few years, as had his brother Lucius. Galba just stared straight ahead into the middle distance, his gaunt, patrician face struggling to conceal the disgust that he evidently felt at the ancient institution of the Senate being addressed by a stuttering and slavering fool.

Any thoughts about what Galba was doing seated with the Vitellii were pushed from Vespasian's mind a moment later when his gaze alighted on the man responsible for his two-year exclusion from the human race: Paelignus. The runt of a procurator almost yelped in surprise as their eyes met; Paelignus evidently had no idea that Vespasian was alive, let alone back in Rome, and the way his eyes flicked around the chamber, as if looking for the nearest exit, brought a smile to Vespasian's face. He nodded at him politely, the smile becoming toothy, and wagged his fore-finger at him a couple of times, as if admonishing a naughty child. He was going to enjoy this, Vespasian decided; he would make him suffer before he killed him.

A communal gasp of shock jerked Vespasian back to the matter of Claudius' speech. Claudius had paused and the few in his audience who had been paying some sort of attention were staring at him with unbelieving countenances while the majority of the Senate were trying to ascertain from neighbours the cause of the astonishment.

Vespasian turned to Gaius, next to him. 'What did he say, Uncle?'

'I've no idea, dear boy, but one look at the expressions of Pallas and Narcissus should be enough to tell you who has gained from whatever it was.'

Narcissus had the closest Vespasian had ever seen to a smirk on one corner of his mouth, whereas Pallas' right eye was twitching irregularly.

'However, I shall g-g-g-go further than that,' Claudius went on. 'I p-p-publicly thank my adopted son, Nero, for being pr-pr-prepared to shoulder the responsibilities of my office had I been called to the F-f-f-ferryman; but now ash my natural son, Britannicush, approaches the time when he shall take the toga virilish, Nero has no need to worry himself about taking on the onerous tasks of the Pr-pr-pr-princeps. I release him from that duty with my gratitude and I know that as my adopted son and son-in-law he will support Britannicus when the time comes and be a shoulder of strength for him to lean on.'

Claudius paused again, no doubt thinking that there should be some acknowledgement of the fair and just sentiments that he had expressed. However, there was nothing but a low mumbling as men checked with their neighbours that they had heard correctly.

'I think the time is coming very, very soon,' Gaius muttered.

Vespasian just stared at the fool on the curule chair as he continued to hasten his own death by an ill-judged, drunken speech; Gaius had not exaggerated Claudius' mental decline.

'That b-b-b-being the case, I feel that it would be right of me to d-divorce my wife, Agrippina, and replace her with someone lessh partial to also act as a guide for Britannicus after I am gone, so I would ask you, C-c-c-consh-script Fathers, to put your minds to thinking of a suitable candidate; someone of high birth, with intelligence, feminine skills and b-b-beauty would pleashe me.'

'I can almost hear the sound of Agrippina mixing her potions,' Vespasian whispered.

'This must be the longest suicide note in history,' Gaius ventured, staring with barely concealed incredulity at Claudius.

'I would also ask you, C-c-conscript Fathers, to conshider what rewards should be voted Nero and Agrippina for their service to the Empire; b-b-bronze statues in the Forum, perhaps? Or maybe a gift of land in one of the provinces; perhaps both. I leave it to you. In the meantime, until Britannicush's fourteenth birthday, you should treat Nero as my heir and honour him as you would honour me. Conscript Fathers, I thank you all for your k-k-kind attention and look forward to hearing the results of your d-deliberations.' With that he rolled up his scroll and looked around the Senate as if he was expecting thunderous applause for one of the most dexterous and far-sighted pieces of politics ever announced in the ancient chamber.

All that met him was utter and silent astonishment.

And then one senator, less dumbfounded than all the rest, slowly began to clap and then stopped suddenly, realising that to show support for Claudius' announcement was to invite a death sentence from Nero who would now surely be emperor, if not in a matter of hours then certainly within the next couple of days.

Of that, everybody in the room was sure; even Narcissus, who now stared at his patron with undisguised horror. Pallas, next to him, had his face set resolute; his timetable had just been brought forward considerably.

With a quick glance between them, the two freedmen jumped up from their chairs and walked from the Curia, one on the left-hand side, the other on the right, so that they left at the same time but not together. Claudius watched them go, twitching in confusion, and then got to his feet, steadied himself on the arm of his chair while taking deep breaths and then lurched out after them.

The senators, pleased finally to be able to do something that could not be construed as being for or against the Emperor's announcement, got to their feet and feted Claudius' departure with a mighty chant of 'Hail Caesar!', each convinced that this was the last time they would see this emperor in the Curia.

As Claudius left the building the Junior Consul brought the session to a close as no further business could possibly be contemplated that day, for the priority of the senators would now be securing their positions during the transfer of power.

'Extraordinary,' Gaius said as he folded his chair. 'He must have drunk more of the new vintage than he poured in libations this morning; it's the only explanation for such suicidal behaviour.'

'He was never a politician at the best of times, Uncle, let alone when drunk,' Vespasian pointed out. 'He won't realise what he's done until he feels the poison burning in his throat. I suppose we'd better spend the rest of the day writing our speeches in praise of Nero.'

They joined the stream of senators making for the doors and, like their peers, struck up an enthusiastic, but inane, conversation about matters of little worth as if nothing of import had occurred in the Senate House that day.

'I imagine you know why I wanted to talk with you, Lucius,' Vespasian said, seated at his desk in the tablinum early the following morning. Hormus stood in his normal position at his shoulder, taking notes.

'Yes, patronus; Magnus has told me all about the team,' Lucius replied, 'and I know for sure that the Green faction-master would be very interested in seeing them and if he approves then he would happily take all five into the Greens' stables. He has a similar arrangement with a couple of other private owners.'

'At what cost?'

'I'm afraid that I don't know anything about the financial side of it, sir; I'm just in charge of the stables' security.'

Vespasian studied his client for a few moments; he was a few years older than Vespasian. Lucius' hard twenty-five years in the IIII Scythica and then life as hired muscle for the Green racing faction had taken its toll: he was battered and bald but still brawny. He owed Vespasian his life when, as a military tribune with the IIII Scythica, his patron had come up with a face-saving way of only executing one of the two men charged with striking a superior officer during a disturbance in the camp; Lucius had been the lucky man to draw the long straw. 'Who is the Green faction-master at the moment?'

Lucius' surprise showed on his face. 'Eusebius, sir.'

'I don't take any interest in racing,' Vespasian said, explaining his ignorance. 'Take a message to Eusebius: tell him I would like a meeting and ask him when would be convenient.'

'Yes, patronus; I'll have your answer at tomorrow's salutio.'

'Thank you, Lucius. You will stay and witness my son's coming of age?'

'I'm honoured, sir. And may I say how good it is to see you back in Rome; I never once doubted that you would return.'

Vespasian inclined his head to his client, thanking him and dismissing him with one gesture. 'It would seem that he still shows gratitude; he attended my uncle almost every day while I was away. Let me have a look at Ewald's list again.'

Hormus passed the list of clients who had drifted away during Vespasian's time in the East.

Vespasian perused it and then handed it back to his slave. 'Seven of them turned up this morning, begging forgiveness, which I was happy to grant; that just leaves one: Laelius. I cannot abide ingratitude, Hormus.'

'Especially ingratitude to a man as generous as yourself, master,' Hormus said with genuine feeling.

'Compose a letter to my brother; tell him the situation and have Sabinus cancel the chickpea contract with the ungrateful shit. Also, if his son is still serving as a military tribune in one of his legions, ask Sabinus to send him home immediately without giving him a reason; that should give Laelius a lesson in gratitude.'

Hormus gave a grim smile. 'Yes, that should do it, master.'

'I'll sign the letter after Titus' ceremony. Also, send a note to Caenis to tell her I'll be with her at dusk.' Vespasian got to his feet. 'And find out to whom Laelius has now pledged his dubious loyalty.'

Hormus brandished Ewald's list. 'It says that here, master.' He ran his finger down the names. 'Marcus Valerius Messalla Corvinus.'

Vespasian took a fold of his toga, draped it over his head and then bowed to the *lararium*, the altar where the images of the *lares domestici*, the household gods, were kept. He then turned to face his son standing next to him. 'This is the last time you will be addressed as a boy.' He lifted the leather thong of the *bulla* over Titus' head; this was the phallic charm that the boy had worn since birth to ward off the evil-eye. 'I decree that from now on, my son, you, Titus Flavius Vespasianus, are a man. Take up a man's duty, dignity and honour and go out into the world and thrive in your own right to your greater glory and to the glory of the house of Flavius.'

Titus bowed his head in acknowledgement of his father's wishes.

Vespasian then placed the bulla on the altar and arranged around it five small clay statuettes that he took from a cupboard next to it. He stretched his arms out, palms upwards, muttered a short prayer, and then filled a shallow bowl with wine from the altar jug. Standing with the bowl in his right hand he poured a libation over the altar in front of the largest of the figures, the *lar familiaris*, which represented the founder of the family. He then motioned his son to join him next to the altar and gave him a sip of wine, before draining the rest himself and setting down the bowl.

Removing the toga from his head he turned to address the crowd of clients watching the ceremony, Gaius, Magnus with three of his erstwhile brethren, Tigran, Sextus and Cassandros, amongst them; Flavia sat before them, tears in her eyes, with her arm around their daughter – Domitian had been judged too ill-behaved to attend – and Britannicus stood next to them. 'I ask all you here to witness my decision to grant adult status to my eldest son.'

There was a chorus affirming that was indeed the case.

Vespasian then signalled to Hormus, who stepped forward with a plain white toga virilis, the sign of an adult male citizen, and began to drape it around Titus. When Hormus was done, Titus covered his head with a fold of his toga and, standing in the prayer position with his palms turned to the heavens, pledged himself to the house of Flavius and to its guardian god, Mars.

As the prayer was recited, Vespasian looked over to Britannicus; tears were streaming down his long face, inherited from his father, as he watched his friend complete the ceremony that, even at his young age he still had the maturity to realise, he would never, for political reasons, be allowed to celebrate.

Vespasian wondered for a moment what sort of emperor the doomed boy would have made and then remembered that he was the product of a fool and a power-mad whore. Britannicus was evidently no fool and so therefore, unless nature was going to be completely overruled, once he fully matured sexually he would probably display all the licentiousness of his mother, Messalina; perhaps he even had the potential of making Caligula look like a man with nothing more than a mildly overactive libido.

As Titus came to the end of his prayer, Vespasian dismissed the thought from his mind as irrelevant: no one could ever know what sort of emperor Britannicus would have made.

Rome was in a festive mood, ready to celebrate the Augustalia. Wreaths of flowers and laurels adorned the many statues of Augustus throughout the city and crowds of loyal subjects of the Julio-Claudians were waiting to give thanks for the founder of the dynasty's victorious return from the Civil War in the East, sixty-three years previously. All were heading for the Porta Capena, the gate that led out to the Via Appia. There, in the Temple of Fortuna Redux on the slope of the Caelian Hill just above the gate and in the shadow of the Appian Aqueduct, they would watch their Emperor, in his role as the Flamian Augustales, lead the prayers and sacrifices to his deified predecessor. But this was just a prelude to the main events of the day: the racing and the feasting.

'You needn't worry any more, Vespasian,' Britannicus said as they headed down the Quirinal Hill with Vespasian's and Gaius' clients following in attendance. 'Titus has nothing to fear from his association with me now that he has become a man.'

Vespasian failed to see how the difference in rank would protect his son walking next to him, upright and proud in his toga virilis. 'Agrippina is a spiteful woman.'

'She is; but Seneca, Domitius' and my tutor, is not a spiteful man.' Britannicus was evidently still unable to refer to Nero by his adoptive name.

'But what power does he have?' Gaius asked as Magnus and his erstwhile brothers, beating a path for the company through the holiday crowds, slowed in the face of the bottleneck at the entrance to Augustus' Forum, clogged with citizens laying small gifts at the feet of his statues.

Britannicus looked up at Gaius. 'It's not so much that he has power, it's that he has influence and he's using that influence to ensure that he will retain the luxuries that accompany it for as long as possible. Seneca knows Domitius' character only too well; who could fail to spot his excesses?'

'Your father, for a start,' Titus pointed out.

'My father's an idiot and will be dead by this time tomorrow because of it.' Britannicus spoke without a trace of emotion. 'But Seneca has managed to persuade Domitius that if he wants to rule for the rest of his *natural* life, rather than just five years like Caligula did, then he will need to restrain himself when it comes to his subjects' lives, wives and assets. If he does so then he'll be free to live a life of artistic indolence, seeing as he's starting to persuade himself that his mediocre artistic talent is the greatest ever bestowed upon any man. Meanwhile, Seneca, Pallas and Burrus take the policy decisions that they are all far more qualified to make rather than a seventeen-year-old youth who's not allowed to let go of his mother's skirts because he is her only remaining political asset and is tied to her by incest.' The party moved on again as the entrance to Augustus' Forum cleared; all around, people were shouting praise to the man who had brought about the longest period of peace free from civil strife that had been known for more than a hundred and fifty years. 'When Domitius has me murdered the deed will only be acceptable if it's seen to be for the good of Rome. But if he kills Titus or any other of Rome's sons along with the one already lost then he will be seen as someone who acted out of spite, like his mother, rather than someone who acted, reluctantly, out of necessity. Seneca will make sure that Domitius understands that; so Titus is safe.'

'Put like that, you may be right, dear boy,' Gaius said, evidently forgetting exactly who he was talking to. 'But how can we believe that Agrippina will have the same discipline?'

'Because she has no hold on power other than through Domitius and, although it will stick in her gorge to do so, she too will understand the need for restraint. After I'm dead, she will have done her job securing her son in power and Domitius will have no use for her; she will have to be very careful about what demands she makes of him. If she becomes too dominant then Domitius might just realise that he doesn't need her any more.'

Vespasian felt an admiration for the youth who could talk so dispassionately about his inevitable death and seemed unafraid to face it. 'Why don't you run?'

'Where to? Some stinking tribe outside the Empire? Or perhaps to Parthia? The first thing anyone would do when they find out my true identity is sell me back to Domitius and then he'll be well within his rights to have me executed for treason.' Britannicus shrugged, looking resigned. 'No, my defiance is willingly accepting the lot served to me by my fool of a father. I take consolation in the facts that he will die before me and that Narcissus, the man who ordered the execution of my mother, will also be waiting on the other side of the Styx when I arrive.'

Vespasian could see the depressing logic of Britannicus' argument: however he looked at it, he was doomed. But maybe he was right about Titus. Now that he was back in Rome, Vespasian decided that the person he needed to cultivate was the man who would hold the reins of the next emperor. 'Do you think, Uncle, that it would be beneath our family's dignity for me to become Seneca's client?'

'Without a doubt, dear boy; but when did that ever stop anyone from trying to secure their position?'

Vespasian, for the first time, found some enjoyment in watching the chariot teams hurl themselves around the sand track of the Circus Maximus; he even found himself willing on the Greens – although this did not translate into actual cheering. He began to look forward, with genuine anticipation, to the prospect of seeing his team of beautiful Arabs leaving the rest of the field behind as they stormed to victory, but more than that, he was looking forward to seeing Caenis that evening. Her naked form came to his mind, her smile enticing him with the prospect of an exhaustingly adventurous time in her bedchamber. However, his daydreaming was regularly interrupted by the almost surreal goings-on in the imperial box, just ten paces to his right.

Claudius had arrived in a litter at the Temple of Fortuna Redux and this had not been solely because his legs were weak; as he dismounted it had been obvious to all that he was still drunk – drunker, even, than he had been the day before. The shame of his fellow priests – Galba's in particular – had been plain for all to see as he slurred his way through the prescribed prayers and then botched the sacrifice so that blood spurted all over his toga in what everybody knew was the worst of omens. However, those senators who had been present in the House the day before were not at all surprised that he should be the subject of a portent of death. Nero, now almost fully grown since Vespasian had last seen him, his sunset hair radiant and now matched by a downy beard, had stood on the temple steps making extravagant gestures of concern and alarm for his adoptive father. He had ostentatiously mouthed every word of the prayers as if coaching Claudius through them; each time the Emperor managed to complete a whole line without a slur or a stutter, the Prince of the Youth made a show of breathing sighs of relief that the gullible in the crowd – a large majority – took to be heartfelt and genuine.

Once the rites had been completed Claudius had been, almost literally, scooped up by Pallas and Burrus, placed back in his litter and equipped with sufficient of the juice of Bacchus to last him for the four-hundred-pace journey to the Circus Maximus. Despite the shortness of the trip the jug had been empty upon his arrival, but Agrippina, awaiting him in the imperial box, had seen to his refreshment requirements as soon as he entered and had since hardly stopped feeding her drink-sodden husband wine of a very undiluted nature.

Agrippina, Nero, Pallas and Burrus were now acting as if nothing were amiss as Claudius, having summoned Paelignus to the box to play dice between races, could barely remain upright in his seat and seemed to be in considerable difficulty each time he attempted to cast his throw.

The crowd, though, took little notice of the inebriate in the imperial box as they urged on the great-hearted equine teams seven times around the *spina*, the barrier running almost centrally down the middle of the arena upon which were mounted the bronze dolphins that marked the passing of each lap. Twelve races of twelve teams, three from each of the factions, were cheered on that afternoon and the celebrations for the winners were raucous; however, they were loudest for one team, when the neutrals and sycophants in the circus joined the Prince of the Youth in his extravagant poses of joy on the four occasions that his beloved Blues were first to tip the seventh dolphin.

With theatrical aplomb the dashing, current heir to the Purple presented the huge prizes to the triumphant Blue charioteers, basking in their glory as if he himself had driven the winning team. From the back of the box, the boy with whom Claudius, in his befuddled mind, planned to replace the glamorous poseur looked on unnoticed by the crowd as his rightful position was unashamedly usurped.

As Nero finished presenting the final prize of the day to the victorious Blues both his mother and Pallas conferred with him. He glanced at Claudius, then over to the senators' enclosure and then gestured, with studied melodrama, for quiet; almost a quarter of a million people obeyed the request.

'People of Rome,' he declaimed in a voice that was husky and far from strong. 'My father,' he paused and indicated with a flourish the bewildered sot oblivious to what was happening as he struggled to read the dots on the dice of his latest throw, 'invites you all to feast at his expense this evening. Tables have been set up throughout the city and will be supplied with food and drink for four hours. He wishes you the joy of the Augustalia!' Standing side-on, Nero held one hand to his heart and extended the other out and up and then turned slowly to take in the entire screaming crowd. With a flick of his wrist and a downward motion of his arm, he silenced them and turned to the senators' enclosure. 'As a personal favour to him, my father requests the company of all senators of Praetorian or consular rank to join him for an intimate dinner at the palace. He expects you there at your earliest convenience.'

Vespasian swore to himself now that his first meeting with Caenis in nearly three years would have to be postponed.

Nero turned back to the crowd and struck a heroic pose, hands on hips, one foot forward, head held high and eyes gazing valiantly into the distance as his adoptive father was helped to the exit, leaving Paelignus, for once, staring at two large piles of winnings, one silver and the other gold.

'I can't imagine that he was in any state to make that invitation,' Gaius observed, watching Claudius being restrained as he lurched to embrace his natural son as he passed.

'No, Uncle,' Vespasian replied, 'it was Pallas and Agrippina who made it.'

Gaius looked over to Agrippina who now held her son's right arm high in the air as if he had won a race. 'Oh dear, dear boy, oh dear.'

CHAPTER XVIIII

'N-N-NONE OFF YOUSH shup-p-p-ported me!' Claudius muttered, returning to his favourite topic of the evening and pointing a trembling finger around the palace's vast triclinium, built by Caligula. 'N-n-none of yoush wanted a cr-cr-cripple for your Emperor.'

Not one of the hundred or so senators present bothered to gainsay him; instead they picked in embarrassed silence at the delicacies set on the tables before them and tried not to notice the fact that their Emperor had wet himself.

Agrippina laid a soothing hand on Claudius' arm and plied him with yet more drink as slaves padded about bringing in fresh dishes and clearing those either empty or cold.

Nero, on the couch to Claudius' right, took no notice of his drunken adoptive father, preferring instead to alternatively feed titbits to his wife and be fed the same by his slightly older friend, Marcus Salvius Otho.

Vespasian and Gaius reclined to the Emperor's left, sharing their couch with Pallas; both trying to think of any small talk with which to bridge the uncomfortable near-silence now shrouding the room as Claudius took slow, methodical sips of his refilled cup until it was dry. The feast was in its fourth hour and no one, apart from Nero, could have claimed to be enjoying themselves.

'Where's Narcissus?' Vespasian eventually asked, turning to Pallas.

'He's gone to his estate near Veii to try to help relieve his gout.'

'Voluntarily?'

'Agrippina did suggest that it might be *very* good for his health, if you take my meaning, as Magnus would say.'

'Indeed he would and I do.'

Vespasian cast his eyes around the sombre gathering of Rome's élite as Claudius slurred on, spiralling down into introspective self-pity as only a man well into his cups can do. Again he noticed Galba was next to the Vitellius brothers, reclining on the same couch, all three of them looking openly disgusted at Claudius' appearance. As Vespasian began to wonder again just what Galba and the Vitellii were doing together, a pair of pale eyes, which seemed vaguely familiar, caught his gaze; they belonged to a huge man reclining on the couch placed next to Galba's. The man raised his cup and drank to Vespasian; not wanting to appear rude, Vespasian returned the toast unable to work out where he knew the face from. His hair, clipped short, and clean-shaven face accentuated a vast, bony head, supported by a bull neck that in turn protruded from a powerful torso.

'Who's that?' Vespasian asked Pallas out of the corner of his mouth as he lowered his cup.'

'Hmm?' Pallas looked up. 'Oh, don't you recognise him? Try adding long hair and moustaches.'

It took Vespasian a couple of moments. 'Caratacus?'

'Tiberius Claudius Caratacus, citizen of Rome, recently awarded the rank of praetor and now looking no different from any other Romanised barbarian.'

Caratacus smiled over to him as the recognition of his old enemy spread over Vespasian's face.

'He's a particular favourite of Nero's,' Pallas explained, whispering. 'He likes to have him around to remind everybody of his magnanimity in recommending his pardon. Caratacus is also—'

The arrival of another course interrupted the Greek as Claudius, roused from his melancholy by the smell, blurted, 'Ah, mushrooms! At lasht something I can trusht.' He downed the contents of his cup in celebration and then held it out to Agrippina to refill.

The company laughed sycophantically at the poor attempt at wit and then busied themselves in making appreciative noises in anticipation of the tasty dish. Conversation suddenly escalated as all began discourses on the safe topic of mushrooms and their preparation.

An elderly female slave placed a large bowl, with care, on the table in front of the Emperor and Empress, adjusting its angle slightly once it was down. Claudius looked at it with wine-stained drool oozing from his mouth as Agrippina dipped her fingers in and took a small specimen from her side of the dish and savoured its aroma. 'They're good, my dear,' she said before placing it in her mouth.

Claudius watched his wife eat, his eyes struggling to focus.

Agrippina swallowed and smiled at her husband. 'Delicious.'

Claudius grabbed one from his side of the bowl and chewed on it with gusto as Agrippina helped herself to another; all around the room people tucked into the dish and the atmosphere relaxed now that the Emperor seemed to be more content.

Claudius heaved out a huge belch and then took another couple of slugs of wine before choosing the largest and juiciest of the mushrooms on his side of the bowl and held it up to Agrippina, slurring what Vespasian took to be a phallic joke, judging by the Empress's dutifully coy reaction. Claudius put the head to his lips and licked it suggestively and then pushed it slowly into his mouth before withdrawing it. Uncharacteristically, Agrippina simpered, but her eyes remained hard, focused on the mushroom. She rubbed Claudius' thigh and whispered something to him; her mouth then pouted and her head tilted in the affirmative with the promise of a treat to come.

Claudius bit the mushroom in half, slavering on its juices. He swallowed and stuffed the remainder in as Agrippina recharged his cup even though it was not quite empty. A thunderous burp announced the disappearance of the last mouthful; it was quickly washed down with the full contents of the cup. Agrippina immediately refilled it, spilling some over Claudius' unsteady hand; conversation throughout the room had grown more animated.

Vespasian sipped his wine and nibbled on a mushroom as Gaius, next to him, tucked into their bowl with undisguised relish; Pallas, to his other side, tensed, his hand, white-knuckled, clutching the edge of the couch. Vespasian looked to see what had startled him.

Claudius' body spasmed, his face a slimed rictus; the contents of his shaking cup slopped over Agrippina who laid a soothing hand on his cheek. The palpitations ceased, his face relaxed and he slumped down, his chest heaving for breath.

Silence spread like a wave throughout the room as people realised that the Emperor had collapsed. Nero stood and looked down at Claudius in wide-eyed, open-mouthed horror with the back of his right hand on his brow like some tragic actor seeing the lifeless body of a lover.

'My husband has drunk his fill!' Agrippina announced looking down at the prone form next to her. 'He has, after all, drunk enough to sink Neptune himself in the last few days.'

Nervous laughter greeted this bald statement of fact, indicating that no one present believed for one moment that it was an alcohol-related incident; however, everyone knew that they would be able to swear to this cover story.

Agrippina turned to an elderly slave woman whom Vespasian recognised as the same woman who had served Claudius his mushrooms. 'Fetch a bowl and a towel.' The woman bowed and padded off as Agrippina got to her feet, a picture of unworried calm. 'I shall have my personal physician attend him to apply an emetic.' She clapped her hands and four bulky slaves appeared from the shadows around the edge of the room and surrounded Claudius' couch. 'I suggest that we curtail our revels; goodnight.'

No one disputed this, although all felt that revels was too strong a word to describe the evening.

'Not you two,' Pallas said as Vespasian and Gaius rose to leave, 'there should be witnesses to the Emperor's sudden and catastrophic change of health. Stay here and compose your speeches for the Senate tomorrow.'

Vespasian sat down on the edge of the couch and looked around the room; it was emptying of senators apart from six others: Paetus, Mucianus, Corvinus, Galba and the Vitellius brothers. Vespasian now understood why they had been seated together: Pallas had drawn on a cross-section of the Senate to secure Nero into power; a consensual conspiracy with support from all sides would be the most plausible of witnesses to Claudius' 'sad and untimely death'.

Gaius evidently realised this too. 'Oh dear, dear boy, oh dear.'

'The Emperor has most certainly overconsumed, causing a disproportionate amount of phlegm in his humours; he must vomit some more.' The bearded Greek physician looked up from his patient satisfied with his diagnosis.

Claudius lay, breathing heavily, on the couch; a pile of vomit, as foul-smelling as it was colourful, was next to his slack mouth.

'What will you give him, Xenophon?' Agrippina asked with a voice laden with concern.

'Nothing; the best thing to do is to tickle the back of his throat.' Xenophon rummaged in his box and brought out a goose feather; he moved Claudius' head away from the vomit.

'Clear that up,' Agrippina ordered the waiting, elderly female slave.

The woman came forward with a towel and a bowl; she placed the bowl on the couch next to Xenophon and began to scoop up the vomit with the towel.

Xenophon waited, idly playing with the feather, rubbing its tip around the bowl. With the vomit collected the woman placed the full towel into the bowl and took both away.

Xenophon tilted Claudius' head towards him and opened the jaw. Very delicately he inserted the feather deep down into the throat and wriggled it around; Claudius suddenly convulsed but Xenophon kept the feather in. With a second convulsion the feather and another full slop of vomit were expelled. Nero shrieked as if he had never seen someone vomit before; he put a protective arm around his wife and Otho put a protective arm around him. Claudius seemed to breathe more easily.

Xenophon repeated the procedure and the Emperor vomited again; Nero shrieked again.

'That should do it,' Xenophon said. 'He should be moved to his bed now.'

'Thank you, doctor,' Agrippina said as if a huge weight had been lifted. She signalled to the slaves, who lifted Claudius from the couch. As they bore him away he suddenly spasmed a couple of times and cried out in a strangled cry before his arms flopped down beside him, touching the floor.

Agrippina screamed and rushed to his side; Xenophon followed as Vespasian and the rest of the senators watched the dumb-show. Nero howled at the gods, reaching up with his right hand in desperate supplication. Xenophon grabbed Claudius' wrist, checking for a pulse and then put his fingers to the side of his neck. After a few moments he looked at the Empress and shook his head slowly.

Agrippina drew herself up to her full height and with the most regal expression on her face turned to the witnesses. 'The Emperor is dead; we shall prepare for the succession.'

Nero stood, his hands half-raised and his eyes staring from beneath arched brows as if miming shock. 'But Mother, I'm not ready for such a burden.'

Behind her in the shadows the slave woman showed a hint of a smile and slipped away as Burrus and Seneca appeared with an escort of Praetorian Guardsmen. 'Come, Princeps,' Burrus said, addressing Nero; a half-smile of triumph flickered briefly across Agrippina's face.

Nero fell to his knees, his hands clasped between his legs. 'Oh, to be worthy of that title. Where would you take me?'

Seneca held a hand out and helped Nero up. 'We shall escort you to the Praetorian camp where you can await the Senate's confirmation of power.' He turned to Pallas. 'Is everything in place?'

Pallas looked at Vespasian and the other senators who had just witnessed the completely deniable public assassination. 'Yes, Seneca; Galba will summon the Senate soon after dawn and Vespasian will lead their call begging Nero to accept the heavy burden of the Purple.'

Vespasian parted with Gaius at the latter's front door at the eighth hour of the night and headed, despite the lateness of the hour, to Caenis' house. He was admitted immediately by the huge Nubian doorman and was surprised to find lamps still burning and the household still up as he walked through the vestibule.

'The mistress is in her study,' Caenis' steward informed him with a deep bow. 'She said that you were to go straight in.'

Vespasian thanked the man, walked to the last door on the right-hand side of the atrium and opened it; light flooded out.

Caenis looked up from behind her desk; it was covered with scrolls. Crates of scrolls and wax writing tablets were piled all around the room. Without a word she jumped up and ran to him, throwing her arms about his neck as he lifted her off her feet. With their lips glued firmly together he walked her back over to the desk and lay her down, scattering scrolls left and right. Still without saying a word they ripped at each other's clothing until they were unimpeded and then, with no pause for any intricate delicacies, began the urgent business of pleasuring each other.

'Narcissus had them sent over just before he left Rome,' Caenis said in answer to Vespasian's question about the scrolls, none of which remained on the desk. 'They contain his entire collection of information on senators and equites as well as his correspondence with all his agents throughout the Empire.'

Vespasian kneeled up on the desk and looked around the study, which resembled a well-used storeroom. He shook his head in amazement. 'This is invaluable. Why did he trust you with it?'

Caenis sat up and kissed him. 'Because, my love, I wrote a lot of these whilst I was his secretary; he concluded that he'd be giving away fewer secrets if I looked after them for him than anyone else.'

'Look after them?'

'Yes; he knew that they would be stolen if he left them in his apartments at the palace after Agrippina advised him to leave Rome; he didn't have time to hide them properly so he arranged to have them sent here in secret. He asked me to keep them safe either until he comes back to Rome or until his execution, in which case I'm to burn them to prevent them falling into Nero's or Agrippina's hands.'

'Or Pallas'?'

Caenis raised a conspiratorial eyebrow. 'That could be up for negotiation.'

'So you won't burn them?'

'I'll burn most of them; it'll be too dangerous to keep it all. But you're assuming that Narcissus will be executed.'

'Agrippina won't let him live now she's had Claudius murdered.'

Caenis took the news calmly as she stood and began to try to bring some sort of order to her dress and coiffure. 'Already? That was quick; Narcissus thought he'd have another half a month or so.'

'No, she did it just over an hour ago; a poisoned mushroom to incapacitate him, as if he'd had a seizure after eating and drinking too much, followed by a poisoned feather stuck down the fool's throat by the doctor pretending to be treating him. It was perfect; made to look like he died of overconsumption. I could even swear to that myself.'

'Then we'd better get to work.' Caenis indicated to Narcissus' intelligence. 'I want to find some material worth keeping before we light the bonfire.'

Vespasian was exhausted by the time the twelfth hour of the night commenced but the loss of sleep had been more than compensated by a small collection of very revealing documents that both he and Caenis judged would be rash in the extreme to burn. He rolled up a scroll concerning the enormous bribe paid by the Vitellius brothers' father, Lucius Vitellius the Elder, to have a treason charge dropped just before his death from paralysis three years before.

With a yawn he put it back in its crate. 'I should go, my love; I need to freshen up before my clients arrive.'

Caenis looked up, with tired eyes, from a wax tablet. 'Did you know that Narcissus planned to have you executed along with Sabinus if you failed to find the Eagle of the Seventeenth in Germania?'

'Nothing surprises me. I can't say that I'll mourn Narcissus after he's gone; he enjoyed using his power too much and made my life very difficult on a number of occasions.' He leant over and kissed her on the mouth; they lingered a few moments before breaking apart. 'I'll see you later, my love, after Gaius and I have persuaded the Senate to seal the fate of the Julio-Claudian family.'

Vespasian and Gaius walked down the Quirinal in the thin light of a damp October dawn, two days before the Ides of that month, escorted by their clients; members of the South Quirinal Crossroads Brotherhood preceded them armed with staves ready to beat a way through the more crowded parts of the city.

'The lads managed to regain control of the area,' Magnus informed Vespasian. 'Tigran told me that it didn't take long; it's hard for a brotherhood to hold two areas because the locals don't believe that they would show enough respect for their crossroads lares and start to become obstreperous.'

Vespasian grunted in an attempt to sound interested in the doings of Rome's underworld but his tired mind was busy with the speech he knew that he must soon deliver and with the order and purpose of all the other speeches as explained to him by Pallas the night before.

Magnus pressed on unperturbed. 'But, strangely, this lot didn't make any effort at all to secure their position. After a couple of days it wasn't safe for them to walk around after dark and then it was just a question of a couple of well-chosen murders followed by an attack very similar to what they did to us and they were forced to fuck off back whence they came.'

'Where did they come from?' Gaius asked.

'Now that's the interesting thing. They weren't from a neighbouring area like I originally assumed; they came all the way from the eastern end of the Aventine.'

Vespasian's mood was not improved by the start of a steady drizzle of rain. 'What's so interesting about that apart from the fact that Sabinus lives over there?'

Magnus looked at Vespasian as if he were a slow but amiable child. 'Because, sir, it confirms a possibility that we were contemplating. Why would a brotherhood from the far end of the

Aventine bother to try to take over one on the other side of the city on the Quirinal? It don't make any sense unless their objective wasn't a takeover. As was pointed out at the time: why did they attack at the precise moment that the imperial secretary and the Junior Consul were having a *secret* meeting? So if you or Narcissus or both of you were the real targets, the East Aventine lads must have been put up to it.'

'Of course they were put up to it; but by whom?' Lack of sleep made Vespasian's remark sound terser than he had meant it to be.

Magnus looked offended. 'Just because you've been up all night, or should I say, up Caenis all night, there's no need to be sharp with me.'

'I'm sorry, Magnus.'

'Yeah, well. Anyway, what you may not know is that since the Palatine became the exclusive abode of the élite there are no brotherhoods there in the modern sense of the concept because there aren't people there who need our … er … help, if you take my meaning?'

'No poor people to terrorise, you mean?'

'Now that ain't fair, sir. Anyway, the residents look after the crossroads lares themselves, so the nearest places to the Palatine where you would find a brotherhood in the very real sense of the word are the Via Sacra or … '

'The Aventine!'

'Precisely, just the other side of the Circus Maximus. Now I ain't saying that it was definitely someone on the Palatine who paid the East Aventine to do it, but I imagine that those lads have quite a close relationship with their betters living on the opposite hill, at least with the more unscrupulous of them, that is.'

'Which would be most of them. I think you may well be right, old friend. So what are you going to do about it?'

Magnus chuckled. 'Me? Nothing. I ain't involved with the brotherhood no more. However, as you know, my mate Tigran is now the patronus and he does listen to the advice of those older and wiser than him.'

'And what advice did you give him?'

'I suggested that he might see if he could catch one of the Aventine lads and persuade him to answer a few questions.'

'That's very good advice.'

'I thought so too and, talking of good advice, Lucius is back there.' Magnus indicated to the crowd of clients following them down the hill. 'As you didn't have a salutio this morning he hasn't had the chance to tell you that Eusebius will send someone to inspect the Arabs today and would be honoured to have a meeting with you to discuss them; Lucius wants to know when and where.'

Vespasian thought for a few moments as the Curia came into view with scores of senators swarming up its steps, leaving crowds of clients milling around waiting for news of proceedings within. 'Tell him I'll come out to the Greens' stables tomorrow; I want to make sure that they're good enough for the team.'

Magnus rolled his eyes. 'The Greens' stables not good enough? As if!'

The rumble of agitated voices filled the Curia as the Senate awaited the arrival of the Junior Consul to call the meeting to order. Rumour and counter-rumour circulated on a tide of apprehension as those who had been present when Claudius had collapsed informed others of the circumstances. Confirmation of his death had not been given and all were afraid to react one way or another for fear of insulting Claudius if he still lived by talking of the succession or insulting his successor by expressing a hope that he was indeed still alive. It was therefore with great relief to all that the Consul arrived, stilling conversation, and began the process of deciding whether the day was auspicious for the business of Rome, which, two goose livers later, it was pronounced so.

Vespasian carried on running over his speech in his head as prayers of thanks to Jupiter Optimus Maximus were said and the sacrifices were cleared away.

'Servius Sulpicius Galba,' Marcus Asinius Marcellus said, once he was seated in his curule chair, 'for what reason have you summoned the Senate on a day that we were not due to sit?'

Galba rose to his feet, bald, muscular and sinewy; his eyes glared around him, his jaw jutted forward and he held himself rigid as if he was about to address troops who had severely displeased him. 'Tiberius Claudius Caesar Augustus Germanicus,' he bellowed, causing those around him to wince, 'died in the early hours of this morning.' With that he sat back down as if he had just announced the name and position of the most junior of magistrates for the upcoming year.

Uproar was instantaneous as all vied to be loudest in their grief for the departed Emperor. Vespasian, prepared for this moment, strode to the centre of the floor and demanded the presiding Consul's attention.

Marcellus stood, arms outstretched, roaring for silence, which was slow to come, but eventually the senators settled with all eyes on Vespasian standing in their midst. 'Titus Flavius Vespasianus,' Marcellus said, his voice rough edged from yelling, 'has the floor.'

Vespasian composed his face into the most sombre of expressions. 'Conscript Fathers, I mourn with you.' He looked around, catching the eye of many in his audience so that they could see just how deeply he felt. 'But the time for grief must be postponed for the good of Rome. Rome must have someone to lead her in her mourning. Before we succumb to the deep sorrow that we all feel let us first do our duty to Rome as her responsible Senate.

'Let us remember the indecision and inaction with which we, to our shame, marked the passing of the last Emperor; our prevarication caused the Guard to nominate Claudius, not this ancient House.' He turned full circle, gesturing with one hand to take in the entirety of the Senate. 'We were all of us to blame. Let us on this occasion, Conscript Fathers, reassert our authority with a decisive act; a course of action that none here can deem wrong as it was clearly stated to be the will of the late Emperor, just three days ago in this very House. Let us call upon the Emperor's son, who, in accordance with Claudius' wishes expressed in here, remains his heir.' Vespasian paused, contemplating the consequences of his next line for Titus' friend. 'Britannicus has not yet come of age! Let us therefore call upon Nero Claudius Caesar Drusus Germanicus to come to this House at his earliest convenience. Here, Conscript Fathers, we shall ask him, no, beg him, to take up the Purple so sadly lain down by his father. If we can persuade Nero to shoulder the onerous burden of power, then, Conscript Fathers, we would have done our duty. Then, and only then, would we be free to mourn!'

Vespasian walked to his stool amidst thunderous applause as Gaius waddled out into the centre of the House, the nervous sweat lining his top lip betraying his unease at being so conspicuous.

Again Marcellus called for silence and when it was manifest he gave the floor to Gaius. 'Conscript Fathers, my nephew has displayed two of the qualities that have made us Romans great. Unselfish dedication to duty and the ability to suppress deeply felt emotion in order to best serve the Senate and the People of Rome. I second his motion but I would add one more line to it: that, should Nero be gracious enough to grant our pleas, then we should thank him by voting him all the honours and titles that we voted Claudius throughout his reign so that he should begin his rule in no less dignity than his father's ended.' With a dramatic flourish of his right arm above his head, Gaius moved back to his seat next to Vespasian as applause came from every senator, each, no doubt, wishing that they had been the first to have moved such a sycophantic motion.

'That seems to have got them going, dear boy,' Gaius observed as he sat down with a flurry of hands patting his back and shouts of agreement in his ears.

'We were only doing our duty,' Vespasian replied, just managing to keep a sombre countenance.

They sat, with the rest of the Senate, nodding, murmuring, applauding or shouting in agreement where appropriate as, first, the two Vitellius brothers extolled Nero's many virtues and the likelihood of him ushering in a golden age, and then Gaius Licinius Mucianus expounded at length on the necessity of coming to a decision very quickly. He was followed by Lucius Junius Paetus who begged Marcellus, with great rhetorical eloquence, to call an immediate vote; but before the Consul could do so, Marcus Valerius Messalla Corvinus took to the floor.

'Conscript Fathers,' Corvinus declaimed once he had received permission to address the House, 'should we come to an agreement on this matter I would suggest that we contemplate how we carry our request to Nero. We can't send too many delegates to the Palatine otherwise there would not be enough of our body here to welcome Nero when he arrives.' Corvinus paused for a few moments as the senators reflected on the difficulty of getting the balance right. 'I propose, therefore, that we remove these problems by sending only one man. Naturally the obvious choice to go should be the Junior Consul, who in the absence of his colleague is the most senior magistrate here. But then, Conscript Fathers, should not the most senior magistrate be waiting here at the bottom of the steps to greet Nero and escort him in?' There were murmurings of agreement and worried mutterings that it was vital for the Senate to start off with a favourable relationship with the man they planned to make emperor.

'Pallas said that he was meant to be nominating Marcellus to go, not blocking him,' Vespasian hissed out of the corner of his mouth. 'What's he doing?'

'Building up his part, is my guess,' Gaius muttered back. 'He hasn't had any preferment since you had Pallas save his life after Messalina's death; Agrippina still can't forgive him for being the harpy's brother.'

'Ah! But if he comes with the request from the Senate she might; is that it?'

'Something like that.'

Corvinus opened his arms to the House. 'So whom should we choose, Conscript Fathers?'

As Corvinus shamelessly beseeched the House, Vespasian regarded his old enemy, recounting the wrongs that he had done to him and his family; and then, as the senators began to call on Corvinus to deign to accept the task, one detail, one small memory of what Sabinus had told him about Corvinus, years ago, caught his attention. 'Quick, Uncle; nominate me.'

Gaius looked at him, surprised.

'Now!'

With a shrug, Gaius got to his feet. 'Consul!'

'Gaius Vespasius Pollo has the floor.'

Gaius waddled out into the middle as Corvinus glared at him. 'Senator Corvinus has made an excellent point and we should be grateful to him for his perception. However, I do not judge him to be quite the right man for the job. I believe that we have one amongst us who would be ideally suited to such a task. A man who is, unlike Corvinus, of consular rank; but more than that: a man who has not been present in the city for almost three years and so therefore can be said to be removed from all the arguments and politics that have dominated the issue of the succession recently. I propose Titus Flavius Vespasianus.'

As the proposal was seconded by Paetus and a vote was called and passed, almost unanimously, Vespasian felt Corvinus' eyes boring into him and the malice that they conveyed; he was, most certainly, breaking his oath to conduct himself as a dead man in Vespasian's presence. However, that did not surprise him as, if he had guessed correctly, it was not the first time that Corvinus had broken that oath.

CHAPTER XX

Nero leant on Otho's arm, trying to draw breath; he threw his head back, his sunset locks flowing with the motion, as he pinched his temples with the thumb and ring-finger of one hand. Eventually he inhaled, gasping, and Vespasian wondered how much longer the Prince of the Youth would be able to keep up this show of overwhelmed surprise.

Vespasian glanced around the atrium of the Praetorian prefect's quarters in the Guard's camp, outside the Viminal Gate. Agrippina, Pallas, Seneca and Burrus waited patiently as if such a ghastly display of overacting, which would put even the most melodramatic actor to shame, was a normal way to react to something totally expected; however, none of them would meet Vespasian's eye.

'I must compose my speech.' Nero's voice, husky at the best of times, was gravelled with emotion.

Seneca stepped forward and pulled a scroll from the fold of his toga. 'Princeps, you already have.'

Both Nero's hands came up, his thumbs touching the tips of his middle fingers, delight now upon his face. 'Ah! So I have.'

Seneca handed the document over. 'I'm sure it's a master-work, Princeps.'

'It is, it is,' Nero affirmed as he read through it.

'Your skill with words is unsurpassed.'

'Apart from musical talent; and if I were to put the two together ...' Nero looked up to the ceiling, his eyes wistful, and then returned his attention to the scroll.

All stood in silence as Nero finished perusing the speech. 'I shall answer the Senate's call and come at once, Senator Vespasian.'

'You honour us, Princeps.'

'But what to wear? What to wear, Mother?'

Agrippina smiled at her son, reaching out and stroking the ginger down on his cheeks. 'Your steward has a selection of suitable attire ready for your inspection in your rooms.'

'Mother, you think of everything.' Nero kissed her on the lips and then grabbed Otho's arm again. 'Come, Otho, you shall help me decide; I mustn't keep the Senate waiting.'

Vespasian watched the chosen Emperor almost skip from the room and wondered just for how long his antics would be tolerated; but he surmised that the innate sycophancy of the senatorial and equestrian classes would mean that his behaviour would have to deteriorate to the levels of Caligula before the whisperings would start. He then got a taste of what was to come as Agrippina turned to Burrus and, with a cold smile on her lips and malice in her dark eyes said, in almost a purr, 'Send a turma of Praetorian cavalry to bring Narcissus back to Rome.' As Burrus saluted and turned to go she added, 'And remove Callistus from his position as secretary to the Law Courts; on a permanent basis.'

The killing was about to begin.

Four hours later, after Vespasian had sent repeated messages back to the Senate assuring them that Nero was coming once he had finished changing, the senators rose to their feet and applauded the Golden Prince after he had, with great verbosity and many shows of reluctance, accepted their pleas. Tears of gratitude were evident in many an eye in imitation of the tears rolling down Nero's cheeks, as he slowly rotated with both hands pressed to his heart so all understood just how acutely he felt the emotion. Resplendent in golden slippers, a purple tunic embroidered with gold thread, a wreath of laurels worked from thin foil of the same metal and bracelets studded with all manner of precious jewels, Nero showed his modesty by sporting a plain white citizen's toga. Of his humility all could be certain as Nero approached the Consul and, kneeling before him, pleaded to be allowed to address the Senate once again.

Fighting against a look of bemusement that kept on flickering over his face, Marcellus gave the floor to the new Emperor. Nero drew himself up to his full height, which was average, and passed his pale blue eyes over his audience, before arranging himself into the classic orator's pose with his left arm across his midriff, supporting the folds of his toga, and his right down by his side, his hand clutching a scroll. Once he was happy with his stance, he heaved a couple of sobs and then cleared his throat of the heavy emotion before launching into a speech that within a few paragraphs had surprised everyone by its fair-mindedness and conservatism. All could see it bore no resemblance to his character and yet none wanted to disbelieve what they were hearing.

Nero affirmed the authority of the Senate, hoped for the consensus of the military, avowed that he had no animosities, brought with him no wrongs to be righted nor any desire for revenge and promised that he would not be the judge of all law cases and, also, that there would be no bribery within his household. As Nero talked on into the afternoon, Vespasian's mind turned to his revenge. He scanned the lines of senators, each looking as if the weak, husky voice addressing them was the most beautiful sound in creation, and soon found the object of his hatred. Paelignus again almost jumped from his stool as he felt Vespasian's gaze upon him and then turned into the full venom of his stare. As Nero worked himself up to a rhetorical climax, referring often to his scroll, Vespasian bathed in the thought of Paelignus' humiliation and then death until, having peaked with the announcement that after Claudius' funeral the following day he would meet with the Armenian delegation waiting in the city and, in one move, restabilise the Roman East, the Senate rose and cheered the Golden Prince who was now their Emperor.

The Junior Consul stood and motioned for silence. 'Princeps, we have all been moved by your words that have so finely expressed the principles of just governance. I would propose that we should have your speech inscribed on silver tablets to be read out every time new consuls come into office as an example to all. What does the House say?'

With a unanimous cheer, accepting this inspirational way of honouring such a fine piece of rhetoric, the Senate hailed their Emperor. The cheering and applause went on and on as Nero graciously accepted it, again and again, with lavish hand gestures and expressions of modesty until, no doubt fearing for his dinner being ruined, the Junior Consul brought it to an end. 'We look forward to taking our oaths to you tomorrow morning, after the funeral of your father. Until then we thank you for your time and will offer up prayers to all the gods of this city to hold their hands over you.'

Nero was too overcome to be able to reply; he walked with a quivering lower lip to the open doors of the Senate House. There, on the threshold, stood his mother, banned from entering the building because of her sex; Burrus stood behind her with a waiting guard of Praetorians. Nero threw himself into Agrippina's arms and they embraced as if both were in rapturous joy.

'What is the password of the day, Princeps?' Burrus asked as the couple released one another.

'The only password possible, Burrus,' Nero replied, gazing at Agrippina. 'Excellent mother.'

Burrus saluted and signalled to the guards to move aside as Nero walked forward to a thunderous ovation from the people of Rome, gathered in their thousands in the Forum. The Senate filed out behind Nero to share in the acclaim that the Golden Prince was receiving. Vespasian joined them, with Gaius, and watched the undeserved outpouring of love by the people, wondering for how long the words that Seneca had put in Nero's mouth would stick there.

'You shouldn't have done that, bumpkin,' a voice said in his ear.

Vespasian did not turn around. 'I thought you were meant to be dead, Corvinus.'

'I think that you noticing me alive in the Senate House this morning nullifies my oath.'

Vespasian still refused to look at Corvinus. 'Seeing as you have miraculously come back from the dead, tell me, Corvinus, where are you living in this life? I seem to remember that in your last life you lived near my brother; that's how you inveigled your way into his confidence and found out the whereabouts of Clementina so you could take her to Caligula. Are you still there?'

'On the Aventine? Yes. What's that—'

'East Aventine?'

'Yes.'

Vespasian spun round and fixed Corvinus with a look of naked hatred. 'You haven't been dead to me at all, have you, Corvinus? You tried to have me killed and make it look like I was a victim of a brotherhood takeover. After I had Pallas spare your life, I consider that to be extremely ungrateful behaviour.'

'It's a humiliation to be in the debt of a man as low-born as you.'

'How did you know I'd be there in Magnus' tavern at that time, Corvinus?'

Corvinus sneered, turned on his heel and walked away.

'What was all that about, dear boy?' Gaius asked, almost shouting over the growing tumult.

'That, Uncle, was about a bastard who refuses to stay dead. I can see that he's going to need a little help next time.'

It seemed to Vespasian that Nero would soon have the whole of Rome constantly shedding floods of tears as he watched the weeping Emperor, with Britannicus and Octavia Claudia following, bearing the casket containing Claudius' ashes to Augustus' mausoleum the following morning. Set on the bank of the Tiber on the north of the Campus Martius, the circular marbled building was capped with a conical roof that supported a statue of the great man who had commissioned it; it was the final resting place of all Rome's Emperors and most members of their family. As Nero passed under the ring of cypress trees and then on through the gate guarded by two pink granite obelisks, Vespasian reflected that yet another member of the Julio-Claudians had failed to live out their natural life; even Augustus was rumoured to have been poisoned by his wife Livia so as to ensure that her son Tiberius inherited, and here was history repeating itself, although this time it had been a feather rather than a fig which had been the poisoned vessel.

The funeral party disappeared into the gloom of the interior and the people howled out their grief, not for Claudius' demise, but for their new Emperor's loss. They cared not for Britannicus nor for Octavia Claudia; they only had eyes for the dazzling Golden Emperor, as he now had become in their minds. They mourned with him now as they had mourned with him throughout the morning while he had eulogised Claudius from the podium next to his funeral pyre. Surrounded by actors wearing the funeral masks of the imperial family, he had praised Claudius for his scholarship, his extension of the Empire, his legal aptitude, all in the very vaguest of terms, careful that the words he used would not make it impossible to better each of Claudius' achievements in short order. Claudius' vices and afflictions had been forgotten, as had been his natural children, previous wives, powerful mother, Antonia, and grandmother, Livia. Nothing had been said that could overshadow or reflect badly on Nero and Agrippina. She sat to one side of the podium, on a dais, at the head of the women of Rome's élite, Flavia and Caenis to the fore.

And the people had loved Nero; they had loved him because he made them do so by his seemingly open personality and his ability to express his emotions. But those who knew him and those who had seen him up close understood, like Vespasian did, that was just an act, a veneer.

And so, as the Senate and the people of Rome took their oath to the new Emperor, once he had emerged from the mausoleum with his duty to his predecessor done, those who appreciated the truth of the matter repeated the ritual formula with apprehension, wondering just what the false exterior concealed and hoping that, whatever it was, it would do them no harm. However, some, Vespasian included, had paid attention to what Nero's natural father, Gnaeus Domitius Ahenobarbus, had said upon being congratulated on the birth of his son: that a child of his and Agrippina would have a detestable nature and would be a public danger. It was with this knowledge and the firm belief that the Empire could not stand another Julio-Claudian who fitted that description that, once the ceremony had finished and Nero had been cheered off, Vespasian walked towards the

Greens' stables to meet Magnus and Lucius, smiling to himself and thinking of ways to keep safe during what would be, to say the least, an unpredictable reign.

'Well, that seemed to go very well, I'd say,' Magnus said as he, Lucius and Vespasian walked across the rectangular exercise yard, lined with stables and workshops, at the heart of the Greens' stable complex. He looked with admiration at the horses being exercised, either singly or in teams of two, three or four. 'Eusebius seems to be a very reasonable man.'

Vespasian found it hard to completely agree with that observation. 'It's a fairish price,' he said grudgingly.

'A fairish price? The Greens pay for the cost of five horses' upkeep and training and you get to keep sixty per cent of their winnings; I'd say that is beyond fair, never mind fairish.'

'I wanted seventy-five.'

'You wanted ninety when you arrived here and, had me and Lucius not have explained that a figure like that would just make you look stupid, you would have been slung out on your arse as a time-waster; in the nicest possible way that a senator can be slung out on his arse, obviously.'

'Obviously. But now the deal's done I think I'm going to enjoy it.'

'Then you had better make good your promise to Malichus,' Magnus reminded him, 'otherwise there'll be nothing but bad luck following your team. It normally takes three or four months for a team to settle in so you should have it done by February; they won't race before then.' He clutched his right thumb between the fingers of his right hand and spat as a precaution against the evil-eye cursing the team that he hoped would make him a fortune on their first outing.

'I'll do it in the next few days while Pallas is pleased with me and Nero's in a beneficent mood. But first I need to go to the Forum and watch our new Emperor try his hand at eastern diplomacy.' Passing out through the stable's gates he left Lucius a small token of his gratitude and, with Magnus, headed across the Campus Martius, past the Flammian Circus to the Porta

Fontinalis, in the shadow of the Capitoline Hill, where the Via Flammia entered the city.

'How dare you block my way!'

Vespasian instantly recognised the voice emanating from within a crowd obstructing the Porta Fontinalis.

'I've been summoned by Agrippina to pay my respects to the new Emperor.'

Vespasian could not see Narcissus but his imperious voice, so used to command, was unmistakable.

'And I've orders to detain you here, Narcissus, until the Praetorian prefect arrives.'

Vespasian assumed that was the voice of an Urban Cohort centurion in command of the gate's watch as he pushed his way through the crowd to see what was occurring.

'You should refer to me by my title of imperial secretary, centurion.' Narcissus' voice had dropped; a sign, Vespasian well knew, of deadly threat.

But the centurion was not intimidated. 'My orders are to keep you here while I send a message to Prefect Burrus and, specifically, not to use your former title.'

Narcissus' face registered a hint of fear as Vespasian succeeded in pushing through the crowd to get next to the freedman, seated in a one-man litter; his expression brightened somewhat upon seeing Vespasian. 'You must help me through the gate, Vespasian.' He indicated to the four Praetorian Guardsmen accompanying his litter, lounging in the sun against one of the tombs lining the Via Flammia and making no effort to progress through the gate. 'My escort refuses to overrule this ... this ...' He struggled to find a word to describe the centurion. 'Underling.'

Vespasian sensed the rising panic in the once all-powerful freedman and, despite everything that Narcissus had done to Vespasian and his family during his time as imperial secretary, he felt a certain sympathy for his predicament. However, he knew that there was nothing that he could do to save the man without jeopardising his own safety. 'Do you remember, Narcissus, after

Caligula's assassination when we were negotiating for my brother's life?'

Narcissus frowned, surprised by the change of subject. 'What of it?'

'You asked me what a life was worth and I replied that it depends on who was buying and who was selling.'

'Yes, and I said that market forces are always at work. What's your point?'

'I would have thought that was obvious: market forces have ceased in your case; you have no currency to buy with. Your life is worth nothing now, Narcissus.'

'Not unless I try to buy it with information. My records; Caenis has got them, as I'm sure you know by now. You could try and negotiate with Pallas and Agrippina on my behalf, after you've removed anything concerning you and your family, obviously.' Narcissus' eyes gleamed with hope. 'There's enough information there to execute almost all the Senate and a lot of the equestrian class.'

Vespasian's sympathy evaporated as the Greek contemplated buying his life with those of hundreds of others. 'I thought you gave them into Caenis' care to keep them from Pallas and Agrippina?'

'I did, just so as I could use them at a time such as now. So you see, Vespasian, market forces are still at work. Will you help me?'

Vespasian thought about it for a few moments. 'What do you have on Paelignus and Corvinus?'

Narcissus looked at him conspiratorially. 'Ah, I see; a fair price. Not much on Corvinus but enough on Paelignus to see him dead. When his father died last year, he left half his estate to Claudius; a sensible precaution as you know. However, Paelignus falsified how much the estate was worth so that Claudius received less than a quarter of what he should have. It's in my records.'

'Good. I'll extract that record before Caenis and I burn the rest.'

Narcissus blanched in terror. 'Burn them? But what about me?'

'Narcissus, do you think for one moment that I would be party to Agrippina having the hold of life and death over more than half of the men of importance in the city? It's going to be bad enough without that over the next few years; I'll not add to the murder. And you were wrong about her, by the way. It was Tryphaena behind the embassy, which was why Pallas knew nothing about it.'

'How do you know that Pallas knew nothing?'

'Because he was as curious as you were about what I found out in the East.'

'You were working for him all along?'

'I took the commission from both of you but I was working solely for myself; it just so happens that it was more to my advantage to share my findings upon my return with him than with you.'

'You treacherous bastard!'

'I learnt from the best, Narcissus.'

A loud voice cut through their exchange. 'Tiberius Claudius Narcissus!'

Vespasian turned towards the direction of the shout to see Burrus stomping through the gate accompanied by a Praetorian centurion holding a sack. Narcissus recoiled as if he had been punched.

Burrus stopped in front of the litter. 'Get out!'

'I am a Roman citizen and have the right to appeal to Caesar.'

'He knows that and he told me to tell you that you are more than welcome to exercise that right and he will be very happy to commute the sentence from decapitation to death by wild beasts; it's up to you.' Burrus drew his sword. 'Centurion!'

The Praetorian centurion dipped his hand into the sack and pulled out a severed head by its ear.

'Your erstwhile colleague decided not to exercise his right to appeal,' Burrus informed Narcissus as he stared in horror at the bloodless face of Callistus. 'If it's any consolation, Nero did express regret at being able to write as he signed your death sentence.'

Narcissus stiffened; it was as if he had found a new strength in his helplessness. 'So the most I can hope for is a clean death.' He stepped out of the litter, calmly accepting his fate.

'We'll burn them thoroughly, Narcissus,' Vespasian assured him.

'You're right; it will be for the best. If I were a betting man, my money would be on you to survive, Vespasian. And who knows to where a long life might lead.' He walked forward and knelt before Burrus, extending his neck. 'There is nothing else to say, my life is at an end.'

It was swift and clean. The sword caught the sun as it was raised and flashed when Burrus sliced it down. With a communal intake of breath from the crowd and a brief grunt from Narcissus, it cut though skin, flesh and bone, in a shock of blood, the edge so honed that Burrus' arm hardly juddered as the blade swept Narcissus' head from his shoulders to roll to the feet of the four Praetorians lounging against the tomb. The body stayed kneeling, rigid, for a few moments, disgorging its contents in great spurts as the heart pumped on, weakening with each contraction. The thigh muscles soon gave out and the husk of what had once been the most powerful man in the Empire slumped forward, dead at the entrance to the city that had given him, an ex-slave, his freedom, wealth, influence and, now, bloody execution.

'Take him away!' Burrus ordered the four Praetorians.

Vespasian stared at Narcissus' face as his head was picked up; his eyes were still open. He remembered how the Greek had forced Sabinus to execute Clemens, his own brother-in-law, as part of the bargain that would spare his life; he smiled at the neatness of the retribution and then, as the head was carried away, his eyes rested on the tomb that had, up until now, been obscured by the Praetorians. He stared at it for a few moments and then broke into a laugh.

'What the fuck are you finding so funny?' Magnus asked.

Vespasian pointed at the tomb and read the inscription. 'Valerius Messalla.'

'So?'

'Even from beyond the grave that harpy still gets her revenge on Narcissus for ordering her execution. Agrippina wouldn't allow her to be buried in Augustus' mausoleum so she was put in her family tomb. Narcissus was executed next to the last resting place of Messalina.'

Magnus blew through his teeth. 'Sometimes you have to give the gods credit for their sense of humour.'

'I suppose this is Pallas' way of doing for Nero what he and Narcissus did for Claudius with the invasion of Britannia, dear boy,' Gaius concluded as they watched the deputation from Armenia approach the raised tribunal in the Forum Romanum where the Emperor waited, seated on his curule chair, to give his first public judgement of his reign; Pallas, Seneca and Burrus all stood next to the tribunal ready to offer advice to their charge. 'A proper invasion of Armenia, rather than the half-hearted ones we've had so far.'

'It's what Tryphaena planned,' Vespasian agreed. 'Except that I doubt that her nephew Radamistus has managed to cling on to power if Vologases has done what he intended.'

As the delegation of ten bearded and betrousered Armenians approached Nero, bearing rich gifts, there was a stirring in the crowd. From the opposite end of the Forum, surrounded by Vestal Virgins, came Agrippina. There was a gasp from all who could see her. Her hair was piled high upon her head and flashed and sparkled with jewels; her purple stola flowed down to her ankles and shimmered as if made of silk. But it was not these details that caused the shocked intake of breath: her palla was pure white, chalked white, and had a broad purple stripe, in imitation of a senatorial toga, and in her right hand she held a scroll as if she was about to give a speech. Behind her walked a slave with a curule chair.

'She's going to place herself next to the Emperor and receive the delegation as if she were a man,' Vespasian said as the magnitude of Agrippina's ambition became apparent.

'Oh dear, dear boy, oh dear.' Gaius' jowls and chins wobbled in outrage at the thought of a woman being so forward. 'That would be the end: women making decisions in public; unthinkable.'

Seneca and Burrus evidently held the same opinion; they called up advice to Nero as Agrippina came nearer and nearer. Pallas then joined the two advisors, giving what appeared to be a contrary opinion and, after what seemed to be a short but heated debate, he was rebuffed by the Emperor, who rose from his seat and inclined his head to Seneca and Burrus.

As Agrippina approached the tribunal, Nero descended the few steps and met her at the bottom. 'Mother! How good of you to come and support me.' He embraced and kissed her, making a great show of filial affection to warm the hearts of the crowd. 'Over here would be the best place for you to watch from.' He held her elbow in a firm grip and steered her away from the steps as Seneca indicated to the slave with the chair to place it down by him, next to the tribunal. Agrippina, with a fixed smile on her face, allowed herself to be seated with much courtesy by Burrus as Pallas stepped back, disassociating himself from the struggle for precedence. Agrippina's eyes flashed first at her son, as he remounted the tribunal, and then at Seneca and Burrus.

'I think Agrippina has just declared war on her son and his two advisors,' Vespasian observed to his uncle.

'I saw the look too, dear boy, and that's a struggle that a woman cannot win; not even that one. I think Pallas' days are numbered.'

Vespasian nodded slowly. 'Yes, it really is Seneca's time now.'

'I'm pleased that we have finally got the chance to meet,' a voice said as Vespasian contemplated the best way to approach Seneca.

He turned and saw a huge man now standing next to him. 'Caratacus!'

'I have not presumed to invite you for dinner, Titus Flavius Vespasianus, being ranked only as a mere praetor and you of consular rank.'

Vespasian took his old adversary's proffered arm and grasped it firmly; it was as if he was clutching an oak branch. 'I must apologise to you, Tiberius Claudius Caratacus, for neglecting to pay my respects but as I'm sure you're aware ...'

'You have only been back for a few days and they have been eventful. It's a sad time for us all.'

Vespasian was surprised by the statement; he could not tell whether Caratacus was referring to Claudius' death or Nero's ascension and decided not to respond one way or the other. 'I'm sure we have much to talk about concerning the conquest of Britannia.'

'A conquest that is far from over.'

'So I believe; it should make for an interesting dinner conversation.' Nero got to his feet to officially welcome the Armenians; Vespasian lowered his voice. 'I shall be making a tour of mine and my brother's estates soon. I should be back after the Saturnalia at the end of December, we shall dine then.'

Caratacus inclined his head. 'It'll be my pleasure, Vespasian,' he said before disappearing back into the crowd.

The speeches had been long and formal and the people's interest had waned as the sun had fallen and the crowds had thinned out to the point that it had become noticeable. With an eye to the possibility of completely losing his audience, Nero interrupted the latest in the line of Armenian delegates in the middle of an impassioned speech about his country's love of Rome and Rome's new Emperor and hatred for all things Parthian, which, considering his eastern attire, was raising more than a few eyebrows.

As soon as it was clear that Nero was about to speak the background chatter that the Armenian delegates had been forced to fight against immediately died down. The Golden Emperor got to his feet and graciously indicated to the Armenians to rise from their bellies, from which position they had voluntarily made their cases. For quite a while Nero made a great show of contemplating everything he had heard, scratching his downy beard, rubbing the back of his neck with a pained expression on his face and then gazing into the middle distance over the heads of his adoring audience, seeking inspiration from afar.

'I have made my decision,' he eventually announced. 'This golden age shall have peace and I shall soon be able to close the doors of the Temple of Janus. But before that happens we shall have war!' He stood with one hand in the air and the other on his hip, the soldierly image of a general addressing his troops, and the crowd roared their approval. He silenced them with a swipe of his raised hand. 'I shall prosecute this war in a firm and positive way and not in the haphazard, half-hearted manner of my father, who despite his many qualities could not be considered martial.' As the crowd cheered their agreement to this point Nero signalled to Burrus to hand him up his sword. Nero held it aloft. 'I will give Gnaeus Domitius Corbulo, our most competent general in the East, full powers to resolve the Armenian question and beat the Parthians back to their homeland. He shall report only to me and shall have the benefit of my advice.

'And so I shall deal with our external problems, safeguarding the sanctity of Rome's borders; but whilst doing this I shall also address an internal infestation: I have been told that there were a few, this morning, who refused to take their oath to me, your Emperor. These people, I have been informed by Lucius Annaeus Seneca, do not acknowledge me as the supreme authority in the Empire but, rather, some crucified criminal called Chrestus. Find them for me, people of Rome; root them out and bring them to me for judgement and sentence. Together, my people, together we shall fight our enemies within as well as without and together we shall be victorious.'

Vespasian looked at Gaius as the people screamed their love for their Golden Emperor; he smiled. 'Now he's united them with common enemies both here and abroad, Uncle. He'll secure his position and then we shall see how he handles absolute power.'

'I'm sure we will, dear boy; let us pray to the gods of our houses that *we* don't get to see too closely.'

'I've found it!' Caenis said, handing an unrolled scroll across the garden table to Vespasian. 'It's all there: the clause, the amount of the bequest and then the original valuation of Paelignus' father's estate as registered in the will at the House of the Vestals. It specifies its actual size in terms of land, goods, chattels and cash. Narcissus must have had this stolen.'

'Or paid the Vestals for it.' Vespasian read through the scroll, smoke from the bonfire occasionally wisping into his eyes. 'But this doesn't tell us how much was paid to the imperial treasury.'

'It doesn't need to. All bequests made are logged and filed at the treasury; you just have to get Pallas to cross-check what was received from Paelignus against what's in that record.'

Vespasian looked at the valuations, did some mental arithmetic and then whistled. 'I make the total value about twenty million denarii, which means that Claudius should have got ten but only received a quarter of that. Paelignus swindled the Emperor out of seven and a half million. That'll do nicely.' He slapped the scroll down on the table.

Caenis pointed to the rest of Narcissus' records that they still had not read through. 'Do you want to carry on looking through?'

Vespasian glanced at them and then across at the bonfire consuming the rest. 'Burn them, my love. I've got what I need on Paelignus and we've got a few other useful things too. If we keep too much, it might become apparent to somebody just exactly what Narcissus did with his records.'

Caenis signalled to her steward to carry on feeding the fire. 'How are you going to explain to Pallas how you come to have an original valuation that had been lodged with the Vestals?'

'I won't; and I also won't be giving it to Pallas, as it would seem to me that his time is coming to an end. I'll use this to buy favour with Seneca. For this he'll be more than happy to get Nero to grant Malichus his citizenship and then, I imagine, he'll come to an arrangement with Paelignus that he pays the balance of what he owes to him in return for his silence on the matter.'

'I thought you wanted him dead.'

'I do, but it might be amusing to ruin him first; see how he likes a couple of years with nothing, just as I had.' He got to his feet, smiling at the thought. 'Have your people pack your bags, my love; we'll leave for my Cosa estate tomorrow after I've seen Seneca.'

CHAPTER XXI

'I GOT BACK to Rome just before the Ides of October,' Vespasian said without any preamble as Hormus showed Laelius into the tablinum, 'and here we are two days before the Ides of February. Why has it taken four months for you to come and pay your respects to me, Laelius?'

Laelius stood before the desk, looking uncomfortable and sweating slightly despite the chill of a February dawn. He rubbed his hand over his now completely bald pate and essayed an ingratiating smile. 'I have only just heard of your return, patronus, as I've been away on business.' He spread his hands and shrugged as if it were unavoidable.

'For four months over the winter, Laelius? Bollocks! You've been in the city and I know it.'

'But you were touring your estates.'

'Ah! In order to know that you must have been here. Anyway, I got back from my tour in the New Year. I'll tell you why it's taken four months to visit me: it's because, with the bad winter they've been having in Moesia, it's taken four months for my letter to get to my brother and then for the news to get back to you that he's cancelled your chickpea contract and dismissed your son in disgrace. Is that nearer the mark, Laelius?'

Laelius cringed and twisted his hands.

'And all the time that I was away you didn't pay me the twelve per cent that you promised me from your business even though I kept my part of the bargain and had your equestrian status restored and got your son a post as a military tribune.'

Laelius hung his head. 'I'm sorry, patronus; I believed you to be dead. I'll pay you everything I owe and raise your percentage to fifteen if you can have your brother restore the contract to me.'

Vespasian turned to Hormus. 'Is Magnus still here?'

'Yes, master.'

'Ask him to come and join us.'

As Hormus left the room Vespasian gave Laelius a friendlier smile. 'It's not the contract or the money that you owe me that I wish to discuss at the moment.'

'What do you want, patronus?'

'How many people do you call patronus, Laelius?'

'I don't understand.'

'Don't you?' Vespasian mused as Hormus came back in with Magnus. 'Magnus, Laelius is having trouble understanding me; would you help him to focus his attention?'

'My pleasure, sir.' Magnus grabbed Laelius' right arm and pulled it high behind his back.

'Have I got your full attention now, Laelius?'

Magnus forced the arm up a bit more and Laelius nodded vigorously, grimacing with pain.

'Good. Now, the last time I saw you I granted you a favour, did I not?'

Another vigorous nod.

'And yet once that favour was done you took the earliest opportunity to cultivate a new patron. What was his name, Laelius?' Vespasian raised his eyebrows at Magnus who applied even more pressure.

'Corvinus!'

'Corvinus,' Vespasian repeated in a reasonable tone; he was enjoying this. 'And for how long have your been courting Corvinus?'

'I don't understand, patronus!'

Vespasian's eyes hardened and he pointed at Laelius' shoulder. Magnus grabbed it and twisted Laelius' arm further up his back; there was a loud tearing sound and a pop. Laelius screamed.

'Would you like Magnus to dislocate the other one for you?' Vespasian asked pleasantly. 'And he will, if you don't tell me just for how long you've been in Corvinus' pay.'

'Five years, patronus.'

'I think that we can drop the pretence of you calling me patronus, don't you? Now, the last time you left this room someone came in for an interview straight after you: do you remember him?'

Laelius whimpered, holding his damaged shoulder. 'No, patronus.'

'The other one, Magnus, now!'

Magnus reacted in a flash and within moments Laelius had fallen screaming to his knees with both arms hanging useless at his side.

'It's the elbows next, Laelius. Do you remember who came in after you?'

'Yes, but I don't remember his name.'

'Agarpetus; he was Narcissus' freedman here to organise a meeting between me and his patron. And you listened at the curtain, didn't you?'

'Yes,' Laelius sobbed.

Magnus' expression changed as he understood the implication; murder shone in his one good eye.

Vespasian held up a hand to stop his friend. 'What did you do with what you heard, Laelius?'

'I told Corvinus.'

'Told Corvinus? Now why would you do that?'

Laelius looked up at Vespasian, his eyes pleading for his life. 'Because he paid me to tell him anything interesting that I heard while I was in your house.'

'Do you know what he did with this information?'

Laelius shook his head.

'Tell him, Magnus.'

'He had the East Aventine Brotherhood attack the South Quirinal Brotherhood.'

'That's exactly what he did,' Vespasian agreed. 'In an effort to have me killed; but, instead, quite a few of Magnus' brothers lost their lives. I imagine the South Quirinal would like to see justice done.'

'Very much so; but they wouldn't be anxious to see justice done quickly, if you take my meaning?'

'Oh, but I do, Magnus, I do.' Vespasian was now enjoying this even more than he had anticipated he would when he had made the connection between Corvinus knowing when he would be in Magnus' tavern and Laelius. That had been over a month before and since then he had been savouring the prospect of Laelius coming to plead for his chickpea contract. 'But you are no longer a member of that brotherhood so it's not really your argument any more. We wouldn't want murder committed for no reason, would we, Laelius?'

A flicker of hope showed in Laelius' eyes. 'No, patronus.'

'So when will be the next time you see your former brethren, Magnus?'

'In the Circus Maximus in an hour or so to watch your team race for the Greens for the first time.'

'Now that is convenient. Laelius lives in Red Horse Street just off the Alta Semita.'

'I know it well, sir, so do Tigran and the lads.'

'And once you've told Tigran and the lads that Laelius was responsible for the deaths of a few of their brethren and their temporary eviction from their tavern, how long do you think it would take them to find Laelius' house?'

'My guess is that for the pleasure of revenge for something like that they would forgo the racing and be there within a half-hour.'

Vespasian made a show of doing some arithmetic. 'I would say that you've got precisely an hour and a half to get out of Rome, Laelius. Goodbye.'

Laelius looked wide-eyed at Vespasian and then realised that he was indeed letting him go. He stood, grimacing at the pain in his shoulders, and then ran from the room with his arms flapping uselessly beside him.

'Follow him, Hormus, and don't let anyone open the door for him; let him try and work that out for himself.'

'Are you really going to give him a chance, sir?'

Vespasian shrugged. 'Do you think that the lads won't get him?'

'Of course they'll get him, even if he runs to Corvinus.'

'Well, then, after what he did, he deserves to live his last few hours, or days, in terror of the inevitable.'

'What do you want to do about Corvinus? I could get the lads to torch his house for him.'

Vespasian contemplated the offer briefly. 'No, but thank you, Magnus, it was a kind offer; he's so rich that it would hardly inconvenience him at all. I'll think of something suitable in due course.'

Magnus grinned. 'I'm sure you will. In which case, I think it's time we went to the circus, sir.'

'So do I, Magnus; and now that Seneca has persuaded Nero to grant Malichus his citizenship I think the gods will look kindly on my team. I've a feeling that this is our lucky day.'

Magnus grinned. 'I believe you may be right; after all, it's already started off so pleasantly.'

The sight of Caratacus being admitted to the imperial box reminded Vespasian that he wanted to share, over dinner, their reminiscences of four years of fighting each other. But as the Britannic chieftain was greeted by Nero, who was enthusing about the scale model of the Circus Maximus and comparing its details to the real structure surrounding them, Vespasian returned to his inner battle and looked down at the purse in his hand, struggling with himself and his inability to part easily with money.

'I've put ten aurii on them, dear boy,' Gaius, sitting to his right, informed him, holding up the wooden bet marker that he had just received from the bookmaker's slave with whom he had placed the bet.

Vespasian was appalled. 'That's five times the annual salary of a legionary, Uncle. What if they lose?'

'Then I shall blame you because they're your horses. But if I win, then I'll get eight times my bet because no one fancies the Greens' third chariot with a team that has never raced before.'

Vespasian looked back down at his purse and weighed it in his hand. Despite the fact that he had driven his team himself a few times in the Flammian Circus and was well aware of their prowess, he was still finding it very hard to lay his first ever bet.

Flavia, seated to his left, snorted in derision. 'You'll have as much chance of getting him to place a bet on his own horses, Gaius, as you would of getting him to pay for your upkeep if you made the mistake of marrying him without a dowry. Fortunately

I didn't make that error.' She smiled in a goading manner and brandished her bet marker. 'Fifteen denarii of *my* money on *your* horses, dear husband.'

Vespasian was taken by just how much his wife was becoming like his mother; given another few years, he surmised, she would stand a good chance of being just as cantankerous. He felt relief that he had forbidden Vespasia Polla to accompany him and Flavia back to Rome, after they had visited her in Aquae Cutillae for the Saturnalia, ostensibly on account of her frailty and the cold; in reality it was because of their souring natures rubbing each other. Dealing with two such women on a daily basis had been intolerable; whereas the month that he had spent with Caenis at Cosa had been very tolerable indeed.

Titus leant over his mother and rubbed Vespasian's arm, bringing him back to his present dilemma. 'Come on, Father, it's just a bit of fun; I've put down five denarii.'

'Five! Where did you get that from?'

'It's part of my allowance.' Titus cocked an eyebrow before adding, 'Quite a large part seeing as you're the one who sets the level of it.'

Vespasian did not take offence at his son's remark; he knew that, although it was an exaggeration, there was more than a grain of truth in it. He sighed, pulled a coin out of his purse and handed it to the waiting bookmaker's slave. 'One sesterces on the Green number three chariot. What will I get if I win?'

'Two denarii plus your original stake, master,' the slave replied, taking the bronze coin. With great ceremony he placed it in his bag before recording the wager in his ledger and then handing the numbered marker to Vespasian.

As the slave walked off to report back to his master, based with the other bookmakers at the rear of the senators' enclosure, Titus handed him a silver denarius. 'That's for managing to keep a straight face.'

Vespasian punched the air and screamed incoherently as the leading three chariots skidded, in clouds of dust, out of the turn into the last of the seven laps, almost level. Only the Red supporters in the circus remained seated as their three chariots lay in mangled wrecks scattered around the track. The Blues, Whites and Greens, however, had jumped to their feet to urge on their teams for the last desperate effort. But those who were yelling the loudest were the people who had put their money on the outsider: the unknown Green team. The team had caused a stir around the circus during the parade before the race; supporters of all factions had marvelled at the quality of the Arabs. Even the Emperor, who was no mean judge of horse-flesh, had been impressed and had interrupted showing off his new set of finely carved ivory chariot models to Caratacus, seated with him, and summoned Eusebius, the Green faction-master, to the imperial box. Vespasian had felt Nero's eyes rest upon him a couple of times as they discussed the team.

But now Vespasian was lost in the excitement of the race as the three leading chariots shot down the straight on the other side of the spina to the delirious roar of a quarter of a million people. The *hortatores*, the single horsemen who guided each chariot through the dust, wreckage and chaos of the race, reached the turning post at the far end of the spina for the last time and, signalling frantically at a party of track slaves, trying to rescue a trapped Red charioteer from his shattered vehicle, to take shelter within the tangle of wood and thrashing horses, made the turn and then pulled aside to leave the final straight clear for the three remaining teams.

With the White on the inside, taking the slower but sharper turn, the Blue and the Green charioteers whipped their teams to speed them around the outside at the fastest possible pace, negating the White's advantage of taking the shorter route. As the three chariots levelled out they were almost in a line and with no more turns to go it was all about fitness and pace. And as the roar of the Green supporters, seated mainly on the left-hand side of the great entrance gates, increased to storm-like proportions, it was obvious which team had the most of both those qualities; qualities that Vespasian knew very well from his amateur efforts with them.

But now they were in the hands of a professional.

With seeming effortlessness the four Arab greys lengthened their stride and almost glided away while the White and Blue drivers, their leather-strapped chests heaving with the exertion, slashed their four-lashed whips over the withers of their teams to no discernible effect. The Green supporters howled their joy as the seventh dolphin tilted and the Green charioteer raised an arm in a victory salute.

'They weren't even at full stretch by the end!' Gaius yelled in Vespasian's ear. 'That could be the best team in Rome at the moment.'

Vespasian beamed at his uncle, his thoughts focused on all the prize money that was now a very real possibility as a Praetorian Guardsman pushed his way along the row to them. With a perfunctory salute he delivered his message: 'The Emperor commands you and your son to join him for dinner after the last race.' Without waiting for a reply the man moved off.

'Oh dear, dear boy,' Gaius said, the joy of winning slipping from his face. 'I've a nasty feeling that I'm not the only one who thinks that.'

Vespasian looked over to Nero and had the suspicion that his uncle was right.

'You must understand, Vespasian,' Seneca said, coming straight to the point, as he met Vespasian and Titus in the palace's atrium, 'that to keep the Emperor ... how should I say? Mollified? Yes, mollified, that's the word, exactly right; to keep the Emperor *mollified* we need to give him what he wants.' He placed an avuncular arm around Vespasian's shoulders. 'If he gets what he wants then we find him far more amenable to acting with reason and restraint.'

'We?' Vespasian asked pointedly as Seneca led him at speed through the once dignified chamber designed, by Augustus, to overawe visiting embassies with Rome's majesty rather than ostentatiously show off its wealth as Nero had evidently decided to do. Hugely expensive works of art were now scattered about the room; not garish and brash as they had been in Caligula's time but, rather, exquisite in their beauty and workmanship. There was, however, vulgarity in their abundance.

'Yes, me and Burrus.'

'What about Pallas?'

'I'm afraid that your friend staked rather too much on Agrippina's support; although, perhaps "support" is the wrong choice of word considering the entirety of what she gives him.' He paused for a short chuckle, his eyes almost disappearing in his well-fleshed face; Vespasian checked himself from asking what support Agrippina still gave Nero. 'But then I expect that you suspected as much as it was to me that you brought Malichus' petition for citizenship.'

'Indeed; and I put myself in your debt knowingly. I trust you have benefitted from the information that I supplied you with.'

'Very much and you'll be pleased to know that Paelignus is er ... "financially debilitated" is the expression that best sums up his position.' Seneca rumbled another chuckle and looked at Titus. 'Learn from your father, young man, he's got political – how should I put it? Ah, yes, that's an excellent word: nous. Yes, political nous is exactly what he's got.' He slapped Vespasian on the shoulder and then gave it a friendly squeeze. 'Now, I shall be candid with you, Vespasian.'

'You want me to give the Emperor my team of horses.'

'I didn't say that. No, no, no, far from it; I didn't say that at all.'

'You said we have to give Nero what he wants.'

'I did; but only if he asks. So if he asks, give him your team.'

'And what will I get in return?'

'Well, well, that's a difficult question. That is ... what's the best word for what that is? Ah, yes: that is an imponderable. Yes, it is. It could be anything from nothing at all to your life itself. That's how things work with Nero; there's very little ... er ... middle ground – for want of a better expression. But, who knows, he may have forgotten all about your horses if the dinner is sumptuous, the lyre player talented and the conversation centres around him, which I shall do my best to see that it does.'

As they walked into the soft music and quiet chatter of the triclinium, Vespasian reconciled himself to losing his team and gaining nothing by it; why else was he there?

'We will have to save our reminiscences for a more private occasion, Vespasian,' Caratacus said, breaking off from a conversation with one of the dozen or so other guests and walking to greet Vespasian as he entered the room.

'Now that I'm back we should make the arrangement.' Vespasian indicated to Titus. 'This is my son and namesake.'

Caratacus took Titus' arm. 'You would do well to follow your father.'

'I intend to do better than that.'

Caratacus threw his head back and laughed. 'That is the joy of sons. You have done well, Vespasian, to instil such ambition in the lad. But what victories could he achieve that are greater than yours?'

'Rome will always be supplying the need for victories.'

'As long as she keeps expanding, yes. But come, we shall drink together and I shall try to forget the fact that for my sons to do better than me all they need do is not lose what they already have.'

Vespasian was surprised to hear no bitterness in the Briton's voice. He took a goblet of wine from the tray of a waiting slave and saw Pallas amongst the guests; the Greek walked over and Caratacus politely stepped aside.

'I thought—' Vespasian began before Pallas cut him off.

'I know what you thought.' Pallas' face was, as usual, unreadable. 'That's why you cultivate Seneca. It is a wise if somewhat ungrateful move; especially after all I've done for you. But whether it will keep you safe from Agrippina or get you the governorship of a province I don't know. Despite what Seneca and Burrus have done to poison Nero's mind to his mother and also me, I've still managed to retain my post as chief secretary to the Treasury; but for how long I don't know. I trust I will not lose your friendship for old times' sake.'

A sudden drop in the conversation followed by applause prevented Vespasian from answering. Nero, surrounded by a colourful entourage, had entered the room followed by Agrippina and two maids; all present joined in a chorus of mighty shouts of 'Hail Caesar!'.

Nero was overcome by his greeting and leant with one hand on the shoulder of a muscular-in-body but effeminate-in-face freedman, while languidly waving the other in acknowledgement. Tears again began to roll down his cheeks and Vespasian wondered if he really was so naturally emotional or had learnt to cry at will or, perhaps more likely, was skilled in the art of applying onion to the eyes.

'My friends, my friends,' Nero said, almost singing the words in his husky voice. 'Enough; we are all friends here.' He turned to his entourage. 'Here, my darling boy.'

Britannicus, escorted by a brutish man in the uniform of the prefect of the Vigiles, came out of the crowd, evidently burning with shame and anger and unsurprisingly so: a blond wig in which blooms had been woven had been forced upon him; his eyes, cheeks and lips were heavily made up and the tunic he wore was of the finest linen but barely long enough for modesty.

Titus reacted as if punched and then made to move forward but was immediately restrained by both Vespasian and Pallas.

'Stay, you fool,' Pallas hissed.

'Today is the eve of my darling brother's fourteenth birthday so this evening is the last time he will be accorded the respect of a mere boy. It is a time to celebrate, a time to revel in the joys of boyhood for one last occasion before taking on the responsibilities of a man before he comes to feel the awful weight of responsibility that comes with the toga virilis.' Nero put an arm around Britannicus' shoulders. Vespasian felt as though a blow had landed on his belly before he had had time to tense his muscles: he had forgotten the significance of the date; this evening was nothing to do with his team. He glanced at Seneca but his eyes warned that they were powerless to interfere.

'You are lucky, darling brother, in that as yet you do not have to make the onerous decisions that come with manhood.' Nero turned his watery-blue eyes onto Pallas, and Vespasian saw the hardness and cruelty in them that lurked behind the veneer of emotion. 'That man fucks Mother, did you know that, sweet boy?'

Pallas glanced involuntarily at his lover.

Agrippina went rigid, shock frozen on her face.

Everyone in the room held their breath.

'He even fucks Mother after I've been fucking her and some-times, I've noticed, he's even fucked Mother before me. Do you fuck Mother too, Britannicus?'

Britannicus made no reply but just stared ahead shaking with rage.

'I'm going to punish Pallas for fucking Mother.'

'You will do no such thing!' Agrippina shrieked, coming out of her shock. 'You monster; how dare you turn on me and how dare you turn on Pallas now that we have got you to where you are?' She flung herself across the room at her son only to be restrained by Burrus. 'Let me go, you uncultured brute!'

Nero slapped her, fore- and backhand, around the face. 'Quiet, Mother, you're disturbing my fun.'

'Fun!' She tried to break free from Burrus' grip but he held fast. 'I thought you would be grateful but no, you're no better than your father.'

'And no worse than my mother. But at least I know what I am and have the goodness to hide it most of the time.'

Agrippina hissed and spat like a rabid cat, almost hyperventilating with wrath. 'I'll go to the Praetorian camp and I'll admit murdering Claudius.' She pointed at Britannicus. 'They'll put his runt on the throne and you'll be finished.'

'And you'll be dead, Mother, if you do that. Besides' – he ran his hand through the blond wig – 'little Britannicus is still a boy and should be treated as such. Tigellinus! On the couch with him.'

The Vigiles prefect brought up the knife that had been keeping Britannicus in check and, putting it to his throat, forced the boy to kneel on a couch; his tunic rose over his buttocks and all could see that he wore no loincloth. Nero admired the revealed sight for a few moments and then licked his lips. 'What a delicious boy. Doryphorus, see to me and then ready him.'

The muscled, effeminate freedman fell to his knees and with practised skill very quickly coaxed an erection from his patron. Nero gazed down at it with love. 'Oh that it were not mine but belonged to another so that I could possess such beauty.'

Titus struggled but Vespasian held on to his son as Doryphorus licked Britannicus' anus, moistening it, before Nero, with surprising tenderness, eased his way in to him; Britannicus made no sound.

All in the room not involved stood and watched the act, transfixed, their faces registering horror as Nero raped his stepbrother with growing rhythm and delight; the rightful heir to Augustus' line pounded in public as if he were no more than a dockside whore-boy earning a sesterces. Tigellinus slathered as he held the boy down, staring into his face, and occasionally looking up at Nero and grinning maniacally with sadistic pleasure.

With no more than a grunt and a slight shudder, Nero came to a climax and then sighed deep with contentment. Pulling himself free of Britannicus and slapping a buttock at the same time, he looked around the room, beaming. 'That's how to treat a boy. Let's eat.'

Nero licked his fingers and then looked at Pallas, frowning, as if recollecting a dim memory. 'Of course! I was in the process of punishing you for fucking Mother.' He took another quail from the platter before him and pulled a leg free. He turned to Seneca, reclining to his right on the couch. 'You claim to have an eye for appropriate justice – what do you think his punishment should be?'

Seneca cleared his throat and wiped his lips to give himself a few moments' thinking time. 'Princeps, in our long hours of study together over the years I have tried to steer you on the path of justice rather than er ... shall we say chaos? Yes, chaos will do admirably. We cannot have chaos, and chaos comes from injustice. Pallas here has served both you and your father well, for that he deserves reward. However, he has also, how should I put it? Compromised, that's it, compromised himself with your mother, and for that he deserves punishment. So from those two conflicting outcomes how can we find justice?'

As Seneca expanded on his theme, Vespasian marvelled that Nero seemed to be listening enrapt rather than struggling to remain focused like the rest of Seneca's audience. Only Pallas, next to him, remained fixed on the discourse as his life was weighed and fate decided. His face remained outwardly placid but the slightest rubbing of his index finger on his cup betrayed a deep anxiety in one normally so at ease.

Caratacus, to Vespasian's other side, sipped his wine, paying no attention to the speech, while Titus and Britannicus both ate methodically and without enjoyment as if just marking time until the whole ordeal was over. Agrippina smouldered on Nero's left, shooting venomous looks at the speaker.

'And so, bearing in mind all of these arguments,' Seneca carried on, drawing to a conclusion, 'including the fact that it was Pallas himself who recommended Narcissus' death in similar circumstances, I suggest, Princeps, that you show a degree of mercy; banish him, put him—'

'I decide the sentence,' Nero snapped, raising his finger in warning at Seneca. 'If I agree with the argument.' Now he went right back to the posing that had seemed to have been forgotten as he had allowed the innate violence within him to run free. After much imitation of a man deep in thought he resurfaced. 'I shall be merciful, Pallas.'

Vespasian felt the Greek relax; his index finger stilled.

'You are banished from Rome but may live on one of your estates close to the city. You may keep your wealth as a reward for your good service to my father but should I need money you will always lend it to me, interest free. However, as punishment for your crimes with my mother you shall play host to her for half of every month. In other words for half the year she shall not be with me, annoying me, but with you.'

Vespasian choked back an involuntary guffaw at the mad logic of the sentence as Pallas got to his feet.

'Princeps, you are just and merciful and I submit to your will.' With a bow to Nero while completely ignoring Agrippina, who was still staring at her son in horror, Pallas left the room, his career in Rome over.

Nero brightened as the Greek's footsteps receded. 'Now, where were we? Ah yes, celebrating my brother's coming of age. We shall have a toast; charge our cups!'

Female slaves who had been waiting in the shadows busied themselves making sure that each of the guests had sufficient before retreating back whence they came.

'To my brother's birthday tomorrow!' Nero shouted, before draining his wine.

All the guests followed his example with varying degrees of enthusiasm. Britannicus, his eyes glazed with remembrance of public buggery, took no more than a mouthful.

But that was enough to make Nero smile as the boy swallowed. 'Which he will never see,' he added, watching Britannicus intently.

Vespasian's innards lurched and he looked at Britannicus who broke into a cold smile of acceptance as he threw another gulp down his gullet, his eyes fixed on Nero, defiance and hatred in them. Behind him a slave woman was staring with the same intensity as she had stared at Claudius while he died; the woman was rewarded by a sudden spasm. Titus grabbed Britannicus' cup from his hand as the spasm repeated, confused by what was happening to his friend who now struggled but failed to draw breath; a rattle emanated from his constricted throat. Titus gaped at him, his face tensed in horror as realisation dawned. Five, ten, fifteen heartbeats the ghastly agony continued as Britannicus' eyes bulged and his lips blued, twitching as they struggled to form a word; his hand grasped Titus' wrist and pushed the poisoned cup up towards his mouth. His lips resolved into a final, twisted smile.

Once more for Vespasian, time's chariot slowed and he felt himself rising as he watched Britannicus slump slowly back, his hand releasing its grip. His heart pounded slow and bass in his ears as Titus stared at the contents of the cup, registering just what it was; he looked down at his friend's lifeless eyes, fixed upon him, before casting Nero a glare of unvarnished loathing. Vespasian screamed, inchoate, as he tried to fly across the room, watching Titus' hand rise even further and the cup slowly approaching his lips. He could see it tilt and the wine within it touch the rim as Titus' mouth opened. The cup rested on his lower lip and the poison began to flow onto his tongue; Vespasian was sure that he saw his son's throat contract with a swallow as his right hand smashed the cup away from Titus' mouth and time cranked back up to her unrelenting speed almost in mockery of how long Titus had to live.

'An antidote!' Vespasian screamed at the slave woman, vaguely aware of laughter behind him. 'What is the antidote, woman?' He grabbed Titus, who was staring down into the pained and dead eyes of Britannicus.

The woman stood motionless, looking towards Nero.

'Two for the price of one, Locusta,' Nero managed to say through his mirth, 'very good.'

Vespasian screamed again for the antidote as Caratacus grabbed Locusta by the throat and lifted her, shrieking, off her feet; the jug she carried crashed to the ground. 'Obey me, woman, and nobody else, for it is in my hands that your miserable life lies. The antidote.'

Locusta reached into a bag hanging from her waist and brought out a phial; Caratacus took it and threw her away to land with a cracking of bones on the hard mosaic floor.

Titus spasmed as Vespasian grabbed the antidote, ripping the cork out with his teeth. He slammed his son's head down onto the still chest of Britannicus and tipped the contents of the phial down his open throat. Once empty he threw it away, pinched Titus' nose and pressed his mouth shut; there was another spasm but then he swallowed. Vespasian looked into Titus' eyes willing him to live, as Nero's laughter still echoed in his ears; no one else made a sound apart from Locusta groaning over a broken arm. Titus' eyes widened in pain, the pupils so dilated there was no colour in them, just black and white. There was another spasm but weaker this time and his face relaxed.

Caratacus pulled Vespasian to his feet. 'Lift him; we must get him out of here.'

Vespasian did as he was told, unthinkingly knowing that was the right thing to do.

'Father?' Titus mumbled.

'You'll be all right; I knocked the cup away before you drank too much and you've had the whole antidote.'

'Who said you can leave?' Nero shouted, his laughter dying.

'With your permission I'm taking them into my care, Princeps,' Caratacus said, helping to lift Titus. 'As you showed mercy to me so I beg you show mercy to this son of Rome. Rome's lost one son already today; do not make her lose a second.'

Without waiting for an answer Vespasian hauled Titus to his feet and, with the help of his one-time mortal enemy, dragged his son from the room, away from the Golden Emperor.

AUTHOR'S NOTE

Between Vespasian's consulship in the last two months of AD 51 and him becoming governor of Africa in AD 63 we know nothing about him. I therefore had a simple choice: skip twelve years – my original intention when conceiving the series – or recount his probable life during that time living in semi-retirement on his estates – dull in the extreme – or insert him into events of the period. Having chosen the third option I once again based the fiction on the writings of Tacitus, Suetonius, Cassius Dio, Josephus and the Bible.

Sabinus was the Governor of Moesia, Macedonia and Thracia during this time.

At the beginning of his biography of Domitian, Suetonius tells us that he was born in Pomegranate Street on the Quirinal Hill.

Tacitus tells us in his history of AD 50 that Caratacus was captured and sent to Rome. However, he also says that he had resisted Rome for eight years, which would place his capture in 51. Seeing as Tacitus often deals with events away from Rome in two-year chunks, it is entirely possible that Caratacus may have come to Rome and delivered his famous speech when Vespasian was consul. As to the speech, I mixed elements of Tacitus' version and Cassius Dio's shorter one.

Tacitus tells of Britannicus insulting Nero by referring to him as 'Domitius' and how it caused Sosibius to be executed.

Corbulo would have been in Rome at that time as he transferred from being governor of Germania Inferior to Asia.

I have combined three examples from Suetonius of how Claudius behaved in court to make the one scene that Vespasian witnesses with Corbulo, so, unfortunately, it's not that far from the reality.

Lydia of Thyatira was the first person baptised in Europe by St Paul; the ceremony happened in the River Gangites at Philippi. Her being tried by Sabinus is my fiction.

Jesus referring to Gentiles as dogs is recorded in both Mark 7:24–30 and also Matthew 15:21–28 in which he also states: 'I was sent only to the lost sheep of Israel.' Make of that what you will.

The story of Paul casting out the demon from the slave girl in Philippi and annoying her owner is taken from Acts, as is the earthquake and Paul's insistence on an apology for the way he had been treated.

Tryphaena had abdicated at Caligula's request and removed herself to Cyzicus where she was a rich and influential part of the community. King Polemon of Pontus was her brother and Radamistus was her nephew; she was also a cousin of both Agrippina and Nero. Her interest in achieving power for Radamistus and Nero, therefore, is historically feasible but is my fiction. The beginnings of the Roman–Parthian war did start off with Radamistus' invasion and usurpation of the throne followed by his murder in the manner described of Mithridates, his father-in-law, and his sons. Julius Paelignus was the procurator of Cappadocia at the time and Tacitus describes him as 'contempt-ible both for his idle intellect and his physical deformity', adding that he was a friend of Claudius who 'added amusement to his leisure time by fraternising with buffoons'. He did invade Armenia with auxiliaries but 'pillaged the allies more than the enemy'. He also transferred his allegiance to Radamistus and encouraged him in his kingly ambitions.

The war gradually escalated and eventually became the conflict in which Corbulo made his name despite the impetuousness of the other commander, Lucius Junius Paetus.

I have taken the liberty of placing Tigranocerta where I have because it suited the narrative. There are at least four possible sites for the town and I just chose the most convenient, which, I believe, is a fiction writer's prerogative!

Arbela, modern day Erbil in Iraq, is considered to be one of the longest continuously inhabited cities in the world. Izates bar

Monobazes was the King of Adiabene at the time and had recently been converted to Judaism by Ananias, according to Josephus. However, it has been argued by Robert Eisenman in his book *James the Brother of Jesus* that this Ananias was the same man as Ananias of Damascus who baptised St Paul. If this was the case then Josephus was mistaken and Izates was not strictly Jewish but had been baptised into an early form of Christianity as preached by Jesus' Jewish disciples.

The audience chamber in Ctesiphon is based on the ruins of a later, Sassanid, structure; however, I imagine that the King of Kings would have conducted his business in a chamber equally as impressive.

Malichus was the King of the Nabataean Arabs and did have a problem with Claudius taking Damascus back into the Empire, it having originally been given to his predecessor by Caligula.

Felix was the procurator of Judaea at the time and was well known for his harshness in dealing with the local populace.

Claudius did address the Senate a couple of days before he died on the subject of recognising Britannicus as his heir; he had also let drop remarks, while drunk, that it was his fate to suffer and then punish the sexual misconduct of his wives. This combination probably led to his death, which, according to Tacitus, was achieved first with a mushroom and then by the doctor, Xenophon, finishing him off with a poisoned feather.

Nero's speech to the Senate is taken from Suetonius and was written by Seneca, according to Cassius Dio.

Tacitus tells us that Nero sexually abused Britannicus and also poisoned him using Locusta's potions. Suetonius relates in his biography of Titus that he was next to his friend Britannicus when it happened and tried to take his own life with the same poisoned cup but failed and became very ill for a while instead. Perhaps this explains his curtailed life. Britannicus was murdered the day before his fourteenth birthday.

Narcissus did have gout at the time and was executed soon after Claudius' assassination. I brought it forward for the sake of the narrative. We don't know what happened to Callistus but he was dead by the beginning of Nero's reign.

Tacitus tells us of Nero's first password: 'excellent mother'. Cassius Dio relates the episode when Agrippina tried to mount Nero's dais and receive the Armenian embassy as if she were his equal. His refusing her was probably the beginning of their split.

My thanks, as always, to my agent, Ian Drury at Sheil Land Associates, for going in to bat on my behalf and to Gaia Banks and Marika Lysandrou in the foreign rights department. To everyone at Corvus/Atlantic for the great effort that they have put in to promoting my books, a big thank you. Thanks also to my editor, Maddie West, and my copy-editor, Tamsin Shelton, for all their hard work on the manuscript to turn it from my ramblings into something comprehensible. Congratulations to Sara O'Keeffe on the birth of Ethne. Finally, thank you and farewell to Toby Mundy, to whom I am greatly indebted for showing such faith in me, and I wish you all the best in the future; and then welcome to Will Atkinson who takes over from Toby at Atlantic.

Vespasian's story will continue in *The Furies of Rome*.